Praise for Mary Wine's Scottish romance

"Hot enough to warm even the coldest Scottish nights...
An addictive tale of betrayal, lust, power, and love with
detail-rich descriptions."

—*Publishers Weekly* Starred Review

"Not to be missed."

—Lora Leigh, *New York Times*
#1 Bestselling Author

"Mary Wine brings history to life with major sizzle factor."

—Lucy Monroe, *USA Today* bestselling author
of *For Duty's Sake*

"Deeply romantic, scintillating, and absolutely delicious."

—Sylvia Day, national bestselling author
of *Pride and Pleasure*

"[The characters] fight just as passionately as they love while
intrigue abounds and readers turn the pages faster and faster!"

—*RT Book Reviews*, 4 Stars

"Lively and exciting adventure."

—*Booklist*

"A must-read… a fast-paced, action-packed, full of adventure story that will keep you turning the pages."

—*My Book Addiction and More*

"Ms. Wine has penned another fascinating tale… an exciting adventure in love (and making love—sizzling hot scenes!), self-discovery, and political intrigue."

—*History Undressed*

"Mary Wine takes you into the rugged Highlands and into the hearts of their kilted warriors."

—*The Royal Reviews*

"The passion Ms. Wine has for this story comes through her characters in ways you'll love to read."

—*Night Owl Romance*

"Solidly entertaining highland romance."

—*Book Reviews by Martha's Bookshelf*

"Once again, Wine delivers romantic banter, excitement, and escape."

—*Starting Fresh*

"What a hot book… if you like to turn up the heat, no matches are required because this volume will definitely light the flame."

—*Bookloons*

Also by Mary Wine

To Conquer a Highlander

Highland Hellcat

Highland Heat

Coming in October 2012

The Trouble with Highlanders

The HIGHLANDER'S PRIZE

MARY WINE

sourcebooks
casablanca

Published by Sourcebooks Casablanca, an imprint of Sourcebooks, Inc.
P.O. Box 4410, Naperville, Illinois 60567-4410
(630) 961-3900
FAX: (630) 961-2168
sourcebooks.com

Printed and bound in the United States of America.
LSC 10 9 8 7 6 5 4 3 2

This one is for the amazing Sylvia Day,
a guru of a mentor and the best friend anyone could ask for.
She's a great writer too!

One

"KEEP YER FACE HIDDEN."

Clarrisa jerked back as one of the men escorting her hit the fabric covering the top of the wagon she rode inside of. An imprint of his fist was clearly visible for a moment.

"Best keep back, my dove. These Scots are foul-tempered creatures, to be sure. We've left civilization behind us in England." There was a note of longing in Maud's voice Clarrisa tried to ignore. She couldn't afford to be melancholy. Her uncle's word had been given, so she would be staying in Scotland, no matter her feelings on the matter.

Better to avoid thinking about how she felt; better to try to believe her future would be bright.

"The world is in a dark humor," Clarrisa muttered. Her companion lifted the gold cross hanging from her girdle chain and kissed it. "I fear we need a better plan than waiting for divine help, Maud."

Maud's eyes widened. Faster than a flash, she reached

over and tugged one of Clarrisa's long braids. Pain shot across her scalp before the older woman sent to chaperone her released her hair. "You'll mind your tongue, girl. Just because you're royal-blooded doesn't give you cause to be doubting that the good Lord has a hand in where you're heading. You're still bastard-born, so you'll keep to your place."

Clarrisa moved to the other side of the wagon and peeked out again. She knew well who she was. No one ever let her forget, not for as long as she could recall. Still, even legitimate daughters were expected to be obedient, so she truly had no right to be discontented.

So she would hope the future the horses were pulling her toward was a good one.

The night was dark, thick clouds covering the moon's light. The trees looked sinister, and the wind sounded mournful as it rustled the branches. But Clarrisa didn't reach for the cross hanging from her own waist. No, she'd place her faith in her wits and refuse to be frightened. That much was within her power. It gave her a sense of balance and allowed her to smile. Yes, her future would hold good things, because she would be wise enough to keep her demeanor kind. A shrew never prospered.

"Far past time for you to accept your lot with more humbleness," Maud mumbled, sounding almost as uninterested as Clarrisa felt. "You should be grateful for this opportunity to better your lot. Not many bastards are given such opportunities."

Clarrisa didn't respond to Maud's reminder that she was illegitimate. There wasn't any point. Depending on who wore the crown of England, her lineage was a blessing or a curse.

"If you give the Scottish king a son—"

"It will be bastard-born, since I have heard no offer of marriage," Clarrisa insisted.

Maud made a low sound of disapproval and pointed an aged finger at her. "Royal-blooded babes do not have to suffer the same burdens the rest of us do. In spite of the lack of blessing from the church your mother suffered, you are on your way to a bright future. Besides, this is Scotland. He'll wed you quickly if you produce a male child. He simply doesn't have to marry you first, because you are illegitimate. Set your mind to giving him a son, and your future will be bright."

Clarrisa doubted Maud's words. She lifted the edge of the wagon cover again and stared at the man nearest her. His plaid was belted around his waist, with a length of it pulled up and over his right shoulder. The fabric made a good cushion for the sword strapped to his wide back.

Maybe he was a Scotsman, but the sword made him look like any other man she had ever known. They lived for fighting. Power was the only thing they craved. Her blood was nothing more than another way to secure what the king of Scotland hungered for.

Blessing? Not for her, it wouldn't be.

◈

Lytge Sutherland was an earl, but he ruled like a prince on his land at the top of Scotland. Plenty of men envied him, but the wiser ones gave him deference gladly, because they knew his life was far from simple. At the moment he was feeling the weight of ten lairds, only half of whom he called friends.

"If the rumor is true, we must act," Laird Matheson insisted. "With a York-blooded son, that bastard James will pass the crown on to an English puppet."

"Or a king who the English will nae war with because they share common blood," Laird Morris argued.

The room filled with angry shouts as men leaned over the tables in front of them to give their words more strength.

"Enough!" Lytge snapped. There were several cutting glares, but Matheson and Morris both sat back in their chairs. The tension in the room was so tight the earl knew he had to find a solution before the men assembled before him began fighting one another. "Let us not forget how important it is for us to stand together, or James will get his wish to disinherit his first son, a young man worthy of our loyalty. If we squabble among one another, we will have to be content with James remaining king."

Laird Matheson snarled, "That bastard has no' done what a king should. He gives riches to his favorites and refuses to punish thieving clans like the MacLeods! It's his fault we're fighting Highlander against Highlander."

"Which is why we're all here, united against him despite half our own kin calling it treason." It was a younger man who spoke this time, and the earl grinned in spite of his desire to appear detached.

"Young Laird MacNicols says it clearly. We're here because we're united—a bond that needs to remain strong. The York lass must be eliminated before she can perform the function James desires of her. We do nae need England's war on our soil."

"We'll have to find her first," Faolan Chisholms said. "Such will nae be a simple task."

The old earl looked around the room. There was plenty of spirit in the lairds' eyes, but thinking the deed done would not gain them success. It would take cunning and strength, along with a healthy amount of arrogance for the man willing to try and steal from the king. Such a man would have to believe himself above failure. The earl was sitting in the right place to find him, for they were all Highlanders.

"I'll find her and steal her." Broen MacNicols spoke quietly—too quietly for the earl's comfort.

"Ye've got vengeance in yer eyes, young MacNicols. Understandable, since James has slighted yer patience by refusing ye justice concerning the death of yer father."

The earl's son, Norris, slammed a fist into the table, sending several of the goblets wobbling. "James neglects us and leaves good men no choice but to feud when their neighbors commit crimes, since he will not dispense judgment upon the guilty."

"I tried to respect the king instead of falling back on old ways," Broen snarled. "I took the matter of me father's murder at the hands of the Grants to the king. The man would nae even see me, much less send an envoy to Donnach Grant to demand me betrothed be returned." He flattened his hands on the tabletop, leaning over it. "I made a choice, sure enough, for I'm here, and I tell ye I will make sure the king does nae get the lass he wants while he refuses me justice for the murder of the woman I was contracted to. She died on Grant land, and I deserved more than a letter telling me she's dead."

Lytge Sutherland nodded and heard several of the other lairds slap the tabletop in agreement. "We place our faith in ye, Laird MacNicols. Find the York bastard, and ye'll have me at yer back when ye demand that explanation from Donnach Grant."

There was a solid ring of endorsement in the earl's tone. Broen didn't enjoy it. His father had been dead for four months, but he still felt the sting of the loss like a fresh wound. He reached up and tugged on the corner of his bonnet before quitting the chamber.

"Ye're in a hurry." Broen didn't lessen his pace as Faolan Chisholms caught up with him. They'd been young boys together, and now fate had made them lairds in nearly the same season.

"There is no reason to sit at a table drinking and talking like old men. I've an Englishwoman to find, since that is the only way I'll possibly see an explanation to me father's death that will nae require spilling blood when the snow melts."

"Aye, Sutherland will nae be giving ye his assistance otherwise, but ye need to know where to look for her before ye ride out," Faolan insisted.

Broen stopped and faced Faolan. "If ye want to come along, ye should have stood up when the earl was looking for men to take on the burden."

Faolan grunted. "Ye did nae give me a chance."

Broen shrugged, gaining a narrow look from Faolan. His friend muttered, "The betrothal was nae complete, and ye know it, Broen. Me own father was set on gaining Daphne for me. The match with her

was a fine one, and we all knew it. Her dowry was
nae yers just yet, nor was the alliance with her clan. I
wanted her too."

"It was me father who died on Grant land after that
bastard Donnach Grant wrote and told us Daphne was
dead. He will nae answer me letters or allow me onto
his land to gain more details. Me men are demanding
justice, which means a bloody summer when we begin
feuding with them," Broen snarled. "So, as it stands, I
have more to lose than ye."

"I know it well. We should combine our clans and
wipe Donnach Grant off the face of the Highlands,
since the king will nae do his duty and give us justice."

Broen laughed, low and unpleasant. "I'll be paying
James back for that slight. Ye noticed I was in a hurry,
and it's the truth I am. A king who will nae keep
us united is one I refuse to be loyal to, so I'm off to
ensure his son inherits as he should. Besides, if stealing
one woman can possibly ensure I can gain an explanation from Donnach Grant that will keep me men from
spilling blood, I'll steal her."

The words came easier than Broen had thought
they would. Surprise appeared on Faolan's face. Broen
turned and continued on toward the doors of the
tower before he thought too deeply about why he'd
chosen service to the earl over securing vengeance for
Daphne himself. He shouldn't need any further details
to honor his men's wishes for retribution.

But that was the old way of thinking. Unity had
its merits, and a good future would only come if the
clans stood together. He needed to think beyond his
own lust for vengeance and consider the innocents

who would die if he was feuding with his neighbors. A mature man recognized that he risked more than his own blood; only lads rushed off with their own glory on their minds.

The afternoon shadows were growing longer, but that didn't stop him from gesturing for his horse. James III was a disaster of a king. Half the Highland clans were feuding because he'd failed to find time to settle disputes, which left the Highlanders to take up ancient ways. The Lowlands were faring little better. The country was splitting in half. James had gone too far in his quest to gain a York-blooded son, though. That rumor was the foulest of all, because it would bring the English war into Scotland.

Not while he drew breath.

The royalists would brand him a traitor, but he'd wear the title proudly. James had a son, one who'd been raised by his mother and would rule well. The lad was grown now, but the queen had died, which cleared the way for James to wed again. The greedy man wanted to annul his marriage to a dead woman and gain himself a York-blooded wife, which would bind Scotland to the bloody English.

It was too much. Too much for Broen to accept from a sovereign he was supposed to kneel in front of and offer his loyalty to. Maybe in France a weakling could wear the crown, but Broen was a Highlander and he'd never kneel in front of a king who wouldn't keep his country united. Or any Scot who would buy himself a bastard daughter of the late king of England. The rumors claimed James had paid dearly for one of the few bastards acknowledged by Edward IV, who had enjoyed having mistresses in spite of claiming to love Elizabeth Woodville. Broen grinned. There was justice for a man—Edward had married a woman famed to be the most beautiful girl in England, but she hadn't been royal-blooded and half his nobles had turned on him.

Well, James III of Scotland may have paid for a York lass, but Broen planned to steal her. He was a Highlander, after all. James would be a fool not to expect it. If the king had taken precautions, the effort might cost Broen his life. He'd take the chance. Life wasn't worth living as a coward too busy sniveling about the wrongs done to his clan to take action. Besides, it was his opportunity to gain Sutherland's backing to put an end to the vengeance being demanded by his clan. There were some who would call him a coward for trying to avoid a feud, but he rather liked knowing he wasn't such a savage as to overlook a possible solution that didn't involve bloodshed. It didn't make him less of a Highlander, only more of a laird, because he had to think of his entire clan before allowing his personal feelings to be satisfied.

Yes, he'd do what he'd promised—or die trying.

❧

"Where is she?"

Clarrisa faced the door as Maud began muttering prayers. The tower was rough, and the rushes on the floor smelled foul. She stared at the rushes. They confirmed she had left civilization behind her in England, where most homes no longer used such, because by winter's end, they were filthy. But the walls

were made of stone, and the men who had met her at
the border were set to watch the doorway, leaving her
nothing to do but face whoever came for her.

She had no reason to be surprised to discover she'd
been shipped to Scotland in the middle of the night.
Her entire life had been one of being told that her
duty was to her family. The war between the York
and Lancaster nobles had claimed so many lives among
the blue-blooded. No child—even one bastard-born
such as herself—was overlooked. Blue blood was
noble, and controlling it the key to which family
would claim the crown.

So Clarrisa stared at the door, waiting to see whom
her uncle had sent her to. The sound of heavy footfalls
came from outside the door, along with soft whines.
The wooden door burst inward, its hinges squealing.

"Hiding, are ye? I expected as much from an
English bitch." James III stopped just inside the
doorway, a couple of hunting hounds at his heels.
One lifted its leg and wet the door frame, telling her
exactly where the stench in the room had come from.
Man and beasts lived together in the keep, and the idea
made her skin crawl.

"I was told to wait for you here." She didn't add
any title, for the moment felt informal. It bothered her
to know she was being sent to him so secretly, so he
might do as he pleased without any protest from the
church. "Which is what I am doing. It is not hiding."

She tried to temper her tone, but his eyes narrowed
before he stepped closer with one fist raised. "Ye'll
mind yer tongue with me, woman, else I'll teach ye
the manners yer York kin failed to. No woman argues

with me. I answer only to God. Why do ye think yer country's nobles are at one another's throats? They crave the same privilege."

Clarrisa lowered herself, remaining down while he grunted with approval. Oh yes, the king of Scotland was everything she expected of a man. The desire to prick his ego gained the better of her. "Forgive me. I simply believed the stories I've heard of Scotsmen— that you were quite different from Englishmen... Obviously only stories." She succeeded in making her tone everything her uncle had always demanded of her, meek and soft. Only she knew she wasn't submissive. She clung to that knowledge and gained strength from it.

"What stories?" He lowered his fist, a spark of interest lighting his eyes. He wasn't a bad-looking man, but he had servants aplenty to see to his grooming. Clarrisa wasn't impressed with his fine clothing. She'd suffered men like him her entire life, arrogant males who believed it their right to have fine things and full bellies while their servants shivered for want of a cloak. A maid watched from the door frame, easing back until the darkness swallowed her. She clearly didn't want any of the king's attention, which told Clarrisa exactly what sort of man he was, one to be avoided, because he'd take what pleased him and never have a care for the suffering his desires inflicted on others. And her family had sent her to him.

"Do nae go silent now, lass. Ye have stoked me curiosity."

"Oh... well... I should have kept my lips sealed. The church has warned me time and time again not to listen to what brazen women say men enjoy. Pious behavior is the path to salvation," she offered in an innocent tone.

"It's also damned boring. It's colder in Scotland, lass. A man needs fire in his bed sport."

"So I have heard..." Clarrisa allowed her words to trail off to a whisper. For certain, she had heard stories, but what had drawn her to the whispers to listen intently were the hints of how to control a man when the world was run by them. The man eyeing her was a king, and his men guarded the tower, but he watched her like a boy anticipating a sweet. "I am sure women's conversation would be of little interest to you."

James grinned, lust brightening his expression. He walked around her, inspecting her from head to toe.

"She'd better be a virgin." He directed his words toward Maud. The older woman drew up proudly.

"She's been guarded well, as befits the daughter of a king. The girl is simply nervous and saying things she's no true understanding of."

"Bastard daughter, but Edward's blood in a son is what I need. Royal blood is valuable, even when it's illegitimate." He reached out, and Clarrisa lost her grip on her composure. She slapped his hand away before he touched her. James snickered at her.

"Ye've been given to me, and ye'll be grateful, for I hear young Henry Tudor is set to kill off anyone with any claim to the English throne, now that he's wed himself to Elizabeth of York."

"He hasn't crowned her as his queen," Clarrisa muttered, unable to suppress the distaste in her tone. Henry VII was using his new wife to further his ambition. Elizabeth of York had no more say in her fate than Clarrisa did. They were both daughters of the late Edward IV.

"Why should he? The man had himself crowned Conqueror King, something nae done since William the Bastard. The York family has been defeated, which is yer family. In spite of the fact that he's English, I like young Henry," he insisted. "I believe it's the Scots blood in him. There is no mercy in him, no' even for a fair lass such as yerself."

Clarrisa lifted her chin. "I agree, and he'll take Scotland if given the chance because of it."

James contemplated her for a long moment, his expression hard. "Which is why I want a son who will be kin to Henry Tudor's son. Such a son could be very useful." He lowered his attention to her breasts and sat in a chair. "I liked our topic better before we began talking of England and its cursed nobles." He licked his lower lip. "What sorts of tales did ye hear from women of experience?"

Clarrisa fought to conceal the nausea twisting her insides. She lowered her eyelashes, and he took it as shyness, chuckling with male smugness. He rubbed his groin, enjoying being vulgar. "Come now, girl… What tales? They don't mean shit if you cannae impress a man with them. Where's that spirit gone to now, I wonder? Ye're the one who claimed she was nae hiding from me."

He was toying with her, and it sickened her more, but she didn't let fear take hold of her. Instead she felt superior to him, because lust didn't rule her.

"Oh… well… let me see." Clarrisa tapped one fingertip against her lower lip, mimicking the gesture she'd seen other girls use on the knights when they wanted their attention. It worked perfectly, snaring James's gaze instantly. "There was one I recall rather well about how a man enjoys having his... weapon polished." She trailed her fingers over her chin and down across her breasts. Maud made a choking sound.

Being a virgin didn't mean she was blind, after all. Her father's kin had kept her skirts from being lifted, but they hadn't stopped her from witnessing the vulgarity around her. Men seemed forever caught between their lust for power and their craving for female flesh.

"Get out, old woman. Ye've delivered her, and she will nae be leaving this chamber a maiden. Yer task is completed."

"I almost forgot the most important part of the tale..."

The king swallowed roughly, his attention intent on Clarrisa. "What might that be, lass?"

Clarrisa offered him what she hoped was a flirtatious look. "I have to bathe you first."

James frowned. "Why?"

"Because that's what the harem women do in the Far East." She rubbed her hands together suggestively. "To show their masters just how much they adore them. Some of the girls said the knights of the crusade brought back tales of how those men were pampered by several women all at the same time... I always wondered..."

"What?" he demanded. James was on his feet in a moment, his eyes bright with anticipation.

"I am simply curious to see if a man can truly hold back his nature long enough for me to bathe him."

"Ye doubt it?"

Clarrisa nodded and watched him lick his lips. "I do. None of the other girls had ever met a man who could last. Yet the Moors are fabled to be able to linger while their slave women rub them—and the Moors last all night long."

James caught her close, pulling her against his body. "That's on account of the fact that they never tried with a Scotsman, lass. I've got what it takes to let ye use yer spirit on me. I'll stand fast while ye polish me weapon from tip to base."

He pressed a foul kiss against her lips, grabbing her bottom with one hand before he spun her loose.

"Go on with ye, lass. Fill a tub and make it ready for yer master."

His men guarding the door grinned at her as she hurried past them. Their lurid looks didn't bother her—she was far more interested in the relief flooding her. Maybe it was a small freedom, but she wasn't stopped on her way away from the man who believed he owned her. As far as her kin were concerned, he did. The men winking at one another as she passed them believed the same thing.

Well, she was out of the chamber, and she'd find another way to escape the fate she'd been sent north to endure. She just wished she knew how she was going to do it.

~

"You've gone mad."

Maud was shaking with wrath, but Clarrisa didn't give her much of her attention. She had other matters

on her mind, such as how to keep the king of Scotland
from breeding her like a prized mare.

"The way you were talking, it's a wonder he hasn't
sent you out into the darkness like a cheap whore, for
that is what you sounded like."

"I've no liking to be viewed as a cowardly sacri-
fice. If it means you are displeased with my words,
so be it." The words slipped past years of instruction
to hold her tongue. She dumped the bucket of water
she'd hauled from the kitchen into the tub that sat
in front of the fire Maud was building up to warm
the room.

Maud turned, pointing a poker with a glowing red
tip at her. "What would ye rather have? Henry the
Seventh of England is hunting down every last drop
of York blood. Where can you make your future but
here in Scotland?" The old woman spit out the words
with clear distaste. "At least you are bound for the bed
of a king."

"He has three sons born in a legitimate union. I will
be naught but his whore; my children, illegitimate."
She offered Maud a sincere look. "It is not so kind a
fate to be born without the blessing of the church. I
would not wish it upon anyone or willingly thrust it
upon a babe. I'd be a selfish creature to think only of
my gain."

Maud stabbed the poker back into the fire. A
shower of crimson sparks flew up before dying in the
cold night air.

"True, but the king wants to be rid of Margaret of
Denmark's sons. He is trying to annul the marriage. I
hear his sons are plotting his murder, so it's fitting he

should be looking to take you as his leman so he can have more sons."

"She's dead and buried," Clarrisa insisted.

"Aye." Maud crossed herself. "But kings do not obey the same rules as other men. James wants the marriage annulled, and he's sent gold to the pope to see the matter resolved." Maud turned and considered her. "You might do very well for yourself if you please him. Perhaps I am wrong to judge you. Scots do like fire in their women. Your brazenness might be just the way to keep his attention."

With a wimple wrapped around her head and under her chin, Maud looked like a bride of Christ, or a bitter abandoned mistress. Clarrisa picked up the empty bucket and hid her smile of amusement. It wasn't wise to make an enemy of the woman, even if she was no more than another person trying to see Clarrisa's worth.

It seemed to be the way of life among the nobles. Clarrisa turned to the door and went down the narrow stone steps. There was only a single candle flickering near the base of the stairs. Considering that the king was in residence, the tower was strangely quiet. The single servant she'd spied in the hallway had not returned.

But James III was a king with many unhappy subjects. Margaret of Denmark had been a popular queen. James was quite the opposite, earning the anger of many of his clans because of his lack of justice. Not that his people's discontent would save Clarrisa from what her kin had sent her to do. She hooked the bucket onto a rope and sent it down the well opening. Her fingers ached from the frigid water, but she preferred it to what the rest of the night would offer.

She had been brazen, but she refused to repent. If her words delayed the distasteful event planned for her, she'd happily be thought as any number of sinful creatures. Everyone she had ever met thought something of her, and most of the time their ideas weren't kind. They judged her, when it was her father's sin that had brought her into the world bastard-born. But kings and nobles often believed they had rights beyond what the church said they did. Her mother had been a knight's daughter, and when the king took her to his bed, she had had no right to refuse.

Clarrisa stopped while pulling the bucket back up and listened. Something filtered through the stone walls, some sound she couldn't quite identify. She held still, waiting for another hint, but all she heard was the wind. The bucket was almost to the top, and she gave the rope another tug to complete its journey. She unhooked it and turned away from the well.

The bucket's contents went spilling onto the floor. Where before there had been nothing but empty space, men now stood in the darkness, cast half in shadow; huge figures that sent a shiver down her spine.

"Christ Almighty! That's cold."

A portion of the floor was missing and the rushes gone as a trapdoor showed how the men had got into the tower. One huge form climbed out, shaking his head and sending water flying.

"Why are ye the one screaming, Shaw? I expected the lass to do the yelling." In spite of his teasing words, there was a solid core of strength in his tone that sent her back a step. He was clearly accustomed to being obeyed, and the men coming up through the trapdoor all looked to him.

Shaw growled and wiped more water off his face. "She's holding her tongue so as to no' warn her lover, that bastard James, that we're here, Laird."

There was only a single lantern lit to help her see to her chore, but the light flickered off Shaw, illuminating the determination on his face. His hand rested on the hilt of a dagger tucked into his worn belt.

"He is not my lover, nor do I want him for such." Her voice quivered just a tiny amount. Clarrisa forced herself to face them. She'd not die a sniveling coward.

The laird chuckled, but it was not a pleasant sound. "There's a fact I plan to ensure does nae change by stealing ye away before His Royal Highness notices ye are taking too long with his bathwater. But if ye're speaking the truth, ye can prove it by coming along with us without a fuss."

His hair was longer than the English wore theirs, some of it resting on his broad shoulders. It was light colored, but the candlelight illuminated copper in it. For a moment she was tempted, relief filling her, but the way Shaw still gripped his dagger made her hesitate. Her thoughts raced, and her heart did too.

"Steal me… To what end? You can murder me here as easily as on the banks of a river."

He shook his head, drawing a short grunt from Shaw. The laird snapped his head around to stare at his man. "MacNicols do nae settle their disputes by spilling the blood of women. We're set to prevent her from becoming the king's leman. Stealing her will satisfy that need."

"She's Edward the fourth's bastard. His blood is a threat to us all," Shaw countered. "One best dealt with permanently, I'm thinking."

"We'll be ending the matter once we've taken her to the Highlands."

Highlands… The Scottish laird might as well have said Hades, for the Highlands were a place where only uncivilized clans lived. The people were barbaric; they stole women from one another like Moors.

But it would be preferable to becoming the king's broodmare.

She was tempted but also torn, because she could see the argument shimmering in Shaw's eyes. Escaping into the hands of men intent on murdering her wasn't a kinder fate. Clarrisa turned to run, but it was too late. A hard hand clamped around her arm, dragging her to a stop before her skirts stopped swirling.

"Here now. Ye'll have to be missing out on treating James like a Moor, for we do nae need England's feud spilling into our royal line," her captor informed her.

"I want none of it either—"

Shaw looped a length of fabric around her head. It was thin enough to slide right through her open teeth and gag her. Clarrisa reached for it, frantically trying to keep it from biting into her skin, but she was too late. A few twists and it was knotted firmly in place. "Get her down the passageway before anyone guesses what we're about, lads."

Whoever the men were, they plucked her off her feet like she was a child. She struggled, unable to master her fear as they handed her to the men still below the surface of the kitchen floor. There was nothing but darkness, which sent a bolt of terror through her.

"Ye might have tied her up, Laird. She's got claws as sharp as a hawk."

Her grasping hands sank into sleeves and plaids, but she was yanked away. Shaw followed her, and she heard the trapdoor being slid back into position. The light from the kitchen went with it, leaving her encased in blackness.

"That maid had best keep her end of the bargain and right the rushes, or our game will be ended quickly," Shaw muttered.

"She'll do it," the laird muttered while carrying Clarrisa through the narrow passageway. "She has as much to gain as we do by making sure the king does nae get a York-blooded son."

Clarrisa twisted and turned, but she was held firmly by her captors. Her dress was a tangled mess, and she felt the night air brushing her knees above her stockings. Her braids hung like ropes—her hat lying wherever it had fallen—but the gag kept her braids from being stepped on. Helplessness almost strangled her, but there was nothing to do but suffer it.

They set her feet down in a thicket, where the trees were dark shapes in the night. There was the musty scent of fallen leaves being disturbed by their passing, but the branches only allowed some of the moonlight to illuminate the ground. She shoved frantically away from the laird, only to hear the man chuckle at her efforts. He caught one of her braids and pulled her back toward him. Tears stung her eyes as pain bit into her scalp, a soft moan the only sound that made it past the gag.

"Best for ye to stay close to me, lass. Me men do nae care to keep ye alive." He leaned close so she could hear his soft words. "I've no liking for harming a female, but I'll be taking ye. How much discomfort ye want to suffer is up to ye."

The solid authority was back in his tone, but his tone lacked the suspicion she'd heard from Shaw. Part of her wanted to grasp that idea close, but she needed to be practical. She could not trust him, yet she longed to, because he promised her life.

There were more of them now. She could see the white puffs of their breath with the help of moonlight. She hadn't heard them, not even with the leaves on the ground.

Highlander. It was a word she'd been raised to fear. The clans inhabiting the upper portions of Scotland were the most fierce. No sane person ventured among them. She retreated without thinking, simply because the idea of going to the Highlands was so horrifying.

There was a short grunt from the laird. "Wrap her up, Shaw. Her claws do draw blood."

The hand holding her braid released. "Hold her steady for me."

The group suddenly faced her. Her arms were pressed against her body as a length of fabric was wound around her. Around and around it went, until she was swaddled like a babe.

"Now, let's be done with this bit of work, lads," the laird muttered before her feet left the ground again.

It was all so simple, so quietly done. The Highlander

hefted her over his shoulder with an ease she might have admired if the man weren't abducting her. Clarrisa found herself straining to hear the sounds of pursuit, but there was nothing but the wind. It blew through the trees, rustling the leaves enough to cover the escape of her captors. The only sound that came at last were the soft footfalls of a horse. Her captor tossed her up and over the back of the beast without so much as a grunt.

He swung up behind her, and she watched him dig his heels into the underbelly of the horse to send it forward. It was as though the men blended together with the darkness, for there wasn't a hint of hesitation from any one of them. Even the horses surged forward as though they were accustomed to nighttime rides.

Fate had a misplaced sense of humor for granting her the escape she'd longed for in the form of such men. She should have been afraid, but the truth was that she was too relieved to be free of James's lust to feel anything else. Even the idea of going to the Highlands was losing its sting as she watched the tower grow smaller and smaller behind them.

But once it was gone, she shivered and dreaded just what fate awaited her at the hands of the MacNicols laird.

* * *

Her jaw ached.

Clarrisa worked her mouth open and closed a few times before she opened her eyes. The sun wasn't truly risen yet anyway; darkness still surrounded her. Pain shot through her head, and she lifted her hand to rub at her forehead with a frown—she couldn't recall what she'd done to injure herself. Her mouth felt drier than during a sweltering August day, and her memory returned with a clear recollection of how being gagged had felt. The thing was missing now, but it seemed the fabric had dried out her mouth.

"Ye sleep like a babe. Unconcerned, as though the world is a peaceful place. Maturity should have taught ye differently, but I suppose I cannae be expecting any royal offspring to know much about life's harsher edges."

Laird MacNicols was a giant. He squatted, the edges of his plaid just brushing the ground. She gained a glimpse of his well-made boots with antler-horn buttons running up their sides before he muttered something to Shaw in Gaelic.

Fear twisted through her, because Shaw's eyes were icy and she recalled clearly what he wanted to do with her.

Shaw was leaning against a rock, his long sword cradled across his lap. "She's the one, sure enough. The only other was wearing a wimple and well past her prime. Saw them both get out of that wagon meself."

The laird had blue eyes—startling with how intense they were. His hair was fair but streaked with hints of red. It hung down to his shoulders, with a section of it braided to keep it out of his eyes. There was an uncivilized way about him that had nothing to do with the common clothing he wore. It was in his eyes and the corded muscles so clearly visible in his arms and legs. He was not a man who had others do his bidding.

But his sword was fine. The pommel was clearly

visible beyond his left shoulder, and the rising sun illuminated the gold hilt. A blue sapphire winked at her from where it was set into a crest that included a rampant lion—a noble creature. Only men with noble blood could use such an animal on their belongings. It meant he was more than just a clan laird. He had blue blood flowing through his veins.

The sight sent her struggling away from him, but the fabric still bound her. His lips twitched up, amusement sparkling in his eyes.

"Now, why the hurry to place distance between us, Clarrisa of York? Did I nae see to yer comfort quite nicely?"

"Your man wants to slit my throat. Why wouldn't I want to be away from you?"

He shrugged. "Shaw believes it a necessary thing, since yer kin seem to think we need their troubles spreading here to Scotland." His grin faded. "Something I am nae in favor of either."

"Neither am I."

Surprise flickered in his blue eyes. "The way I heard it, ye were fixing to wait on our king like some fat pasha from the Far East."

There was thick disapproval in his tone, and he stood. He was dismissing her—condemning her, actually. She struggled and sat up, in spite of the fabric binding her.

"You understand naught," she sputtered. "It was a ruse, to delay him."

He returned his dark blue gaze to her, but there was a slightly mocking arch to one eyebrow now. "Well then, lass, I'm listening sure enough. Why do nae ye explain to me what ye're doing in me country and with me king?"

Why was she begging?

Because she wanted to live.

Heat stung her cheeks because she was ashamed at just how easily she had been reduced to whimpering. It wasn't the first time she'd had no one to depend on except herself. She drew in a deep breath and tried to collect her courage.

"I was sent here by my family. The ruse gained me freedom from the tower room your king intended to use to breed me like a mare." The sting in her cheeks doubled as she spoke. "So... you see... we desire the same thing."

He bent his knees so he was able to scrutinize her once more on the same level. He had his share of arrogance, but what surprised her was the enjoyment lurking in his eyes.

"Do we now?" he muttered softly. "I have to doubt ye on that, since ye turned to flee from me."

"I couldn't willingly go with you when one of your men wants to kill me."

He shrugged again. His lips parted and his teeth flashed at her when he grinned. "I told ye it would nae be happening, and I am laird." His expression hardened. "But ye are still the natural daughter of Edward the Fourth of England and might be well accomplished in the art of twisting words."

"I am hardly the only child he is rumored to have fathered outside his marriage." She struggled again against the fabric binding her, feeling too helpless by far, being caught in its folds.

"I hear Edward acknowledged ye, which means a great deal considering how rare noble blood is becoming due to yer War of the Roses."

He reached out and grabbed the fabric beneath her chin. A moment later she was standing. Her feet shifted, her balance unsteady because her toes had gone numb sometime during the night.

"Henry Tudor has wed Elizabeth of York. The War of the Roses is finished now, because York and Lancaster are united," she explained.

"But Henry has nae had her crowned queen, and ye are here, brought under cover of darkness to a lone tower where James of Scotland sneaks away to meet with ye. Now, that is suspicious, lass, and no mistake. But it is also dangerous for me and me clan, for we have enough troubles without ye giving James a son with York blood. Ye tried to flee when I offered ye freedom, which means ye might well be intent on becoming a powerful queen through yer son."

"I told you why I tried to run."

He chuckled, but it wasn't a pleasant sound. "Am I to trust ye, then?" He stepped closer, maintaining a firm grip on the fabric to keep her in place. "Will ye offer to bathe me with yer delicate hands, Clarrisa? To show me how adept ye are at common chores? From what the young maid told me, ye claim to have more practice at polishing men's weapons. Mind ye, I am no' saying I would nae enjoy ye proving yer gratefulness in such a fashion."

Her jaw dropped open, but the sound that emerged was a snarl. Full of rage and frustration, she actually lowered her chin and tried to bite the hand securing her in front of him.

"I shall not! You're a fiend to suggest such a thing."

He laughed at her, jerking his hand away before she sank her teeth into his flesh. She stumbled and would have landed on her backside, but someone caught her floundering body from behind, and her face burned bright red as she listened to his men enjoy her shame. Someone yanked the length of wool off her, and she spun around like a child playing in a spring meadow. When the last of the wool plaid fell away, she was dizzy. Her captor gripped her wrists while she struggled to maintain her balance, and wrapped a length of leather around them. He knotted the ends firmly before giving a satisfied grunt.

"I am Broen MacNicols, and ye will be leaving, lass, but ye will be traveling with me to the Highlands where I can be sure ye are nae adding to the troubles in me country. Give me men any frustration, and I'll let them keep ye bundled like a babe."

"Brute," she accused. "Uncivilized… Highlander."

He offered her a wink and a grin, which sent her temper up another few degrees.

"Mount up, lads. We're too close to England for me taste. The stench sours me stomach."

❧

Beast.

Broen MacNicols was uncivilized.

Clarrisa felt her cheeks stinging with another blush, only this time it was born of shame. Her behavior had matched his. She had no idea where such an urge had come from—biting a man was the reaction of a street strumpet. For heaven's sake, she could read and write!

But she'd wanted to bite him; the urge had swept through her faster than any reason might intercede. Perhaps her mind had broken under the stress of the last few days.

She scoffed at her thoughts. There was nothing unhinged about her reasoning. It had been her temper, flashing brighter than a fire catching summer straw. Besides, she was too young to be insane. That idea made her smile. Madness hadn't taken hold of her— for that would have been a blessing. At least insanity would have kept her from worrying about the right and wrong of what her blood kin wanted her to do. Well, their ambition had landed her in Scotland and on her way into the Highlands, it seemed.

Clarrisa twisted her hands again, in spite of knowing that the leather binding her wrists would hold steady. Pain sliced through her skin, reminding her that she would be the only one suffering for her struggles—but she seemed unable to master the urge to chafe against her bonds periodically.

The day grew warm. Her escort unbuttoned their doublets and oversleeves, grinning as the wind flapped their shirtsleeves.

Broen MacNicols wasn't like any of her noble kin. He didn't ride in the center of his men but took the high ground and then pushed his stallion to move faster than the rest of them so he might appear on the opposite side of a gorge. He was always in motion, even when he pulled his mount up to give the huge beast a moment of rest. In those brief times, his eyes moved constantly. His profile was harsh, his jaw square, and his cheekbones high. Every winter tale she'd ever heard of wild Scotsmen rose from her memory to go along with the sight of him sitting so confidently with his knees peeking from beneath the edge of his kilt.

Highlanders, actually. The Lowland Scots were more like the English. Highlanders were different. When they came down to fight, history changed.

Maybe she was exactly where she needed to be. It was a dangerous idea, but one that tantalized her too. She had no way of knowing if her situation was improving or not. The only thing that was clear was that Broen pushed them north the entire day; even sunset didn't stop him. When he did call a halt to their journey, the moon was fully risen, and Clarrisa slid from the back of her mare gratefully. Her legs trembled, and every joint ached, but she stomped at the ground to restore her circulation.

Her mare eagerly left her to go and drink from the nearby river. All the horses surged toward the water, many of them flicking their tails.

Clarrisa turned in the opposite direction.

"Now where do ye think ye're heading?"

She jumped and stumbled back a pace. "You needn't appear in my path so suddenly."

Broen tilted his head to one side. "So are ye saying I should make sure ye see me on me way to head ye off?" He propped his hands on his hips. "That's something ye English have been wishing for a long time, but we Highlanders will never bow to yer desire to know exactly what we're about."

The suspicion in his tone threatened to send her temper flaring again, but the absurdity of having to explain her needs to him made her shake her head instead. "If you cannot understand why I might be set on seeking out some privacy after all day on the back of that mare, you must be as dull-witted as I've heard Highlanders are. Or do your women hike their skirts and relieve themselves among you?"

His amusement evaporated, but she caught the hint of regret in his blue eyes, because many of his men were relieving themselves. He reached out and caught her upper arm to turn her away from the sight. "I am nae used to having women along, and for that, I owe ye an apology. Go on, but understand that keeping sight of ye is important. I suggest ye become accustomed to me company."

"When it snows during summer," she muttered, too relieved to make her tone mild.

He chuckled. "Ye might decide ye like me. Many a lass has done so..."

There was a slim hint of heat in his voice now. She found the idea of his liking anything about her unsettling; a tingle raced down her spine at the thought, one she needed to kill quickly. "Well, I doubt I shall become one of them."

She hoped so, anyway, but the man walked in front of her once again. He was attractive in a way she'd never encountered before. The night seemed to fit him, the moonlight enhancing his rugged features.

"You are simply not to my taste."

Liar...

One golden eyebrow rose mockingly. "Now why

would ye go and say something like that and dash me hopes that ye might lavish me with personal attention like some eastern harem laird?" His lips curved in a sensuous manner, sending a second jolt of sensation down her back. "Ye're truly testing me, lass, for a Highlander enjoys a challenge more than just about anything."

He was grinning at her. She should have considered the expression arrogant, for it was, but instead of becoming annoyed, a warm tingle rippled across her skin. He was too intent, too keen, and she feared he could read her feelings right off her face.

"I am not challenging you, sir. All I crave is to be out of your sight." She sounded breathless and grabbed the front of her skirts to go around him. The man let her move until she was even with him before reaching out and securing a hard grip on her forearm. Once more he loomed over her, his greater height making it necessary for her to tip her head up so she might maintain eye contact with him. Another tiny shiver went down her spine.

"Now, lass, do nae be unkind. Cannae I enjoy the idea of a fine-looking woman such as yerself attending me while I'm saddled with the chore of keeping ye from starting trouble in me country?"

"No, you cannot," she insisted before pushing at him. He was as immovable as a mountain, and she gained not even an inch for her effort.

"Well now, Clarrisa, ye do nae control me thinking, and that's a fact." His voice had turned deep and husky.

"I have no say over what you do at all." Nor over how he affected her. "There is something you have in common with my English kin."

He frowned, his eyes darkening, but for some reason the look on his face didn't remind her of her uncle's displeasure. When she looked into Broen's eyes, she didn't find the same arrogance, only solid disapproval.

"I do nae care to be compared to the English, Clarrisa."

There was a warning in his voice that pleased her. It should have frightened her, but instead she discovered she enjoyed knowing he wasn't happy with her. At least the knowledge killed whatever strange emotional response she'd been struggling against. Yes, it was much better to be at odds with him. "I seek privacy; if you allow me that, we need not converse."

"Something ye shall nae have until I can be sure ye are secured inside a solid tower."

Horror arrived at last, stealing her thoughts and leaving her gasping. Thoughts of the boy princes and the fate of those with royal blood who were locked away for safekeeping rose up to torment her. Those young princes had died because others coveted their power. No one ever saw them again, except as ghosts. "Now, do nae be looking at me like that. I am nae a monster." He released her, a sound of disgust reaching her ears. "But I cannae have ye giving James a York-blooded son."

"So you will lock me up…" Her voice was a mere whisper, her throat feeling like it was swelling up.

"A few of me countrymen believe slitting yer throat is a better solution, as ye have already noticed. Kindly recall I am nae one of them."

"There is little kindness in this entire affair."

She stumbled away from him, forcing herself to stop when he began to follow her. Horror was making her shiver, and she detested its powerful hold. She raised her chin and clenched her jaw. "Well then," she ground out, "if you lack the courage to spill my blood, step aside and allow one of your men to do the deed. I have no taste for living in fear."

She might be foolish to say so, but it was what she truly felt in that moment. Her words were bold and brash, but they filled her with a steady confidence that cut through the terror. "I'm going up behind those rocks if you need to point the way to Shaw. If my throat is going to be slit, at least I shall not die with my robes soiled like a babe."

She turned her back on him. It took every bit of courage she had to not look over her shoulder, but she pulled up her skirts and climbed to the outcropping of rocks, making it behind them before her nerve deserted her.

※

"I never thought I'd witness ye taking those sorts of words from any man—much less from an Englishwoman."

Broen sent a cutting look toward Shaw. "She has courage, so I'm feeling generous."

His cousin hooked his hands into his wide belt. "Ye mean she's arrogant, which is in keeping with her kin. Young Henry is doing this world a service by ridding it of York blood. Power hungry, the lot of them."

"I do nae kill women."

Shaw made a low sound. "She'll whelp more greedy sons to keep the war going into the next generation. I wear the same colors ye do, but there are exceptions to every rule."

"No' to honor, Shaw, and ye'll be remembering that while I'm laird of the MacNicols."

"Which will nae be for much longer, if James has his way. We'll all be breaking bread with the English if a prince of Scotland shares the same blood as the heir to the English throne. She looks very convincing, but she's no' innocent, and ye can bet everything ye have on it. Did nae ye listen to what she was planning to do for James? 'Treat him like a Moor' is the way I heard it. Those men have palaces full of women all fighting one another to place their children at the top. Scotland has no need of such savageness." There was heat in the man's voice, a rage fueled by blood spilled through the ages.

"Ye think I have no feeling for the suffering the English have inflicted upon our kin, Shaw?" Broen turned to face his cousin. "Ye seem to forget it was my father who lost his life to the Grants."

"A wrong done to all MacNicols—which ye have yet to claim vengeance for."

Several of his men were listening now. Broen could see their eyes glowing with the same rage in Shaw's voice. He battled against it himself.

"We'll be feuding with the Grants, and no mistake, if I cannae gain a reasonable accounting from Donnach Grant for me father's death. James cannae be taking issue with me for fighting when he refuses to do his duty and bring that bastard Donnach to justice for stealing me bride and putting our men to the sword when me father went to talk terms." His men nodded, but Shaw remained still, his expression hard.

"This woman is another matter. The earl sent us

after her, and her fate is Norris's to decide. I stole her
so the earl would force Donnach to meet me, because
I will nae see yer mothers weeping until I've done
me best to avoid feuding. Stealing one woman for the
earl is better than beginning a feud without knowing
I've done me best to avoid it. Do ye want to see yer
mother wailing over the body of one of yer brothers?
There will be death if we go looking for vengeance.
Do nae doubt it."

Shaw nodded at last. "I suppose that's why ye are
laird and no' me. I did nae think on the matter quite
that way."

Broen watched his men nod in agreement, but he
was far from feeling settled. Norris Sutherland might
very well agree with those who demanded Clarrisa be
eliminated permanently. Her blood was too precious,
too dangerous in the unstable world they all shared.
But she had spirit, and there was a lack of arrogance in
her eyes, which had him looking back to where she'd
taken refuge behind a large boulder. Shaw would call
him a softhearted fool, and maybe it was true, but
taking her life held no appeal.

She was no beauty but wasn't too hard on the
eyes. Her hair was blond, and the sunlight had turned
it golden. But what captivated him was the way she
moved. The curve of her hip when she walked or the
manner in which she chewed on her lower lip when
she was trying to decide what to say to him. Or the
way she'd watched him throughout the day. He'd felt
her blue eyes on him as though she were touching him.

Bloody hell.

He shook his head, wondering when he'd lost sight

of what was best for his clan. Clarrisa was rumored to be one of several bastards of the last English king, Edward IV. The man had fallen in battle, and his cousin Henry Tudor was now crowned. Henry had wed Edward's legitimate daughter, but he hadn't made her queen yet, which left the nobles wondering if there was still power to be grabbed.

James Stuart was thinking exactly that. A king had responsibilities, and James III liked to ignore his too much for Broen to follow him.

It made him a traitor in the eyes of many Scottish nobles. Broen would wear the title gladly. His father had died while sitting at a negotiating table, and the king had sat in his castle and done nothing. James wasn't worthy of his loyalty, and the man would never get the York-blooded son he sought either. Not while Broen was laird of the MacNicols.

Of course, with the way the country was, nothing was for certain. It might be his throat slit instead of Clarrisa's—or maybe both. There were too many men whose loyalty was uncertain. Did they follow the king, or seek to see his son placed on the throne of Scotland so a new era might begin?

Well, he knew where he stood. A man was only worth as much as his honor. Clarrisa was going to Sutherland land, but she was going alive.

And he could just bloody well forget what her lips looked like.

❧

"Why did ye pull on that leather? Did ye really think the knots would give?"

Clarrisa turned to find Broen watching her. He hadn't stepped out into the open, which fit his character. She lowered her hands, killing the urge to inspect the damage she'd done to her skin. The skin itched and burned, confirming she'd torn her flesh.

"Doesn't every captive pray for deliverance?"

He moved forward, looking like he was materializing from the shadows. He hadn't buttoned his doublet and seemed quite at ease in the chilly night. The edge of his kilt fluttered gently in the stirring breeze. He moved silently and stood before her, while she was still satisfying her curiosity about his person. He captured her forearm once more and raised her wrists.

"Praying is hoping God will strike down yer enemies. Struggling is failing to have faith in his power to deliver ye." The moonlight reflected off a small dagger as he slipped the blade under the leather and jerked it upward. "I know a few priests who will take issue with ye for nae waiting for the divine hand of the Almighty to free ye."

His tone was playfully mocking, renewing the rush of heat that seemed to happen anytime he was near her.

She stepped back and brushed the coils of leather from her wrists. "I know more who will protest your intention to murder me, which made it a fine idea to take a hand in my own fate."

He slid the dagger back into the top of his boot. The worn leather ended just below his knee, and she could see the edge of fur peeking out. Her toes were frozen, and she was envious of the sturdy footwear.

"I believe I know a few priests who would condemn ye for going to the bed of a man who is nae yer husband. A fine thing for me to interfere with," he insisted.

"It wasn't any idea of mine." Her uncle would have beaten her for such an admission, but the man in front of her was lawless, and it seemed to be affecting her. "It was my uncle's scheme and your king's. I've already thanked you for removing me from it. We should stop trying to agree with each other."

Broen folded his arms over his chest and studied her for a long moment. She actually felt the weight of his judgment. It needled her, making her realize she cared what he thought of her. She shouldn't—*wouldn't*.

He grunted. "Aye, maybe ye've got more sense than I do, lass. We'll be parting ways soon enough."

His words shamed her. She felt her cheeks brighten with a blush. His gaze touched on the color for a moment before he shook his head.

"Now, there's why I'm torn. Ye seem genuine in yer innocence." His eyes narrowed. "Which may be a skill ye've been perfecting since ye learned to walk. Most likely so, from what tales I've heard of English nobility. The females are a sly lot."

Clarrisa glared at him, lifting her chin to look at him directly. "Maybe you are planning to use my blood for your own gain. That's a skill Scottish lairds learn early, I hear. Highlanders only have loyalty to their own clans."

"I am a Highlander and proud of it." The amusement vanished from his eyes. She should have been satisfied to hear the disgruntlement in his voice; instead, all she felt was needling guilt for being so insulting. Her mother would be ashamed of her.

"We're getting nowhere with all this talk," he informed her in a low tone that did little to disguise his frustration.

"Of course you believe so, for it would be much easier for you to deliver me to my imprisonment if you weren't made aware of how unjust it is."

"Unjust?" He uncrossed his arms, making him huge once more. Sensation snaked down her spine, and she was suddenly foolishly aware of the man for some reason. Clarrisa stepped back, a warning rising from somewhere deep inside her brain. She wasn't even sure what it was telling her—to escape, or that Broen MacNicols was dangerous.

"Life is nae fair. No man has an easy path. Even royal blood carries with it burdens. I'll nae pity ye for having to shoulder what every man does. I'm taking ye into the Highlands even if ye try to talk me to death along the way."

He reached out and clamped one hand around her forearm. He pulled her behind him on his way back down to where his men were resting. She couldn't rightly call it a camp, for there wasn't a single tent. Several of the Highlanders had pulled their swords off their backs and raised their plaids to cover their heads. They were nestled against tree trunks, where the branches were thick. Some had dug up fallen leaves and piled them over their laps so they practically disappeared. The horses were nowhere in sight; the younger boys who'd ridden with them were gone as well.

"We'll nae rest long, just enough for the horses. Sleep while ye can."

He tugged her right into the thicket. She had to raise her free arm to protect her face from being scratched. Once they reached a thick tree trunk, he released her.

"Sit, or I'll tie ye again."

Clarrisa sank to her knees, watching him as he pulled his sword free. He raised his plaid and sat down, before leaning back against the tree. She gasped when he reached out and grabbed one of her braids.

"Closer, lass. Yer hair is nae that long." There was a renewed hint of amusement in his tone. She ground her teeth with frustration, but he didn't grant her any mercy. He looped her braid around his wrist and grasped the end inside his fist. He tucked his arm beneath the length of his plaid, pulling her closer.

She ended up sitting next to him with only a tiny space between them. Broen closed his eyes, granting her privacy, even if it was of an odd sort. The man had ahold of her hair, for Christ's sake, something that struck her as intimate. Only little girls and brides wore their hair loose. She stared at him, because she'd always imagined that when a man touched her hair, he would be her husband. *Or her lover…*

Clarrisa chided herself and ordered her imagination to be silent. Circumstances were grim enough without her appearing to be drawn to her captor. Still, at least she was free of his piercing stare. She leaned back against the tree, longing for her cloak, which lay forgotten in the tower chamber. At least she could pull her knees closer to her chest, which allowed her toes to take shelter beneath her skirts.

Her thoughts wanted to whirl, but exhaustion was

nipping at her. She closed her eyes, hugging herself
for warmth. Her head was uncovered, and the chill
of the night made her long for her hat. Silk ribbons
were threaded through her braids like a bride's, and
her dress was made of linen, too lightweight for the
Scottish night.

Still, she preferred the chill to the demands James
would have made of her. Many would call her
foolish, but her body was the only thing she had;
her virtue, her single possession. But she would not
go so far as to say she preferred Broen's company.
No, she would not. Yet she was grateful her wrists
were no longer bound. Her sleep became restful; the
knowledge that Broen was near actually granted her
a feeling of security.

Better the devil you know…

She didn't know Broen, but he'd freed her when
it would have been easier for him to leave her tied.
Actions so often spoke more of a man's nature than
what he proclaimed. Her uncle had liked to tell her
what her place was, often imposing duties on her to
reinforce his demands. His face faded away as she
turned toward the warmth of the man next to her.

For the moment, it was all she needed.

❦

"I warned ye, Laird."

Clarrisa jerked awake as the man she was leaning
against erupted into motion. She went rolling across
the fallen leaves, gaining a few scratches along the way.

"Ye're mad to startle me, Shaw!" Broen snarled.
He had his sword unsheathed and in hand before he'd

finished speaking, but Shaw reached out and grabbed her by the nape. He dragged her to her feet and threw her several yards.

"She was pressed to ye like a well-satisfied whore." Shaw was shaking with rage. "No doubt she thinks to warm yer cock and secure herself a Highland laird, since we've ruined her plans to have the king."

"I plan no such thing."

"Be silent, Clarrisa." Broen's voice was deadly. It shocked her into shutting her mouth when her pride still stung. The MacNicols laird kept his sword steady, leveled at his clansman. Broen moved on sure feet, keeping his knees bent as he changed position to stand in front of her. "Ye're shaming yer mother, Shaw MacNicols."

"And ye're disgracing yer murdered father by allowing this scheming English jade to rest her head on yer shoulder."

Clarrisa felt her face flame with a blush, for sometime during the night, she'd ended up leaning against Broen. "It wasn't planned. The man had hold of my braid."

Broen snorted. "Do ye ever do what ye're told, woman?"

A few of his men chuckled, and even Shaw snorted with enjoyment. Clarrisa felt her temper ignite.

"Oh yes, my lord." She lowered herself prettily, exactly as Maud would have approved of. "I obeyed my uncle, who sent me to that cursed tower where your king planned to use me." She rose and glared at the men watching her, but mostly at their laird. "Doing what I'm told has brought me to this place where there isn't a trusting soul in sight, so I believe I am done with it."

She was casting out a challenge but didn't care. The man was a barbarian; the least she might do was match her behavior to his. She stumbled out of the thicket, not knowing where she was going, only sure she had to move because there was so much emotion coursing through her.

She'd slept against him.

The knowledge rose in her mind. Her cheeks continued to flame as the night replayed in her mind like a well-memorized fireside tale. There was a fleeting recollection of her nose warming at last and deep satisfaction as she'd huddled close to his body heat. She was going to burn in hell. Or die of shame where she stood. Maybe expire from pure frustration. Possibly—*Enough!*

But frustration began to burn her alive as she heard the MacNicols retainers laughing. She fumed and turned to face them, but whirled back around when she caught sight of them roaring with amusement.

Highlanders. Only Highlanders would be entertained by uncivilized behavior.

Broen wanted to be furious. For certain, he needed to make sure his men knew he was strong enough to lead them. But he lost the battle to maintain a stony expression and sheathed his sword while softly laughing at his cousin.

"Well now, Shaw… she's got you pinned with yer own words." His cousin scowled, but the rest of his men were still amused, laughing outright as Shaw scratched his head. "Admit it, Shaw, or get yerself a pair of breeches and move to England, where men do nae have any sense of humor. It's for sure ye need one in the Highlands."

There was more laughter, and Shaw finally grinned. "Aye, ye've got a point there. I never met an Englishman with a good nature. Laird."

Broen nodded in acceptance of the single word. He walked past his cousin and clapped a solid hand on his shoulder before continuing on after Clarrisa. She was nowhere in sight, but a fresh set of tracks led to the rocks she'd gone behind the night before.

His men were leading the horses back over the rise, dawn turning the horizon pink. His young squire handed him the reins of his stallion. Broen watched the lad check the saddle. It took getting accustomed to—allowing another to see to things, like his horse, but the lad wouldn't be given his own horse until he proved himself by caring for the animal of another man first. Even as the laird's son, Broen had done the same.

"I understand what the lass was saying." Shaw stepped up, his own reins held in a firm grip. "I'm nae so dense as to no' see she was sent by her kin, or that having Sutherland lending his name to our argument with the Grants will be a great benefit."

"And I'm no' so prideful as to no' see ye have the best for the MacNicols in mind," Broen muttered. "I made ye one of me captains because ye are nae afraid to tell me what ye truly think. Only the English are foolish enough to ride into battle with arse-polishing men at their sides."

Shaw nodded and grinned, clearly pleased with Broen's words. "I do speak me mind." He pointed at Broen. "She was draped over ye, but now that I'm thinking on it..."

Broen glared at his kin. "What's on yer mind, man?"

"Well... yer head was resting on hers. Such a pretty picture it was too. Warmed me heart."

His cousin laughed at the groan Broen offered him. Shaw mounted and smirked at him. "Now, I do believe ye told me a Highlander needs his sense of humor, Laird."

Broen gained the saddle and controlled his stallion's motions as he glared at his cousin. "Aye, that's a fact, but it's also a fact I've no liking for this situation at all."

It was a sobering thought, one that brought tension back to where it'd been digging into the center of his shoulder blades. He guided his stallion up the hill, dreading running down his captive. But he'd do what was necessary.

Instead, he pulled up his stallion, the animal side-stepping because it wasn't accustomed to his stopping him so soon after starting. Clarrisa was standing just over the ridge, with the dawn illuminating her. From her head to her toes, she wasn't very tall, and her limbs were what he'd call *delicate*. Twin golden braids hung down her back, and the lightweight fabric of her dress was wrinkled. Everything about her was fragile, except the look she aimed at him.

He swore he could have warmed his hands over the fire in her eyes. Disheveled and chilled, she should have looked defeated. He should have been battling pity for her plight. Instead, Broen discovered he admired her—more than just admired. His feelings were building, gaining strength as Clarrisa lifted her chin and stood her ground. As he guided his stallion forward, she didn't change her demeanor. She kept her blue eyes steady and her chin firmly set.

"Are ye ready to ride, lass?" His voice had turned husky, betraying his fascination with her. She lifted a hand and took the one he offered her. The woman didn't lack strength. She stepped onto a boulder before using it to spring onto the back of the horse. He could have lifted her—had expected to—but found himself guiding her more than pulling her from the ground.

She settled behind him, grasping his belt to secure herself. Broen bit back the demand he wanted to issue to her to answer his question, because it felt a lot like flirting. Now there was a difficulty he didn't need. His clan didn't need Clarrisa among them, with her royal blood to draw other lairds onto MacNicols land seeking to steal her.

But his emotions didn't want to listen to reason. Curse his feelings—and his own nature.

Two

"THERE'LL BE A WARM FIRE AND SUPPER AT
Raven's Perch."

Relief swept through her, but Clarrisa didn't allow
herself to be carried away by his promises. Broen
had to stop his stallion from nipping her mare. He'd
allowed her back into her own saddle halfway through
the day, no doubt to keep his horse from exhaustion.

"Ye're a hard one to please if you cannae even smile
at the idea of a hot bowl of stew, maybe even bread."
He tried to tempt her with a soft tone.

But she needed to protect herself. Broen was too
likable. She'd never suffered such attraction to a man
before. She wanted to return the smile on his lips, but
he'd only see her responses as proof that he had the
skill to bend her to his will.

"Hard? Oh aye, I believe there shall be hard and
sturdy walls at your Raven's Perch for me as well.
What a charming idea to know I'm so near to my
prison." She looked away from the MacNicols laird,
unwilling to expose her despair to him. Everything
she knew was far away, on the other side of the

border. It was best to remember she was not among friends. Every confidence she muttered might be used against her.

"We'll pass the night, lass, and that is all. Do ye wonder why I doubt ye when ye say ye wanted no part of the king's plan for ye, when all ye do is spit at me?"

She lost her resolve to ignore him and turned to see him watching her. The last of the sun was turning his hair fiery red.

"Can you not understand? I have no liking for knowing I'll be locked away because of my blood like the little princes were. Everyone knows they are dead, and yet no one dares say so."

There was too much sympathy in his blue eyes. She turned her attention away again, desperately seeking something to dwell on except her fate. Life was a precious thing and a delicate one. It seemed she had been running from those who threatened her life for too many years.

The land was turning green with new crops. The evening light washed over people in the fields, who were making use of every last bit of daylight to plant. They had their sleeves turned up, and sweat marked their shirt collars, but their faces clearly displayed good cheer when they looked up to see who passed on the road.

They were people with hope. The season in front of them held opportunities, and she envied them. She'd always expected to marry at the direction of her relatives but had never considered it to mean she would have no joy or respect. Keeping herself pure was her duty, but she couldn't help feeling that her uncle had failed to do his by bartering her to James for nothing more than bed sport.

There were women who took lovers for the pleasure and nothing else. She worried her lower lip, because her thoughts had turned wicked. *Ah… but enticing nonetheless.*

Broen didn't answer her. He gave his stallion the freedom to take the lead. Clarrisa watched him go, staring at his back without shame. Wicked, perhaps, but who knew if she'd ever have the chance to indulge her curiosity again? She was suddenly too conscious of how many hours she'd squandered. She wanted to wring every bit of enjoyment out of each moment she had left.

She watched the way Broen turned his stallion sideways so he might see all of his men. There was an intensity about him that sent a ripple of sensation across her skin. His doublet sleeves were buttoned behind his back, and the chill of the approaching night didn't seem to bother him.

Highlander. She had never really considered the word as a title rather than a slur. Yet she discovered herself recognizing Broen and his men as more than the thugs that her kin had so often told her the Highlanders were. They were not rabble without order, but men endowed with strength that she couldn't help but admire. They also had honor. It was evident in the way they followed their leader, and even more prominent in the way Broen thought of his country instead of how much he didn't care for the part he was playing in her misfortune.

You don't know he doesn't care for what he's doing to you…

But she could have sworn she felt it when he stared into her eyes. He was not blind to her fears; his heart wasn't hardened by arrogance and his assumption that she should serve his desires because it was his right.

She liked that knowledge too much. Felt it dissolving the distrust she was trying so hard to maintain and leaving her wondering why it mattered if she liked him.

He stirred something inside her...

Heat rose to her cheeks. Broen looked at her, and she turned away to hide the stain. Her emotions would lead her to ruin if she didn't force herself back to being disciplined. Fascination had led more than one person to despair, for the world was very unforgiving. Broen was a Highlander, and she was English. They were both duty-bound to dislike each other.

Another ripple of sensation went down her back in defiance. She bit her lip harder in reprimand.

The next rise showed them a small town. The newer houses rose two stories and sat nestled against a rocky section of land with well-worn tracks from carts. Up on the high ground was Raven's Perch. It was an imposing structure of three towers, two built in front of the tallest. They were surrounded by an impressive curtain wall that extended a half circle, beyond which was a sheer drop to the ocean. In days gone by, the rocky section of land would have held another wall to form inner and outer baileys. Clarrisa looked again at the tallest tower and noticed the stone was of a lighter color. It had been built at a different time and most likely from the wall that had once enclosed the town.

Riders met them in the center of the rocky

ground—more Highlanders, wearing their swords across their backs as the spring breeze pulled at the edges of their kilts. They were serious, but their leader offered his hand to Broen. The two men clasped each other's forearms before the men surrounding them lost their somber expressions.

"So ye managed it, did ye?" The leader of the welcome party stared at her. He kneed his stallion forward until he was closer. "There's a tale there, to be sure. I do nae think James let her go easily."

This Highlander studied her much the same way his king had, as if she were a mare. Clarrisa bit her lip, trying to keep her opinion to herself, but failed. "And you Scots think yourselves so different from the English."

The leader of the welcoming clan was dark haired with midnight black eyes. His chin was covered in dark stubble, giving him a rakish look. Surprise registered on his face before he leaned forward to glare at her. "Ye do nae see a difference, lass? Now, that's the first time I've met a blind Englishwoman. Cannae ye see me knees, or should I let me kilt ride up a bit higher to test yer courage?"

Clarrisa softened her expression, calling upon years of experience appearing meek when she was nothing of the sort. "Men thinking themselves so superior to women that they simply talk of them as though they are not even present... Well, that is something my English kin do very well." Her eyes swept the group of retainers listening so intently behind him. "I see more similarities than differences."

She could feel the tension in the air and Broen

glaring at her, but she maintained her position, refusing to duck her chin.

"I'm Faolan Chisholms. Me uncle is the Earl of Sutherland. Does that please ye?"

Clarrisa shook her head slowly. "No, it simply offers me another example of how much you have in common with the English nobility. They are all quick to tell anyone who they are related to, all that much better to attempt to frighten them into submission."

Faolan's men didn't care for her tone. They frowned at her, some scowling. Faolan did neither. The man considered her with a stony expression while fingering the reins resting in his hands.

"Well, it seems we'll have plenty to discuss over supper, for I've got a lot of relatives. Some of them are a little less in favor with the church than others, because they were nae born under the blessing of marriage. But here in the Highlands, we're a bit more concerned with blood. Especially royal blood."

There were grins among his men. Faolan lifted his hand, and they parted. He shifted his attention to Broen.

"I can see why ye are nae in a hurry to get inside and bask in front of me hearth. This York female has a heat I can feel all the way over here. It's a wonder ye don't have blisters on yer face, man."

"My hide is thicker than yers, it seems," Broen stated arrogantly. "Seems a good thing I went to fetch her, since ye are wilting beneath her slicing tongue."

Faolan grunted. "Ye haven't proved anything of the sort."

Broen reached over and snared her reins before she realized what he was doing. "I snatched the prize me uncle wanted, when there were plenty who claimed it was undoable."

Broen rode beneath the raised gate and into the inner yard. Faolan and his men followed. Clarrisa held tight to the bridle of her mare but turned to look back, feeling as if a huge stone were pressing down on her chest. She was off her mare before the men finished dismounting. Boys ran forward to take the animals, and her mare happily followed one to a stable.

A firm hand clapped around her upper arm. "Do nae let Faolan ruffle yer feathers, lass," Broen said. "I keep my word. We'll pass the night here and no more."

She shot a hard look at him. "I cannot trust you." But she hated how much she wanted to. It wasn't logical, and she needed to be logical.

Broen pulled her closer, his voice dipping so his words remained private. "Ye struck me as more intelligent than that, Clarrisa. There were others who would have happily taken ye from the king in order to please the earl, and no' many of them would have left ye alive. Best ye trust me, for the time might come when I'll need ye to follow me willingly."

His blue eyes were guarded now.

"You have left me alive so you can take me to your overlord. It sounds as though you took the challenge in front of others. That is not so trust-inspiring." She kept her voice low so her words wouldn't drift.

"I did, because it was the best thing for me clan and country." The grip on her biceps became soothing. "And I would nae have done so if the threat yer blood poses were nae so great."

"So I cannot trust you, because I am only a threat to you." There was regret in her tone, and she witnessed it in his eyes before he moved her forward toward the largest tower and its arched doorway.

"I suppose that's fair enough." There was a gruffness to his voice she might easily have believed was remorse. It did not matter if it was. The brute was still tugging her toward Faolan Chisholms like a prize taken in battle. How he felt about her plight wouldn't change her fate.

"Come now, lass. Me hospitality is nae so wanting that ye should need to be pulled across the threshold." Faolan appeared beside her and settled one of his arms around her waist. "Ye would nae want to hurt me feelings."

"Enough of this." She surged forward, walking into the large hall that lay directly inside the doors. It was full of tables, most of which were occupied by Faolan's clan members. Supper was being served, but everyone stopped eating to stare at her.

"Broen MacNicols has come to pay us all a visit! Bring up a cask of cider," Faolan announced.

A cheer went up, and the meal began again. Faolan went down the center aisle, clearly the master of the tower. Men reached up, tugging on the corners of their knit bonnets, and women nodded as they continued to serve the tables. Broen received the same respect, which sent a tingle down her spine. She'd been overly bold with him, and it was clear there wasn't a soul in sight who would refuse to follow his commands.

She was at his mercy, but she still wasn't ready to repent. Her fate would be the same no matter how she faced it. The only thing she held power over was how she went to it.

The cider cask arrived, and another cheer went up. This one was louder, with the men pounding their mugs on the tabletops. Faolan had reached the head table. He pressed his hands on its surface and waited for his men to finish expressing their appreciation. Faolan considered her as his captains lined up shoulder to shoulder behind him. Broen stood beside him, the feathers in their bonnets all pointing upward to denote their rank. The two lairds had all three feathers raised; their captains each had one raised and the other two lowered.

"I'll bid ye a good night, lass." Faolan pointed at two of his retainers, and the men pulled on their bonnets before starting toward her.

"I hope you choke on your cider," she answered sweetly. "And wake up in a privy."

There were several gasps from the women, but Faolan grinned at her. "Ye really need to stop teasing me so brazenly in front of me men, lass. I'm sorely tempted to tame ye."

"Another trait you have in common with the English—thinking women are so impressed with any man's effort in her bed to ever become tame."

The women giggled now, and it was clear many of them agreed with her.

Instead of becoming irritated, Faolan grinned. "Ah, but ye see, lass, being a Scotsman means I'll be arriving in yer bedchamber to prove I am no' just spouting empty promises. By morning, ye'll know the difference between me and those English who sent ye up here a virgin."

Heat blazed across her cheeks. The hall erupted
into laughter, the tables being pounded once more.
Faolan slapped Broen on the back and roared with his
amusement. The retainers set to the task of escorting
her from the hall battled to maintain stern faces, but
their eyes twinkled with mirth.

Clarrisa began to lower herself. It was a habit that
had been instilled in her as a child, but she froze
halfway down and straightened back up. Broen raised
an eyebrow at her audacity and almost looked as
though he admired her daring. It would be insane to
think he respected her rudeness. Foolish as well, for her
fate rested in his hands. Or perhaps his friend's—she
wasn't sure, for it was Faolan's men who flanked
her now and his holding in which she was secured.
Not that it mattered to her. One Highlander laird or
another, it made little difference. She refused to allow
herself to think of Broen or his promise that he would
not murder her. He hadn't, so the man had kept his
word. She could expect nothing else from him.

Maybe he'd handed her over to a man who would
spill her blood. Such was a common way of dealing
with offended honor among men.

She walked slowly, frustrating her escort, but they
seemed loath to touch her. Her feet shuffled on the
stone floor, and she turned her head to look out of the
few openings in the stone walls as they passed. Most
were archer's slits—thin cross-shaped places where
there was no stone. The night air blew in, and she
filled her lungs with it, fearing it might be the last fresh
air she breathed.

The young English princes had gone into the

Tower of London and never been seen again. She shivered, saying a quick prayer for their souls. They'd only been boys, but the Lancasters had convinced their mother to allow the boys into their care.

The retainers took her up two flights of stone steps. The sounds from the hall diminished until all she heard was the wind whispering through the arrow slits.

"Here, lass. The chamber is sound and clean enough." The door hinges opened easily, proving the chamber was kept in good repair. The iron hinges were huge and would have squealed without attention. At least the floor wasn't covered in rushes. It was solid stone but appeared to have been recently swept.

"Now, do nae be making a fuss. Ye heard me laird. Inside with ye."

"I know who to blame for my circumstances." Clarrisa crossed into the room and was sure the air was colder inside. The tiny hearth in the room was dark and cold. "My own kin."

Confusion crossed the face of the older retainer. He reached up and scratched the side of his gray beard while contemplating her words. He held up his hand to silence one of the others who had grumbled over her words, and the man snapped his lips shut instantly, proving age was respected even in the Highlands.

A tiny hint of civilized behavior where she'd always heard there was nothing but savageness.

"Kindly do not berate me for disrespecting my noble uncle." She turned her back on him and tried not to let him hear her sigh. Somber was the kindest word she could think of to describe the room. "But I hardly think his plans for me… decent. Even if it is my place to obey him."

Bleak was a better word, but if her spirits sank any lower, she feared she'd give in to the urge to pity herself. She shouldn't even be talking to the retainer but couldn't seem to halt the words. Fear was trying to rise up and strangle her, fear of being alone and forgotten inside this stone room. How long would it be before she believed being murdered would be preferable to her fate of incarceration?

"I'll get one of the lasses to fetch up some supper for ye. A good meal will cheer ye up a bit. No need to be so discontent."

Clarrisa turned around to stare at the older Chisholms retainer. "That would be most welcome."

He nodded. "Aye, well, seeing as how ye are nae unleashing yer temper on me… 'tis the decent thing to do. Even if ye are English."

Highlander pride. It rang clear and solid in his voice.

She smiled as the door shut, enjoying the sound of his voice ringing in her ears. Her enjoyment faded as silence surrounded her. A small bed was built into the corner of the chamber. The bench she sat on was the only seat. Off in another corner was a small but serviceable table whose top was scarred with cuts and ink. No inkwell was in sight, nor parchment, but such items would be kept locked away, for they were expensive. Had someone enjoyed their labor inside the room? A secretary maybe, one given a room inside the castle as a mark of his position within the laird's household. She stood and walked to the table, gently running her hand across the surface, pausing at one ink stain. What a strange contrast to what the chamber was for her.

She sighed, wandering in one circle and then another.

❧

"The lass is mine to take to yer uncle." Broen spoke quietly, but Faolan heard the edge to his tone.

"The threat she brings to Scotland is shared by many. She's secure here. If ye take her out, someone might take her from ye."

Broen stared straight into his fellow laird's eyes. "Do ye think I would have bothered to ride across land held by royalists, or that I'd order me men to take such a risk, if there was nae a damned good reason? Do nae insult me, man. She's my prize, taken for the benefit of us all—but mine, nonetheless. Ye had the chance to join me, but do nae insult me ability to get one lass across the ground between yer land and mine."

Faolan lifted his mug but never swallowed any of the cider. The man was making a show of drinking with his men while ensuring his wits remained sharp. Faolan glanced at his own mug, still three-quarters full of cider, before standing. There was a gleam of knowledge in his eyes when he looked at Broen, one Broen returned. Being laird now that his father was gone meant keeping one step ahead of half the clans surrounding his. He and Faolan had been inseparable as boys, but as men, they had to keep their clans' interests foremost in their thoughts. Suspicion was knotting his gut, because there was something in Faolan's eyes that was just as hard as his own determination to have Clarrisa remain his prize.

That idea rubbed his temper in a way that stunned him. The irritation went deeper than pride, and he'd be a liar if he didn't admit it.

Faolan raised his mug. "I've enjoyed yer company, lads, but Laird MacNicols and I have important matters to discuss."

Many of the men raised their tankards to their laird before turning back to dice and card games. A piper was beginning to play, along with several drummers. It was the time of night when the Chisholms retainers relaxed, the only time of day they allowed themselves the luxury of being at ease. Broen's own men were quieter and merely sipping at the cider. The MacNicols retainers wouldn't be at ease unless they were secured behind the walls of their stronghold, Deigh Tower.

"Ye know the way of it well, Broen." Faolan led him down a well-lit hallway. Both men still looked at the ground to check for shadows before going too near a connecting corridor—no fortress was fail-proof, as Broen had proven when he'd stolen Clarrisa.

"But ye should also know me family has more to lose if the king gains a York-blooded son," Faolan continued.

"Now, I will nae agree with ye on that point." Broen followed Faolan into a chamber. He recalled it well from when it had belonged to Faolan's father. Faolan smoothed a hand over the edge of the large table. A large chair sat behind the table, one worthy of the laird.

"I remember standing next to ye while me father scowled at the pair of us over this table." Faolan sat in the large chair. "I still find the chair a bit uncomfortable for that very reason. I expect me sire's ghost to arrive at any moment and begin giving me hell for the time I spend chasing the lasses instead of doing what he'd sent me to do."

"Aye, I know what ye mean. Both our sires spent plenty of time trying to tell us how important the responsibility of being laird is, but it's far more pressing when ye must feel the yoke yerself," Broen muttered. But he didn't let his guard down; suspicion was still raising the hair on his nape.

"Exactly. Hearing me father warn us to always remember what we were to become was nae the same as having to curtail me own desires in favor of what is best for me clan." Faolan frowned. "Which brings us back to the matter of young Clarrisa and the good that can come from having her here at Raven's Perch."

"I stole her, so I'll be the one finishing what I began. If ye wanted the duty, ye had the chance to speak up when yer uncle put the matter to us." Broen didn't sit in the chair his friend gestured to. Every muscle in his body was too tight. "Do nae betray the trust between us, Faolan. I would nae have ridden here if I doubted ye were a man I can call a friend."

"Me position as laird is nae as secure as yers, Broen."

Broen snorted. "Ye have a distorted view of me position, man. The Grants would love to know I've ridden off me land, so they could burn enough of me villages to believe they would have a chance at taking control of me clan. A few of me men would like that as well, because it would give them the chance to start the feud they are demanding from me."

"Donnach Grant is nearing the end of his days."

"Not soon enough for my taste. The fact that he's getting old only promises that I'll be hearing his son Kael has returned, a man whose loyalty none of us is sure of," Broen insisted. "I stole the lass, so tell me where ye had her taken."

Faolan stood, tension evident in his stance. "Wedding Daphne was the only issue we ever fought over."

Broen nodded. "True enough. Until now, it seems."

"Ye are nae the only one who wants justice for her death." There was a warning in Faolan's voice.

"I am no' blind to that," Broen muttered softly. "But ye welcomed me here as a friend, so let me finish what I promised yer uncle I'd do, because forcing Donnach to meet me and explain what happened will give us both the answers we seek."

Faolan shook his head.

"Curse ye, Faolan."

The Chisholms laird laughed, but it wasn't a pleasant sound. "I am that, Broen. Cursed for certain, for I swear to ye I've seen young Daphne's ghost."

A shiver went across his skin, for there was a light in Faolan's eyes that made it plain the man believed what he was saying.

"Ye mean ye've dreamed about her, man." Broen softened his tone, commiserating with his friend over the topic. "Understandable, considering—"

"It was more than a dream," Faolan interrupted. "It was so real it scared me."

An uneasy silence filled the room. Faolan's face was drawn tight with tension as Broen swore softly.

"I would have called any man who accused ye of being afraid of anything on this earth a liar."

"Except we are nae talking of anything natural." Faolan sat back down, looking older than his years for a moment. "I do nae want to believe it meself, and ye are the only man I'd confess it to, but I swear that woman is haunting me. In the darkest hours of the night in my dreams, I see her in a stone room wearing naught but a pure white robe…" His voice trailed off as he looked like he was captivated by the vision once more.

"It's clear ye believe what ye're saying, so it's best I take Clarrisa to Sutherland so we can both hear the explanation of how Daphne died. Only that knowledge will end this."

Faolan slapped the tabletop. "Nay! It's clear I need to settle accounts, so Daphne can rest in peace. She haunts me, so I must be the one."

"Ye are nae making sense, man," Broen argued. "Clarrisa has naught to do with Daphne's fate."

Faolan straightened. "She does, and it's me she's haunting, so I must be the one to take the York bastard to me uncle."

Broen looked closely at his friend and noticed the dark circles beneath his eyes. The emotion in his friend's eyes burned brighter than what he'd ever felt for Daphne. It was a truth he didn't care for, but he couldn't ignore it either. Clarrisa's face surfaced from his memory, her blond hair shimmering like a spring morning. She was far more fetching than he'd admitted to himself… *Oh Christ.* He didn't need that sort of trouble. Broen shook his head. Faolan snorted.

"I mean what I say, Broen. I'm taking Clarrisa to me uncle to satisfy Daphne. Since she's haunting me, ye can just make yer peace with my decision on the matter."

"If Daphne is truly haunting Raven's Perch, it will take more than delivering one Englishwoman to the Highlands to get her to leave."

Faolan grunted. "I suppose ye know a thing or two about ghosts walking the halls of yer home."

Someone used the heavy brass knocker set on the door.

"Come," Faolan barked. There was a hint of uncertainty in his voice, which drew a sound of disgust from Broen.

Distrust between them was a new thing—a sign of the troubled times, but it was also a result of Daphne. Broen tried to recall her dark eyes and the way they'd seemed irresistible the last time he'd seen her, but what surfaced instead was the memory of the last look Clarrisa had shot him, her blue eyes full of spirit and determination in spite of the burly Chisholms retainers flanking her petite form. There had also been a hint of regret, but he was better off not noticing that. He needed to recall that she was English, nothing else. But it seemed good sense wasn't prevailing, because his thoughts lingered on that last look she'd sent him. He itched to take action, feeling the walls around him closing in.

"Where did ye put her?" Faolan asked his men.

Broen jerked his attention to the men who'd entered. Both tugged on the corners of their bonnets before the eldest spoke. "I put her in one of the kitchen storage rooms. She did nae give me any trouble, so I thought to spare her the dungeon. That's a right frightful place for such a slight lass."

Faolan frowned, appearing as though he was going

to argue. The elder of the two men looked surprised, but his years gave him the courage to speak plainly. "Those storerooms have solid doors and bars. The lass cannae be going anywhere unless someone lifts it for her."

"It would take a man, too. We used a heavy bar, one of the new iron-wrapped ones," his companion added.

Faolan grunted. "I suppose ye're correct. There's lasses aplenty sleeping in the kitchens too. Well done, lads."

The retainers left, the older one looking glad to be done with his laird's bidding. Broen watched as Faolan waited for his men to leave the room before he emptied his cider mug.

"Ye think I've gone mad."

Broen shook his head. "Nay, I think ye believe what ye say ye saw, but I'd be sorely tempted to tell ye it would be disappointing to hear ye spent the night in that chair because ye feared another encounter with Daphne. As far as specters go, she's a fair bit better than the one I've got at Deigh Tower."

Faolan chuckled, returning to the good-humored man Broen called friend. It didn't last, though; Faolan's grin faded until he was once more somber.

"Aye, that spirit walking yer halls is a mean one, and no mistake. Too bad ye did nae have a sister or three. If yer father had promised one to the church, maybe Deigh would be peaceful."

"I'll just have to make me own way, as ye will." Broen made to leave but heard Faolan stand behind him. Broen turned and raised an eyebrow at the suspicious look being aimed at him. "I've had little sleep since I left yer uncle's home, Faolan, and I do nae plan to be gone from me own lands much longer."

Faolan nodded. "I do nae want to make an enemy of ye, Broen."

"Then have done with this nonsense about you delivering the English lass to quiet Daphne's spirit. I'll gladly help ye discover who caused her soul such unrest just as soon as I deliver Clarrisa to yer uncle so I can gain that information from Donnach Grant. Me men are demanding a feud, Faolan, something guaranteed to give me plenty of sleepless nights thinking of the men who died because I failed to be a good-enough laird to maintain peace."

Broen watched his friend clench his hands into fists until the knuckles turned white. "Think on it, man. If Daphne is disturbing yer sleep, she's needing the same justice me own father does. Such a thing does nae come from making a prisoner of a wee English lass—even if I went and stole her, because I agree it was the best thing for us all. Honor is nae satisfied through women."

"Ye have a point, Broen. I'm nae blind to it." But his tone made it plain he wasn't willing to agree. "We'll talk more in the morning. I've missed too much sleep recently to be making sound decisions."

Broen nodded before quitting the room. His men were leaning against the walls in the hallway. Shaw watched the doorway. Broen lifted his hand to keep the man silent while placing some distance between Faolan's study and himself.

"What are ye thinking, Laird?"

Shaw asked the question quietly, but Broen could

feel the weight of his men's stares. No one was at ease, nor did they have any liking for Faolan's desire to keep their prize.

"I'm thinking we'll nae be getting any sleep tonight, lads. I'm feeling chilled, too chilled to remain here." Eyebrows rose, along with the corners of his retainers' mouths. "Gather up the rest of the men and send them out on their way home under the excuse I do nae need all me men here."

"And how will we make our way past the gate?" Shaw asked.

"First we'll get the lass," Broen answered. "There's nae point in thinking on how to pass the gate without her."

And he wasn't leaving without his prize. There was sure to be a priest or two who'd frown at him over his pride, but Broen didn't pause. He made his way down the stone hallways, pinching out half the candles as he went. He left a few flickering in the darkness to make the staff think the wind had blown them out. Pitch blackness would have announced his plans. The hall was still full of merriment; the cider barrel, not yet empty. There were more pipers playing now, and couples were dancing now that the cider had made them all merry.

"Go on, men. I'll join ye when I have the lass."

～

The supper the Chisholms retainer brought her was cold, but it didn't stop her belly from rumbling. Her hands shook with anticipation as her nose picked up the scent of the broken bread sitting on top of the bowl. A small ceramic pitcher of milk was left on the table before the door closed once more. With no candle, the room became nothing but shadows. Slim fingers of golden light from the hallway teased her from beneath the door. They didn't penetrate even halfway across the room.

Well, she didn't need to see her meal. Sitting on the narrow bed, she broke off some of the bread and tasted it. Spring was new, so the flour would have been ground from last year's harvest. But it wasn't musty or stale, proving the housekeeper knew her craft well. Unlike the staff in the keep in which Clarrisa had met the king.

Clarrisa tried to slow down, because she heard her own lips smacking. Maybe it was the darkness or the fear that she'd never see the sky again. Every sound hit her as louder, more intense while she consumed the meal. The milk was chilled from being stored in the cellar, the pottery cold against her fingers. She forced herself to leave half of it in the pitcher in case no one remembered to bring her breakfast.

Her thoughts wanted to whirl like a snowstorm, but with her belly full, her body longed only for rest. She lay down and pulled the single blanket over her body. Damn Maud for insisting she dress in summer linen to better display her curves. She doubted James had cared what she looked like; it was her blood he was drawn to.

What drew a man such as Broen to a woman?

She was mad to think on such a topic, but her mind was half-gone into slumber, and discipline seemed to have vanished. An image of him crouching down near her surfaced from her memory and followed her into sleep. What surprised her was how much she was drawn to the details that set him apart from civilized men. She should detest him; instead, she dreamed of him.

❧

"Come, lass…" The voice was husky and dark. Her eyes flew open as Faolan's promise to prove himself to her filled her thoughts.

"You will not have me!" She shoved at the man sitting on the edge of the bed. He stumbled, giving her the opportunity to kick the blanket aside. "I am sick unto death of everyone's desire to be in my bed."

"Be silent, woman."

"I will not help you commit this atrocity, Faolan Chisholms." She picked up the pitcher and flung it at him. He moved faster than she did, clearing the path she sent the pottery sailing along. It smashed into the stone wall, shattering into bits.

A hard hand grabbed her and sealed her next retort behind it. He yanked her up against his body as she struggled to escape. There was too much iron strength in the man holding her. She strained with all her might but remained held securely.

"'Tis Broen, and I've come to—"

His identity was too much for her to bear. It must have been her dreams of him while falling asleep, but her cheeks flamed and her heart raced the moment he revealed his name.

"Ye bit me," he accused in a soft snarl. For a moment the iron cage of his arms opened as he shook his hand.

"I thought you were that devil of a friend you handed

me over to." Clarrisa sent her best punch toward his face. Pain erupted all along her arm when her knuckles connected with his jaw. "Well... I will not submit to him or you or your king! Do you hear me?"

"Sweet Christ, half the castle heard ye," he swore in a raspy tone. "Quiet down before ye truly have to deal with Faolan. He's got a notion to keep ye, but I am here to keep me promise to ye."

Broen pushed her against the wall, pressing his body against hers from head to toe. One moment she was trying to rub some of the pain from her hand, and the next moment the huge lout was closer to her than any man had ever been. Except for him during the last few days.

He smothered the rest of what she had to say with his palm. "I came in here to help ye, but I need the Chisholms to stay in the hall and nae come down here because they hear ye howling like a scalded cat."

She curled her lips back, intending to take the largest chunk of flesh she could out of his hand, but he yanked his hand away.

"Would ye quiet down?" Shaw spoke from the chamber door. "Someone is sure to hear... Ah... well now, I don't think we've got time for that sort of convincing, Laird."

Clarrisa snarled. It was the most uncivilized sound she'd ever made, but it suited the moment.

"I'm trying to keep her from raising the alarm."

Shaw grinned at her as Broen pressed his hand against her mouth again. "Well now, the gag worked well enough, if ye ask me."

A strangled sound made it past Broen's hand.

Clarrisa strained against him but only managed to feel just how hard his body was.

"Curse it all."

Broen suddenly leaned in so close she could feel his breath against her cheek. Her skin prickled with awareness, which raced along her flesh, raising goose bumps. She'd never been so aware of how a man smelled or felt. Every breath pulled the details deep into her senses and unleashed a torrent of sensation. It was shocking, but pleasurable too.

"Listen to me, Clarrisa…" His voice sent a shiver down her spine. It was raspy and commanding, bringing to mind the moment she'd contemplated what sort of woman he'd be attracted to. "I'm here to offer ye a choice."

The candles from the hallway flickered in his eyes as he stared into hers.

"Aye, something ye have nae had from me before, and I'll admit ye have the right to scratch me for appearing in the darkness." He lifted his hand away, slowly at first, clearly not trusting her. He still had her pinned against the wall with his body.

"Ye can come away with me now, or wait here to see if Faolan decides to make good on his boast to prove himself to ye."

He pushed away from her, and another ripple of sensation traveled down her body, only this time it was lament. She wrapped her arms around her body, trying to console herself. It was foolish to feel anything but relief, yet she hugged herself tighter.

"I don't trust you, Broen MacNicols."

But he's never hurt you…

He'd moved to the center of the room. "Do nae ye, lass?" He closed the gap between them once more. His warmth enveloped her, and his body pinned her arms in place between them. This time he raised her chin, cupping it in one hand. His breath teased her lips, the delicate surface registering an insane amount of notice from so slight a touch.

"Feel how smooth yer skin is, lass?" He trailed his fingers across her neck. "Nae a single cut. Better to place yer faith in me than anyone else surrounding ye at the moment."

His fingers lingered on her skin, sending heat across her cheeks. For a mere moment, it looked like his attention had settled onto her lips. Her mouth went dry, and her breath froze in her chest. Would he kiss her? *Would she kiss him in return?*

Neither happened. Broen stepped back, but it seemed like he hesitated.

Fool! Would you have him drawn to you?

"Trust me, Clarrisa. I'll see ye to the Highlands alive. Ye have me word on that."

He extended his hand, palm up, and waited for her to place her hand in his. Her throat felt like it was swelling shut, far too tight to allow even a single breath through.

"Has this cell endeared itself to ye, then?" He looked around and grunted. "No' even a candle spared for ye."

"I know it well." But she still didn't like hearing just how defeated she was.

The candlelight from the passageway allowed her to see his eyebrow rise mockingly. "But ye are nae sure I am any better a choice? At least I will take ye out into the night, where the air is fresh. 'Tis yer choice, and ye need to make it now." He turned and took a step toward the door.

Need pulsed through her, pushing aside everything else. She felt like he was being torn away from her, and she couldn't endure the separation.

"Oh... damn us all. I'm coming... Bro—" His name lodged in her throat. It seemed such an intimate thing, to speak his first name; simply thinking about it reawakened her desire to know what his kiss was like. He stopped, and she almost ran into him, stopping so abruptly her skirts collided with his legs. He cupped her chin once again.

"Why does me name stick to yer tongue? 'Tis simple enough to say."

She stepped back, lifting her chin to remove it from his grasp. Not that she might have eluded his touch if he weren't in the mood to allow her to. He loomed over her, making her more conscious of how much more strength he had than she. She felt vulnerable yet strangely impatient to prove she could meet him in every contest of flesh there was.

Insane... She'd lost her wits completely...

"Laird MacNicols."

He took a step toward her. "That is me title, no' me name, Clarrisa."

Shaw cleared his throat. "So sorry to be interrupting... Laird, but if the two of ye do nae mind, I'd appreciate no' ending up in Laird Chisholms's dungeon tonight because ye cannae wait for a more secluded place to circle each other."

"We are not circling," Clarrisa insisted with a backward step.

Broen muttered something under his breath and reached for her. He circled her waist with one hard arm and pulled her into the hallway. "Shaw is correct about one thing, lass. Time is precious tonight."

She pushed at the arm holding her to him. "I've made the choice to follow you. There is no need to hold me."

He looked at her, and his lips curled into an arrogant grin. "But that's the part I'm enjoying. Ye're a fine-looking lass, Clarrisa."

"No, I'm not. My uncle often lamented my lack of beauty."

She reached up and pressed a hand over her lips when she realized just how personal an admission she'd made.

"Well now, this is nae the first time I've disagreed with an Englishman, but I do believe I feel more strongly about it than ever before."

The night air was no longer cool, because she felt like her entire body was blushing.

He found her pleasing to look at?

She shook her head. Now was not the time for girlish flights of whimsy.

He held up a finger in front of his lips before sweeping her down the hallway. She picked up her feet faster, lifting her hems so she might hurry away from what had been her cell. Broen and his men moved swiftly, but with a silence that was unnatural. The sounds from the hall grew louder before Broen led her around a corner and away from them.

"Now would be a good time to share with me yer

plan for getting out of here, Laird," Shaw said and turned to look at her. "With her, that is. No doubt the Chisholms at the gate know their laird is intent on keeping her."

Shaw reached out and pulled something from a peg on the wall. It was a length of fabric used by the maids when the weather was foul. "Best cover yer head and look a bit more Scottish, or we'll have wasted our time in getting ye out of that storage room."

"Oh... yes." She shook the length of plaid; the wool fibers were surprisingly soft against her fingers. With a few twists, she had it draped over her head and around her shoulders. She shivered in eager anticipation of being free.

Broen slipped a wide leather belt around her waist and buckled it.

"You shouldn't be so familiar with me." Because it was tempting her to touch him in return.

His eyes narrowed. "And ye should hold yer tongue more often. Yet both of us seem to have difficulty with keeping to the places the church says we should. Do nae admonish me when ye are nae willing to lower yerself in front of me and grant me the respect my gender is due."

"You'd consider it an insult if I did." Her response was reckless, but it felt good to speak her mind. She'd been holding back her true words her entire life. "You would know it was insincere."

His hand remained on the belt buckle, and she felt the weight of his stare even as the light behind him made it impossible for her to see his expression clearly.

"Ye have a fine talent for judging men." He

transferred his grip to her wrist. "I do nae care for false pretense, and the king was easily led by a few words of promise. I wonder if I should admire yer skill or listen to Shaw when he's telling me ye're scheming because ye know no other way."

"If that were so, I'd be whimpering and trying to lull you into thinking I was helpless."

His grip tightened around her wrist. "Aye, that might have worked, but Shaw was correct, lass." He leaned in, twisting her arm so she couldn't bend it and back away from him. So simply, so easily he secured her in place. His breath teased her cheek, sending a shiver down her back. "We'll be needing to escape before we return to circling each other."

Her temper flared, but he turned to look at the yard they needed to cross. "I have no intention of circling you… Highlander…" It was more of a title than a place from which he hailed.

She saw him grin, the expression full of mocking confidence. He looked toward the gate and back at her.

"On the other hand, lass, if ye want to leave Raven's Perch… maybe we should circle each other a bit closer to ease our way through the gate."

A tingle of anticipation went down her spine. "What do you mean?"

He lifted one hand and beckoned her toward him with a single finger.

～

"Yer father made a bargain with the last of the York nobles in England." The crown prince of

Scotland listened to Alexander Home with a dark-ening complexion. "He planned to breed a son on one of Edward's bastards, a son who—"

"Who would be kin to Henry the Seventh of England and in a fine position to set me aside." He stood and paced across the fine Persian rug covering the floor. "What happened to the girl?"

In spite of his youth, his tone was steady. Princes had to mature quickly or they would end up dead like the two English ones had.

"She was stolen. We believe by the Earl of Sutherland's order."

"You hope." Young James watched Lord Home stiffen at his tone and chided himself. His father's mistake was not giving respect to those who served him, an error his mother had taught him to avoid making. "I hope so as well," he amended. "Forgive me. I worry for the future."

"As do we all." Lord Home held up a letter to see the ink better. "Your father failed to bed the girl; that much is certain. The keep he selected is loyal to our cause. The maids helped Laird MacNicols steal the York bastard away. My sources tell me yer father paid a great deal for the girl."

"MacNicols"—James paced a few more times—"came seeking justice a few months past. My father refused to see him." The prince turned to pace back across the carpet.

"Your memory serves you well, and it seems your father's failing has added another Highland clan to our side." Lord Home sounded very pleased.

"Yet the York bastard is very dangerous to us, even

if she's held by loyal hands." James's tone made his distaste clear, but he still aimed an unwavering look at Lord Home.

"If she is even still alive."

The prince weighed his answer while fingering his fine velvet doublet. "We must be sure. It is sad to hear my father is still not ready to be the king Scotland needs. I so hoped he'd mend his ways, as many do near the end of their days." He nodded, obviously needing to convince himself of the necessity to go after an innocent. The boy was young, but not too young, which was why men were willing to follow him.

The prince drew in a deep breath. "See that the bastard has no chance to be used against the unity of this nation. We have no need for alliances with England."

James nodded before leaving the room. Margaret of Denmark had raised her eldest son to be a prince. There was a solidness about young James. It was a quality Alexander was willing to follow. James was noble, but also a true Scotsman, which was what the country needed.

Alexander pulled a piece of parchment from his writing desk, dipped a quill into the inkwell, and began writing. He frowned at the word *York* after he'd written it. Scotland didn't need ties with England! James III was a poor king and not even worthy of being called a Scotsman, in his opinion. Too many times, the king had fled to England for shelter—England, the sworn enemy of every Scot. Such actions were too much to overlook, too much to ignore. Alexander refused to give his loyalty to a king who sided with the English. Well, if Laird MacNicols had the York bastard, the man would surely want something in exchange for her, but Alexander wasn't willing to let any laird have such power over the Prince. So Lord Home was writing to Laird Grant, because there was one thing certain to make MacNicols yield the York girl, and it was also something Home knew Laird Grant could not refuse to relinquish to him. Lord Home kept his position as royal adviser by keeping a small stash of favors owed to him by Highland lairds. It was an important part of making sure the young prince ended up with his birthright. It was a service James III had forgotten Lord Home once performed for him. Home intended to make sure his former master regretted losing his loyalty.

He held up the letter so the ink would dry. He could hear his men following the prince out in the hallway. At fourteen, James needed to be watched carefully, or he'd end up being poisoned like his mother had been. The time was nearing; Alexander could feel it. With spring beginning to melt the snow, the king was falling into his old habit of doing whatever pleased him, no matter the repercussions. Even his royalist followers wouldn't be able to protect him when the rest of the Scots rose up in rebellion, not when it was clear he was making alliances with England yet again. The prince was naive enough to hope for a peaceful resolution, but Alexander knew they were well past such a thing. Soon the Highlanders would come down, and the matter would be decided by strength and steel.

While James III lived, the York girl threatened

them all. Laird Grant owed Lord Home a large favor, and it was time for him to pay the debt. The Highland laird wouldn't be happy to receive his letter, but Alexander signed his name to it anyway. He folded the letter before lifting the candle and holding the flame beneath a stick of sealing wax, which puddled onto the folded edges of the parchment. He replaced the candle before closing his fingers into a fist and pressing his signet ring into the cooling wax.

Alexander smiled. Things were really quite perfect. Laird MacNicols was a man with an Achilles' heel, one Alexander knew the secret to obtaining. The York bastard would be handed over, and the threat her English blood posed to Scotland would be destroyed.

Alexander felt satisfaction warming him. The best part of the plan was that Broen MacNicols would be in his debt after he provided the justice the king had refused the Highland laird. Donnach Grant would be free from his debt, but Broen MacNicols would be in it. Yes, a wise royal adviser keep the important men in his debt. A more-perfect solution there couldn't be.

&

"What do you mean?" Clarrisa asked suspiciously. Broen MacNicols's tone was too playful by far. He was fighting back a smirk too, while amusement danced in his eyes.

He pointed at the gate. "It's a fair bet those Chisholms retainers have heard who ye are and that their laird wants ye to stay."

Disappointment slammed into her so hard she gasped.

"If you knew such a thing, why did you bring me out here? To torment me with what I cannot have?"

He lost the battle to maintain control over his expression. His teeth flashed at her in a wide grin. "Clarrisa, lass, ye have spirit, to be sure, but ye're lacking a healthy sense of humor."

"Ye'll need one in the Highlands," Shaw added.

She propped her hands on her hips, but Broen looked at Shaw. "Get the horses and make sure the retainers at the gate see ye enjoying what yer laird is about. Let them think ye've had a bit too much cider."

"Ye have nae told me how ye're planning on getting past them..." Shaw appeared confused for a moment before Broen slid his arm around her body and pulled her against him once more.

"I'm going to let them think I have a mind to tryst."

The burly retainer snorted before tugging on the corner of his bonnet. "Come along, lads. Let's make this good. I've a mind to get me feet back on MacNicols land."

Tryst...

The word shocked her, but it also set off a pounding deep inside her that seemed to urge her to abandon reason and join in with the night shadows and some unseen wildness lurking beyond her sight.

An insane idea... one she needed to resist... of course...

"You cannot simply touch me," she insisted and pushed at his arm.

She might as well have not spoken, for Broen ignored her, his arm binding her securely to his body. Shaw and the other men left, leaving her alone with their laird. Light flickered over them from the wall torches, but it struck her as strangely intimate—for sure her position in Broen's embrace was. What shocked her was how much she didn't detest being held against him. Broen was hard; his body, solid next to hers. She should have been repulsed as she had been when the king leered at her, but delight was stirring in her belly, sending heat through her veins.

Insanity…

She flattened her hands on top of his chest. "What do you think you're doing?"

"Making a good show of it, lass. We'll nae be making it past that gate otherwise," Broen muttered against her hair while he watched his men.

Shaw began laughing. He slapped one of the other MacNicols retainers on the back, while they all chuckled in the middle of the open yard.

"Hurry now, lads… Our laird is nae in the mood to wait now that he's found himself a friendly lass to go moonlight riding with!"

Her cheeks heated instantly.

"Come now… Get those horses! We'll have to be making sure no one takes advantage of him being distracted by something so charming!"

The younger MacNicols retainers began to appear with horses. Shaw continued to jest and lifted his head to look at the Chisholms men on the walls.

"Here now, lads! Me laird wants to prove his worth! Raise the gate, for we're off to see the forest by moonlight!"

Shaw slurred his words, and the other MacNicols laughed too loudly. They stumbled as they led the horses forward, and the Chisholms retainers grinned at them.

"The gate guard is watching us, lass," Broen whispered. He cupped the back of her head, angling her face so that it looked like they were preparing to share a kiss.

"Broen—"

"Ah… at last me name comes across yer sweet lips." He placed a kiss on her cheek. She trembled; couldn't stop herself. She watched recognition flash in his eyes as the hand cradling the back of her head slid down to gently massage the corded muscles of her neck.

"So it was all bluster," he whispered, but there was the ring of judgment in his tone. "Ye were playing a dangerous game with the king, lass. His temper would have been hot, and no mistake, if he'd made it down to that bath."

"I'd have managed… if there had been no other choice."

He blew out a breath that sounded like a soft snort. Her pride bristled as sensation raced up and down her body. Nothing made sense, and her thoughts were whirling too fast. Like she was watching a blizzard and knew there were thousands of snowflakes, but they were swirling too fast to see individually.

"Release me." She didn't wait to see if he'd comply with her demand but pushed against his chest to gain what she wanted.

You want him to kiss you…

No, she did not!

"The Chisholms are still watching, and that gate has nae lifted yet." He moved his hand gently along her nape. Prickles of enjoyment raced through her. "We're going to have to help Shaw convince them we're set on trysting."

Trysting…

"No—we're not." She sounded too breathless, too husky.

"I am nae so sure, lass… but I am sure I want to know what yer lips taste like."

"You mustn't…"

He smothered the rest of her denial beneath his lips. The kiss was firm and demanding but not hurtful. For some reason, she was positive he was being conscious of how much strength he used against her mouth. He maintained his grip on her nape, using the hold to keep her in position for his kiss. She'd thought heat was filling her veins before, but now it raced through her like a flame consuming parchment. She gasped, and he took advantage of her parted lips to deepen the assault.

It was truly an attack, but one that opened a door inside her she'd never noticed before. Behind it lay desires that came flooding out, and all of them produced even more heat. She wanted to kiss him back, mimic his motions, because the teasing actions of his lips felt so delightful. A shiver shook her, and his fingers moved once again to soothe it.

"Easy, lass… 'Tis but a kiss."

"But… you shouldn't—"

Something flashed in his eyes that looked very much like the disappointment rippling through her now that he'd lifted his mouth away from her own. She longed for more, but he suddenly scooped her up and cradled her against his chest. Her belly twisted with excitement, the raw display of strength affecting her far differently than she would have expected.

Instead of being frustrated by her helplessness, she felt compelled to boldly match him.

"Come with me, sweet lass, and I'll make good on me promise to chase ye through the woods like a Highlander." Broen spoke in a rich timbre laced with good humor. "Ye there... Lads, be sporting now and let me ravish this charming creature the way only a Scotsman can!"

There were sounds of laughter from the wall before the gate began to rise. Broen reached his stallion and released her for the moment it took him to gain the saddle. He reached down for her, shielding her from the sight of the Chisholms retainers. She hesitated, because in his eyes she witnessed the same desire that needled her. A flickering flame sparked to life by the kiss he'd pressed against her lips so briefly. It felt branded into her soul, the moment pounded deep into her mind.

She'd never forget him... or his kiss.

Or how much she wanted another one.

She gasped, startled by how deep her desire ran. It was as if she didn't know her own nature and was just now being forced to face it. The Chisholms retainers weren't doing anything to keep their voices low. She was actually grateful to them, for their conversation covered her gasp.

"They will nae be cold..."

"Nothing like a moonlight romp to make a man feel welcome..."

Broen let her feet down as he reached for the reins of his stallion and swung up onto the back of the animal with a grace that impressed her. No mounting blocks for this noble laird; he was as strong as the men he commanded.

Shaw and the others mounted, the squires gratefully handing over the animals so they might hurry back to their warm beds.

"Come, lass." Broen's voice was deep and full of something she wanted to avoid naming, an emotion that paired exceptionally well with the excitement still brewing in her belly. The moonlight cast him in silver, and he offered her his hand. For the moment, he appeared more legend than man, but her body was still warm from his flesh.

"Now she thinks on what her father will say in the morning..."

"Is nae that like a lass? All sweet kisses until the moment comes to make good on what she's been promising..."

Their smugness sent her reaching for Broen's hand. Her lips still tingled, but she'd trust him over the man who'd so boldly threatened to prove his worth to her before locking her in a cell. Broen pulled her up behind him.

"Hold on to me, lass, and hide yer face. They'll think naught of yer wanting secrecy."

But what would he think of her clinging to him?

You'll like it, just as you enjoyed his kiss...

Maybe, but at least Broen was riding toward freedom. The horse surged beneath her, and the night air stung her unprotected hands where they rested on his belly. It was a surreal moment as they passed through the gate, and the Chisholms retainers chuckled. The night was dark and speckled with moonlight. Nothing made sense, for the fortress behind them was everything she'd been raised to think of as secure. But for the moment, the man taking her into the dark unknown represented more security than all three of the stone towers of Raven's Perch.

His Highland home was suddenly more welcoming than England.

Three

THEY DIDN'T SLEEP.

Broen urged them forward, only taking time to allow her to transfer to her own horse once his men joined them. The mare hurried ahead of the stallions lined up behind it, carrying her weight easily in spite of the rough ground they covered.

Dawn cast its light over newly plowed fields and the farmers who rose early to begin planting. The last of the snow had melted, filling the rivers they crossed with roaring white water. They took the horses across carefully, but the water was high and wet her to the waist in the deepest rivers.

But the sun was warm when it rose completely. The wind died, but the motion of riding rippled her dress to help dry it. In spite of the fact that the sun began to dip on the horizon when they neared another river, Clarrisa considered slipping off her horse to swim across, because it had been too long since she'd bathed.

Such would be foolish, a risk she didn't need to take, but she smiled anyway, allowing her mind to toy with the idea instead of dwelling on the approaching night.

There was something about darkness and Broen MacNicols. The combination was proving to be intoxicating.

You're thinking foolish thoughts...

Yes, she was, and a half dozen lectures from her childhood rose to needle her with warnings of how wickedness would lead her to damnation. Her smile grew wider.

"I did nae expect to see such a pleasant look on yer face."

She jumped, startling her mare. The animal side-stepped, moving too close to Broen's stallion, which was right beside her now. The stallion snorted and made to nip the mare. Broen muttered something in Gaelic while trying to control his horse.

"Oh fie." Her mare wasn't waiting to see if Broen could master his stallion. It bolted. Clarrisa leaned low and thanked the saints for the fact she was in Scotland, where she didn't have to ride sidesaddle. She gripped the mare between her thighs, matching the pace the animal set. Her heart beat faster as the wind burned her cheeks.

She laughed when at last the mare began to slow. Perspiration had appeared on her forehead, and she raised a hand to wipe it away. The mare slowed at the top of a ridge, the last rays of the sun illuminating the valley below. A river cut through it, the roaring sound filling Clarrisa's ears.

A hard arm slipped around her waist and hauled her off the back of the mare in a flash.

"Ye're insane, woman," Broen hissed at her while holding her in front of him and keeping a hand on the reins.

The need to be bold surfaced, as though it had been waiting for the opportunity. Being held so close to him, able to smell his skin, ignited the urge so quickly there was no time for thinking.

"You're the madman here." She aimed a vicious shove at him, arching her body away from his. "Dragging me off my mare like some Highland savage."

His arm didn't slacken, not even the slightest amount, but his eyes narrowed. Clarrisa glared straight back at him, trying to master the urge to giggle. She was far past the age of giggling, for heaven's sake, but he saw the amusement glittering in her eyes, and she watched his blue eyes light up with something very similar.

"I was perfectly capable of managing the mare."

"Is that so, lass?" He slid his hand up her back to press her torso against his. "If ye are so adept, why did yer mare take off? A competent rider would have kept the animal under control."

"A capable man would have held his stallion in check, or was that your way of having an excuse to handle me?" She was being bold and had no idea where she'd learned to talk so brazenly, only that it excited her.

His eyes flashed with something that looked very much like he was rising to meet her challenge. The arm around her tightened, and she suddenly noticed they were out of sight of his men.

"If ye understand what being handled means, Clarrisa, I assure ye, I have only begun to handle ye."

His voice was low, but the promise was clear as a church bell. His attention lowered to her lips, setting off a longing inside her to have done with arguing with him.

Kissing him promised far more pleasure.

She shook off the wicked thoughts. "Enough. You appeared beside me like a specter, and it was your stallion that misbehaved by attempting to bite my mare. Yet I am not surprised, for it takes after the uncivilized nature of its master."

She offered him a soft laugh, but it sounded nervous. He didn't join her in amusement this time; his eyes darkened, making her feel too hot to remain so close to him. The heat would soon affect her reasoning.

"Aye, I'm uncivilized, and that's a truth I'm proud of, but I do admit to enjoying handling ye."

She shouldn't have liked his confession so much.

She froze, her fingertips resting lightly against his chest. She noticed how much she enjoyed touching him. Her stare settled on his, those blue eyes seeming deeper and more intense than she'd noticed before. Her belly twisted with nervous excitement as a quiver rippled across her skin. His shirt and doublet were open at the neck, allowing the garment to split and bare his skin. She moved her hand up so that two of her fingertips were resting on his warm skin. Such a simple touch, yet she felt it so intensely her breath caught.

"You should put me down." Her voice was a mere whisper, the words feeling as though they were choking her.

"That is nae what either of us wants, Clarrisa."

He smoothed his hand up her spine, sending out a flood of sensation. She was keenly aware of him. Time seemed to slow, ensuring she might experience every tiny motion. Details flooded her, the way his fingers cupped her nape one at a time, until he was gently gripping it. She heard the way his breathing deepened and became rough. She saw the way his nostrils flared slightly before his attention slipped to her lips and hunger glittered in his eyes.

"Ye want me to kiss ye."

"Do not, Broen." She turned her head away. "It isn't right."

She was pleading, but not because she feared he'd take what he wanted. It would be so much simpler if he did, easier for her to absolve herself of responsibility.

But it would make her a coward.

He blew out a harsh breath and used his grip on her neck to turn her face back toward his. Anticipation raked its nails down her spine. When she looked back into his eyes, it was clear she was inexperienced in the ways of passion, for what she'd witnessed before had only been the beginnings of hunger. Now desire blazed in full force in his eyes, and she recognized it in spite of all the times her uncle's men had shepherded her away from situations where she might have learned about passion.

"What is nae right is selling ye to a man twice yer age and expecting ye to give him a son without him giving ye the respect of wedding. A maiden deserves such respect."

Emotion threatened to strangle her. It was too thick, and she failed to smother a sob that rose from deep inside her in the only place she was free to admit what she truly felt. But she rebelled at the idea of sharing it with him. Between them was only the merest shred of trust, not nearly enough for her to allow him to see her heart.

"Yet it is common enough. I am hardly the first daughter to be bartered for the betterment of the family name. Release me now, Broen." She pushed at him and arched to dislodge his grip on her neck. "I do not want you touching me."

He grunted. "Liar," he accused softly.

She jerked her attention back to his face, stilling for the moment. "I do not lie."

His lips lifted in response, but the grin wasn't mocking; it was arrogant. "No' intentionally, I'll grant ye that."

"But… there is no middle ground when it comes to dishonesty," she muttered, too breathless to suit her demand he release her. Deep and husky, her voice betrayed just how much she was enjoying his embrace.

"There is when ye have no concept of what it is ye're feeling, Clarrisa."

He moved his hand, gently stroking her nape. Delight raced down her body, raising a trail of goose-flesh as it went. Even her nipples contracted into hard points.

"Ye do nae understand why ye're trembling or why a simple stroke makes yer insides twist…" He smoothed his hand over her nape again, and sensation spiked through her instantly. "Or why ye keep having to look away from me to avoid staring at me lips…"

Oh God, she was…

He turned her face toward him with a sure grip once again. His gaze lowered to her lips, focusing on them as the delicate surface tingled with anticipation.

"You're toying with me," she forced out.

He chuckled, low and deep. With the light fading,

the moment took on a more intimate feel, because the night had ever been the sanctuary of lovers.

"I am guilty of that charge." His grip was still solid on her nape. She was held immobile and at his mercy. "And a few other things too, lass, like wanting to tempt ye until ye kiss me back."

She wanted to protest, but he didn't give her the chance. Broen kissed her with all the force of the passion burning in his eyes. His mouth claimed hers, possessing it without mercy. She twisted, unable to decide how to bear all the sensation erupting from the kiss.

A reckless urge rose for her to press closer to him. It encouraged her to be bold and touch what she wanted while arching back to offer her breasts to him. She wanted to feel every bit of his hardness against her, pressing closer until there wasn't any space between them. She slid her hand into the opening of his shirt, marveling at the enjoyment she gained from being skin to skin with him.

He pressed her lips open, and she lost the will to consider what she was doing. She gripped his shirt, pulling him toward her. She captured a soft growl with her lips and felt the vibration with her hands as it shook his chest.

"Sweet Christ, woman—"

Clarrisa cut him off this time, reaching up to cup the side of his jaw and turn his face back toward her kiss. Satisfaction blossomed inside her—that boldness that had needled her since the last kiss cheering her on as she tried to mimic his motions. She tilted her head so their lips might fuse more completely, pressing her mouth against his while teasing his lower lip with the tip of her tongue. Another growl surfaced from him, but his grip on her nape moved up until he'd captured one of her braids. He gripped it and took command of the kiss again. Her thoughts spun out of control, but she felt more than she'd ever imagined she might. Pleasure and delight swirled through her with such brilliant intensity she broke away before it drowned her.

"I shouldn't have kissed you." Shouldn't have, because now she wanted more, and her discipline was long gone.

Surprise registered on his face, but she slipped out of his distracted hold and slid down the side of the horse. It was much farther to the ground than she had thought, and her ankle collapsed when she tried to make it take her weight. The stallion let out a snort as she struggled to regain her footing so close to its flank.

"Don't be foolish, woman," Broen growled. The stallion turned in a circle as Broen fought to command the strong-willed creature. When he brought the animal around, his knuckles were white from the grip he used to control the beast. "This is a full stallion, Clarrisa. Ye ride well enough to know better than to slide down its side like that. He could crush yer skull with his hooves."

"It would have been more foolish to remain atop him."

She turned her back on him but whirled back around when she heard his curse. There was a warning in his tone, as sure as the night had closed around them.

"Let me be, Broen MacNicols. Maybe you're thinking I'm free with my favors, but I'm a maiden still."

He smothered another word of profanity. "That's plain enough."

The man was furious, his tone condemning. Clarrisa propped her hands on her hips. "You don't need to sound like it's something I should be ashamed of."

He tilted his head. "Cannae ye just be content with the fact that I believe ye are pure?" He muttered something else in Gaelic while looking to see where her mare had gone.

Frustration was shredding her. "I don't know what I want from you," she explained.

"A solid truth if ever I heard one," he groused. "Come back here. Yer mare is out of sight."

Part of her wanted to obey, but the sheer intensity of what his kiss had unleashed inside her made her shake her head. "I'll walk."

"Are the pair of ye finished?"

Shaw's voice hit her like a blast of winter wind. She turned to look up the hill, where the burly retainer sat on his horse. He was sideways, looking away from them, but he'd obviously noticed they were no longer embracing.

Broen kneed his stallion forward until the animal stood near her. He leaned down, his shoulder-length hair falling low enough to brush her shoulder.

"'Tis for sure we are nae finished, lass. No' finished even by half."

He reached down and grasped the wide leather belt that secured the Chisholms plaid around her waist. With a hard tug, he pulled her off the ground and sent her halfway over the back of the stallion. She shrieked, but he paid her no mind, pressing her down in front of him.

"We're just getting started, and that's me promise to ye, lass."

Hard and determined, his voice carried a promise.

~

"The little lass has daggers in her eyes for ye."

Broen shot Shaw a deadly look, but amusement sparked in Shaw's eyes as he grinned.

"I thought ye wanted to warn me away from her and her scheming ways. Ye're sounding like a woman with all yer mind changing."

Shaw shot him a look Broen wasn't interested in suffering, but Shaw was right.

"This business irritates me."

"I've noticed, Laird," Shaw replied. "As a matter of fact, so have the lads."

Broen looked over his men. Most were sleeping; the only ones still awake were set to watching Clarrisa and the road. Broen felt his chin tingle. He'd just wasted precious time that he could have spent sleeping to shave—for a woman.

For an English woman.

There was no way to ignore the fact. It frustrated him and rubbed his temper, but the three-day growth of beard on his face had left the faintest of pink abrasions on Clarrisa's delicate skin. Fatigue was pounding in the back of his head, and what was he doing? Preening for a female. And not even for Daphne.

He stopped for a moment, his temper cooling. He could recall Daphne MacLeod's dark eyes but hadn't thought of her during the days he'd been away from his land. Somehow her memory had slipped aside. He'd believed he couldn't live without her, but obviously he could. The only saving grace to the knowledge was that she wasn't waiting back at Deigh Tower for him. Women had a way of knowing what men were thinking when they were alone with them. He certainly didn't wish her dead, but he didn't want to think he'd have broken her heart. It was a cruel trick of nature that made men unable to do the same.

Clarrisa opened her eyes, staring straight at him and proving his point. Maybe they weren't alone, but it felt like there was a connection between them. He muttered a curse. Maybe Daphne was beginning her torment of him, but in the form of an Englishwoman whom he had no business wanting.

Much less shaving for.

❧

Heat licked its way across her cheeks. Clarrisa lowered her chin so more of the Chisholms plaid would cover her face. She didn't need Broen noticing her blush. It wasn't for him.

Yes, it is…

She cringed. Why did he have to be so handsome? She was mad to notice, but there seemed to be no way to ignore him. With a shake of her head, she forced herself to look away from his newly shaved face, but she felt his attention on her. The blush burned hotter as sensation spread down her body. It happened faster this time, her skin somehow more sensitive. The feeling settled in her breasts again, drawing her attention to how much she'd enjoy having him nuzzle them with his newly shaved chin.

Clarrisa!

She actually trembled at her ideas.

Carnal ideas…

Oh, they certainly were, and for the first time in her life, she truly understood what the lectures in church had been about.

Wicked… Temptation… Wanton…

All of them leading toward one thing: sins of the flesh.

There were longings clamoring for attention inside her that both frightened and delighted her. But in all honesty, it wasn't true fear, at least not the sort she would have expected. This was an unease, an ache that unnerved her because she wanted to satisfy it. She closed her eyes, but sleep eluded her. Instead, the memory of Broen's kiss tormented her. Her body remained sensitive; her nipples, hard and needy.

The Highlander was a curse, after all, just as she'd always been told their lot was.

～

"Ye're a fine lad."

Laird Chalmers MacLeod smiled as his man handed over the sealed parchment he'd taken from the messenger Lord Alexander Home had dispatched to Laird Grant. He paid the messenger well to make sure he read messages from Lord Home, no matter to whom the man was writing them.

"I can nae stay too long," the messenger muttered.

"Easy, lad. Ye've done the deed now." Laird MacLeod turned over the letter and stared at the seal. "Lord Home will nae notice another day, considering how far ye had to go with this." He used the English pronunciation of *lord* on purpose. "Make no mistake. Ye have me gratitude for bringing this to me. Home is a traitor, and a power-hungry one too. He only wants the boy on the throne so he can rule through the lad."

Laird Chalmers MacLeod held the letter over a single candle flame. He kept it far enough away to ensure the paper didn't scorch, keeping the wax seal facing up. The room was silent except for the scuff of the messenger's boots against the stone floor when the man failed to mask his nervousness.

Laird Chalmers MacLeod didn't allow his attention to be distracted; he concentrated on the wax, waiting for it to glisten just the tiniest amount. When it did, he set the letter on the tabletop and pulled out the dirk that was tucked into his boot. It was small, with a thin blade that he always kept razor-sharp just in case an assassin sneaked close to him. He slid the steel tip beneath the warm wax and gently lifted it from the parchment without tearing the seal. Then he leaned close and blew on the wax to harden it once more. It was a careful process, but once the wax no longer glistened, he was able to unfold the letter and read it.

Chalmers growled. The other men in the room wanted to know what the letter said, but he left them in ignorance. He waved the wax above the candle's flame briefly before pressing it back into position on the folded letter.

"Take it to Laird Grant."

The messenger flinched at his tone. "Aye, Laird." He turned and quit the room before taking time to inspect the seal. There was no hint it had been opened. He tucked it back inside his doublet and hurried

toward the kitchen for a hot meal. Chalmers found
his own appetite lacking. War was brewing, one that
would pit clan against clan. By summer's end, Scotland
would either have a new king or an old one with no
living son. There was no way to know which side
might win, so he was keeping friends on both. It was
a wise thing to do for a common man such as himself.

⁓

"There it is, lass. Deigh Tower."

There was unmistakable joy in Broen's voice.
Clarrisa turned to look at him. She realized she'd
never seen him truly happy. He was now. His expression was radiant, and his eyes glistened with happiness.

"Do nae fret, Clarrisa. We've only one ghost."

She frowned. "I am not afraid of you and your
Highlands. Kindly stop trying to scare me."

Except the place did look like the perfect home for
a specter.

His stallion refused to be still, prancing in a circle
because it smelled the familiar scent of its home. Her
mare was eager to be back inside a stable too. The
animal hurried forward, carrying Clarrisa past Broen.
She heard him chuckling and bit back the retort that
sprang to her lips. She needed to avoid talking to the
man. Any interaction with him was dangerous.

Heat teased her cheeks, but there was no help for
it. The best she could do was let the mare have its
way. The animal took her to the top of a ridge—one
more in what had come to be an uncountable number
they'd crossed. Deigh Tower wasn't much to speak of,
simply a stone tower rising from the landscape.

At least that was the way it appeared until she crested the ridge. Below her, the tower sat in the center of the valley. It was built on a solid stone base that rose like a table and was surrounded by walls that were three stories high, on top of which were battlements. She could see the men stationed in the lookouts and the torches burning along the walkways. The walls formed a hexagon with thick keeps at each intersection to withstand cannon fire. Beyond the rock the fortress sat on, the last of the day's light shimmered off a loch. The water lapped the rock foundation, and she could hear the rivers flowing down the other side of the valley into it. The water emptied from the loch and made its way down the valley past a town.

So clever—from the other side of the ridge, it looked like a single tower. Anyone attempting to attack the fortress would have to ride down the sides of the valley, completely exposed to the battlements. Set on a base of stone, there would be no tunneling under the walls. Deigh Tower was impressive and formidable. The sight also made her throat tighten, as though a noose were closing about her neck.

The sun was setting, and she hadn't eaten since morning. She'd wrinkled her nose more than once throughout the day as she caught a whiff of the stench her skin had developed. Her braids were frizzy, and the linen dress wrinkled horribly, while every muscle she had ached. But she still pulled up on the reins, reluctant to willingly enter what might well become her prison.

Broen scooped her off the back of the mare in what

was becoming a familiar motion. He had her seated in front of him before she had managed to do more than sputter.

"Deigh is a fine place, so do nae let the fact that it means ice in Gaelic make ye think it's a cold place to live."

Her mare was happily speeding up once more, now that it was free of the weight of a rider. Clarrisa tossed her head, and the stallion snorted at her.

"It seems I am nae the only rider who takes after the temperament of me horse, sweet Clarrisa."

She turned her head to take issue with him. "I am not your sweet anything." She tried to shove him, but they were too close for her blow to have any true strength. "And if you try to bite me—"

"Ye'll what?"

There was a challenge in his tone, one she was sorely tempted to brave, but she turned to face forward and his chest rumbled with his amusement.

"You're a brute," she accused.

He caught her head and turned her face back to his. The amusement had vanished from his face. "The king would have shown ye brutality, but I have nae."

She shook her head, his grip irritating her almost beyond her endurance. "Think you I care for bruises or strikes?" She laughed at the surprise on his face. "You haven't heard a word of complaint for the aches in my body from the pace you've set, or the wounds festering on my wrists."

He reached for her wrist, but she shoved at him, making it necessary for him to clamp her tightly to his body or lose control of her.

"Damn yer stubborn nature, Clarrisa. Why do ye accuse me of being a brute?"

They rode beneath the raised gate, cheers coming from the men on the battlements. Somewhere a bell began to toll, and then another and another, until the entire fortress echoed with their chiming. She turned to look where they were going, part of her actually grateful to him for taking the choice from her. It was weak of her to think in such a way, but at least she was honest. Broen rode into the inner yard and pulled the stallion to a stop.

"I'm waiting for an answer, Clarrisa."

His arm was still tight around her body, binding her to him. More and more people came out of the doorways to welcome their laird back. Children pointed at her as their mothers leaned toward one another to whisper about her.

"Release me, Broen. You've taken me where you wished, and I owe you no obedience, nor must I hold my tongue in your presence." There were plenty who would tell her how foolish such words were, but she was oddly past caring.

"Is that so?" he demanded in a low tone meant only for her ears.

"It is. It's wiser too. We respond to each other too much."

It was an admission, but she heard him pull in a harsh breath. His arms tightened, reminding her of their embrace at Raven's Perch. A shiver raced down her back.

"You know it's wiser, Broen. You did not take me for yourself." But she wasn't sure if she wasn't saying it out loud in order to believe it herself.

She pushed against him, half fearing he'd refuse her. Broen freed her, but a large retainer caught her around the waist before she was halfway to the ground.

"A Chisholms lass, is it?" a MacNicols retainer asked.

"No," she answered.

Her English accent sent the retainer back away from her. Broen chuckled as he jumped down and hooked an arm around her waist.

"This is young Clarrisa, me guest at the request of the Earl of Sutherland." He gripped the belt holding the plaid to her waist and brushed the plaid back from her head to make sure his men got a good look at her face. "She'll be staying, and I will nae be pleased to hear any of ye have allowed her past the gate."

More than a hundred people leaned closer to peer at her. Broen stood half behind her as they studied her.

"I can stand my own ground," she snapped before turning to face him. "I am no coward."

He raised an eyebrow. The same man she'd awakened to find watching her while she slept. She felt the weight of his authority. He was master of the fortress, his word law to every living soul watching them, but she still wasn't willing to return to the meek manners that had seen her following her family's orders to go to Scotland.

Instead, she lifted her chin and offered him her best interpretation of the grin he so often vexed her with. "I need no help to face down those intent on helping you imprison me."

The crowd grew silent and pressed in closer to see what their laird would make of her refusal. For a moment, a gleam of appreciation appeared in Broen's eyes, but it transformed into a flame of challenge so quickly she didn't have time to step back before he moved.

"Be careful how ye label things, lass." His tone warned her that he was willing to match her defiance of convention with some of his own. "Because I might be of the mind to prove ye right." He lowered his shoulder and tossed her right over it. A cheer went up as his people began to clap and whistle.

Her temper exploded, and she refused to hang over his shoulder like some prize. But the moment she straightened, he smacked her bottom. The shock of it sent her back over his shoulder, and he turned in a swirl of kilt to carry her up the steps and into Deigh Tower.

"I'm owing me overlord for sending me after this one, lads!"

Broen didn't stay on the ground floor. He climbed several flights of stairs before bursting through a door. Several women gasped before laughing at the sight of him carrying her like a sack of grain.

"I've brought ye something," he announced before tossing her off his shoulder. For a moment she was cradled in his arms, against his chest like a babe. She caught just a glimpse of his grin before he tossed her into something.

"Holy Mother of Christ!" she shouted as she landed in a tub full of water. It splashed up in a huge wave as she frantically tried to control her landing. She ended up sprawled on her backside with her feet in the air and her arms grasping the sides of the tub. Water soaked her body, covering her to midchest because the tub was so large.

"So ye do know how to curse." Broen stood with his hands propped on his hips. The sword pommel with its sapphire glittered above his left shoulder, while his golden hair was still only held out of his eyes by a single braid, and his doublet was open to the waist. He looked as wild and untamed as he had the first time she'd seen him, and she felt like scratching his eyes out. In fact, her hands curled into talons as she began to push herself out of the tub. He planted a hand in the center of her chest to keep her on her back.

"Ye'll learn, Clarrisa, to respect my will here. Display that wild streak of yers too publicly, and I will be happy to tame it... so all can witness it."

The women in the room smothered their laughter.

"You will never—"

He sealed the rest of her denial beneath a kiss. He grasped a handful of her wet clothing and lifted her so he could silence her with his lips. It was hard and demanding. But enjoyment still raced through her even as she began to throw water at him. He shook his head when he straightened, flinging water from his hair.

"I accept yer challenge," he announced before looking across the room. "Me guest does nae like the way she smells. It seems I've brought home one of the few Englishwomen who does nae like to stink. Bathe her."

It was an order. Every woman in the room lowered herself immediately. If looks could kill, Broen MacNicols would have died right there in front of her. Instead, she watched the pleats of his kilt swaying before he disappeared behind a solid door.

"Brute!"

She might as well have saved her breath, for the

only thing her shouting did was renew the laughter surrounding her. Four maids began stripping off her shoes and stockings as she tried to climb out of the tub. Her dress had soaked up so much water her exhausted body refused to stand under its weight. She would have protested as the women began to remove it, but she was too busy sighing with relief.

Brute... Highlander. The words seemed to mean the same thing.

❧

"Ye're better off no' seeping in such dark thoughts."

The woman speaking had Maud's years but her voice lacked the pinched tone the English matron had always used.

"I'm named Edme."

Clarrisa lowered herself. She was already finishing the respectful gesture before she realized how long it had been since she had offered anyone a gesture so polite. It seemed ages. Somehow she'd completely lost track of time since Broen had taken her.

"Ye have pretty manners, a credit to yer family," Edme muttered. The woman had on a sturdy wool dress with a piece of the MacNicols plaid held on her right shoulder with a silver brooch. A belt secured it around her waist. On her head, she wore a knit bonnet similar to the one Broen wore. Clarrisa decided she liked it better than the pressed linen caps her uncle made the servants in his household wear.

"Not really. They had me trained to please whoever paid the most for me." Clarrisa covered her mouth with one hand, horrified by how bitter she sounded.

"What of yer mother? Mothers teach their children manners because it is their duty. We'd be savages otherwise."

Highlanders were savages. At least, she'd heard it said many a time. Clarrisa bit her lip, clamping down on the impulse to be surly.

"My mother died when I was only a few winters old. I only recall her face because my uncle had a miniature of her and he allowed me to see it sometimes." When he was in the mood to impress upon her what fine things might be hers if she caught the eye of a titled man. Clarrisa began pulling a comb through her drying hair once more. Anger and discontent were brewing inside her, but it was becoming impossible to direct her feeling completely toward Broen. She certainly detested the man for treating her like a sack of grain, but she was still grateful to him for taking her away from the Scottish king's plans, which left her standing in a swirling cloud of discontent. She had no idea what to hope for. Not having anything to look forward to left her feeling like the ground was giving way beneath her feet.

"Here now. I've brought ye some supper. A full belly will lift that dark humor from yer face. Ye look bone weary and half-starved. I'm nae surprised. The laird travels quickly when he's off his own land, a good habit in times like these when we are nae sure which clans are royalist." The older woman brought a tray forward and placed it on the small table near the fire. "Sit here until yer hair is dry. The Highlands are no place for wet tresses after nightfall."

"Your laird tossed me into the tub." Clarrisa had

to set down the comb because the scent of food had set her hand to trembling. Her belly rumbled, low and loud. She had never smelled food so enticing before. Her mouth actually watered.

"Aye... I've heard the tale several times over already." Edme lifted the cover off a soup terrine, and a puff of steam rose. "Never known the laird to give up his hot bath for a lass before. Right kind of him."

"Kind—"

Edme raised an eyebrow at her tone. Clarrisa shut her mouth with a click of her teeth. A small smile appeared on the older woman's lips.

"Yer mother would be proud of ye," she decided with a nod.

Clarrisa shook her head and reached for the spoon lying neatly beside the bowl. "If you've heard the tale, you know my behavior has been less than perfect."

The stew was still hot, thanks to the heavy silver bowl someone must have warmed before ladling the meal into it. She sighed as she swallowed and scooped up another spoonful quickly. She was too hungry to control the urge to eat fast.

"Ye're in the Highlands. Spirit is respected here. Ye'd nae have survived the trip if ye did nae have enough of it."

Clarrisa stared at Edme as she turned and went to the room's huge bed. The feet were carved like lion's paws, and two full rampant animals dominated the headboard. Edme tugged down the coverlet, exposing creamy linens.

"Is this Broen's chamber?"

The spoon was halfway to her lip as she noticed the

fine table and chairs near the window. Costly squares of glass were set into the windows, and the tub was an overlarge one.

"As I told ye, the laird gave up his bath for ye." Edme came back toward her. "But it's good to see that dressing robe used. The laird never wears it, mind ye. He's young enough no' to be bothered by the chill of night. Still, some of the younger maids find it shocking when they see him walking about in naught but skin after his bath."

Naught but skin?

Her eyes went wide as heat rose in her cheeks. She stuffed another spoonful of stew into her mouth to prevent voicing some careless comment. The dressing robe was thick. Even with only a chemise beneath it, she was warm.

"I've told ye plenty of times, Edme, no' to put the lasses to work hauling water up here. I'll bathe in the bathhouse."

Clarrisa dropped the spoon and stood. Broen stood near the doorway, wearing only his kilt and a shirt that had its collar lying open.

"What are you doing here?" Clarrisa demanded.

He lifted one eyebrow. "It's me chamber, as Edme just told ye." He walked toward the bed and placed his sword on two iron poles protruding from the stone wall. The pommel lay within reach of the bed.

"Ye're the laird now. Privacy is yer due," Edme muttered while inclining her head.

Broen wasn't watching his clanswoman. His blue eyes were on Clarrisa. The chamber was lit only by candles now, the fire in the hearth no more than a glowing bed of coals. The golden light danced off drops of water left in his hair.

"I admit, Edme, yer persistence in continuing me father's tradition of bathing up here came in right handy tonight."

"I disagree," Clarrisa informed him. Her voice trembled, and she bit her lip before adding more to her statement. She needed to find her composure, and quickly, before the man decided she was besotted enough by his charms to fall easily into his bed.

His kisses certainly scatter your wits...

Broen chuckled. "Well now, Clarrisa, I'm going to call ye fickle, for ye railed at me about how ye did nae care for the stench our journey had left ye with."

"That was not an invitation for you to carry me to your chamber like some prize. After all, I was telling you about the wisdom of us remaining separated."

"That does nae mean I agreed with ye, lass." He closed the space between them. "Ye're me prize, sure enough, one that will help ensure the king cannae begin any new trouble."

"Why are you not loyal to your king?" It would have been better not to ask. Learning about him would only make it so much harder to maintain distance between them.

All traces of teasing left his face. "A king must earn his loyalty by dispensing justice when his nobles come to him. Me father was murdered in cold blood, and James refused to even see me. I will nae follow him when he's so selfish as to leave such a grave matter undecided, which will lead to feuding. I want justice, no' having to listen to the mothers of me retainers weeping because their sons are run through this summer now that the Grants know the king will allow them to get away with whatever they want. I and me men will have to protect our own, or blood will flow."

"How will bringing me here help?"

"Me father died on me neighbor's land. Donnach Grant will nae face me to explain what happened, which leaves me men demanding vengeance. Me overlord was willing to trade the favor of backing me cause if I made sure the king did nae get the York-blooded son he craved."

Anger smoldered in his eyes, and she struggled against the wave of compassion that swept through her. "A just cause, but I should be free to leave now that you have prevented your king from using me, not kept here by your order."

He crossed his arms over his chest and considered her for a long moment. "To go where?"

"Well"—she searched her memory—"I have a cousin who would most likely welcome me."

"A relation who does nae obey the will of yer uncle?"

Her uncertainty must have shown on her face, because Broen scoffed at her. "Where would ye end up next time? In whose bed, lass? Or beneath whose blade?"

Heat licked across her skin as she noticed that his bed was too close for her comfort. The knowledge that they were in his chamber refused to be pushed aside. She suddenly realized Edme had left silently. "Not yours, Broen MacNicols. You can put the thought straight out of your head."

She sputtered and moved to step away from him, but he snaked out his hand to grasp her wrist. The bench she'd been sitting on toppled over, raising a cloud of ash when it landed in the coals of the fireplace. Broen pulled her against him and away from the coals before she truly had time to fear being singed.

"Who is thinking of bed sport more, lass? If ye were nae dwelling on it, ye'd have insisted no one wanted to spill yer blood. Instead yer mind only heard me speaking of beds." He was warm, just as she remembered, and her body eagerly approved of being in contact with his. "Ye kissed me back, Clarrisa, with passion hot enough to burn."

"That does not mean I am content with being in your chamber."

He had her arm twisted up behind her back. For a moment, the embrace tightened, pressing her breasts against his chest. Her nipples contracted, the soft globes compressing. A soft gasp escaped her lips when sensation went shooting through her. She'd never realized her breasts might feel so much enjoyment.

"Shall I court yer contentment?" He leaned down until she felt his breath against her lips. "Shall I test yer resolve to resist returning me kiss once again, lass? Ye failed but a few hours past. A lover is something most women never get the chance to enjoy. Are ye sure ye want to turn yer back on the opportunity? There is passion between us, lass. It is no' a common thing. Ye think me unwise, but I know how rare this sort of flame is."

She shivered with the knowledge and felt heat licking at her insides. Need began pricking her with tiny demands that rejected her reasons for denying what she craved. But the growing intensity frightened her.

It would overwhelm her so easily…

"Do not make this a matter of your pride, Broen. My purity is the only thing I have. I was sincere when I thanked you for taking me away from your king. Please do not behave like him."

He lifted his head, pressing his lips into a firm line. In his eyes, there was a conflict, one that burned brightly before he released her and turned to lift the bench out of the hearth. She shivered once more, this time from loss.

"Ye wound me with yer words, lass. For all that ye accuse me of being a brute, I have no desire to have ye gaining evidence to support yer claim." He turned to consider her. "At least no' when it comes to the matter of sharing me bed. I stole ye to prevent war, and ye'll stay here until the earl aids me in doing what needs doing. Leave, and I'll run ye down. That's a promise."

His tone held the authority she'd so often heard in her uncle's; the difference was that Broen seemed to deserve it. She wasn't sure where such an idea had come from; it was completely foreign to everything she'd been raised to believe. Her gaze settled on the open shirt that revealed the light hair covering his chest. He was the barbarian she'd always heard Highlanders were, but he didn't lack integrity. In many ways, he stirred more admiration inside her than any Englishman she'd ever met.

The wilds of Scotland were tearing her away from civilized thinking, just as she'd heard they would. There was no other explanation for the yearning to argue with him in the hope he'd impress his will upon her once again.

"Edme will have turned down the bedding in the chamber at the end of the hallway. Go on with ye now, before I'm tempted to bury me hands in yer hair. Ye're a tempting woman, Clarrisa." He studied her from narrowed eyes. She lowered herself and heard him mutter a curse.

"Now ye offer me respect?" He opened his arms, looking like he was preparing to pounce. "Why? Because ye fear following yer passion so very much? Or do ye believe I am such a savage I do nae value a lover who chooses me of her own free will?"

She rose back to her full height. "I offer you respect because you earned it by granting me a choice."

Her words were low because she was trembling. Longing was burning in her belly, teasing her with how good it felt to be in his embrace. She was tempted to surrender to the moment, take the pleasure that might be hers, and forget all the reasons why it wasn't a wise idea. His words beckoned with the promise of what delights she'd find in the arms of a lover as opposed to the man her kin had sent her to.

It felt so very good to be in his arms...

He chuckled softly and with an unmistakably menacing sound. "The idea of luring ye into me bed is beginning to tempt me more than I care to admit."

She backed up a step, having to gather a handful of the dressing robe because it was so long in the back. "You should keep your attention on the reason why you stole me. It sounds as though you have many important matters to attend to, Laird MacNicols."

His gaze traced her flowing hair. The strands swayed softly every time she moved. The only time she allowed men to see it unbraided was May Day, and it was strangely intimate to notice the way Broen appeared to enjoy the sight of it.

"Aye, but there's something between us, and that's a fact, lass." Now there was a warning in his eyes, something she recognized out of pure instinct.

"Possibly…" She could have bitten off her own tongue for allowing him to hear how much she feared the way he overwhelmed her, so much so, she was lying to cover it.

She turned and moved toward the door but felt him following her—stalking her, really. She glanced over her shoulder and saw that he was keeping pace with her. What stole her breath was the hunger flickering in his eyes.

"It is lust, common and to be avoided." She stopped and faced him. "Surely there is a priest somewhere nearby who will happily lecture you on the merits of pious behavior."

She could certainly have used a good lecture to restore her resolve.

He reached forward and right up the sleeve of the dressing robe. He clasped her bare arm, below where the chemise ended at her elbow. For one moment, their skin touched as he slid his hand down to her wrist. He pulled her hand up and placed a kiss against the back of it.

"Surely there is a reason ye are trembling, lass, and I'd much rather ye listen to me explain why."

She pulled her hand away, but he'd awakened every

inch of her skin. She shuddered, feeling the touch all the way down to her toes. "We cannot."

Must not…

Clarrisa turned her back on him. It was a foolish way of escaping, but she wasn't thinking anymore. His touch reduced her to reactions. Heat blazed across her cheek, and he reached out to stroke the scarlet stain when she turned to glance back at him.

"Broen…" She went to step forward but was too close to the door. Broen moved up behind her, flattening his hands on the surface of the door. She was pinned between his arms, but he wasn't actually touching her. Yet she was so keenly aware of him.

"We can, lass. There is no one here to judge us."

She felt his breath against her hair. He inhaled and made a low sound of approval. She'd never felt attractive before, but that single sound filled her with confidence. For the first time in her life, she felt the desire to bare her body for another. There was no shame, only need. The heat in her face spread down her body, touching off anticipation. Every inch of her longed to be touched, kissed—or anything else he wanted.

"But I want a lover, Clarrisa, and I believe ye need time to think on that choice."

She felt him move away from her, granting her the freedom to leave or stay. The power of choice was overwhelming. He chuckled at the wide-eyed look she sent him. "Think on it, lass, for I find I enjoy knowing I earned yer respect just a wee bit more than proving ye truthful when ye call me a brute."

He went back to the bed and sat on it, patting the

space beside him suggestively. "If ye want to know why ye're trembling, ye'll have to come to me of yer own free will. Do ye nae want to be the one who decides whom ye yield yer maidenhead to?"

"I don't want an invitation to your bed because you pity me." He did too. Behind the glitter of desire, she saw it clearly.

"It's far more than that, lass." He stood, and she trembled.

"But you do pity me and my plight." She shook her head. "I see it in your eyes."

He didn't offer her any excuse, only held up his hand with his eyebrow raised.

It would be so simple, so satisfying to know her uncle hadn't been the one to decide whose bed she occupied. But she did not want pity.

"I'm not a coward, nor am I willing to take shelter beneath pity. I'll bear what I must."

He didn't care for her answer, but admiration gleamed in his eyes. "Then ye'd best get on to yer chamber before the sight of yer flowing hair tempts me to try my hand at seducing ye."

It wasn't an idle threat, and part of her wanted to linger, just to lift the decision from her hands.

But he deserved better from her. Broen deserved a lover who was as bold as he was. Clarrisa opened the door and frowned when she failed to find anyone there. "Am I free here?"

He laughed at her. "Ye have the same amount of freedom I do. Me clansmen always keep watch on the stairs, for they fear I'll end up dead before I have an heir. Ye may go to the end of the hall or stay here.

But if ye go to that chamber, close the door and stay in there. Argyll will no' bother ye inside the chamber."

"Who is Argyll?"

"The ghost of Deigh Tower."

She wanted to argue with him, but the look of anticipation on his face made her clamp her mouth shut. It wasn't easy to resist the urge. She choked on her retort as she stepped into the hallway.

Ghost. Truly the man must think her a weak-kneed fool to take to cowering inside her chamber for fear of a ghost.

She sighed. It was most likely true. Broen no doubt had been raised to believe Englishwomen were no better than she'd been taught to think of Highlanders. The last few days had opened her eyes, but that didn't mean his had been. He was still laird and her captor. At least she'd not been so foolish as to give in to her yearnings.

The chamber at the end of the hall held all the comforts she might wish for. Edme had lit a lantern, and its light spilled over the floor cheerfully. The night was still chilly, but not cold enough for a fire in the hearth. Wood was neatly stacked inside it in case she should change her mind. Such was a luxury, for every resource used inside a tower was accounted for.

Clarrisa smiled when she spied the mirror. Oh, she knew full well it was vanity, but she adored being able to see her reflection. The mirror was placed in the corner, near a large wardrobe. Framed in silver, it showed her entire length.

Her hair was becoming…

She shook her head to dispel the vain thought but

shivered as she recalled the way Broen had buried his face in her tresses. She turned and gazed at the way the strands fell to below her bottom. Newly washed, her hair was curling. It was mostly blond, with darker streaks. Maud had lamented those, declaring them a flaw.

Broen hadn't seemed to mind. Of course, he'd also been set on luring her into his bed.

She turned and looked at the bed. It was beautiful, and yet she frowned, thinking of Broen. She was mad; there was no other explanation. Edme had turned back the covers, revealing creamy sheets. The coverlet was stuffed with goose down, drawing a sigh from her exhausted lips. The bed ropes creaked slightly when she crawled onto the mattress. Her cheeks were still burning as longings needled her flesh. She lay back, trying to ignore the clamoring in her body. How was it possible to want a man so much when she knew so little about him? Perhaps she might understand if she had harbored affection for him, but there was no way she could believe herself in love with him.

Whatever the cause, she slipped away into slumber before she thought the matter through. The days of travel had taken their toll, refusing to allow her to ponder her circumstances any further. But the longings settled into her dreams.

He could have overwhelmed her. Should have.

Broen snorted and tossed his shirt onto the table. He flexed his arms before reaching for his belt. At least stripping brought him a measure of contentment, even if true satisfaction was going to be denied him. His cock was hard. The damned thing ached, but what soured his disposition was the fact that he craved Clarrisa. *There* was a curse.

Three floors down, he'd find more than one willing lass to ease his desire. Why did he have to have a taste for the Englishwoman sleeping down the hallway?

He grunted and lay down. His bed was soft and warm. Sleep should have come easily after the time he'd been on the road, but it eluded him. Instead, he contemplated Clarrisa. She was his prize, yet he wanted more from her. His bed felt empty without her, but he didn't lament allowing her to leave. What he truly longed for was for her to choose him. Perhaps he was a blackguard for wanting to have her for a lover, but at least he was not so much of a brute as to overwhelm her. Doing so wouldn't have been too difficult.

That thought made his cock twitch. It hardened even more in response to the memory of the way Clarrisa had responded to his kisses. Her innocence was to her credit, but what kept him from slipping off to sleep was the way she'd risen to the challenge of kissing him back.

He wanted her. Plain, simple, and blunt.

Brute…

He was one, indeed, and his fiery English captive liked that quality best of all.

Four

"I BROUGHT A FEW THINGS DOWN FROM THE STORE-rooms." Edme's voice sounded far away. Clarrisa struggled to wake up, her eyelids feeling too heavy.

"Yer dress is filthy and too lightweight for this early in spring." The older woman was followed into the room by four other girls. They all wore a length of the MacNicols plaid down their backs.

"As soon as ye've dressed and eaten, the cobbler is expecting ye. These shoes are nae hardy enough for the Highlands."

"Oh… thank—" A sneeze interrupted her. "Excuse me—" Several more followed. By the time she had mastered the urge, her head ached.

"Tell the cook to brew up something for the laird's guest. She's caught a chill."

The other women turned to peer at her, but a sharp snap from Edme's hand and they went back to their duties. Edme came closer and laid a hand on Clarrisa's forehead.

"Little wonder ye've got the fever. Riding out in naught but summer linen."

"I'm well enough."

Edme humphed softly. "Ye're young and will likely heal quickly. All the more reason to get ye some proper clothing and footwear."

Clarrisa had been too busy trying to force her mind to work to notice the dresses. When she stood at last and rubbed the sleep from her eyes, she gasped. Three dresses were spread out on the table. Each was a jewel tone, sapphire, emerald, and ruby. They were made of costly velvet, with silk edging and even sleeves of brocade from France on one. The women carefully arranged them, touching them with the same care they might have used while dressing a queen.

"Those are far too fine." She still walked closer to the garments, unable to resist the urge to finger one of the velvet sleeves. So soft and plush, her fingertip glided over the surface and left a trail as the fibers bent ever so slightly from the weight of her touch. "Fit for a princess."

"Ye are the daughter of a king," Edme said. "So, 'tis fitting."

The velvet lost its appeal instantly. "My grandfather was a knight and gave the king lodging one night. My sire decided the hospitality included his host's daughter. When my mother birthed a daughter, the king settled a purse upon my grandfather, acknowledged me in the shire church, and never returned." She turned her back on the rich velvet dresses. "I am no princess and have never lived as such. I'd be worried about ruining such fine cloth."

But she did have a chill. Her nose was stuffy, and her head ached.

"Well then, I'll fetch ye some wool dresses. They'll be warmer." Edme draped the dressing robe around her shoulders before pointing at the velvet dresses. The remaining girls carefully picked up the gowns and carried them from the chamber as if they were babes.

"How did ye come to be under yer uncle's direction?"

Clarrisa jumped, startled by Broen's voice. It seemed she had dreamed of the man most of the night. She'd woken too many times to count, no doubt the true reason she was suffering a chill. "I thought you said this was my chamber. Shall I not be granted privacy here?"

He stood in the doorway, frowning at her tone. "I hear ye're suffering from my lack of attention to yer needs. Yer health is something I take personal interest in. So nae, ye'll no' have privacy when it comes to such important matters."

"I never said I was suffering." She tugged the belt of the dressing robe into place and knotted it. "And I am quite well, so you need not waste your time."

Edme drew in a stiff breath. "I know a fever when I see one. She has a chill, and no mistake. Ye'll mind me or risk having it settle into yer chest. Yer youth will nae protect ye if that happens."

Clarrisa lowered herself. Shame tugged at her for disrespecting Edme in front of her laird. The quarrel she had with Broen was private. Besides, making an enemy of Edme wasn't a wise idea. Broen might be laird, but Edme ran the house. She could make life at Deigh Tower comfortable or not, depending on her whim.

Edme nodded. "I needs speak with the cook meself,

to make sure she brews up what I know works best. Our cook is young but has a fair talent." She nodded to her laird before leaving the room.

Edme's departure left them alone again. Clarrisa waited for unease to begin nipping at her, but it didn't. Instead, there was only a sense of acceptance and something else she wasn't ready to name. A feeling of faith, which could so easily be mistaken for trust—a mistake she couldn't make.

Broen moved forward, his keen stare studying her. "Ye should have told me ye were cold. I'm used to riding with me men, but that does nae excuse me for overlooking yer needs." He stopped and picked up one of her discarded shoes. It was made of only thin leather and constructed with fashion in mind, so the sides were open. The ribbon rosette decorating the front of it was muddy and crushed. The once-bright ribbon used to tie it closed was torn and crumpled from the hard journey. He dropped it with a sound of disgust.

"Why would ye obey yer uncle if he had nae raised ye as yer blood deserved?" Suspicion edged his words, but not the coldness she'd heard before. "Did ye send the finer dresses away to lull me into compassion for ye?"

Her pride bristled. She didn't want to answer him, but she realized it was only because he was demanding. For once the choice was hers and hers alone to answer. That knowledge gave her satisfaction, but she needed to master the urge to argue with him, and quickly, before she ended up in his embrace again.

"My uncle sent his men to claim me after the two princes were taken to the tower… for safekeeping…"

Broen grunted. "Elizabeth Woodville was a fool to allow both her sons to be placed inside that fortress. She had nothing once that was done."

There was a hard certainty in his voice that bothered her. "She thought she was safeguarding them by agreeing with the lord protector. Besides, princes belong to the state."

"Still… a fatal mistake."

Clarrisa bristled under the smugness of his comment. "Many a woman has placed her faith in the titled men around her, only to discover her trust misplaced when those men decide to follow their own agendas. Better for a woman to refuse to trust men, because they serve their own purposes first."

He drew in a stiff breath, her words finding a soft spot. "Ye're here for the benefit of me people. Being laird means I consider their welfare above everything else."

So she could never trust him. It was a hard truth that punctured the fragile faith she'd somehow cultivated in him. At the moment, Broen was every inch the laird of the MacNicols. His kilt was pleated evenly and secured with a belt sporting fine tooling. The corner of his plaid was held on his right shoulder with a large silver brooch, and there was a matching one on the side of his bonnet. Three feathers were held in place by that brooch, all of them pointing upward.

He watched her inspect him, his blue eyes darkening. Tension drew her muscles tight. For a moment, the space between them felt filled with some force almost too great to resist. It pulled at her, trying to move her toward him, where they might abandon the issues between them.

Broen felt it too, a glint appearing in his eyes. His nostrils flared the tiniest amount, but she noticed it, her attention shifting to the physical display. He stepped forward, and her chest tightened, the air trapped inside her lungs. He cupped her chin, and that simple contact threatened to scatter her wits.

"The sort of trust I'm seeking from ye is far more personal, Clarrisa." He brushed his thumb over her lower lip, sending a surge of desire through her. "Think what ye may about me, but remember, lass, no other man would grant ye the choice." He slid his hand across her cheek, and he gripped her neck a second later. So quickly his touch went from teasing to controlling. A warning flashed in his eyes, one she understood perfectly.

"My choice is no." Her voice was steadier than she felt. His grip tightened, just enough to let her know she'd wounded him again, but his lips twitched.

"Ye've no' made up yer mind, lass."

"Yes—"

His kiss sealed out the rest of her denial. Hard and demanding, his mouth took control of hers, pressing until she opened her lips to allow his tongue to sweep inside. He closed the distance between them, the harder surface of his body feeling perfect against her softer curves. This wasn't a soft or teasing kiss. It was a bold challenge, one that swept aside her reason. Desire flared, bright and hot enough to burn away every bit of resistance. She reached for him, gripping the doublet when laying her hands on his chest wasn't enough. She wanted more; needed to be closer.

Broen broke the kiss, using his grip on her nape to hold her back when she would have followed him.

"Think on that, lass." He squeezed her neck once more before releasing it. "A man interested in only his own agenda would have had ye last night." His eyes flashed with hunger. "It would nae have been hard, and I was tempted."

She aimed a brutal shove at his chest but only gained a smug chuckle from him when he backed up. "Then why didn't you press your advantage?"

He sobered. "Trust is nae something any man can demand from a woman. It must be earned."

"It isn't earned by locking me inside your keep and invading my privacy," she insisted.

He chuckled, his lips curving arrogantly. He reached out and stroked her cheek once more, until she shook her head to dislodge his hand.

"Stop touching me. I cannot make a clear-minded choice when you keep acting so—"

"Uncivilized?" he finished for her. "I'm beginning to appreciate the fact that ye do nae listen to me advice, Clarrisa." His eyes twinkled with merriment. "For I do find I enjoy it when ye lavish such praise upon me."

"Uncivilized is an insult."

He spread his hands wide and cocked his head to the side in a mocking bow. "Nay, lass. To a Highlander, it is praise."

She sneezed, and he frowned before turning to leave, but he paused in the doorway and looked back over his shoulder.

"It is also a challenge."

The man was impossible. Clarrisa snarled softly as she tried to ignore the sound of his laughter echoing in the hallway as he left her.

Impossible… brute. But he could have had her.

The truth was shameful, but oddly stimulating. Anticipation was brewing inside her once more, the excitement building like it did before a holiday. There was no way to hide from it. Insulting the brute wouldn't save her from knowing it was her own failing that had allowed his advances to gain notice. But she did smile as she called him a brute, because the word fit him very well, to her way of thinking.

So she would have to find enough work to drive every thought from her mind. Edme returned and offered her a strong brew. Clarrisa drank it quickly, glad to be able to hand the empty mug back to the head of house. One of the maids placed a tray on the table and held out a chair with a plush-padded seat cushion.

Clarrisa looked at the tray for a long moment. "I can eat in the hall with everyone else."

"No' without something to wear," Edme muttered. "The laird is already smitten enough with ye. Besides, think on the difficulty that will arise when he sees his men admiring yer shape through that thin dressing robe."

Two of the maids laughed. Clarrisa felt her cheeks burn. "He is not… smitten. He was but teasing me…"

"And ye're so quick to defend him," Edme pointed out as she studied the bright spots of color decorating Clarrisa's cheeks. Her lips curved in a knowing manner. "Sit down and break yer fast."

"But… I'm English. Aren't all Scots, and Highlanders

in particular, known to detest English blood simply because it's English?"

"No' when it's flowing through the body of a sweet young lass. Scots, and Highlanders in particular," Edme mimicked Clarrisa's accent as she quoted her, "never fail to admire a fair lass."

The maids laughed, no soft sounds muffled behind their hands but full sounds of merriment.

"That is... Well... I mean to say..."

Edme held up a wrinkled hand. "Save yer blustering, lass. I know what I saw."

Clarrisa dropped into the seat, defeated by the woman's confident tone.

He wasn't smitten; he was filled with lust.

So are you.

The tray held a bowl of porridge. Clarrisa began eating it to shut out her own thoughts. Once she had finished, one of the maids began to comb her hair.

"Really, it isn't necessary to wait upon me. I am not accustomed to service," she muttered while trying to take the comb from the girl's hand. The girl wasn't much older than Clarrisa, but she grinned confidently while refusing to give up the comb.

"Then enjoy it and stop telling me how to direct this house." There was a hint of amusement in Edme's tone now.

Clarrisa eyed her, but the woman didn't relent. Edme watched as the girls combed, braided, and pinned up Clarrisa's hair. Clarrisa sighed once it was done, for it felt as though it had been ages since she was neat.

Dresses made of wool arrived, but they were still

finer than Clarrisa would have preferred. Dyed rich
shades of blue and gold, the wool was woven tightly
from thin threads. Edme snapped her fingers, and two
of the maids removed the dressing robe. Clarrisa felt
the sharp gaze of the head of house taking note of
her size as well as every other detail of her body. It
wasn't a new experience, but her belly quivered with
apprehension because she just couldn't help thinking
the older woman was deciding if she was fit for her
laird's bed.

"The blue, I believe."

The blue dress had a cranberry underdress. Made
of linen, the undergown had straps that came over
her shoulders. It was quilted across the front in tiny
rows with stiffened reeds inserted into the channels to
support her breasts. Hooks and eyes were closed down
her front before the overdress was lifted and dropped
carefully into place. Once the back laces were tied, the
dress fit reasonably well.

"We'll set the seamstress to work on a few others,"
Edme muttered. "Let Ardis in now."

One of the maids opened the chamber door. A
man with a long white beard stood there with two
younger men behind him. He tugged on his bonnet
before walking into the chamber. One of the men
held a wooden box, which he set on the floor, while
the other man carried a stool, which he set it in front
of Clarrisa. Ardis sat down.

"Ardis is the cobbler. He'll make up some sensible
boots for ye."

The box was opened, and Ardis took the tools his
assistant handed him—a measuring tape and even a

sheet of costly parchment. He carefully recorded the measurements of her feet before tracing an outline of each of her feet.

"I'd have been happy to come to your workshop."

Ardis stood and shook his head. "A lass of royal blood does nae belong in a cobbler's shop."

"I'm bastard-born."

He stroked his beard as his assistants picked up his stool and closed the workbox. "Blood is blood."

He was gone without another word, while Clarrisa was still trying to decide on a way to argue with him without disrespecting his greater age.

"Now that's done, we'll take off the dress so ye can rest." Edme's voice rang with authority.

"Oh... but really... I'm not tired." Clarrisa turned to avoid the hands of the maids.

"Ye're fighting a chill," the head of house declared.

If they disrobed her, she'd be imprisoned in the chamber as surely as if the door were barred. "I'll sit by the window... and read. I simply don't want to be in bed like a child. It's only a hint of a chill."

The maids stopped trying to catch the ends of the laces and waited on their mistress to decide. Edme tapped her foot several times before nodding.

"The sight of the fields being turned can be a hopeful one. No doubt it will encourage ye to heal quickly."

The maids moved to the windows and opened the shutters to allow the sunlight in. Clarrisa sat down and suffered their pushing a padded stool beneath her feet, while another offered her a selection of books. She took one without looking at the title.

"I truly am not fragile."

Edme looked unconvinced. She snapped her fingers, sending the girls toward the rumpled bed. They set it to rights before lowering themselves and quitting the room. Clarrisa listened to their steps fade away before looking at the book in her hands. For once, she wasn't interested in a new book, which was surprising because one of the few things she'd adored about living with her uncle was his collection of books. But he'd known it and had often restricted her access to the costly volumes whenever he was of the mind to discipline her.

Break her will was more the correct way to say it...

It didn't matter. She was about as far from her uncle's castle in Kent as she might be. The Highlands were a place no English army ventured, which left her with the task of freeing herself—if she truly wanted freedom.

Did she?

Or did she want to choose Broen...

With a hiss, she stood and placed the book on the seat of the chair. The brew from the cook had eased the pounding in her head, but the result was that she was thinking much too clearly. Alone with her thoughts, she'd become easy prey for Broen if she did nothing but recall his kisses. She would drive the man from her thoughts with work. Her shoes were neatly placed in the wardrobe. She gave them a shake before putting them on.

Deigh Tower was in good repair. From the stories she'd heard, she had expected dank and smelly corridors. Instead, the solid stone walls were covered with smooth plaster. Every ten feet along the walls were iron torch holders that each held a length of iron with its end wrapped in dried stalks from the last harvest.

The stalks were coated with pitch, the dry material soaking up large amounts of the black substance. At night, they would burn well and far longer than wooden torches.

Such was a modern design. The wind did whistle through the arrow slots, but it carried the sweet scent of spring, no noxious odors from slime accumulating in the dark corners. In fact, the hallway was well lit with windows that had their shutters open. She hurried past the master bedchamber, Broen's voice ringing in her ears.

Fate was determined to hound her, it seemed, for her lips tingled. She felt anxious and her senses keener.

Trust him? Not likely. The man was too good at the game of seduction.

The stairway was narrow, but still wider than the ones in her uncle's home. It made sense, for Broen and his retainers were burly men, every one of them wide-shouldered and tall. That portion of the tales of Highlanders was proving true; they were formidable men.

She needed to find some work. Her mind wanted to dwell on Broen MacNicols, no matter the consequences.

She smelled the great hall before she saw it. At the bottom of the stairs, the scent of roasting meat filled the air. Preparations for the midday meal would be well under way. She made it to the entrance of the hall and frowned when the MacNicols women there all lowered themselves.

"I am not worthy of such respect."

The women didn't respond to her, only studied her for a moment before continuing with their duties.

They switched to speaking in Gaelic too, shutting her out completely.

Well, she'd not allow their perception of her station to keep her from finding something to occupy her hands. There was always work aplenty in spring.

But every time she tried to help, some MacNicols woman would take away the chore. Frustration nipped at her, but the challenge of outwitting them became greater. She went into the back kitchen and began to scale fish. She'd finished two before she was discovered and the remaining fish taken away.

"Yer hands are too soft, lady," the cook muttered with a meek look but a touch of superiority in her tone. For as much as she'd always heard Highlanders were men of amazing strength and audacity, she'd never considered what type of women lived among them. The MacNicols women were good companions to Broen and his retainers, it seemed.

That only reinforced her need to rise to the challenge of besting them by having her way.

"No, my hands are not soft, because I am not lazy. My day has always been full, and I see no reason to change honest habits. There must be chores I can help with," she insisted and lifted her hands to show the cook. The woman only shook her head.

"Does nae matter. Yer blood is royal. The chores in this kitchen are too lowly for ye."

She might have continued to argue with the woman, but more and more of the kitchen staff were taking notice. The cook was their superior, so they'd not go against her word. It was better to see if she might find someplace where the opinions of the older

women didn't reach. Besides, if she forced the cook to
bend, she'd only be proving that she was owed obedience because of her royal blood.

It was a frustrating tangle to be sure, one that made
her pity true princesses, because their lives must be so
very limited by what everyone around them believed
they should or shouldn't be doing.

Down a corridor came the sound of singing.
Clarrisa followed it to find a long workroom with
spinning wheels and two looms. So early in spring,
there wasn't any wool left to card or spin. The only
woman in the room was working the loom.

"There is fine linen on the table to make the laird a
new shirt," she called out over the cloth she was weaving.

A wife made her husband's shirts, or a mistress or a
lover, for the undergarment was an intimate thing. It
showed devotion to labor on something no one else
would see. Handling the fabric that would rest against
his skin… She shook her head to dispel the image. The
MacNicols woman grinned at her, but the expression
resembled a smirk too much for Clarrisa's taste.

"I will not make Broen a shirt," she blurted out,
too flustered to keep her voice even and composed.
The Highlands were truly driving her mad, sucking
every civilized behavior from her while destroying her
self-discipline.

The woman smiled. "But ye use his Christian name
so easily."

The insinuation sent a blush back to her cheeks.
The maids had clearly carried the tale of Broen's
kissing her far and wide. Clarrisa sighed on her
way out of the spinning room. It was no different

in her uncle's castle—or any castle, for that matter. Everyone knew everyone's doings very soon after they happened. It made her temper sizzle to think everyone assumed she belonged in Broen's bed.

Even the brute himself.

"Ye are supposed to be resting, Lady Clarrisa." Edme was in the hallway with several maids trailing her. Clearly the woman was busy, for many of the maids had rolled parchments in their hands.

"I am not tired, nor are my hands too soft for work." Clarrisa held her chin steady. It was time to show the MacNicols head of house that she was also not a child easily bent.

"I'm a Highlander, Lady Clarrisa. I know what sturdy hands look like," Edme declared while her staff watched intently. Clarrisa stood her ground.

"I am also not accustomed to being addressed by the title of 'lady.'"

Edme tilted her head. "On that we disagree, for yer blood is blue, which entitles ye to the title of 'lady,' even if ye were nae afforded it before now. Even we in the Highlands know how titles of nobility work. Blood is blood. Being born the daughter of a peer means ye are a lady."

"Perhaps, but my uncle forbade any member of his house to address me so. He feared I'd forget my place." She'd learned long ago to ignore the shame her uncle had meant to inflict with such a dictate. If she didn't care, he couldn't hurt her feelings. "I was raised to be useful. I do not know how to be idle while the sunlight is squandered, and I do not want to learn such a wasteful habit."

"Well now, there is something ye might help me with. A task no one else has the knowledge for."

There was a gleam in Edme's eyes that made Clarrisa leery, but the promise of something to take her mind off Broen MacNicols was too much to resist. Her suspicion grew as Edme led her back up the stairs toward the chamber she'd slept in. The woman was just as much a Highlander as her laird, for she would not be bested.

Well... neither would Clarrisa accept becoming the pampered plaything for the laird of the keep. Edme continued to the next floor. "Like any good head of house, I like to keep a strict accounting of what is inside the keep." Edme opened a door to reveal a room crowded with chests of all shapes and sizes, many of them locked. There was a rattle of keys as Edme took a large key ring from one of the maids.

"The things in this room came with the laird's grandmother or as gifts from her relatives." Edme sent the maids toward the window shutters. Once opened, the morning sunlight illuminated dust floating thickly in the air.

"She was bound for marriage with an Englishman when the laird's father brought her here." Edme made a soft sound. "She followed her heart and married him."

"If she wanted to stay here, why didn't she open these chests?"

Edme's expression turned sad. "She never got the chance. Fate had other plans. She died of childbed fever, but her relatives wouldn't believe the husband she'd wed without their permission when he wrote to them of her passing." Edme spread her hands wide. "So the gifts came, and the laird's grandfather was too full of grief to open them. Now that he's gone, it's time to open them, but they are gifts for a noblewoman. Perhaps ye can help me identify what they are."

A chill swept down her spine. The neatly stacked chests belonged to a woman long dead. She wandered in a circle, trying to decide which chest to open first. A sense of adventure filled her as she settled on one. She began humming, enjoying being needed for something beyond the blood flowing through her veins.

Indeed, being needed for the knowledge inside her head and the order she might bring was a fine thing indeed. Who might have thought she would find such a place among the uncivilized Highlands of Scotland?

"Ye sit too often in the darkness, Father."

Donnach Grant erupted out of his chair, but not with anger. The few men near him were startled because they had fallen asleep waiting on him to retire.

"Kael! My son! It's about time ye found yer way home!"

The Grant retainers all relaxed when their wits had cleared enough to recognize their laird's son—his only son—and Donnach embraced him heartily.

"Ale and bread. Someone rouse the kitchen lasses!" Donnach watched his son strike a flint stone to light one of the candles. The wick caught, casting a warm circle of light.

"Now… what brings ye home at last?"

Kael Grant sat down with a satisfied groan. "Ye know I stayed away to keep the other clans wondering what side I was on."

Donnach nodded. Two women brought them mugs of ale and a platter of sliced cheese with a round of bread. Kael tore the round in half and aimed a charming smile at one of the women.

"Be a sweetheart and bring me some fine Highland butter. I swear even the grass in the Lowlands is inferior to what we have here." She melted beneath his charm, and he reached out to pat her bottom. She laughed, low and sultry, before hurrying off to fetch what he desired.

"Ye rogue. Answer yer father's questions before ye start chasing the lasses."

Kael offered him a smug look before tearing off a piece of the bread and stuffing it in his mouth. He washed it down with a large swig of ale.

"That's an interesting tale, Father." Kael abandoned his playfulness, sitting forward to keep his words from drifting. "Seems Lord Home is sending ye sealed letters." Kael reached into his doublet and withdrew a parchment. "More interesting is the fact that the messenger took it to Laird MacLeod."

Donnach Grant growled, gaining a few looks from his men. They were enjoying the unexpected ale but still diligently watching his back. "MacLeod is a royalist. Home trusted the letter to a traitor."

"A dead one."

Donnach nodded and broke the seal on the parchment. He'd not spare any pity for a man who wasn't loyal to the laird he claimed to serve. Shadow dealings and taking letters to the wrong man were worthy of death in his opinion. Any man with honor would have the courage to stand up and be clearly counted on the side he was on.

"I sent his sword back to MacLeod, and his head to Lord Home."

Donnach Grant grunted approvingly. His son was a man, one he was proud of. But the letter from Lord Home captured his full attention. He'd known it would arrive one day, but that didn't lessen the impact.

"What's amiss?" Kael inquired.

"There are times I wish ye were nae a grown man, Kael."

"So ye could tell me to respect ye and no' ask why ye are frowning so darkly?" Kael chuckled, but it wasn't a friendly sound. "Times such as these need more than politeness."

"Aye," Donnach muttered, scanning the letter once more. He finished and held it over the candle flame. The corner caught, and the fire spread quickly up the page. He dropped the letter on the table and watched the fire turn the letter to black ash. Once all hints of color were gone, he smothered the smoldering remains with a plate.

"I owe the man." Donnach looked his son straight in the eye. "Something ye do nae know I owe him."

Donnach watched his son grow deadly serious. "I suppose 'tis a good thing ye are here. Ye need to know what happened with Daphne MacLeod and Laird MacNicols."

❧

"I know knitting needles when I see them, but why are those so small?"

Edme wasn't the only one who wanted to know the answer. The maids who always seemed to be hovering about the head of house stared at Clarrisa, eager to hear what she had to say.

"They are for knitting stockings."

Edme furrowed her brow. "With how narrow those are, the hose would be thin and of little substance."

Clarrisa picked up one of the five needles. Made of silver, it was polished to a high luster. "You knit lace stockings with them. The idea is to, well... to have skin visible..."

Surprise filled Edme's expression, along with a knowing gleam. She cast a look at one of the maids, both of whom were chuckling softly.

"Well now, perhaps ye should knit a pair. I wager the laird would enjoy seeing ye wear them."

The needle tumbled from her fingers. Edme laughed as a maid retrieved the needle. "The look upon yer face, lass—it takes me back a few years. To a time when I was foolish enough to believe all the prattle the church tries to fill our heads with about abstinence and about pleasures of the flesh being so sinful. Age gives us the wisdom to know life is best lived to the fullest. Once ye pass up an opportunity, it may nae cross yer path again. Regret is far worse than sin when it comes to a man who stokes yer passion. Dressing to please him only doubles the enjoyment..."

Edme was still chuckling as she went out the door, the maids following. Clarrisa stood still, the last of the sun coming through the windows.

Passion...

She should have been able to dismiss the idea quickly and with disdain, yet she didn't. She turned to gaze at the needles and reached out to finger one. Heat warmed her cheeks, but this time she felt no shame, only a rising sense of urgency to reach out and grasp the opportunity in front of her.

She truly had taken leave of her senses.

The admission didn't bother her. She lifted the wooden tray the needles were in and reached for a thin piece of wood stored below that had silk cord wound neatly around it. There were a dozen of them, all in different hues.

Double the enjoyment. Would it truly? Her body was slowly warming with just her thoughts, the memory of Broen's kiss fanning the flames. She'd be a liar if she claimed she didn't enjoy it, and a coward for shying away from her feelings.

Maybe she didn't need to worry so much about the pity she'd sensed in him.

She took a stiff breath and reached for one of the needles. Tugging the end of the cord loose, she began to cast on the stitches, knitting them carefully until all five needles were being used.

She might not be ready to decide if she wanted to trust Broen MacNicols, but she refused to act the coward. Besides, there was a sense of satisfaction filling her as she decided what she wanted to do herself instead of following the dictates of her greedy kin.

The stockings might come in handy, but Broen MacNicols wouldn't be hearing such a thing from her. The man was too presumptuous by far.

She smiled, and her husky laughter echoed through the chamber.

Yes, let the man enjoy the challenge of wooing her, for she planned to make sure it tested him.

"Is she healing?"

Edme didn't answer quickly. She lowered herself first, and Broen suspected the woman was toying with him.

"Yer guest is well. Her youth is no doubt helping her to be rid of that chill so quickly."

Broen frowned and then noticed how many of his men were watching him intently. The spot next to him at the high table was vacant, left empty for Clarrisa, but she had not appeared. Everyone was waiting to see what he'd make of her absence.

He pointed at Shaw. "Make sure the men know not to allow her past the gate."

"Aye, Laird, no' a one of them will miss that bonny face, should she venture too far from the tower."

Broen crushed the bread in his hands. More than one gaze went to the scattered mess he made. Some of his men leaned closer to their comrades to whisper.

"I've matters to attend to."

He stood, and the hall filled with the sounds of scraping of benches as his clan stood as well. He ground his teeth in frustration, for he'd told them not to stand every time he did, but traditions died hard in the Highlands.

Like his fascination with Clarrisa. Her kiss clung to his lips. His mind had wandered during the day, and he'd had to fight the urge to climb to the old ladies' solar to see what she was about. But she was an Englishwoman—and not just any Englishwoman. His uncle would send for her. When that happened, his fascination with her would leave a scar—a deep one, if he didn't learn to control his desire for her. She'd been the wiser one to reject him, an action he could learn well from. His need for her defied his understanding. There were willing women he could take his desire to, and a half dozen offers from neighbors who would like to secure an alliance with him through marriage to one of their daughters. But he was neglecting the chore of settling on another bride.

Aye, instead he was acting like a beardless youth fascinated with his first woman. Hell, he hadn't even bedded her yet and still his thoughts had shifted to her more times than he could count during the day.

It was bloody annoying. He was a Highlander and didn't need an Englishwoman in his bed. He needed to thank the woman for refusing him; she obviously had more sense than he did.

But her lips tasted fine, and she smelled better than any woman he could think of…

He stopped when he realized he'd climbed to the third floor and was on his way to her chamber. A curse rolled past his lips, but he still opened her chamber door and peered inside. She'd left the window shutters open, which cast moonlight over her sleeping form. He was beside the bed before he really knew what he was about. Standing there as she slept was a torment, but one he enjoyed too much to turn away from.

Her hair was braided, the long blond strands secured with a length of cord. The dressing robe was draped over the edge of the bed; only a chemise covered her skin. He reached out and trailed his fingers along the edge of that single garment. Clarrisa muttered in her sleep and shifted toward his touch. She kicked at the bedding, pushing the coverlet lower. He stared at the swells of her breasts and lost the battle to keep his hand away from them.

So soft yet firm… His cock rose beneath his kilt, throbbing with the desire he'd pushed aside all day.

But he'd only wanted Clarrisa.

She sighed, and he found the sound unmistakably pleasurable. His cock throbbed, and he cupped one of her breasts, grinning almost savagely when she arched. An enjoyable torment, indeed. It seemed they both suffered from it. Her eyelids fluttered, lifting only halfway.

"Why do you invade my dreams, Broen?" Slurred with sleep, her voice was a bare whisper.

He leaned down, smoothing his hand over the swell of her breast. "Because ye summoned me with yer longings, lass."

She sighed and closed her eyelids. "I think about you too often…"

Her breathing deepened, and his frustration returned, but he smiled with satisfaction too. She couldn't banish him from her thoughts either. Such a revelation should have convinced him she was a curse, one he'd be wise to get rid of at first light, but the idea of sending her to his overlord tore something inside him.

He straightened, the emotional reaction making him wary. Men who succumbed to loving a woman often made poor decisions. It was a point worthy of contemplation and possibly action. It would be wise to put distance between them.

But he leaned down and placed a kiss against her cheek before pulling the coverlet back up to protect her from the night air. He caught a whiff of her scent, and it sent a flood of desire pounding through him.

Sending her off to Sutherland would be best, but he wouldn't enjoy doing it.

❧

He was near. So very close.

Clarrisa could smell Broen. The scent of his skin touched off a ripple of need that settled in her belly. Her body twisted, unable to rest peacefully. She craved something, some form of satisfaction.

She sat upright, jerked out of her slumber. Instead of waking in a fog, her wits were sharp. The bedding was a rumpled mess, and her braid frizzy from her tossing.

Broen—although she wasn't sure if it was fair to blame the man for her obsession with him. Maud had often lectured her on the enchanting powers of the barbarians who inhabited the Highlands. Looking them straight in the eye was a sure way to allow their pagan devil magic to work its will on her.

Clarrisa laughed. She couldn't help it. Along with Maud's words came the memory of how haughty the matron had sounded when she was handing out lectures. Pride was also a sin, but the older woman hadn't seemed to recall that teaching from the church. With a shake of her head, she pulled the tie off the end of her braid. She worked the plait free and walked toward the table where the comb lay.

The moon was full, casting its yellow light across the floor of the chamber. Nearer to the window, she could see the stars twinkling in the night sky. The moon was more than halfway across it, but morning was still several hours away. Her chemise fluttered in the night breeze. Her skin was chilled, but not uncomfortably so.

Heat was still burning inside her from her dreams of Broen.

She drew the comb through her hair, wrestling with the admission that she was longing to go to his bed. Alone in the darkness, it seemed easier to admit her dark cravings. The church certainly had that portion of their teachings correct; the night hours were the time for spells and sinfulness.

She brushed her hair into a soft cloud, the braid having given it fullness. She placed the comb aside and gave in to the urge to slide her hands down her body. Her breasts were so sensitive, and her nipples were hard, and it wasn't due to the cold. She enjoyed the feel of stroking the curves of her hips, and a soft throbbing began between the folds of her sex. So dark and wicked, but it felt completely right in that moment, so good, so satisfying.

The chamber suddenly felt cold, but the delicate fabric of her chemise didn't flutter from any breeze any longer. She hugged herself and shivered, feeling the chill bone-deep. From the corner of her eye, she caught something moving across the mirror.

She whirled to face it but found no one in the chamber. The hairs on her nape stood up as she was sure she heard a deep male chuckle.

Twisting back to face the mirror, she saw a shadow shift behind her.

Argyll—the ghost of Deigh Tower…

Broen's words rose up as clearly as a church bell

as she heard something scrape across the corner of the room.

"Sweet Christ!" she shouted before bolting toward the door.

"Get away from me!" she yelled as she ran, her heart pounding. A full scream erupted from her when she ran into a hard body; hard arms clamped around her instantly. Fear coursed thickly through her, and she fought with every ounce of strength she could muster.

"Here now…"

She slammed her palm up into the hard jaw of the man holding her. He cursed and released her.

"Goddamn it, Clarrisa…"

She recognized Broen's voice, but it wasn't enough to override the pressing need to flee. She was covered in sweat, her heart feeling like it might burst through her chest, but she also felt stronger and faster than ever. She ran down the hallway, not caring that the floor scraped her bare feet.

She slammed into more men. They grumbled and clamped their arms around her. They jerked her to a halt, twisting her arms brutally. She gasped, the pain tearing through the fear clouding her judgment.

"Easy, lads… 'Tis our English guest."

She couldn't seem to stop struggling. The delicate fabric of her chemise tore, and the sound echoed in the silence.

"There… there is someone… in my chamber…" She panted, her lungs struggling to keep up with her racing heart.

Light came up the stairway, and the heavy steps of more retainers filled her ears. The two men holding her pushed her toward the newcomers as Broen turned and went into her chamber. She was pushed up against the wall, and the man who held her jerked his hands away when he realized how little she wore.

"Get up there and protect the laird's back," he ordered the men behind him. He glanced back at her once he'd given his order but looked away with a sputter. Clarrisa looked down and realized the torch illuminated every curve of her body. Even her nipples showed through the thin fabric. She gasped and hugged herself to cover what she might. It was far too little, and she leaned against the wall, trying to decide what to do. Down the stairs was the hall where most of Broen's retainers slept. They'd be on their feet now, worried the castle was under attack.

There was clothing back in her chamber, but a shiver shook her the moment she considered returning.

"There is no one," Broen muttered as he re-appeared. His sword was in hand, but she looked away because he was wearing less than she was. The man was in nothing but his skin.

"I heard... I'm sure I heard..." Her cheeks were blazing, but she refused to be thought of as a foolish child frightened by her own imagination. "I was fully awake and on my feet..."

"Argyll does nae enter the chambers..." the retainer near her muttered.

"Well, he did enter my chamber. You promised he wouldn't." Her mind finally cleared completely, causing her to contemplate just what she'd seen.

Suddenly she wasn't so sure. Edme's potion had been potent.

Broen grunted and set his sword inside the open door of his chamber. "As flattered as I am to hear ye believe me so powerful, Clarrisa, I do nae have the ability to control the spirits."

She snapped her gaze back to him but turned away because she was too tempted to look down the length of his nude body. "Maybe I didn't see… I am not sure anymore…"

Broen's retainers began muttering, offering their opinions. Her eyes went wide when she realized how many men were observing the moment. She looked back at Broen, desperate to escape. He was watching her, and his eyes narrowed when she locked eyes with him. He reached out and captured her wrist. His grip didn't hurt, but it was solid. With a firm tug, he pulled her away from the wall and down the few steps to his open chamber door. She ended up stumbling into his chamber after a sharp jerk and a slap against her bottom.

Laughter erupted in the hallway.

"My thanks, lads, for seeing to me welfare. Ye'll have to forgive me for hiding the lass. She's nae dressed for visiting."

The MacNicols retainers laughed, a few adding comments that kept her cheeks burning brightly.

"I'd like to have the lass dressing like that to see me…"

"Found her quite pleasing as she was…"

"Do nae change for my sake…"

She stumbled a few paces from the door but froze when she couldn't see into the dark corners of the chamber. Her need for modesty struggled against the fear rising from the memory of having heard a spirit speak to her.

"Argyll has never been seen in this chamber."

She jumped but bit her lip to contain the cry that tried to escape. Clarrisa lifted her chin, forcing down the lump in her throat. "It... He simply surprised me."

"He frightened ye," Broen muttered in a soft voice.

"No, he did not, and you're a—"

"Brute?" Broen finished for her. His tone turned menacing. He captured her wrist again and pulled her hand up until he could press her palm to his jaw. Along the side of it, she felt the warm presence of blood. "Ye're the one who drew blood tonight."

A soft cry made it past her lips. "Sweet Christ..." Everything began to crumple; her reasons and logic. There was only the warm skin beneath her palm and the scent of metallic blood in the air. She stepped toward him, delighting in the feeling of having his heat wrap around her. She smoothed away the blood and stretched up onto her toes to kiss the spot it had escaped from.

He groaned, the sound striking her as complimentary.

One kiss seemed too little. She pressed another and another against his jaw, until she was trailing kisses up to his ear. She didn't want to stop and reached up to wrap her hands around his neck and tilt his head so she might continue.

"Clarrisa... ye're testing the limits of me control..."

His voice was husky and shook just a little. That tiny confirmation that she affected him as much as he did her sent the passion she'd toyed with back into a full blaze.

"Good, because you've been driving me mad, and you promised to explain why you make me tremble."

He caught her face, framing it with both hands. The small amount of light coming in through the windows reflected off the glitter in his eyes.

"I was warning ye, lass."

She moved her head, needing to feel his hands moving against her skin. Delight rippled down her body, and she felt her nipples contract into hard points.

"You were daring me to stand fast and allow you to be my lover."

He drew in a stiff breath. She placed her hands on his chest, spreading her fingers and shivering at the feel of their skin meeting.

"Why are ye the only English lass who does nae quiver in me presence? I was going to send ye to me uncle at dawn."

Her hands formed into fists, frustration making her ache. "Then do it, Broen MacNicols, and prove yourself a blackguard for kissing me when you were only toying with me."

She shoved him away from her, hissing with disappointment when he released her face. But he caught the sides of her chemise and ripped it upward in a crack of cloth. The garment fluttered to the floor like a wounded bird as she gasped.

"I have no' yet begun to play with ye." He caught her, moving faster than she expected. In less than a moment she was secured against his body, her curves meeting his harder form from chin to toe. Against her belly, his cock was rigid. The spot hidden by the folds of her sex began to throb once more, this time her passage joining the demand to be touched.

"But I promise to mend me ways immediately. Ye

tremble because ye want me inside ye, and I'm hard because I want the same thing."

His mouth captured hers, the kiss bold and hot. Whatever she'd been thinking to say scattered into bits of thought too tiny to notice. What drew her attention was the flood of sensation flowing over her. She kissed him back, seeking out more heat. He caught a handful of her hair, combing his fingers through the strands before gripping them near her scalp. She was helpless, but feeling his strength heightened her enjoyment. In some corner of her mind, she liked knowing how strong he was.

"I want more than just to get inside ye," he growled against her mouth, trailing kisses along the length of her neck. She trembled, never realizing how acute a simple touch might be.

"What else?" It wasn't a proper question, wasn't something she should even think, but the rules of the civilized world seemed impossibly far away.

He chuckled, the sound dark and dangerous. She was free for a moment, his hand slipping over her shoulders and down her chest until he was cupping each breast.

"I wanted to cup these last night and nuzzle against them before kissing their tips."

Knowing what he was going to do intensified the moment. Anticipation tightened in her belly, making it difficult for her to breathe. Broen kissed her collar and then lower, following the same path his hands had forged. He selected her left breast first, kissing the top of it before nuzzling against it.

He slipped his arm around her waist again, this time

using it to support her when he bent her back so that her breasts were thrust up.

"Close yer eyes, lass, and just feel. I'll not let ye fall."

She struggled to comply, wanting all her senses to help her understand, but it wasn't a moment for thinking. She leaned her head back, feeling the ends of her hair against her calves. It felt like she was free, truly unbound for the first time in her life.

She gasped when he claimed her nipple. His lips felt hotter than she'd ever believed a man's mouth might be. It was too much, and she tried to straighten.

"Ye cannae deny me such a treat, Clarrisa."

He scooped her off her feet and carried her to his bed. For a moment, she recalled the first time she'd seen him, when she'd thought him a barbarian. He placed her among the rumpled bedding, pressing her onto her back against a blanket of her hair.

"Nor deny yerself the pleasure it can give ye."

He cupped her breast once more, leaning on one bent elbow as he lay beside her.

"Breasts are for feeding babes."

He laughed. She was beginning to recognize the tone he used when he was in the mood to tempt her, and excitement brewed inside her. He leaned down, the ends of his hair teasing her skin. "But first they are meant to be handled by a lover to help entice ye into allowing him inside ye."

He sucked her nipple back into his mouth, cupping her breast as he did it. She arched, her body rising to seek what it craved. A moan crossed her lips as she reached for him. She suddenly wasn't close enough to him. Need became a living force inside her, and the only thing it craved was contact with him. She gripped his shoulders, pulling him closer.

"Exactly like that, lass."

He slid his hand down her body, teasing the smooth skin of her belly before continuing on to the soft curls growing on her mons. She shied away, but he pushed her back and settled his fingers in the curls. "The best place of all for a lover to stroke."

She shivered, but not from cold. Anticipation threatened to overwhelm her, possibly even leave her mind broken when it had run its course. That didn't seem to matter. Her clitoris was throbbing, its name rising in her mind from some half-heard gossip—a few comments muttered in husky tones before the more-experienced women of her uncle's household had noticed she was near.

Broen found it, pushing the folds of her sex aside until his fingertip rested gently on top of it. Pleasure spiked through her. She jerked, lifting her hips and gasping when even greater delight resulted from the friction.

"Ye felt that, did nae ye?" He was challenging her now. He rubbed a bit harder, producing a pleasure that began to satisfy the raging hunger inside her.

"Lift yer hips in time, lass. I promise it will yield what ye've been trembling for."

There was an urgency building inside her. Nothing but reaction remained in her mind. There was the pleasure each stroke produced and the increasing need to move faster. She clamped her thighs around his forearm, frantic to maintain the pressure against her clitoris. He didn't deny her. He pressed harder and rubbed faster in response to her demands. There suddenly wasn't room in her mind for distracting things like sight. She arched and closed her eyes as her fingers clenched the bedding. Every muscle in her body grew tense, feeling like they might snap. Beneath his finger, pleasure tightened until it burst in a blinding shower of white-hot delight. In spite of the bed beneath her, it felt like she was falling through the air, her body suspended inside the pleasure for a moment that felt endless. It twisted through her, biting into her before dropping her back into reality, where she struggled to draw breath. She'd cried out but only noticed it now as an afterthought.

"That's what ye craved from me, lass." He was smug and arrogant. She opened her eyes, the urge to be reckless overpowering her.

She reached down, closing her hand around his length. "And what is it you keep kissing me to gain, Broen MacNicols?" He groaned, the hard flesh in her grasp jerking slightly. She rolled onto her side, pushing him back as she worked her hand from the top of his weapon to the base.

"I may be a virgin, but I know men want more from women than to pleasure them." The bed shook as he flopped onto his back. The moonlight showed her his expression and his gritted teeth.

"Do yer worst, lass. I have nae stopped thinking about yer promise to polish a man's weapon. Show me the courage that had ye holding back a king's lust for power."

She slid her hand back up to the crown of his cock. "So long as it is Broen asking me for such a thing and not the laird of the MacNicols demanding a service."

"I'm foolishly admitting how captivating yer words are to me."

"Well then, let me see what condition your weapon is in…"

Her attention lowered to the cock in her hand. She looked directly at it, refusing to shy away in deference to rules of modesty. She was sick unto death of being told what she must be. For the moment, she was Broen's lover. She let herself feel bold, granting herself the freedom to act on her impulses.

She stroked his length, listening to his breathing to judge her pace. The skin was softer than she'd believed a man's cock might feel. His chest rumbled with a groan, one that satisfied her.

"Now I'm truly a blackguard." Broen abandoned his lazy demeanor, drawing a creak from the bed ropes as he turned and flattened her against the bed. "But I am no' sorry to see ye grinning so smugly."

He pressed a kiss against her lips. He settled over her, spreading her thighs with his hips. She didn't have the chance to protest, even a halfhearted one. His mouth demanded a response she was only too happy to provide. Hot need renewed its insistence, churning deep in her belly. The satisfaction he'd given her with his finger seemed insufficient somehow, and she yearned to gain true release.

"But I've failed the challenge ye set, sweet Clarrisa, for I cannae stand fast while ye toy with me any further." The head of his cock nudged the folds of her sex, pushing them open as it began to enter her passage. His eyes narrowed as the muscles along his neck corded. "I've dreamed of ye too often."

His voice was strained. She felt the same level of urgency, every muscle tightening until it was almost unbearable. The intensity of the moment was over-whelming. He thrust forward, sending his length into her. Pain tore through the pleasure of the moment. She recoiled, trying to avoid the torment, but Broen had her firmly pinned, his body keeping her in place as he withdrew and thrust again. This time his cock trav-eled deeper, lodging completely within her. The pain bled away, until only a dull ache remained that was overshadowed by the satisfaction spreading through her from being impaled.

"That will be the end of the pain, lass."

She surprised him by laughing. His expression told her he was stunned.

"Why are ye laughing, woman?"

She savored the word *woman*, knowing without a doubt she was no longer a girl. Broen snorted, and his body shook as though he was straining to hold back. He muttered a word in Gaelic that she didn't understand, but his tone made it clear it was profane.

"Trust ye to laugh at me attempts to be considerate."

He pulled free, distracting her with a rush of enjoy-ment. When he thrust forward again, his hard flesh slid against her clitoris, filling her with delight.

"Would you rather I were weeping?" She lifted her hips to take him completely. "Or that I admit I enjoy being here?"

He brushed the hair from her face, soft, soothing touches that were tender. "That's why ye drive me insane, lass. Yer spirit is as bold as mine."

His voice had turned husky, almost harsh, but she

wasn't interested in gentleness. She did feel bold. A wildness was brewing inside her, and it urged her to move—faster—and Broen seemed to feel it too. She grasped him to her, using her entire body. She rested her hands on his shoulders and pulled him closer. She gripped his hips with her thighs, rising to meet every downward thrust. Each time he buried his length inside her, the hunger raging within her doubled, possibly tripled. She was beyond being able to understand anything. There was only need and response.

"That's it, lass… Ride with me." The bed ropes groaned as he thrust hard against her. "It will be worth the effort. I swear to ye."

"Sweet Christ…" She was cursing, but her body was beginning to spiral out of control. Every thrust threatened to unleash something she knew she wanted, but that she suspected might tear her in two. She didn't care. They strained against each other, her fingers becoming talons, her nails digging into his skin. He moved faster, unleashing the burst of delight she'd sensed was coming. It jerked her into its hold, ripping away every thought while roaring through her. The pleasure was on a scale beyond her experience. Encompassing and blinding, it commanded her completely.

"That's the way, lass," Broen snarled before burying his cock inside her. He growled, the sound low and primal, as his body shook. She felt the spurt of his seed burn the walls of her passage, which set off a second ripple of satisfaction. This one was milder but deeper, and she lifted her eyelids to lock stares with her lover. In that moment, there was only the pair of them.

Society didn't matter, didn't even exist. There was only her lover and the scent of their sweat.

Absolutely nothing else mattered.

⁓

Clarrisa wasn't the only one who slept soundly for the rest of the night. Broen rolled over and pulled the bedding around them, but that was the last conscious thought he recalled. Normally he woke several times a night, when noise from the training yard woke him. The bed was still encased in darkness, the bed-curtains drawn to shut out the light. With a snarl, he sent the one nearest him swinging into the post and landed on his feet.

The chamber door was closed, but the window showed him full daylight. He stared at the light, disbelieving the proof that he'd even slept through the church bell tolling the morning Mass.

Clarrisa was nowhere in sight.

Frustration sent a few more words past his lips that would have gained him a penance if the priests heard, but he didn't care, didn't give a damn what celibate men of the cloth had to say about his feelings for Clarrisa. He grabbed a shirt and took a few moments to pleat his kilt. The chore felt endless, and for the first time he regretted not allowing Edme to serve him as she wanted. The damned kilt would have been pleated and waiting for him to buckle it around his waist if he hadn't forbidden his head of house to wait on him. He shook his head, trying to dispel his frustration.

Edme wasn't to blame. He was. Along with his lack of discipline. But what needled him most presently was the fact that Clarrisa had left his bed and he'd remained sleeping like a fat pasha. Such a lapse of awareness could get him killed. Most lairds had retainers at their chamber doors, because an assassin could come in many forms—desirable female flesh included.

Would you rather I weep?

Shame nipped at him, the soft words from the night whispering across his memory. Suspicion was an ugly thing. It twisted a man until he lost perspective completely.

His men were waiting on him. The two retainers posted at the foot of the stairs battled to maintain blank expressions. Neither of them succeeded very well.

"Where is she?" he growled.

"The English lass?"

"Yes, the English lass," he snapped.

His man smirked before smoothing his lips in response to Broen's dark expression.

"She went off to Mass. Young Arawn and Gahan followed her."

Broen stopped himself from replying quickly. Uncertainty was boiling inside him. It was an emotional state he wasn't comfortable with. In fact, he couldn't recall ever feeling so unsteady over a woman before.

He should send her north. It would solve a great many difficulties and gain him the favor of his overlord. But the churning feelings inside him rebelled, threatening to bubble over.

He needed to discover her game first. Aye, that was what he wanted. Once he heard her confess her reasons for lying with him, it would be simple to let her go. It was unlikely he'd enjoy knowing why she'd not pushed him away. Perhaps Shaw was right; she was trying to secure herself a place.

Would that be so terrible?

He drew a stiff breath, trying to convince himself that the answer was yes. Part of him was certain it was, but there was a growing sense of just not caring why she was near, so long as she was.

The daylight hours went by too quickly. Clarrisa set to work with the other MacNicols women. They tried to take the chores from her, and she snapped at them. Their eyes widened, some of them narrowing immediately with outrage, but she refused to be run out of the kitchen. She couldn't afford to have time to think.

Her thoughts were too heated to ponder, or too shameful. Her passage was sore, reminding her often that she'd fallen from grace. Maybe the ache would be easier to endure if she could truly repent, but she wasn't sorry. An unrepentant soul was bound for damnation. *Maybe.*

She doubled her efforts, unwilling to face her mental dilemma. She should be ashamed. She was ruined, but she felt more alive than ever.

"Have ye defeated that demon of yers yet?" Edme asked, her tone full of knowledge. The head of house was oddly free of anyone trying to gain her attention. "The laird is fighting the same one, I believe," Edme continued with a knowing gleam in her eyes.

"There's no reason why he should be." Clarrisa slapped a hand over her mouth with shock. Edme could have her lashed for such an admission. The role of head of house included keeping morality in check. But a need to stand firm in the face of her deeds took control of her, and she removed her hand. "I lay with him by my own choice."

The words were easier to say than she had expected, and satisfaction filled her once she'd said them. Maybe she was ruined, but she was not a coward.

Edme smiled and shook her head. "I would nae have suspected me laird of wrongdoing, but I admit yer confession shames me for nae questioning the matter."

"Why?"

Edme inspected the spices Clarrisa had been grinding with a pestle. The older woman lifted the mortar and peered intently at the cinnamon, judging the fineness of the grains before she set it back on the table.

"I should question it because ye were brought here against yer will." When Edme lifted her head, there was a shimmer of understanding Clarrisa hadn't expected. "There was a time, when I was a young lass, that a man stole me away."

The older woman grew silent, her attention moving to the window and the setting sun.

"What happened?" She was being intrusive but couldn't seem to shame herself into silence.

"Men can be harsh." Edme's voice was thick with emotion. She drew in a deep breath and turned her gaze away from the window, as if she was turning her back on the memory.

"I think ye know the difference I am speaking of. It's that knowledge that makes ye so honest with me about something many might judge a transgression. But I recall what it was like to learn the difference between a man who considered me his property and one who wanted to share the delights of being me lover." She shook her head wistfully. "I recall very well being unashamed of me choice. The priests at the church would be more pleased with me if I had repented too, but I will never cry shame over me choices. I only hope for mercy when my days come to an end."

"Was the man who stole you a MacNicols?"

Edme nodded. "I was born a Grant but choose to live a MacNicols."

"Why?"

The older woman frowned. "Because I learned something from the man who stole me. I learned the same lesson I see on yer face, Clarrisa of the York family: the knowledge that yer blood believes ye naught more than a bargaining tool. The laird's father was a good man. He did nae allow his men to mistreat women, but more important, he offered me the invitation to become his lover. I'd not have had any choice of who was in my bed if I returned home." She smiled with satisfaction.

"But you didn't explain why you should have expected Broen to treat me harshly."

Edme considered her long and hard, moving her gaze slowly over her face and neck, looking for any dark marks. "Me laird is a good leader. Fair and fearless. Noble too, a true man of his word." Her tone lowered. "But the nature of a man when he's with a woman is something ye cannae know about until ye experience it. A man with a fine reputation among his clansmen can be unkind when lust controls him."

"Your laird isn't one of that sort."

Edme smiled, but it wasn't in approval; it was an expression shared between women who took their chances. "It's good to know he is truly his father's son. I'm proud to be his mother."

Shock rippled through Clarrisa, and Edme laughed softly.

"Aye, ye heard me. Broen is me natural child, even if there are few who know it left alive these days."

"But why—" She struggled to find the words that weren't insulting.

Edme interrupted her. "Because it was what I wanted. The chance to belong to no one but myself was offered, and I took it. Remaining the laird's leman gave me position and kept me from having to return to me family, who would have begun shifting through the offers for me to find the most advantageous one for their interests. Many consider me a poor daughter for no' doing me duty, but staying offered me the choice to decide what I wanted from me life." Disgust edged her words, and Clarrisa discovered herself agreeing with the woman wholeheartedly. Edme offered her a satisfied look.

"I gave him a son, and fate was kind enough to make it so his legitimate wife never conceived even a daughter. Only the church is displeased with me, but I am content." Her expression became serious once more. "Much more so now that I know me son treated ye well. I needed to know."

The older woman's eyes sparkled with happiness and satisfaction. Clarrisa discovered herself envious of Broen for having a parent who was so interested in his morality. Edme had no interest in securing a royal-blooded child for Broen to use for the clan's advantage, and she had issued no warning for Clarrisa to stay away from her son's bed to prevent any threats.

"Mind ye, if ye let me son catch ye so simply, I'll be a bit disappointed."

"He has not caught me," Clarrisa insisted. "I thought I heard Argyll in my chamber, and it frightened me, but I'm not sure if there was anything there except my numbed wits, and well... well..."

"Nature got the best of ye. It happens, lass."

"It will not happen again," Clarrisa insisted. Edme eyed her before waving her toward the door. Clarrisa began to follow, her mind more focused on how to make good on her promise. She would. Somehow.

Liar.

Five

"I'm impressed."

Clarrisa jumped, and the comb fell from her fingers. She turned to glare at Broen.

"Since you have told me this is my chamber, you should knock before entering," she scolded, too kindly.

His lips curved arrogantly while he took another couple of steps into the chamber. The damned man was so large, his stride far too close for her comfort.

"Argyll was my grandfather. It seems I have inherited his lack of respect for announcing his intention to enter yer chamber."

Clarrisa jerked her attention to the mirror, something she'd done often since returning to the chamber. The only man watching her from the polished surface was Broen. His doublet was missing and the collar of his shirt open, as seemed to be his habit.

"Argyll will not unnerve me again. If it was even him I saw." A soft tingle went down her spine, but she wasn't sure if it was from her brush with a ghost or the fact that Broen had come looking for her. "Edme's elixir was laced with whisky."

"He was chasing his mistress down the hallway and forgot the floor wasn't finished, when he fell to his death," Broen revealed. "The servants have sworn he haunts this tower ever since, but I have never seen him."

Heat blossomed in her cheeks as she fought to not look at the bare skin beckoning her. "What is it with the men in your family and their mistresses?"

One fair eyebrow rose. "We're lusty."

"You sound very proud... of that sin."

He shrugged and moved closer. She felt his approach; it rippled across her skin as surely as any wind would have. Remaining on the chair became a battle, but she resisted the urge to panic.

"There are worse things my life requires me to do that I have a skill at." There was a gleam in his eyes which tempted her to join him in his teasing.

She offered him a shake of her head. "I believe I should be the judge of your skill."

She was trying to best him at his teasing game, but challenge glittered in his eyes and he walked behind her. A chill crossed her nape, and she did give in to the urge to stand—having him behind her was too much to endure. But he caught her about the waist and pulled her back against his body. "Well now, lass, ye have an excellent point." His breath brushed her ear as his voice became husky. "But I can be the judge of yer skill, Clarrisa. I'll say plainly yer touch is like fire, and I enjoyed it full well."

"Oh stop, Broen." She sent her elbow back into his ribs and gained her freedom, but he stood chuckling and looking none the worse for wear. "Do you have no shame?"

"None," he insisted. "Only a burning need to know why ye slipped out of me bed before I woke."

His tone hardened, and she realized he'd been cleverly disguising his true mood. Suspicion glittered in his eyes now, and it irritated her.

It also hurt. She lowered her eyelids to protect her fragile emotions.

"I thought you'd be happy not to have me about once you'd had what you wanted." She placed a few feet between them, fighting to maintain her composure. "I do hope Shaw wasn't too disappointed to hear I didn't make demands of you."

"Why did nae ye?" It was a hard question, spoken with enough heat to curl her hair. The fragile trust she'd discovered growing inside her since she spoke with Edme withered in the face of his accusation.

"Oh, I see. You agree with Shaw that I have motives for everything I do."

He crossed his arms over his chest. "Do nae sound so wounded. Everyone has motives. It's part of our instinct to survive."

"Get out," she snarled and pointed at the door. "Go on with you, Broen MacNicols. I want nothing from you. I pray you find the knowledge satisfying."

He frowned, furrowing his brow. "I do nae, woman. Ye'll answer me—"

"I already have," she insisted. "I want nothing from you. Naught at all, so get you gone from my sight."

"The blush on yer cheeks makes ye a liar."

"Allowing you near me now, with your suspicious questions, would only prove you right."

She drew in a stiff breath, her temper flaring bright

enough to burn away her desire. "So go on with you before I tempt you."

He captured her hand and twisted it behind her back to press her against his body. "And I'm a liar for saying I came in here to discover why ye left me bed."

His kiss drowned out her response. For one moment, her temper had her struggling, but he held her still, pushing her lips apart to accept a deeper kiss. All the anger transformed into passion. It happened as fast as summer straw burned. One moment she was trying to yell at him, and the next she heard his shirt rip because she was pulling on it so hard.

"That's right, lass. Take what ye want." He cradled her head, holding her in place with a grip that pulled some of her hair too tight. Tiny points of pain dug into her scalp, but they intensified the need boiling inside her. "Rip it if ye want to feel me skin."

She laughed like a lunatic, enjoying the idea of doing wrong, because she was insane. The shirt split easily, the fabric tearing with a loud sound. She pushed her hands inside the opening and shoved the ruined garment over his shoulders. He had to release her, and his arms became pinned.

"There are some of your orders I do like following after all, Broen." Her voice was deep and husky, astounding her with how sultry it sounded. She buried her face against his chest, working her hands up the ridges of muscle until she found his nipples. She continued up, pressing kisses against his flesh until she found his jaw.

"Ye're in need of chastisement, woman." His voice lacked any true warning, but there was a promise lurking in his eyes when he stepped away from her. A quick pull on the wide leather belt that held his kilt in place and the plaid began to slide down his body. He caught it with a practiced motion and flung it onto the chair where she'd been sitting. The ruined shirt fluttered to the floor before he tossed his bonnet onto the chair as well.

Somehow he was more powerful nude. Clothing was made to impress, but the way Broen stood so confidently in nothing but his skin sent a shiver through her. The man feared no one, not even the harsh environment he'd been born into.

Highlander—it was a title a man earned.

"You're my lover, Broen MacNicols, not my husband, so do not think to chastise me." She felt wonderfully free in that moment. "I'll do what I please, and only what pleases me."

He growled softly, "Nay, lass, I assure ye the pleasure is going to be all mine."

He was smug and arrogant, but excitement went flooding into her belly. Her lips curled back from her teeth slightly, the pure magnetism of him threatening to make her wild. But she would hold her ground. She stepped back toward him, watching enjoyment take command of his expression.

"There can be rewards for the man who waits on his lady's whim." She met his eyes, staring at the flames of hunger. "Rewards you will never sample if you continue to act like such a brute." She rolled the word and watched his eyes narrow.

"Ye should nae be able to make that word sound enticing, but ye do."

She tapped the center of his chest with her finger-tips. "And you shouldn't be about to growl while giving me a compliment."

"Me tone is part of the praise." He tugged the belt of her dressing robe free. "It is nae often I find me control tested."

He pushed the edges of the dressing robe open, and the heavy garment fell to the floor with a soft sound.

"Can you never admit you're wrong?"

His teeth flashed at her before he answered, "No." He tugged her chemise over her head. The night air felt good against her skin, the excitement brewing inside her making her warm. She only had a moment to notice they stood together nude before he scooped her off her feet and carried her to the bed.

"Let's give Argyll something to watch, should he decide to come calling."

She aimed a slap at his shoulder and rolled over, refusing to be pinned. "Little wonder your tower is haunted when you talk in such a way about the dead." She ended up on her knees facing Broen. He climbed onto the bed, looking as though he was stalking her. She knew the bed was smaller than his, but it seemed to sink as he moved all the way onto it. That, or he grew until she was battling the urge to flee. But it wasn't the sort of fear she knew—this was an insane sort of need to run simply because she hoped he'd chase her.

And catch her.

She suddenly giggled, unable to resist the urge to be insane again. A look of surprise appeared on Broen's face before she smashed one of the pillows into it. He yanked it from her grasp and offered her a growl.

"Oh, for heaven's sake," she groused. "You're a Highlander. I've been raised with tales of how barbaric you are, and that measly growl is all I receive for my impertinence?"

"I would nae dream of disappointing ye. 'Course, it will likely bring the boys running again…"

She launched herself toward him, slapping her hand over his mouth. Satisfaction lit his eyes as he cupped the sides of her hips and held her firmly.

"Oh fie."

He forced her back, placing her beneath him without any further effort. He nuzzled her neck, numbing her wits again as passion began to intoxicate her. She was suddenly awash in sensation—every inch of her in contact with him. It was overwhelming, but exciting beyond even her memory of last night. Her body didn't wait to be coaxed into arousal. Passion swept across her like fire in summer.

"Are ye truly dismayed to be beneath me, lass?" He found her neck with his lips. He lingered over the delicate skin, teasing it with tiny kisses that set her clitoris to throbbing. "Admit ye crave me."

"I do, but I want more than to lie beneath you."

He raised his head, the unmistakable look of anticipation illuminating his eyes. "Ye were virgin last night, Clarrisa."

"Virginity doesn't interfere with hearing, Broen, and I've heard as many heated tales as the next girl."

He stroked her cheek, tenderly smoothing over her lower lip before leaning down to kiss her. "Do nae be gullible, lass. Listening does nae grant ye any skill."

She reached down and grasped his cock. His

expression hardened. She could see him battling to recall what they were talking about, and it filled her with confidence. She wanted to send his wits scattering just as he so often did hers.

"If I wanted to lie beneath a man, I'd have done my duty to my family and let your king have his way. Tonight I'll ride you."

He shuddered. She felt the ripple move down his length, and his cock hardened even more. It was now as hard as iron, and she shivered at the idea of being the one to set their pace.

"Ye bait yer hook well, lass. I'm eager to jump at it."

He rolled over, shaking the bed as he settled onto his back. The night air was cold after having his warmth covering her, but she sat up, the freedom to command him filling her with a confidence she'd never felt before. Once more all the rules vanished, and she was able to follow her feelings, her cravings, wherever they took her.

"I don't want to be your possession." And she refused to be intimidated. She rose onto her knees and heard him groan.

"There are advantages to having ye on top, lass. More are being revealed to me as we speak." His gaze was on her breasts. He cupped her hips and helped lift her into position. He held her above him, and her knees sank into the soft bedding on either side of his hips. "Aye, this position has merit."

She should have scoffed at him, challenging him over his comments, because it was unlikely he'd never been in a similar position. But she didn't want to think, didn't want to quibble with him. The head of his cock was burrowing into her passage, and all she wanted to do was sink down until his entire length was deep inside her.

"Easy now… The night is young."

Need was pounding through her, but he maintained a grip on her hips that kept her obedient to his will. She sank inch by inch onto his length, every moment feeling too long. At last he relinquished control, and she rose instantly, up until only the head of his cock was within her and then down until she no longer held her weight.

"I recant, woman… Go as fast as ye like." His voice was husky now, his expression tightening. He guided her with the grip on her hips, helping her to learn the rhythm.

"I'm telling you what I want… Broen MacNicols…" It was nearly impossible to form her thoughts into words, so she stopped trying. She leaned her head back and closed her eyes. All she wanted was to feel the sensations being unleashed by her motions. Every lift granted her light friction, but when she came down, his rod was pressed firmly against her clitoris, threatening to send her into the vortex of pleasure she'd experienced last night.

She craved that pleasure, but she wanted something else too. Forcing herself to look down at her partner, she watched his face, seeking out signs of what he enjoyed best. She adjusted her pace and held the one that seemed to intensify his pleasure. For long moments, they were locked in a battle of wills. He tried to maintain his composure, while she attempted to break it.

"Ye learn too quickly, lass," he growled before pushing her down and turning over with her clasped to his body. He pressed her onto her back and took command of their pace. "But I'll nae be unmanned before I hear ye cry with delight."

"You brute."

He growled at her but grasped her wrists and pulled her arms above her head. His pace was driving her insane, the hard, driving strokes making her mindless. He leaned close to her face, pressing a hard kiss against her mouth as his body drove her closer and closer to climax.

"Aye, and ye enjoy every bit of me brutish nature, because it allows ye the freedom to meet me."

It was true.

She cried out, not sure if it was because of the motion of his driving hips or his words. Everything was tangled inside her mind, and she surrendered to it. Lifting her hips to meet his, moving faster and faster until her heart beat at a frantic pace—it didn't bother her, because it allowed her to feel so much more. Her clitoris was tightening, and the explosion of release beginning to wash over her.

"That's the way, lass. Take yer pleasure." His voice was like a clap of thunder, accentuating the flash of intense light that split her in two. She strained toward her lover, crying as she felt him begin to give up his seed. For a moment that felt endless, they were spinning through the wildness of the storm together. When the wildness released her, she was bathed in satisfaction so heavy she felt pinned to the bed.

But she realized the weight was Broen. He kissed

a trail along her arm before releasing her wrist and then tenderly rolled off her. The only sounds in the chamber were of their heavy breathing. She lay where he'd left her, feeling too spent to move. He reached for her and pulled her next to his body with one solid arm.

"What are you doing?"

He nuzzled against her hair, drawing in a deep breath. "Going to sleep."

"But…" She tried to disengage herself from his body, but he smoothed her back into his embrace and even tugged the bedding over them as though she hadn't tried to escape.

"Lovers lie together long after the hunger is fed, lass." He slid one of his legs over hers, tangling their bodies even more.

She wanted to argue but couldn't seem to form her thoughts into words—at least not any that made any sense. Railing at him for wanting to remain after he'd had her certainly made no sense. Women the world over struggled to overcome the hurt inflicted on them when men used their bodies for release and left moments after gaining it.

So what did it mean when a man pulled her close?

Love…

She scoffed at the word that rose in her mind. It was born in that part of her that wanted to believe in courtly love. Reality wasn't so peaceful. Affection for a husband was a wife's duty, but only after marriage. True courtly love didn't involve physical intimacy.

So what was Broen doing? The man wasn't chilled and in need of a bed partner to keep the Highland night away. He was warm, and she snuggled closer because his heat was inviting. So what…

Her mind refused to continue trying to understand the situation. Instead, she sank into slumber, satisfaction still radiating inside her. Morning would be soon enough to contemplate the issues surrounding her.

❦

"I'm riding out to see Broen MacNicols."

Donnach Grant sputtered and struggled to his feet. "Ye'll do nothing of the sort! That man is set on running through every Grant."

"Exactly why I'm set on clearing up this matter." Kael Grant already had his mail tunic on, and his gillie followed behind his master with his helmet. "Ye may have given yer word, Father, but I'm… reckless. So I'll be riding out to set the matter straight, since ye cannae."

"Ye do nae need to sound so smug. The ploy we've employed was to benefit the clan. No' give ye the freedom to do as ye pleased." Donnach grunted, his face turning red, but he lost the battle to remain on his feet. He dropped heavily into a chair positioned next to his bed because his leg supported him less and less these days.

"This leg is a curse," he muttered. "It keeps me from doing the things I need to."

"This is nae yer duty," Kael insisted. "By the rules of this ruse we've begun, I'm the only one who can make peace with the MacNicols. Ye gave yer word to keep the secret of Laird MacNicols's death, but I did nae."

"Aye, I did, and I will nae break me word. I'm grateful ye came home, for ye're right. Ye are the only one who can ride out and keep Broen MacNicols from spilling our blood. But I do nae like it, no' a bit." He slapped the armrest.

"The only part I like is that I'm able to shoulder the duty of serving ye and this clan, Father. I understand it frustrates ye, but I'm proud to be able to assume me duty as yer son."

Donnach struggled back to his feet. Kael stepped forward so his father could clasp his shoulder.

"I'm proud of ye, Son."

Once outside the master chamber, Kael frowned. His sister, Nareen, stood there, waiting on him. Her lips were lifted in a satisfied smile.

"Ye have too much cunning for a female," he announced on his way toward the yard. Nareen laughed, her voice soft and musical. He turned to look at her. "And ye have all the charm of a siren."

"Ye needn't sound so surly, Brother mine." She paused near the doorway to the yard and pulled her arisaid up to shield her head from the rain. "What good would I be to ye today if I were timid? Ye are nae the only member of this family who likes to receive Father's approval."

Nareen stepped into the rain without a care for it.

"Fate has a misplaced sense of humor for sending ye to this life as a female," he remarked. "Ye have the spirit of a Highlander."

Nareen took the reins of her mare and mounted the animal without any help from the men waiting to ride with them. The mare was a feisty creature and danced in a wide circle before his sister took control. Nareen's eyes sparkled with enjoyment of the challenge.

"Of course I do. Am I nae riding out with ye and yer men?" She scoffed at him with a pout that made her too fetching by far. "Do nae be so dense as to think only men can be Highlanders."

"Ye mistake me, Sister. I was lamenting the lack of feminine graces ye were not endowed with. Finding a man to wed ye will be a chore, to be sure."

"An easier task than finding a bride who will wed ye, thinking ye a man of no position who is naught but a rogue."

"I might take that wager, Sister, and ye know I do nae ever lose when I accept terms. Ye'll find yerself behaving meekly in order to best me." Kael tilted his head. "It might just be worth losing to see ye behaving all sweet and submissive."

"Nothing is worth that." She tossed her raven hair and shot him a sour glance, but she also looked toward the gate. Kael took his helmet from the young lad acting as his gillie and gained the back of his stallion. A priest was offering a blessing to the men who were set to ride out with him.

Maybe he was a fool to forgo kneeling in front of the priest. Broen MacNicols wouldn't be friendly. But the season had changed fully, and there was no longer any time to spare. War was looming over the entire country, which meant he couldn't leave his father with a neighbor who felt he had a justified reason for feuding.

"Let's ride, lads. There are important matters to resolve."

Or die trying.

～

It was a gray morning.

Clarrisa woke to the sound of the church bell ringing. She lifted her head, only to have the bed rock violently as Broen erupted from it.

"It's only Mass."

He turned to glare at her. "That is nae the church, Clarrisa. It's the village bell."

She sat up and listened, hearing the difference in the tones. This bell rang faster, like a cry for help.

"Cover up. We'll nae be alone much longer." He had already shrugged into his shirt and was pleating his kilt.

She heard the pounding footsteps of his men and grabbed the coverlet before they made it to the chamber door.

"Enter!" he snapped before they made it close enough to knock. The chamber door was yanked open, and Shaw came in with others on his heels.

"Grants are riding over the hill, Laird. Looks like Kael is leading them."

"So… Donnach's son has returned at last." Broen's tone was ominous. Clarrisa hugged the bedding closer, certain the temperature had dropped.

"Out," he ordered his men.

Shaw looked confused, switching his attention between his laird and her. Clarrisa was sure her cheeks would catch fire.

"Right, lads… Let's wait in the hallway…"

Clearly Broen hadn't given his men such an order before. They all glanced at her, contemplating why she was pulling their laird's attention away from them.

"Just for a moment, lads."

Broen finished dressing, and his men left. They didn't go very far, for she couldn't hear their footsteps on the stone stairs.

"Come and kiss me, lass," Broen muttered softly, too softly, for he was trying to hide his emotions, keeping his voice low so the tone wouldn't betray him.

Kiss him good-bye...

It was a personal request, one that sent tears to her eyes. He was a proud man, but there was no missing the tension in his expression. It was possible he was riding out to defend his people with his life. She could see that knowledge reflected in his eyes, the solid commitment to do his duty, no matter the cost.

She pushed the bedding aside and went to him. His eyes were bright and focused on her. She felt a connection to him, one which was tugging her closer. It was the need shimmering in his eyes. It pulled her toward him because she wanted to be worthy of how much he desired her.

He reached for her, gently cupping the sides of her face. The kiss wasn't hard; it began slow and sweet, a tentative meeting of their lips. He tasted her, slipping the tip of his tongue along her lower lip before deepening the kiss. She felt his need burning and kissed him back with equal fire, but he set her back all too quickly.

"Stay in the tower, lass."

He'd withdrawn behind his stony expression, the one she remembered well from the first time she'd met him. This was the laird, the man who felt responsibility for the clan resting on his shoulders. He reached over and retrieved the sword leaning against the wall. She hadn't seen him place it there and felt frustration needle her for not realizing the man had come to her chamber with the intent to take her to bed. She'd have been a hypocrite to say she was sorry.

She watched him go and waited until the chamber door had closed before she allowed the tears stinging her eyes to fall. They eased silently over her cheeks while she tried to decipher her feelings.

Did she care if he died out on the hills today? If so, why? Was her concern for herself and what would become of her? Faolan Chisholms came to mind with his teasing—or was it a promise? She wasn't sure.

Or were her tears for the man who'd held her through the night, in spite of every reason he shouldn't have any liking for her?

So many questions and so many tears. There was no stopping them, and she didn't try. The truth was impossible to ignore. Broen MacNicols had touched her heart.

Such the fool she was.

❧

"What the hell." Broen looked across the valley, taking longer than necessary because he was hoping the view might change. It looked as though every retainer the Grant clan had was facing him. They'd brought their shields and axes. Every last man wore mail, and there wasn't an unprotected head in sight. Except one, which was covered only by the Grant plaid. "That bastard Kael brought his sister."

Kael Grant was positioned next to Nareen Grant, and when the man moved forward, his damned sister followed.

Broen cursed but went to meet them. He waited until Kael had stopped his horse.

"I've thought a fair number of nasty things about ye, but never that ye'd resort to hiding behind skirts," Broen declared.

Kael was a worthy opponent, a man Broen knew had earned his reputation. Kael didn't care for the accusation.

"I need to have words with ye. Bringing me sister was the only way I could think to get ye to hold back on trying to run me through before we talked."

"Yer father is the one who's been refusing to have words with me. He's sitting in yer keep like a woman."

Kael surprised him by not taking offense. His sister did it for him. "Do nae insult me father."

"Keep yer peace, Nareen, before young Laird MacNicols takes a fancy to ye. I hear he has a weakness for outspoken women."

Nareen looked shocked, but only for a moment. Flames flickered in her green eyes, ones which Broen admired, but he didn't have time for.

"It's fixing to rain, perhaps yer sister would like to retire inside Deigh Tower, since ye claim ye came for a peaceful conversation."

The rain had already soaked the new spring grass and every last man present. Nareen didn't look ill at ease, and she even rolled her eyes, but minded her brother by making no further comment.

Kael grunted. "If that is what it will take to gain enough time to talk this matter through."

"It is," Broen insisted. "Agree to send yer sister into Deigh, and I'll have to admit I want to know what ye have to say, because it must be good for ye to place yer only sibling in such a position."

"Then she'll go, with her waiting woman to stand

as witness that I do nae have any reason to be swearing vengeance against ye." Kael lifted one hand and sent his young gillie back up to the waiting ranks of Grant retainers to retrieve the woman.

"Now, just one moment, Kael. Ye cannae ask me to go inside his fortress…" Nareen interjected.

"I'm nae asking it. Laird MacNicols is." Nareen fumed. But her brother didn't relent. "A fact that should impress upon ye how close we are to a summer of bloody feuding. I'd only send ye if I felt sure we might resolve the issue and that the MacNicols are reasonable. Ye'll go."

Nareen wasn't happy. She shot her brother a furious look before her matron arrived and they followed Shaw back toward the ranks of MacNicols retainers.

"Ye've got brass balls, man. I'll give ye that, Kael Grant, but do nae be thinking I'm going to be easy to sweet-talk. Now that yer sister is gone, we'll be settling this man to man."

"Daphne MacLeod is nae dead."

Broen felt stunned but not relieved. His temper flared. "Yer father is the one who told me she was. It's the reason me father rode onto yer land."

"Aye. He did nae lie either," Kael continued.

Broen shook his head. "Start making sense, man, or take up yer sword. I'm set to finish this, since ye rode onto me land with yer men outfitted for fighting. I do nae fancy spending the summer wondering when ye'll begin raiding me villages."

"Nor do I, which is why I'm here to set the matter straight. Me men are dressed to defend themselves in the event ye will nae listen to reason."

Broen had to concede the point. "Fair enough. I'm

here and listening. Ye're right. I'd no' have ridden down here if yer sister was nae with ye. So explain."

"Me father wrote and said Daphne was dead to ye."

"Aye, that's true enough. I've seen the letter." And just thinking about it sent his temper still hot.

"She's wearing sackcloth in the convent," Kael muttered. "So… dead to ye."

Broen struggled to absorb the information. It made sense, but he had to shove aside a sense of impending doom, because he was betrothed to Daphne. The sweet memory of the way Clarrisa had come to him and kissed him rose to torment him. The MacLeods might well demand Daphne back from the church and insist the wedding take place. Another feud could result if he refused to honor his father's word on the match.

"Ye're understanding the importance of it. I see it on yer face, MacNicols," Kael continued. "The wedding banns were cried and the contract sealed. It's why yer father made the rash choice to try to take Daphne from the convent. It was a church knight who ran him through for transgressing on holy ground with the intent to steal away a woman who would bring a fine dowry to the church."

"Sweet Christ," Broen swore. "If that bit of news gets out…"

"Aye. Such a thing must never be known, for yer father would be disgraced and possibly excommunicated for the sin of trying to steal from the church. Me father has hidden it, and the knight died this winter of lockjaw. Fate seems to favor ye for the moment."

Broen struggled to control his frustration. It felt like

a noose was tightening around his neck. "I'm no' a coward, man. I'll shoulder what me father did."

"But neither are ye a fool," Kael snapped. "Allowing this to come to light will nae help anyone. The church would demand penitence from ye, and no' just hours on yer knees."

"They'd want gold." A great deal of it. Daphne MacLeod had come with a large dowry; that was the very reason Faolan Chisholms had wanted her too. There was also the alliance with the MacLeods. She was a prize bride. The church wasn't blind to that fact and had killed to protect their claim on her.

"Me father should have left her, but I know he would nae have agreed with me."

Kael nodded. "Me father kept it quiet because the royalists will be making their move soon. I agree with him. We need the MacNicols strong, no' trying to scrap together enough food to survive because one woman decided to disobey her father. Me father is nearing the end of his days and will take the knowledge out of this world."

"What do ye want for the service of keeping quiet?" Broen demanded.

Kael moved his horse closer to Broen's. He reached into his doublet and pulled loose a length of fine blond hair that was tied at both ends and braided.

"Daphne shed her hair in preparation to take her novice vows. So it's time for our clans to have a new understanding. I want the MacNicols strong enough to help restore dignity to Scotland, so we both can marry and raise families. Me father gave his word to remain silent, as demanded of him by the church so ye would nae come to reclaim yer betrothed. They want Daphne's dowry, and no mistake. But I did nae give my word, so I'm telling ye what happened so we can end the rumblings for vengeance from yer men."

It was a pleasant thought. The struggle consuming his country was becoming impossible to bear.

"What of her kin?"

Kael shrugged and pushed the hair back into his doublet. "Chalmers MacLeod is a royalist. I do nae care what becomes of him. It's possible Daphne will outlive her kin because she left them. Only time will tell. For the moment, I'll no' be the one to tell Laird MacLeod of his daughter's choice. We do nae need him marching his men up here."

"Aye," Broen agreed.

Kael tugged on his reins and sent his stallion circling away from Broen. "Think on the matter, Laird MacNicols. The prince needs us more than we need to distrust each other, and I did let ye have me sister. Send her back, or swear ye're going to wed her and save me the trouble of trying to find a man who will share a tower with her. It should be against God's will for a woman to be so beguiling. Mark me words. Half yer men will be drooling like halfwits simply by being in her company for this last hour."

"I do nae know whether to accuse ye of insulting me men or of bragging over yer sister's charms, but I'll send her out."

"Now who's insulting whom, MacNicols? Is nae me sister good enough for ye?" Kael Grant laughed before he rode back to his men.

Broen found himself joining Kael in laughter. In

fact, he laughed so hard Shaw raised an eyebrow, but that didn't stop him.

"So... things are right cheery from the sound of ye," Shaw muttered, obviously confused. He peered at the line of Grants holding shields and swords before looking back at the grin on Broen's face.

"They are indeed, lads. Kael Grant has cleared up the matter to me satisfaction."

Surprise appeared on his men's faces. The ones in front turned to relay the information.

"But how did he do that?" Shaw asked.

Broen sobered. "I'll have to ask ye to take me word on the matter. Someone ride up and tell Nareen Grant to rejoin her brother."

His men were frozen with shock for a moment, but they began to move, relief appearing from behind the dutiful expressions they'd worn since leaving Deigh. No doubt the riders heading up to retrieve Nareen would spread much-needed cheer through the families waiting to see what would happen.

He couldn't lie, but for the moment, it appeared he wasn't the only one looking for a way to avoid a feud. Still, the secret would always be lurking in the background, coming to mind because he knew it would prove a dark day for the MacNicols if it were ever uncovered. It was still an easier burden to shoulder than knowing he was at war with his neighbor.

Maybe he should consider wedding Nareen. Kael would have a strong inclination to maintain his promised silence if his sister's position were at stake.

He rejected the idea as soon as he thought it. Nareen was a fine woman, but Clarrisa overshadowed her. In all her stubbornness, and even her English ways, he still thought of her over the fiery Nareen. He watched Kael's sister ride toward them, leaning low over the neck of her mare and letting the animal take the lead. Her eyes shimmered, and her skirts rippled up too high, showing off her legs, but Nareen never paused. She was one with the ride, enjoying the thrill.

Nothing stirred inside him. It should have—half his men were eyeing her. The other half were thinking of their sweethearts. Just as he was.

It was a sobering thought and a frustrating one, for it unleashed a fear inside him. It would be difficult to keep Clarrisa. More than difficult, it was most likely impossible. Her blood would always be coveted, at least so long as Henry VII ruled England.

"So me visit is concluded, Laird MacNicols. Pity, I had little time to drink very much of yer fine spirits. Yer head of house took a long time to unlock the store she claimed was reserved for ye alone."

"I'll send over a cask of it for yer table, since we're now friends."

She nodded a single time before digging in her heels and sending her mare forward. Her waiting woman appeared well suited to her position, for she rode as well as her mistress.

He watched only long enough to ensure they made it back to their kin. It took discipline, because he was anxious to return to Clarrisa. Every moment they had was suddenly more precious than he'd noticed. He was going to woo her tonight. Plan the steps of her seduction instead of grabbing her like a... like a brute.

A smile lifted his lips when he turned and looked at his men. "Let's go home, lads. We've a peace to celebrate."

They cheered, and soon the bell was ringing in the village once more, but this time in welcome. To be truthful, he'd never been so happy to be riding home.

⁓

"I know me duty. Stop hovering over me," Edme groused. "Ye look like an Englishman all set to beg for his lady's favors."

"I'd think ye'd be more interested in insulting me for no' taking the time to try to impress the lass before this." He leaned over the cook again, trying to see what she was arranging on a platter. The kitchen smelled delicious, but he wanted to see for himself that the feast he'd ordered was fine and pleasing to all the senses.

"Well… ye have a point, I'll admit."

The cook finally waved to the assistant waiting near the hearth with a large domed lid. The lass held it up to catch the heat from the fire. The cook was busy arranging a roasted goose on a platter. She sliced it carefully before motioning to the girl. The girl hurried over with the lid and set it down on top of the meal to keep it warm while it was carried up to the laird's chamber. Such tender meat was a luxury normally reserved for feast days or celebrations. New spring rosemary lent its scent to the roasted meat, and there were dark spots from pepper to complete the lavishness of the meal. It was fit for the daughter of a king or the mistress of the castle.

"Quickly now, else it will all go cold," the cook muttered with a flip of her apron.

The assistants gathered up the meal and began carrying it up to the third floor. Broen followed, trying to decide what was ailing him. The meal smelled delicious, but there was a definite quiver in his stomach. Edme rapped on the chamber door before opening it. The first girl spread a freshly ironed cloth on the table before the serving dishes were set down. Candles were lit, and the scent of beeswax began to waft through the chamber. Clarrisa sat near the window with her back to him.

The cold reception sent a small shaft of doubt through him, but it was most likely she was embarrassed over having been found in bed with him that morning. Edme finished, and he waved her toward the door. She swished her hands to encourage her staff to go ahead of her and gave him a smile before following.

"I understand ye are most likely sore with me for allowing me staff to find us together, but it's something I plan to attempt to charm ye into accepting, because it goes along with being me lover."

She drew in a stiff breath, but he really couldn't tell if his words affected her in any other way, for she was wearing a cloak and even had the hood raised.

"Come, lass... Spit at me... Call me a brute, but do nae waste this fine meal. If I understand courting, ye're supposed to enjoy me offerings before attempting to freeze me."

"Ye've suffered me rejection, Broen, and no' had the opportunity to spit at me." The voice was soft and lyrical. When she turned and lowered the hood, he stared at a face that had faded from his memory. Daphne MacLeod was every bit as beautiful as he recalled, a stunning sight, really. Her features were delicate and almost angelic, but he was not pleased to see her.

"I'm sorry, but I had no choice." Her hair was cut short, proving that Kael was clever, but not a liar.

Daphne shed her hair...

Aye, but not because she'd taken vows as a bride of Christ.

"Where is Clarrisa?"

Daphne flinched, disgusting him because she was too delicate—he far preferred Clarrisa's unwavering courage.

"She's gone with Nareen," Daphne answered.

It was all too simple. Nareen Grant was just as cunning as her brother. She'd held his attention, and he'd never taken a second look at her waiting woman.

"Why?" he demanded. "Are ye daft, woman? Half the Highland chiefs would consider slitting her throat a deed well done."

"I did nae force her to go, but she went after Nareen told her who I was and that we are betrothed."

Rage was beginning to burn inside him. It was hotter than anger, more intense than frustration. "Ye chose the church. Our contract is ended."

Daphne surprised him by propping her hands on her hips. "I did nae want to be a nun and could nae lie to the priest when he asked me if it was truly me heart's desire. He refused to hear me vows until I was more settled into life serving the church, but I will never be content there."

"So ye came here. For what, Daphne? Did it amuse ye to watch me chase ye? Or have ye decided ye are more content to wed me after letting me think ye dead?" Part of him failed to understand why he was displeased to see her. After all, the woman had a handsome dowry to go with her fair features; all he would need to do was wed her to insist her father pay it. Daphne glared at him and pointed one of her delicate fingers straight at the center of his chest.

"I will never wed you," she declared with enough heat to douse some of the flames his temper was burning with. "It sickened me to see ye and Faolan fighting over me. With every meeting, the pair of ye were moving closer to trying to kill each other. Think ye I could bear such a burden?" She lifted her hands into the air. "But I'm wasting me time trying to make ye understand. All ye saw was the alliance with me clan and the gold I'd bring ye and this beauty, which time will dull."

Broen drew a stiff breath. "Mind yer slicing tongue. I'm no' the one who deceived ye. I've the right to be angry. Me father was run through on account of yer choice to no' face me with what ye're saying to me now."

"Yer father was greedy," Daphne accused. "I told him me reasons, and he even agreed that the match with me was poisoning yer relationship with the Chisholms. Donnach Grant had the wisdom to give me shelter, but yer father refused to leave in peace. He came after me because he did nae want to lose the gold me father had promised him when ye wed me. What does gold matter if ye are dead at the hand of one of yer best friends, or I'm widowed because the pair of ye cannae remember ye've been friends since yer milk teeth fell out?" Her face was flushed with anger, and she was moving toward him. "How dare ye lay it at me feet? I am no' some vain English noblewoman so selfish as to watch others die because I crave position and power. I entered the convent to prove life was more important than one wedding."

Broen stiffened, suddenly understanding why he hadn't seen Daphne's face in his dreams. He hadn't ever truly loved her, only the idea of having her as his bride, his possession, exactly as Clarrisa would have been to the king. He'd been thinking of his bride as his property, nothing else. The difference was clear to him now, and he felt it because Clarrisa had come to him with the expectation of nothing more than sharing his company.

He was a fool.

"Yer point is well founded." He shook his head and bit back a curse. "It shames me to admit it, but ye're correct. Faolan and I were acting like savages, and it was no' out of love. We were trying to best one another by bringing home the best dowry."

She scoffed. "I never thought I'd be so happy to hear a man admit he did nae care for me."

"I did nae say that, woman, but I agree what I feel for ye is no' true love. 'Tis the affection of growing up together. But ye've caused trouble now equal to what I was doing with me fighting with Faolan. Ye could have returned without this trickery, which has put Clarrisa in danger."

"No, I could nae." She shook her head. "I pity her, the English York bastard. She has to suffer more than just two men fighting over her."

"Names, Daphne. I need to know who me enemy is, for I'm going after her. Why did Donnach withdraw his support of ye? Who's behind his sending ye back to me?"

"Lord Home sent a letter to Donnach Grant insisting he put me off his land. Donnach owes Home a favor and told me he had no choice but to make good on the debt. Me father is a royalist, and Home is hoping our union will lead to the MacLeod splitting since I do nae have a brother."

"And he wants Clarrisa as well." It made too much sense, for Home was a brilliant strategist when it came to battles. Even the idea of splitting another clan would be attractive to the man. But Home was also opposed to anything English. He'd turned his back on the king because James kept running over the border to England for sanctuary.

Fury boiled through him. "Damn ye, Daphne, for helping her escape Deigh."

Daphne smiled. "Ye're wrong, Broen. I thought long and hard on the matter, and Kael Grant is her only hope, since ye cannae refuse to receive me and Lord Home knows ye have Clarrisa. Sutherland no doubt received a letter too. Would ye hold out against yer overlord, knowing it might cost yer clan the protection being in his good will provides? Clarrisa was nae willing to see ye face that burden. Ye're caught as surely as she is. Donnach owes Lord Home, and ye are betrothed to me. Home will use the contract between us to force ye to give him Clarrisa."

"But Kael has been playing the unpredictable son. No one knows his position for sure," Broen finished for her, feeling like the walls were collapsing upon him. "And Clarrisa cannae return to England, for fear

Henry will have her killed to ensure his bloodline maintains the throne."

Daphne nodded. "Clarrisa made the choice to leave. She could see it was the most logical action."

Broen shook his head, every muscle drawing tight with rejection. "She chose to leave because she does nae trust me, but mark me words, Daphne. I plan to change her mind. Ye should nae have helped her leave the safety of this keep. For that, I am right unhappy with ye."

"But—"

"Ye should have recalled what it meant to ye to have sanctuary granted by Donnach Grant when ye needed it."

"Sutherland will nae allow ye to keep her."

Broen shook his head. "Sutherland might well send me a letter or two, but the man will surely no' waste more effort on the matter. He's certainly no' going to march his men upon Deigh for one Englishwoman."

"But we are contracted. Now that I have been forced from my hiding, the church will force ye to wed me to hide their attempt to keep me—"

"They will no doubt try, but I'll see to annulling our contract, since ye have no desire to wed me. It will nae be the first time such has happened, and ye should have thought upon that before helping Clarrisa to take such a foolish action."

Relief spread across her fair features. It should have needled his pride. Instead, it pleased him. "I still think of ye kindly, Daphne, but it's the truth I prefer ye as a sister. Ye had more insight than I did. Me father should have put the matter to me; this is nae England, where affection is nae something desired in a marriage."

She smiled, and when she did, her face became a radiant vision. Even with her hair barely brushing her shoulders, she was by far the most beautiful woman he had ever set eyes on. But she did not draw him to her.

"Enjoy the meal. I believe ye'll find it lavish after living in the convent."

She scoffed. "Where are ye going?"

"To regain Clarrisa."

⸎

At first sight, Bronach Tower was everything she'd been raised to expect of a Highland fortress. Clarrisa tried to conceal her apprehension but couldn't stop shivering. The stone was dark. Both towers had few windows, and Kael Grant rode across a narrow bridge to reach the gate. Clarrisa followed, looking down to see a river thick with chunks of ice. Falling in would be a death sentence because the current was swift and the banks steep. They had traveled farther north, which accounted for the ice. The winters would be longer and harsher here.

At last, she found something that suited her mood. The towers were desolate, and her heart felt as cold as the water flowing past them. She'd done what had to be done. So why did it feel so horrible?

"Ye needn't look so forlorn, lass," Kael Grant commented. "I might take it personally."

The son of the Grant laird was a man full grown. He was Broen's opposite, with midnight-black hair and dark eyes. There was a gleam in his eyes that hinted at wickedness, but it didn't make her breathless. All it did was make her think of what she'd chosen to leave behind. Broen was a proud man; he'd not follow her. But as soon as she thought about it, she scoffed at herself, because the entire reason she'd left was because Broen couldn't keep her. The facts of the rest of the world were set against them. Not that she could truly expect him to want to keep her. She'd warmed his bed, and men did not feel the same devotion to their bed partners as women did.

Yet another fact set between them.

"We are strangers, so there is no reason for you to take offense. Even then, I'm English. Wouldn't you consider my disapproval a compliment?"

Broen had…

She had to stop thinking about the man. He was bound to another, and she didn't want to birth his bastard children. It was best to leave him now, before her affection grew any deeper. But she felt worse every moment…

Kael laughed and was joined by some of his father's men. "Ye have an understanding of Highlanders I'd nae expect in an English lass." His tone was lighthearted, but there was a flash of warning in his dark eyes that told her he was more focused than his outward appearance betrayed.

"When will we go north to Sutherland?" She needed to set her mind on where her future was headed.

"When I'm ready to."

Her throat tightened, but she forced herself to swallow the lump threatening to choke her. "Your sister claimed you would keep your word."

"I will, when it's safe to travel." He waved two burly retainers forward. "Until me father and I decide upon the matter, ye'll be staying in the solar. Me sister hates it."

"I believe I'll discover myself agreeing with her."

He grinned. "We'll see."

There was a warning in his tone. She found herself wondering if he meant to cast doubt on whether or not he'd take her to Sutherland as Nareen had promised or if he cared about her opinion of the solar.

Not that it mattered. She climbed several flights of narrow stairs before reaching the solar. It was a round room, built across the width of one of the towers. A maid scurried in to open the shutters of the single window.

Dismal indeed, and dank. Obviously no one bothered to open the window's shutters very often. Fresh air blew in, but it brought her no sense of relief. It felt like grief was wringing her heart—which was insane, for she couldn't believe herself enamored of Broen. Not the man who'd...

She stopped, recalling the Scottish king and her uncle's demanding face before she'd left for Scotland. Finally she recalled the look in Broen's eyes when he'd asked her for a kiss. Tears trickled down her cheeks as she lost the battle to resist admitting how much she hated leaving him.

But she'd have been a greater fool to remain. Daphne was his betrothed. They were as good as wed. The only future she might have with him was as his leman. Such a choice might suit her heart well, but she had no right to inflict such a life on their children. They would have no place, as she had no place.

So she'd taken the opportunity to leave. It might well land her in a worse place, but she'd be the only one to suffer. Small comfort, but all she'd receive.

She'd never see Broen MacNicols again.

Except in her dreams.

❧

"Chisholms riders on the ridge!"

Broen cursed, enjoying the opportunity to express his feelings while the priest might allow it.

"I did nae think he'd ride all the way here for the lass." Shaw muttered as he frowned.

Broen stopped for a moment, earning dark looks from his captains. "Since he's here, maybe the day will nae be such a loss."

He headed for the yard, leaving Shaw confused. "What did he mean by that?"

The other captains shrugged before following their laird.

❧

Faolan Chisholms was furious.

He'd brought his retainers and Broen found himself facing a force that looked ready to wage war.

The damned country was dissolving into chaos. Clan was pitted against clan because their king wasn't strong enough to lead. Broen raised his hand, palm forward to indicate a truce, so he and Faolan might talk. It took a moment before his fellow laird mimicked the gesture and rode forward.

"Let's hope yer luck holds," Shaw muttered. "I admit I did a few things when we returned from smoothing things over with the Grants that I've nae received absolution for."

"It's me the man wants to run through. I believe yer soul is safe, at least until ye go seeking that absolution."

His man tugged on the corner of his bonnet before Broen let his stallion have his freedom.

"Ye're a bloody poor excuse for a friend, Broen MacNicols," Faolan snarled.

Broen leaned over the neck of his stallion and shot Faolan a sharp look. "I believe I said the same thing to ye when ye claimed me captive and planned to present her to our uncle when ye did none of the fetching."

Faolan snorted. "I had a fine reason. One I'd expect ye to understand. Our friendship is longer than most."

"But we forgot that when it came to the matter of fair Daphne MacLeod. Look at ye, man, ye're ready to challenge me while reminding me how long we've been friends, and I was doing the same before she was taken from us. But I've had to admit recently that I was fighting over her worth and not the lass herself," Broen muttered. Faolan opened his mouth but shut it without making his argument. The need to disagree flickered in his eyes but he resisted it and drew in a deep breath before replying.

"Ye're correct. I've nae truly thought about it but I was ready to strangle ye over her." His expression tightened. "I still am."

"I'm ashamed to look back at the way we were behaving," Broen responded.

Faolan's captains were getting restless, easing forward to protect their laird as the night wind carried their raised voices to where the Chisholms retainers

waited. Broen's men were looking no more at ease.
The day had worn everyone's nerves raw.

"Ye rode all the way up here to carry on the fight. Do
ye have tender feelings for her or just for her dowry?"

Faolan shook his head. "A fair-enough question.
Ye rubbed me temper, and no mistake. Why have
ye become so content with the situation? Ye left for
England intent on vengeance, as I recall."

"Aye, but I also went to prevent a threat of a
bloody feud."

Faolan's eyes narrowed. "Ye've gone soft for that
York bastard."

"Her name is Clarrisa," he snapped. "And I am no'
soft for her."

"Then why the sudden insight into our sins over
Daphne?" Faolan challenged.

"All right, Clarrisa is responsible for some of me
change in thinking, but I've only known the woman
a short time. Do nae be casting any ideas at me that
include affection for her."

Faolan opened his mouth, but Broen cut him off.
"No' just yet, man. I'm no' adjusting to knowing a
woman can twist me feelings."

"All right, no' now," Faolan agreed.

Broen nodded. "Now, let us get on to what needs
doing. Since ye're here and me friend, I need a favor
from ye."

Faolan's eyebrows rose. "A favor? It's ye who owes
me for slipping out of me castle—"

Broen grinned, and his friend cursed.

"Ye're an arrogant bastard, Broen MacNicols."
He sighed. "What do ye want? And do nae tell me

ye do nae want something from me, for I know the look well. But I can see ye do nae want to ask me, so I'm curious what it is ye want badly enough ye'd ask another man to do it."

"Ye're a smug bastard," Broen countered.

"But I'm correct tonight."

Broen ground his teeth so hard his jaw ached, but there was no help for it. "I need ye to fetch Clarrisa back for me."

Faolan appeared stunned, surprise flickering in his eyes. "Ye mean to say ye've lost the little lass?" He chuckled before tossing his head back and laughing loudly enough to send his men to stroking their beards in contemplation of just what the two might be discussing.

"Kael Grant has returned, and his sister helped Clarrisa escape me keep, while I was up listening to the man explain why I should nae run him through over me father's death."

Faolan sobered. "What did he have to say?"

"Something I'm still contemplating, but it's worthy of stepping back. I'm nae feuding with the Grants for the moment. But that will only stand if I get Clarrisa back. I can go after Kael meself—"

"But it would be far simpler for me to pay the man back for using his sister to do ye a disservice."

Broen nodded. "Exactly. One deception deserves another. Do it for me, and I'll see ye get the opportunity to settle accounts with Daphne."

"How do ye plan to do that?"

Broen tilted his head to one side. "She's inside Deigh."

"She's what?" Faolan growled. "Do nae think to fool me so easily."

Broen stared his friend straight in the eyes. "Ye asked me why I noticed how we'd been fighting over the lass. It was Daphne who pointed it out to me. Kael brought his sister along this morning, and I set her inside me keep while I listened to Kael make his peace. She took a waiting woman, who turned out to be Daphne. Seems she ran to the convent to avoid seeing ye and me at each other's throats. I'm ashamed to admit she was less foolish than both of us."

Faolan simply stared at him for a long moment. "That damned woman needs to be—"

"Respected for thinking about both of us above her own future. I'll be annulling my contract with her. She swears she will nae wed me, because of the harm it does our relationship. Daphne MacLeod has grown into a woman with good sense."

Faolan wanted to argue, but he clamped his mouth shut and his face turned red. "Ye're right. May Christ kick me in the balls, but ye're right." He shook his head. "Daphne is right." He suddenly started laughing. "But I'm damned happy to hear she's alive. Maybe I can sleep again."

"I will nae rest until I have Clarrisa back. Ye can help me or no', but I'm going to regain her."

Faolan studied him for a long moment. "Now ye are the one sounding insane. She's a woman ye've known for a single week. What does it matter if Kael has her?"

"It matters to me because I brought her here, and I will nae see the woman's blood spilled. I stole her to keep a feud from beginning, no' so someone could slit her throat because they believe she's too dangerous to remain among the living."

Faolan nodded. "Aye, I can see yer way of thinking. There is no honor in allowing the little English lass to fall into the wrong hands, and I'm sure I do nae need another ghost keeping me from me rest. Yer Clarrisa may be English, but she has a fire in her that could see her materializing in our hallways if we let her be murdered. I'll see what I can do about getting Kael to welcome me into his keep."

Faolan rode back to his men. Broen watched him go, frustration threatening to drive him insane. But he controlled the urge to ride after Kael. He wasn't a man who enjoyed letting others do things for him, but the world was becoming a bigger place. No clan survived without alliances and making the most of those connections. Kael Grant was unpredictable. For the moment, he had Clarrisa, and the man knew Faolan had been fighting with him over Daphne.

Faolan had a much better chance of making it into Kael's tower. One Broen wasn't sure he had. If he rode up to the gates of Bronach Tower, Kael would know for certain he wanted Clarrisa back. Such an action would expose his Achilles' heel, something a wise laird never did, not even with a man he considered his ally.

But it meant he was reduced to placing his faith in another. When it came to Clarrisa, he didn't care for waiting.

He scoffed at himself, trying to counsel his emotions. There were many reasons for leaving Clarrisa with Kael. With the snow gone, the royalists would no doubt be moving to gain access to the prince. He should be focused on the battle looming ahead. Blood was going to flow; he didn't doubt it. The fact that Clarrisa had been brought to the king would no doubt be even more incentive for the two sides to clash. James had always been too close to the English for any Scotsman to tolerate. Trying to breed himself an English, royal-blooded heir was inexcusable when the man had legitimate sons.

Aye, he should be focused on the powder keg his country was. Instead, he was looking across the hills toward Grant land and cursing Kael for taking Clarrisa.

Actually, she had left of her own free will. The knowledge stung.

He should leave her to the fate she'd chosen, but the kiss she'd given him at sunrise still burned. She was still a prize.

His prize.

Six

"DO YE BELIEVE YE MADE THE CORRECT CHOICE, Clarrisa of the York family?"

Clarrisa stiffened but controlled the urge to jump. She turned smoothly to face Kael Grant. Why was it all Highlanders seemed to be huge? Kael was leaning against the doorway, looking relaxed, but there was a sharpness in his gaze that betrayed just how on guard he was.

"Your sister seemed to agree it was the best action."

Kael grinned, and the expression gave him a rakish appearance. "Which surprised me, for me sister has a wild streak in her." His eyes flashed a warning at her. "I expect Nareen would stay with her lover no matter the circumstances. No matter what I thought of it."

Clarrisa ordered herself not to blush. Kael Grant would not see her jumping at the bait he so skillfully dangled in front of her nose. "Then you are accusing your sister of being selfish and considering no one but herself. I doubt she would thank you for such, and I disagree with you. Your sister did not strike me as a disloyal person."

"Thank ye, Clarrisa. As ye can see, men bluster

just as often here in Scotland as they do in England,"
Nareen announced from somewhere in the stairwell.
Kael laughed, tipping his head back and filling the
chamber with the sound of his amusement. His sister
appeared, clearly vexed by his demeanor.

"And females try the patience of their kin here in
Scotland too," Kael added with a dry hint of sarcasm.

"Aye, for ye see, if I were his mistress, he'd label
me spirited," Nareen announced with a toss of her
hair and not a single hint of remorse for the indecent
nature of her comment.

"Obedience has its place in a mistress," Kael
muttered suggestively.

Nareen frowned, her cheeks flushing with color
at last, but she shook it off quickly. "Get on with ye,
Brother mine." She aimed a solid blow at his arm, and
he recoiled from her but grinned, making fun of her
attempts to chastise him.

Two retainers followed Nareen, carrying a bathing
tub between them. Nareen directed them with a
confident gesture. The men set the tub down and
tugged on the corner of their knit bonnets, but they
were trying to sneak peeks at Clarrisa while offering
respect to their mistress.

"Enough, ye rogues," Nareen muttered. "I've a
mind to go tell the priest about yer roguish peeping."
They offered another tug to Kael before disappearing.

"Ye're a harsh lass, Nareen. I pity the man who
weds ye."

Nareen propped her hands onto her hips as a line
of boys came into the solar with yokes across their
shoulders bearing buckets of water to fill the tub.

"Oh, do ye now? And but a moment ago I thought I heard ye declaring to all how I'd stay with me lover."

One of the boys dropped his bucket, splashing water onto the floor. Kael watched the lad try to mop up the mess while his fingers fumbled.

"If any member of this family is bound for shaming our mother, it will no doubt be ye, Kael. Now get ye gone. This is women's work," Nareen declared.

Kael pushed his lower lip out into a pout, which looked ridiculous on a grown man.

But Clarrisa laughed. "I agree with you, Nareen. Best to begin praying for his soul now. He looks in need of redemption."

Kael raised one finger. "If ye want to know me transgressions, lass, well remember the scriptures do warn ye no' to judge, which means ye'll be needing to be me partner in sin, if ye intend to be in the proper position to accuse me."

"I've been in your Highlands long enough to know pretty manners will not help me survive here. Save your bragging for a woman interested in what you have to offer her. I am going to bathe," Clarrisa informed him.

"Maybe I'm interested in viewing what ye have to offer me." His voice had dipped and was edged with suggestion.

"It would be a waste of your time, unless you have a taste for forcing yourself on women."

He straightened, the amusement fading from his face. She'd offended his honor, but she didn't back down. Her chin remained level as he aimed a hard stare at her.

"So ye have courage, Clarrisa of the York family, something I can admire and it explains why Broen has no' sent ye north." Something flickered in his eyes that sent a shiver down her spine. The man was pure devilment—she doubted there was anything on earth that he feared.

"So now that ye have the information ye wanted, Brother, get ye gone," Nareen insisted.

His lips twitched again, and satisfaction appeared in his eyes. "Ye judged me correctly, Nareen." He kept his eyes on Clarrisa as he spoke and actually reached up to tug on the side of his bonnet before he disappeared.

Another ripple of sensation traveled through her, but this one was warm. Many would label her a fool for enjoying the man's approval, but she did.

"Men," Nareen muttered. "I fail to understand what God was thinking when he created them." One of the maids sputtered. She was young and stared at her mistress.

"When there are no men about, we may be truthful at last," Nareen informed the girl. "They have no tolerance for it, though. Best ye remember that."

Clarrisa laughed. "Your brother might be an exception. I believe he was amused by my insults."

Nareen shrugged. "Possibly. But he's here so rarely, I forget he is entertained by me more than he is offended."

The maids had placed two large kettles on hooks and pushed them into the hearth where they'd built a fire. Water was beginning to boil and escaping over the top. The drops sizzled on the sides of the hot metal. Another set of footsteps was heard on the stairs, and Nareen waited while a woman entered with a clàrsach.

Clarrisa stared at the small harp. "Really, you need not pamper me. I am not a princess."

"Ah... but ye need no' tell anyone such and deprive us of the chance to listen to our harper while we work." The women in the solar laughed good-naturedly as Nareen began to unlace the back of her gown.

A woman set the wooden harp on a small table and pulled a stool up close to play it. She drew her fingers along the strings, producing a magical sound before she began to expertly use the different tones to produce a melody. The chamber began to fill with the sounds of the clàrsach. Clarrisa discovered her toe tapping in time with the tune. There was nothing barbaric about the clarsàch. Yet another thing she'd been raised to believe of Highland customs that wasn't proving true. More than one English noble had attempted to outlaw the clarsàch because it was deeply rooted in Celtic tradition.

"Pleasing, is nae it?" Nareen muttered. She took the dress when it was lifted off Clarrisa and twirled around in a circle in time with the tune. The blue wool fluttered before she allowed one of the maids to take it from her and hang it up.

Clarrisa battled against the urge to hug herself and keep her underrobe on.

"Do nae be so modest. We're all women here."

Clarrisa looked at the chamber door. "I wish there was a bar there."

Nareen laughed. "Because of me brother? Aye,

I know the feeling of wanting to ensure he cannae sneak up on ye." She came forward and helped lift the over robe up from the front. "Do nae worry. I'll deal with him. Besides, Kael has as much boldness as arrogance. He'll no' resort to peeping. There is one of the few things I am sure about when it comes to me brother's nature."

Clarrisa laughed softly. Nareen raised an eyebrow, doubling Clarrisa's laughter. "I actually feel sorry for your brother now. You are a good match for him."

Nareen scoffed. "Do nae. He's a true rogue. Whatever I might do to him, he's earned it in one way or another." There was a sizzle and a splash as the hot water was added to the tub.

"Now in with ye, before it cools. Hot baths do nae remain hot very long here."

Clarrisa realized she was becoming more at ease without her clothing. She stepped into the tub while contemplating the wicked thought. It was really more of an idea, one that had to do with her confidence.

She admitted to enjoying her body. Such a confession would surely gain her a judgment of being sinful, but it was no less true. In spite of a childhood spent being instructed to abhor pleasure of the flesh, no shame prickled across her conscience as the maids helped to bathe her.

It had been delightful to be in Broen's bed.

Tears burned her eyes, and she drew in a stiff breath to dispel them. She had done what was best. That knowledge seemed of little comfort, but she'd continued to remind herself of her reasons and hope time would ease the pain of parting. It wasn't right that she longed for a man she'd known for so little time.

But he knew you more intimately than any other…

She held off the tears until Nareen and the maids were gone. Wearing another dress she did not own, she stood in front of the window, looking out at the day. She had no idea what to do with herself.

Lytge Sutherland growled, "Can no one complete a simple task these days?"

His eldest son peered at him without comment.

"Mind the way ye judge me with yer eyes, Norris. The day will come soon enough when ye'll have to be thinking how every little choice will affect ye and yer holdings."

"I was nae judging ye."

"But ye were nae agreeing with me, boy," Lytge insisted with a soft growl.

Norris sat forward. There was an unmistakable maturity about him, and his body was definitely a man's. Lytge took a large swallow of ale, wondering where the years had gone.

"Aw… do nae say it, Norris. I'm in a foul temper, but I've no' changed me mind on wanting only honesty between us. There are lairds aplenty who will shine me ass and tell me it smells of spring heather, but no' many who will speak the truth."

"Well now… A few more weeks into spring and with the right lass for company, ye might get yer backside to smell of heather."

The maid serving the high table dropped her

pitcher, spilling amber ale across the polished surface of the wood. His father pounded it with his fist, sending the wide-eyed girl fleeing from what she perceived as her laird's displeasure.

Norris waited, an eyebrow raised as his father glared at him. "Maybe no' that lass. She's a bit skittish still. Give her a few years to gain some confidence. I'll see what I can do to help her along."

Lytge sputtered before losing the battle to hide his amusement. "Ye're a wicked boy, Norris. I hear the priests battle between them to see which of their number is forced to suffer yer confessions."

"It's more a matter of which one of them gets the enjoyment of the entertainment I bring to their dull duties."

Lytge sucked in too much ale and choked. "I'm going to end up building them a new wing to the cathedral to save yer soul from damnation."

Another maid arrived to wipe up the mess, this one showing more cleavage than the last. She leaned over while cleaning, offering Norris a clear view of her breasts, before taking her soiled linens away with a sway of her hips.

"Someone has to give these lasses the attention they crave."

"Well, that one will have to find another tonight," Lytge grunted. "I need ye to ride down to MacNicols land and fetch that York lass here. She's got connections to powerful men."

Norris lost his teasing demeanor. "Broen MacNicols is a good man, one I trust. If he has the lass in his keeping, the king will nae succeed with his scheme."

"It is too risky to leave the matter open. Better to have her here, where we control whom she lies down with."

Norris's expression darkened. "Say what ye mean, Father. If ye distrust the man, be plain with me. If ye're hinting at me taking her as a bride, say so. Ye are nae the only one who craves honesty between us."

Father and son faced off for a long moment before Lytge lowered his voice.

"I distrust the situation. Broen MacNicols is free from his contract with the MacLeod lass. He stepped up and stole the York lass, for which I'm grateful. Besides, maybe I'm thinking of wedding the lass meself. Old Lindsey cannae boast such a blue-blooded wife, and I would enjoy putting the man down."

"And Broen MacNicols has no reason to leave the lass untasted." Norris chuckled softly. "Are ye sure ye trust me to deliver her untouched?"

Lytge leaned forward with a smirk on his lips. "No' if ye're any true son of mine. But if it troubles ye, as I said, maybe I'll wed her meself. I can sure think of more vexing ways to needle old Laird Lindsey. Wedding a royal-blooded lass would be one slight I'd enjoy giving."

Norris threw his head back and laughed. Plenty of his men watched, but they knew to stay below the high table. Men of his father's station always had to fear a spy, even from among their own clan members. All it would take was a cousin who had been married into another clan at some point to turn one of the loyal retainers into a source of information during a family feast while the ale flowed freely. So his father and he kept their conversations private.

He pushed back from the table. "As ye command, most respected Father."

Lytge rubbed his hands together while watching his son stride down the hallway.

Norris was pure Highlander, the long pleats of his kilt swaying as he walked. His men fell into step behind him, their scabbards empty because swords were forbidden in the hall. That fact hardly reduced them to being harmless. He chuckled softly and reached for his ale. He was proud to know his retainers hid dirks and other small weapons on their persons. They were Highlanders, which meant they were always ready to defend themselves and their clan. But he was an earl and knew well how to make sure his family fortune was maintained. He'd set his secretary to drafting a letter to Henry Tudor of England demanding a fair dowry for the York bastard. The new king might be irate over the demand, but he'd pay up or risk seeing Lytge wed the girl to one of Henry's rivals instead of keeping her so far north.

Aye, that would do the trick, all right. Henry would rather have the girl secure in the Highlands, making an ally of the Sutherlands rather than breeding up another generation of Yorks to hassle Henry in his old age. If her children were Highlanders, they'd spit on the throne of England.

The serving wench returned, this time offering him a view of her ample chest as she filled his goblet. She didn't shy away from looking him in the eye while she served him and offered him a smile full of suggestion. Perhaps there were benefits to having a grown son to see to some of the important matters, after all.

"Come serve me in me study, lass..."

Her eyelids lowered, and her cheeks brightened. "As ye like, my laird."

Oh, he liked. Lytge felt a surge of satisfaction moving through him that made him feel twenty years younger. He envied his son the conquest he was embarking on, but also grinned at the idea of his lad rising to the challenge. An English lass would no' be simple to lure into bed, but Norris was a master of seduction. A skill he'd learned from his father, Lytge was proud to know. The serving lass appeared only moments after he sat down behind his desk. Her linen cap was missing, and her hair lay like shimmering moonlight across her shoulders. Beneath his kilt, his cock hardened.

Yes, everything was going to be perfect.

Including his afternoon.

∼

"I will freeze in this dress."

Kael Grant looked up but only grinned at his sister's disgruntlement.

Nareen snarled softly, earning a chuckle from her brother. The silk dress rustled when she moved. The soft, delicate shoes looked like they belonged on the feet of a fairy, and she discovered herself longing for wings to help her avoid feeling the chill of the stone floors in the hallways.

"We've guests tonight, ones worthy of pomp and circumstance," Kael reminded her.

Clarrisa used measured steps to move closer to him to reduce the amount of sound coming from her garments. She'd failed to understand just how much work it was to be a queen. Just walking across the court was an effort, and if you failed, the gossips would be sure to repeat your lack of grace.

"Then where is your finery, Laird Grant?"

He frowned. "This is me best kilt, woman. Do nae they teach ye in England what finery looks like in the Highlands?" But his doublet was still only made of leather and the sleeves were hanging behind his back.

"What me brother is saying in his normal brash manner is that he thinks Highlanders above such things as pomp. At least when it comes to clothing," Nareen announced from the doorway. Frustration edged her tone as she joined them with the same careful stride Clarrisa had adopted. "Which is grossly unfair," Nareen accused her sibling. "If I have to suffer these ridiculous clothes, so should ye."

Kael reached out and cuffed her gently on the chin. "One of us has to be ready to keep Norris Sutherland from ravishing the pair of ye."

"Some proper clothing would assist better," Clarrisa announced. Her dress was beautiful, and she'd honestly never worn one to equal it. It was made of jade silk and the back of it flowed behind her. Wide cuffs of lace were set to the sleeves, while more of the rare embellishment ran around the neckline and down the center of the bodice. Even if you made the bobbin lace yourself, it was made with gold wire floss. Hundreds of hours would have been needed to produce the amount adorning the dress. A border of velvet edged the bottom of the gown, too.

Kael surveyed her from head to toe, his gaze slipping over the way the soft silk outlined the curves of her breasts and hips. Heat flickered in his eyes, sending her back a pace.

"Nae, lass, I disagree. Ye are exactly what I need to keep Norris attentive to the supper I'm fixing to serve him."

"Well, ye do nae need me," Nareen announced with a rustle as she turned toward the doorway.

"Stay, Sister. Yer presence is required because ye are the daughter of the laird. Ye'll take yer place as surely as I will, since the son of our overlord is here."

Gone was all trace of teasing in Kael's tone. It was interesting to see how quickly the man could become formidable. Interesting, but it sent a shiver down her spine too. Clarrisa held her silence while brother and sister battled. It was truly a skirmish, for neither wanted to bend. She saw the solid laird Kael was and had so cleverly hidden behind his playful facade.

Nareen flounced back into the room, her silk skirts rustling like a pile of autumn leaves. "I detest it when ye are correct."

Kael lifted her chin and placed a sedate kiss against her cheek. "But I adore ye when ye apply that clever wit of yers to doing what is best for the family."

Jealousy caught Clarrisa by surprise, the hot ripple of longing flashing through her. There had been cousins aplenty in the house where she was raised, but she'd never had any she considered her friends. Only a few dim memories remained of times when she had trusted one of those relations with her true feelings only to experience the pain of betrayal when they told every word of her confessions to her uncle. She'd learned to keep her own counsel early.

"I see yer sister has outgrown her nurse."

The newcomer was a lighter-haired man with hints of copper. His eyes were a startling green that he aimed directly at Clarrisa.

"As if ye're paying any attention to me at all," Nareen groused in a tone so honey sweet it was almost comical. "I could be covered in warts and ye have nae noticed, with the way ye're staring at me, friend."

"I wager there is nae a wart on yer fair skin," their company answered while turning his attention to her. "But I insist on being sure of me facts."

"Ye may insist all ye like, Norris Sutherland, but I am nae impressed with yer father's title, so do nae be relying on it to get this dress off me."

He closed the distance between them and offered Nareen his hand. She placed hers in it, and he lifted it to his lips. But at the last instant he turned her hand over and placed a kiss against the delicate skin of her inner wrist. She lost her composure for a moment, only the briefest of time, before shaking her head.

"Enough, ye rogue." Nareen's voice had turned husky. She jerked her hand away and retreated with a rustle of silk. "I am still nae impressed."

Norris chuckled and offered her a low bow. "Ye never have been, but I still try me luck."

Clarrisa felt a tingle of loneliness move through her. The playful nature surrounding her only seemed to illuminate just how much of a stranger she was.

"This is Norris Sutherland, eldest son of the Earl of Sutherland," Kael announced. "Which is a true shame, for the earl will no doubt be angry with me for running him through…" Kael shrugged. "But there is naught I can do since he's offended me sister."

"Do nae blame me for yer barbaric impulses, Kael."

Norris had her fixed in his sights once more. There was a flicker of satisfaction in his gaze.

"Delighted to meet ye, Clarrisa."

Her name rolled off his tongue with an ease that set her suspicions to boiling. The man was pleased, too pleased for her comfort. He offered her his hand and she laid hers in it. But the smile she gave him when he took the liberty of kissing her inner wrist was equal to his own. She felt nothing more than fleeting enjoyment. It was gone almost in the same moment it happened, and she had no trouble offering Norris a disinterested look.

"Indeed, it is a pleasure to meet you."

She sank down, offering him the rehearsed gesture her uncle so often demanded. What made it bearable was the fact that she meant it not at all. It was merely a public nicety she performed without anyone knowing her true lack of sincerity. Except something flickered in Norris's eyes that she avoided looking at too closely.

"Come, Norris. Me father has had the cook running her staff to near insanity with preparations for yer welcome feast." Kael walked between his guest and Clarrisa, taking her hand and placing it on top of his hand. "Escort me sister. It will give me father something to hound ye about throughout supper, so I may have some peace."

"All the better to flirt with Clarrisa," Norris remarked, but he was happily stalking Nareen. She tossed her head and looked surprised by her own action. She frowned before stomping toward Norris and giving him her hand.

"Let Father say what he will."

Norris chuckled softly. "Sweet lass, with a chill such as that in yer tone, I just might agree to whatever terms yer father offers, because it would grant me the right to woo ye."

Nareen scoffed at him. "Ye would never wed such a lowly woman as myself."

Norris was escorting her down the hallway while Kael pulled Clarrisa along behind them.

"Ye think not?"

Nareen nodded, the torches set to light the passageway making the waves in her unbound hair shimmer. "Yer family has a long tradition of wedding with an eye on advancement. Ye're here because we have the daughter of a king beneath our roof."

"My sister is overly blunt," Kael remarked.

They'd reached the doors of the great hall, and musicians began playing.

"But truthful," Norris remarked with a touch of bitterness. "I'm no' sure if I am more relieved to hear it so plainly or tempted to go home to me father with a different bride than he sent me for." Nareen tried to jerk her hand away but he held her fingers. "Do ye think ye are the only one who likes to do the unpredictable?"

"But then ye'd have me in yer bed," Nareen informed him sweetly.

Norris made a choking sound. "A good point. If I'm going to suffer a match I've little taste for behind the bed-curtains, I'd rather have a match my father would be pleased with. A man needs some happiness in his life after all."

He turned to survey Clarrisa with a cunning look.

There was no more chance for conversation as the music rose. The hall was filled with Grant retainers and their families. Faces were freshly scrubbed, and most of the men had on their doublet sleeves. There were candles in abundance, all illuminating those watching their progress toward the high table at the end of the hall. Little girls gasped and pointed at the way the candlelight danced off the silk dresses. All the while, the music of the harps and bagpipes surrounded them.

It was a moment fit for royalty. When they passed, row by row, the spectators lowered themselves. Norris accepted their deference with a nod and a grace worthy of admiration. At the end of the main aisle was the high table. It was set for a platform, and Donnach Grant stood waiting for them.

"Welcome to ye, Norris Sutherland. 'Tis a fine day indeed now that ye are supping beneath me roof."

Servants pulled the chairs out for them, and Clarrisa looked down at the fine silver plateware.

She preferred the wooden plates at Deigh Tower.

It was becoming annoying the way she thought of Broen so often. She needed to focus her mind on her future. Norris offered an excellent opportunity, for he might offer her marriage and legitimacy for her children.

A lump formed in her throat as she contemplated sharing the man's bed.

Oh for Christ's sake… Love has truly stolen your wits!

Just as Maud had predicted, it would be foolish

enough to allow herself to fall... well, to form an attraction to any man. She'd not admit it was love. No, she most certainly would not.

Liar...

❦

"Come with me." Nareen appeared out of the shadows, her voice startling Clarrisa. Nareen had her skirts gathered up so they couldn't rustle.

"Where are you taking me?" Clarrisa demanded.

Nareen lifted a finger and placed it in front of her lips. She moved closer so they might talk in whispers. "I was nae only taunting Norris. He was sent here by his father for ye."

"He confessed that to you?"

Nareen shook her head. "But I feel it is so. If ye want to be his trophy wife, I'll leave ye to it. Me father can continue to enjoy the goodwill of the Sutherlands if I do nae help ye."

"Why would you help me?" Clarrisa demanded. Maybe the fine wine served with the meal had softened her wits, because she couldn't understand what Nareen had to gain from her offer. Or even what the Scottish girl was proposing. "You're the one who convinced me to leave Deigh Tower because there was no hope of a bright future for me."

"I know, but I've changed me mind," Nareen muttered as she looked down the hallway and gestured for Clarrisa to follow. The men were drinking whisky in the laird's study now.

Nareen disappeared into a dark corridor. Clarrisa hesitated, torn between her desire to know what the girl offered and the reasons she'd left Broen. Her curiosity won.

"What…"

"Hush… We need escape before Norris comes after us. Do nae doubt he will; for all his teasing, he is his father's son. He'll do what is best for the Sutherland. Take home a bride his father will be pleased with and force ye to suffer his mistress because he has no affection for ye." Nareen stopped and pulled Clarrisa close. "It's yer choice, but for meself, I want more from my life than to be bred like a prized mare."

"That is not how you felt when you revealed Broen's betrothed to me." It hurt to say the truth.

You do love him…

Be quiet!

Nareen pulled her down the passageway and on through several others. Clarrisa shivered as the temperature dropped. She smelled the river and shivered again, the thin silk dress failing to protect her.

"Here," Nareen announced at last. "Behind this door is an escape tunnel. It goes beneath the river and will likely be colder than ice."

"You haven't explained why you're doing this."

"Because of the sound of joy in yer voice right now. I saw the way ye looked at me and Kael, like ye'd never experienced a family sharing love. It shamed me, for ye were happy until I shattered yer joy by telling ye Daphne was contracted to Broen."

"She still is."

"Aye," Nareen admitted in a soft tone. "I do nae know what to tell ye to do about Broen MacNicols, but I do know I've no liking for watching the way Norris

Sutherland is contemplating ye with all the calculations of a secretary making sure his columns of numbers add up. So I'm offering ye the choice to leave. Maybe ye want to go back up there and take the position of his wife because it will grant ye respectability, but I believe it a false title, for he'll never be faithful to ye."

"And you want more from life." Clarrisa could hear it in her voice.

Nareen offered a dry laugh. "Pitiful, I know, but I want something more. Something I saw dying in yer eyes when I told ye so bluntly who Daphne is. I let me brother talk me into forgetting about what I've come to feel is more important in this life."

There was a soft sigh. "Well… that's me offer. Go now, or get back upstairs and make sure ye do nae lose the opportunity to make Norris Sutherland dance to yer tune."

Such temptation. Clarrisa watched Nareen hunch down and fiddle with a latch in the dark. The only light came through the arrow slits, and it was meager indeed.

What did she want? Maybe the better question to ask was what did she wish to avoid the most?

"The chance to belong to no one but myself was offered…"

Edme's words rose from her memory, filling her with determination. "I am sick unto death of being what everyone demands of me."

When Nareen stood, Clarrisa embraced her, hugging her tight because she just couldn't hold back the urge.

"I swear you are more treasured to me than any blood kin, Nareen. I have nothing, but if the day comes when I can repay your kindness, I shall."

"Forgive me for tearing yer heart and convincing ye to leave Deigh Tower. It made a hypocrite of me, and I hate myself for it." Nareen squeezed her hard for a moment before pushing her away. "Get on with ye. I can do no more than show ye the way out. There will be cloaks inside, but no light. Ye'll need yer courage to make it to the other side, for it will be pitch-black. The sort that plays with yer reasoning, making ye think there are daemons in there with ye."

She held out a folded parchment. "Take this. Go to the village beyond the woods and seek out me old nurse. She lives beyond the church at the edge of the village. Keep the cloak closed over that silk until ye find her. Her sons will give ye escort back to Broen if ye give her that letter. She will know it comes from me and will do me this service. Good luck to ye."

The doorway was small, only two feet high. The silk dress was a hassle but she made it and Nareen closed the door behind her.

It was cold. Maybe it was the blackness, but Clarrisa shivered and was sure the sensation traveled to the deepest parts of her soul. Panic tried to seize control of her. It sent her heart pounding, and sweat began to bead on her skin.

Courage!

She reached for the walls, smiling when she felt them. Moving along, she searched for the cloaks and found one. She shied away from thinking about how dirty they might be, telling herself they were only musty from lack of fresh air. At least the one she donned was thick. She raised the hood to help warm her head and began walking.

How far was it?

She started to count, for at least it would tell her how far back the door was if she lost her nerve.

You will not!

She swallowed the lump forming in her throat and focused all her attention on counting. She would not allow her mind to think of anything except the numbers; that way, she'd not have the chance to change her mind.

One… two… three… four…

❧

Someone pounded on his door.

Broen sat up, ripping the covers off in a motion so violent he heard the sheet tear.

"Come in."

He pulled a shirt over his head before realizing what he planned to do. Edme had already pleated his kilt, and he grasped the ends of the belt.

Edme entered, a parchment in her fingers. "Norris Sutherland is at Bronach."

Dread twisted his insides. There would only be one reason Norris would be so far south. The man was hunting for a prize.

Clarrisa.

"Tell no one else."

"But…" Edme argued, "it is nae safe for ye to ride out alone."

"One glimpse of me riding with me men and Norris will know what I'm coming for. The only chance is for me to try and sneak into Bronach."

He knew how, but only because Edme had told him of the escape route out of the Grant stronghold.

Lacing his boots took enough time to drive him mad with frustration. Each second felt too long, like a nightmare he couldn't fight his way free of.

His sword slid easily into its scabbard, and he ducked his head under the thick leather harness to settle the large weapon across his back, Highland-style. The keep was silent; the two men set to watch the lower hallway sat near the hearth where they rolled dice to pass the time.

Broen walked past them, making no more sound than a specter. The stable lads were all sleeping with their plaids pulled up over their heads. His skin was hot from the accelerated pace of his heart.

The gate guards were wide awake. They peered down at him.

"Lift it."

They complied, only pausing to consider what was happening after he rode through the gate and no one followed. By the time they realized the laird had left the castle without his escort, the night had swallowed him. The clouds moved to hide the moon, making it impossible to catch sight of him. The captain was going to strangle them both for sure.

Two hundred twenty-four… Two hundred twenty-five… Two hundred twenty-six…

Clarrisa ground her teeth so hard, she expected them to shatter, but she continued to count.

Two hundred twenty-seven…

She hit a wall in front of her. A strangled sob rose from her throat.

Too good to be true.

Maybe she was disoriented because of the darkness. What terrified her the most was knowing the sun would never reach her in the passageway. She'd struggle to find the end until she collapsed into a heap to die in the darkness—like being entombed alive.

Stop it!

Her fingers were on a solid wall. She forced her mind to function past the paralyzing fear.

Nareen had told her she'd need courage, and she had enough to see her way back into the light. She would not die beneath ground.

She slipped her hands along the surface and bent her knees until she was near the ground. The stones gave way to smooth wood, and she shook with relief. It was so overpowering her legs gave out. She landed on her backside in a puddle of silk and musty wool.

But her fingers found the latch. It was bone-chilling cold and slick with something she decided she was better off not identifying, but it was preferable to the costly silk she wore. Smoothing her fingers back and forth along its length, she discovered the direction to move it.

The latch resisted, the damp interior of the passageway having corroded it. She struggled and her breathing increased, but it refused to budge. Courage had seen her to the door, but she needed fate's blessing to make it to freedom. Or perhaps some clear thinking.

Leaning her back against the wall, she struggled to move the silk skirts aside and raise her foot. She wedged it against the latch, gritting her teeth as the delicate slippers offered her little protection. She drew a deep breath and shoved with all her might. Pain bit into her, threatening to steal the strength from her knee, but she persisted. Her cry echoed along the passageway, the pain becoming white-hot. The latch slid.

She cried out again, this time with joy. She scrambled out of the way so she might pull the door open. Desperation drove her to yank hard on the door, even though one of her fingernails began to tear. It was worth the effort.

The night was dark, but not as pitch-black as the passageway. She crawled out, tearing her skirt as she pushed with her feet to propel her body out of what had felt like a tomb. She collapsed onto the dirt, breathing in the fresh air as though it had been years since she'd smelled it.

Thank you… thank you… thank you…

Clarrisa wasn't sure who she sent her gratitude to. God? Fate? Nareen? Or perhaps herself for refusing to allow her fear to rule her. It didn't matter.

She forced herself to stand. She'd come out in the forest a short way from Bronach Tower. She could see the fires along the battlements twinkling like stars.

The woods should have frightened her. There were sounds all around her: the scrabbling of something and the whistle of the wind. But she seemed to have no fear left in her. It felt like it had washed away, leaving her content in a deep sort of way she couldn't completely understand.

Yet it felt miraculous. Empowering and confidence-filling—as if she could do anything she pleased without the fear of failure.

Now all she need do was decide what she wanted. The question confounded her as she closed the door and began walking.

The only thing she was sure of was that she wanted away from Norris Sutherland. She was a thing to him, a material possession. The knowledge stung even more when she recalled how charming he'd been with Nareen.

Many would call her a fool for longing for Broen instead of taking the chance to be claimed by the heir of an earl.

Well... not Edme.

She smiled as she thought of the woman who had borne Broen. Satisfaction filled her as the lights of Bronach Tower faded. She had no idea how long a walk it was to the village, and she began to shiver.

She heard a horse and somehow decided it was Broen. Maybe she was too cold, or perhaps she'd collapsed in the tunnel and was only dreaming of freedom. People went mad in the Highlands at night. The dark hours were the time when witches and ghosts reigned supreme.

She heard the blood rushing past her ears, and the sound of the horse seemed to keep time with her heart. The rider appeared in front of her, cast in slivers of moonlight that fell in tiny, sparkling drops.

A specter... Broen... She wanted to believe he was both. Just for a moment, one perfect moment, everything was as she wished it. She felt him look at her and watched the way he pulled the stallion to a halt. Recognition rose from someplace deep inside her, someplace still warm.

Yes… Her moment of perfection.

"Broen…"

It was her last word before she slid to the ground, her strength spent. She didn't notice when her body failed, because she was locked in her moment of joy.

❧

"What would ye have of me, woman?" Shaw demanded. "Would ye have me ride up to Laird Chisholms and admit I've no idea where me laird is?"

Edme wasn't impressed with Shaw's tone. "Ye must do something. Ye're the head of me son's retainers!"

Shaw froze, along with a half dozen men near enough to hear what Edme shouted. Several younger lads serving as gillies also heard, and their eyes widened.

Edme realized what she'd said, one hand covering her lips as silence surrounded her.

Shaw recovered first. "Well, I suppose I can understand yer nerve now. But I still do nae know which direction to go looking for me laird and cannae ride out now or risk ruining the tracks he left. We'll have to wait until sunrise."

A bell began to ring from atop the gate. "Rider approaching," the guard cried out.

Shaw climbed to the top of the wall and peered over the battlement. The horse that materialized from the early-morning mist was one he thought he recognized, but a lifetime of Highland fireside tales made him question what his eyes showed him.

"It's the laird. Lift the gate," Edme cried.

He was so tense Shaw almost sent his fist into her face because her voice startled him so badly.

"Jesus Christ, woman! What are ye doing on the battlement? Have ye gone daft?"

"Ye're the one lacking sense if ye cannae see the truth which is right in front of ye," she accused.

Broen let out a whistle and several more in a prearranged pattern that sent relief through Shaw.

"Lift the gates, lad! I told ye all no' to worry. Our laird is pure Highlander, and no midnight ride could have an ill effect on him."

The gate lifted, the chains grinding loudly enough to drown out any further conversation. Shaw took the moment to breathe a sigh of relief, but when he opened his eyes, he was staring at Edme, and the muscles along his neck tightened once more.

The laird's mother?

&

"Come back to me, lass."

She smelled him, the scent of his skin. It made her smile, and she snuggled down into the warmth surrounding her.

"Clarrisa…"

She frowned, a pain stabbing through her forehead like a dagger. It grew white-hot, sending a burning pain down her spine. It radiated to every limb, not stopping until even her toes hurt. She didn't want to wake up, not to the pain. She wanted to die in her perfect moment, safe where nothing else existed.

"Ye need to allow her to rest."

Edme spoke softly, but Broen growled at her, "I must wake her. She's hiding in this fever."

"Ye cannae know such a thing."

He didn't know it; he felt it. Just as he'd felt her fear. He clamped his lips shut recalling how easily he'd condemned Faolan. He knew better now. There were ties that made no sense, connections a man couldn't rationalize or even understand. He stroked Clarrisa's scarlet cheek, feeling her slipping away from him as surely as he felt the heat of her skin against his skin.

"Come back."

She muttered something and smiled as her breathing became slower. He heard Edme smother a sob. She reached out and placed a hand on top of his.

"It's time to summon a priest."

"I refuse to give up." He reached for the hilt of the dagger tucked into the top of his boot. "And I refuse to believe Clarrisa would give up." He reached for one of her braids, clamping his teeth tight as he cut it. The second one met with the same fate as Edme nodded approvingly. She needed cooling, and her hair was only keeping her warm. It was a desperate attempt to interfere with fate, but he'd take it since it was his only sliver of hope.

Someone rapped softly on the door, and he turned to see a priest entering. Edme covered her mouth but waved the man inside.

It was a damn thin sliver of hope.

◈

The night was alive.

Clarrisa rose up, not sure how she'd lain down to begin with. It didn't matter, though. She felt so light; her feet didn't even touch the ground. It was a miraculous feeling. Around and around she twirled, until her hair floated away like a cloud, but it didn't matter because she felt so cool and free.

Nothing mattered at all.

❦

"Ye belong to me."

She jerked, trying to flee, but she was paralyzed. Norris Sutherland was no longer charming, but cold and controlling. His face transformed into her uncle's as he loomed over her.

"Ye shall do your duty."

She tried in vain to move again, but her limbs lay useless. Her mouth was parched and too dry to form any words. All she could do was wait helplessly for Norris to take what he would.

No... She wanted more... She wanted her lover...

❦

Rain fell down on her, the drops soaking into her dry tongue. She opened her mouth, greedy for more. More water slipped over her face, easing the tightness and carrying away the heat. She wanted to wake but couldn't find the strength; the task of lifting her eyelids was beyond her. So she drifted off into sleep as the rain receded.

❦

"I've come for ye, lass!" Argyll's voice pierced her slumber, shattering it into a thousand pieces.

"No!" she screamed, sitting up and kicking the bedding off her legs. "Get out of my chamber, you letch!" She stumbled across the floor to the table, fumbling to grip the first thing she felt there.

"Get out!" She hurled the pottery bowl toward the mirror, at the laughing face of Argyll. It smashed, flowing onto the floor like melted silver. "And stay away from me!"

Her entire body shook, her knees knocking together. The chamber door slammed into the wall as Broen kicked it open with such strength.

"I dealt with your ghost," she informed him before he began to chastise her. His face was twisted into an expression of amazement. "Indeed... I did."

Her throat was raw, and her legs refused to support her. All she could do was look at the floor. She was helpless to stop herself from collapsing. Broen caught her, sweeping her off her feet just as her knees buckled. He clasped her close, his arms quivering—she didn't understand why.

"What—"

"Shh... Lass, ye've been at death's door for three days..." He laid her down as gently as though she were a babe. He lifted a small cup from the bedside table and placed it to her lips. The water tasted sweet, and she grasped his hands, trying to tip it faster.

"No' too much, else it will come right back up."

She hadn't realized her eyes were closed. Broen took the cup away when Edme spoke, and she opened her eyes to search for it.

"More," she insisted.

Edme carried a single candle, but that flame was bright enough to make her eyes sting. But that wasn't the worst. She wrinkled her nose when she realized the stench she smelled was coming from herself.

"Lord... I need a bath..." Mortification gave

her the strength to lift one hand and push against Broen. "Go—"

"The stench of hell itself couldn't move me from yer side, Clarrisa." There was a tremor in his voice that drew her hand to his face. Several days of beard covered his cheek, and dark shadows hung beneath his eyes. He angled his head so her fingers cupped his jaw completely, his eyes narrowing with pleasure as he gently gripped her forearm to help her maintain the contact.

"'Tis glad I am to see ye defying what everyone expected of ye, lass." His voice caught, thick with emotion. "Right glad, indeed."

❧

"Do ye think I do nae know ye must have shown her the way out?"

Nareen stiffened, but she didn't jump. There was no need, for she'd been expecting her brother to confront her.

"I know ye are an intelligent man."

Kael moved into her chamber and sent the maids scurrying with a snap of his fingers. A quiver did shake her belly, for Kael kept his emotions hidden behind his carefree demeanor most of the time. That snap was like an outburst, a crack in his impermeable shell. He was furious.

"Ye look surprised, Sister." The door closed with a bang.

"I am. She was but an Englishwoman," Nareen offered.

"One with royal blood," Kael snapped. "Ye are nae a simpleton, Sister. If we offend the prince or the king, we could lose everything."

Nareen flipped her hand through the air, trying to dismiss the importance of the matter. "None will notice her being gone. She was barely here."

"She was here long enough. The Earl of Sutherland will know ye allowed her to go free, and it's very possible he'll assume ye could nae have possibly come up with the idea on yer own."

Nareen crossed her arms over her chest. "Is that what has yer feathers ruffled? The idea that ye shall share the blame? 'Tis the first time I've heard ye worry about gossip."

"This is nae a children's game, Nareen," Kael snapped. "Sutherland could demand ye be lashed."

"I do nae care."

He growled, "That stubbornness will nae protect ye when the leather bites into yer tender flesh, nor will it save ye from the fever that so often follows. Ye've made it impossible for me to protect ye."

Shame came at last, and it was brutal. "Och, Kael. I do owe ye an apology, for ye've always been a fine brother, but I could nae live with meself. No' when I saw the way Norris was looking at her. I just could nae stand idle while she suffered the fate I deplore so greatly."

Kael shook his head, still darkly furious. "Ye insult me, Sister. Gravely so."

Now she was confused. "I do nae understand ye."

A ghost of a grin appeared on his lips. "I would never have allowed Norris to take her. I'd have taken her down to the passage meself once I was sure Norris was settled in for the night."

He turned his back on her, but she flew after him,

hooking his arm and spinning him back around to face her.

"Then ye are misplaced to judge me so harshly simply because I found the opportunity to help her first."

His eyes were glowing with anger. She stared at the heat, mesmerized because she had only seen Kael so close to losing control once before. It was a memory she recoiled from.

"I judge ye, Sister, because it is me place to protect ye and this family." Duty edged each word. "Never once have I asked ye to suffer any ridiculous rule set down by church or state, unless it was for the continued well-being of our kin." He moved toward her, pushing her back with the sheer weight of his outrage. "And in case ye are unclear, Sister, I am talking about matters that affect where our winter food will come from or how our people will deal with the snow if they have no homes because another clan burned them in retaliation."

He froze, drawing in a deep breath. "Ye will leave matters of such importance to me, or at least bring yer ideas to me before acting upon them. Now dress warmly and get into the passageway. Me men are waiting to take ye south to Cousin Ruth."

"Ye're sending me away?" For all that she'd often told herself she wouldn't care if he was displeased with her, it stung fiercely.

"I'm hiding ye, for the guards have spotted Norris heading back this way. No doubt he's failed to find Clarrisa and is likely to demand ye be punished or taken in her place. But do nae make the mistake of thinking that means he'll wed ye. He'll take ye up north and secure ye so his father can demand anything of our father or risk knowing ye suffer for his disobedience. The Sutherlands are earls because they know how to protect their interests. Norris came for Clarrisa, and he will nae return home with naught."

She lifted her chin, refusing to allow the horror churning in her belly to show. "I'll bear whatever he demands."

"Ye shall nae." Each word sliced like a blade. "It is me duty to safeguard ye. Norris will be content with the fact that I sent ye off to an older woman for instruction, or he may have at me, but ye will respect me wishes in this matter."

"Or what?" She was playing with fire, but part of her wanted to know more about this side of her brother's personality. He kept it so private that she found herself facing a stranger.

His lips twitched into a grin, but it wasn't a pleasant expression. Instead it was full of promise. Grim, solid promise.

"I'll have ye bundled like a babe and taken away for yer own good—but I shall be the one facing Norris."

He left her while she was still stunned into silence. Her temper flared, but so did her shame. It was an odd mixture, one that dug deeply into her heart. She'd been selfish, only focused on appeasing her own feelings without realizing the repercussions that might land on her fellow clansmen. Such were the actions of a child—and she was well past the age of being excused for her tender years. Curse the nature of men.

But not her brother. Kael was correct, and she wasn't

a liar. She began to dress in warm wool clothing and
sturdy leather boots. She put a dirk in the top of her
boot before she made her way toward the passageway,
because traveling was dangerous even in the best of
times. She did smile once she was surrounded by darkness, for Cousin Ruth was anything but prim. In fact,
she was looking forward to seeing what the woman
might teach her now that she was less of a child.

It would certainly be stimulating.

Seven

"Do nae fuss about yer hair," Edme scolded.

"I'm not." But Clarrisa didn't turn away from the mirror. Her hair was chopped away at her shoulders, the ends curling upward. "I was simply amazed you trusted me with another mirror."

"Oh well, ye were no' in yer right mind when ye destroyed the last one. There was no reason to punish ye." Edme was followed by two maids, who laid out a meal on the table. "Besides, we're all still rejoicing over yer recovery."

Did that account for the fact that she hadn't seen Broen?

Clarrisa sat and kept the question to herself.

"Sweet Mary…" Edme muttered. Clarrisa looked up to see the head of house staring at her calf, where the dressing gown had flipped aside to show off one of the lace stockings she'd finished. She'd used the scarlet silk, and the contrast against her skin was stunning.

"Since you will not let me out of this room, I thought I'd wear them for a bit. It does take a long time to make them."

Edme had pressed a hand to her chest and seemed

to be considering the lace stocking intently. Her lips rose into a wicked smile.

"Seems ye should be inviting the laird to sup with ye if ye feel strong enough to wear those."

"Invite him?"

Edme raised her gaze to Clarrisa's face, and there was a firm reprimand in her eyes. "Well now, ye did leave him. A man has his pride. I do believe ye'd no' be too happy if he visited the same upon ye. So… if ye wanted to see him, it seems only correct that ye would issue an invitation."

Edme moved her attention to the maids who were straightening the bed. It provided Clarrisa the chance to contemplate what the woman had said.

Had she wounded Broen's pride?

The question made her wince because it made her sound like a milksop without a drop of confidence. She was worthy of a man being upset because she'd shunned him. What shamed her more was the fact that she had failed to consider his feelings while dwelling upon her own.

"Edme, would you please inquire of your laird if he would like to sup with me tonight?"

Edme offered her a satisfied smile. "I will do so directly."

"I think I'll go down to the bathhouse."

"Ye shall nae," Edme insisted. "A bath will be brought up."

"Edme, you are spoiling me by waiting on me." The head of house didn't appear to be even a tiny bit impressed by her pouting. "And these walls are beginning to close in on me. Have mercy and allow me a short walk to prove my legs still work."

Edme's expression softened. "I suppose that is something I cannae refuse ye without being overly harsh." Her eyes narrowed. "But I insist ye take those stockings off first. I do nae need every maid in the keep wearing those. No' a thing will ever get finished, because the men will be following them about like puppies."

Clarrisa laughed, but her tone was husky. Heat had settled in her cheeks and was flowing down to her belly. She was well rested—indeed, she felt strong and quite desperate to embrace life with a renewed vigor.

Every day was suddenly full of opportunities, ones she refused to cast aside because of someone's opinion in some faraway church or palace. But apprehension twisted her belly too. It was possible Broen would want nothing to do with her. He was a proud Highlander, one who had earned his position. She'd shunned him in front of his clan, and such was not a thing easily forgiven.

But as she began to untie the garter secured around the top of her right stocking, a wicked idea began to form in her mind. Why should she be content with gaining his approval easily?

Seduction…

She'd heard the word said in so many different tones: Hushed ones by the fireside, muttered by smiling girls with twinkling eyes. Condemning tones, spoken as a warning by a priest intent on convincing her to follow a path of piety.

She folded the stocking gently and began to undo the second. The two maids were sneaking peeks from across the chamber. Edme snapped her fingers, but the head of house also sent her a wink of approval.

Yes... seduction. Broen MacNicols had overwhelmed her and unleashed passion inside her, so
it seemed fitting to plan his downfall by the same
method. She stood and patted the two stockings gently
before going off to bathe and plan just how she was
going to bring the brute who'd stolen her to his knees.

She'd never imagined she would enjoy wickedness
so much.

⌇

It was possible he'd refuse to come. Clarrisa tried not
to dwell upon the chance of failure because it sent a
shaft of pain through her heart. But it took a great deal
of effort to avoid listing the reasons why Broen might
refuse her.

"Is there a reason ye're wearing a path across that
fine carpet, lass?" His voice still made her tremble.
Only now she smiled, freely enjoying the way she
responded to him.

"I suppose I've been inside too long."

He was clean-shaven once more, but the collar of
his shirt lay open, just as she was beginning to expect
it always to be. Indecision showed in his eyes as he
hesitated in the doorway.

"A wise course of action, considering how ill ye
managed to make yerself by running about in naught
but silk. There is a reason that flimsy fabric is worn
in Italy. The summers there are warm enough for it."
His tone snapped like a judgment, ripping through her
carefully-plotted plans for seduction.

"It was not on purpose, and I do know how to dress
properly for the weather, but it was a result of—"

"Of yer rash decision to leave me protection," he finished with a slicing motion of his hand. She drew in a harsh breath, but he didn't give her a chance to defend herself.

"If ye'd stayed here, it never would have been necessary for ye to walk through a rainy night in that fairy dress. Ye almost became one of the forest spirits, thanks to yer stupidity."

Her cheeks were burning, but not because she was finding it impossible to resist him. "Stupidity is your thinking taking me to your bed means I consider myself your personal pet who does not think of what is best for the future. You have a betrothed."

"I still do, and yet, ye invited me to sup in yer room." It felt like he'd slapped her. She wanted to gasp, but her jaw was hanging open. With a hiss, she turned her back on him.

"What do ye have on yer legs, woman?" She turned to face him, irritated by the demand in his voice.

"Lace stockings—but I'm very sure you will simply tell me how impractical they are and how much of a fool I am to wear them for your benefit." She was acting like a shrew now and didn't really care. Disappointment was cruelly shredding her newly kindled confidence. "So... never you mind what I'm wearing, Broen MacNicols. Perhaps Argyll will appreciate them, since ye prefer your betrothed."

"Do nae put words in me mouth, woman."

His tone had changed, but she was too frustrated to enjoy the victory. "Do not worry. I shall be happy to see you turn and leave before I'm foolish enough to continue with the idea of seducing you."

Surprise brightened his expression right before he laughed. The sound bounced off the chamber walls, infuriating her completely.

"Oh... get on with you! Do you think I care what you think of me? Well... I do not!" She grabbed one of the soft rounds of bread waiting on the table for their meal and threw it at him. Broen was too busy laughing, and it struck him full in the center of his chest.

He jumped and landed in a semicrouch, his hands wide and his eyes trained on her. She'd taken him by surprise, and she enjoyed the surge of satisfaction it sent through her.

"Get out, Broen. I've no more patience for you and your condemning nature."

He straightened but didn't leave. Instead he moved into the chamber and pulled the door shut behind him.

"I told you—"

"But I've no' told ye, Clarrisa, how seeing ye so near to death put me on me knees." His voice had sunk to a deep timbre that drowned the flames of her irritation. "Or that discovering ye'd left me set me thinking on just why I was so angry over yer loss."

"You only wanted your prize back." She was being surly, but her feelings stung. The pain was deeper and more persistent than any she'd ever experienced.

He moved close, his blue eyes flickering with heat. "Oh, aye... That's true enough, but no' because of who yer sire was. I wanted me lover back—me prize." He all but snarled the last two words before rushing her.

"Broen—" She squealed as he clasped her against his body. He cupped the back of her neck as he draped his other arm across her body to bind her to him. Heat swirled through her in a crazy sensation of twisting and turning. She clung to him because it was so disorienting. He was the only solid thing in her world at that moment.

"Clarrisa... stop talking."

He kissed her to enforce his will, but she kissed him back, feeling as though she had a year of longing trapped inside her. The dam burst, her emotions flooding over her, carrying away her irritation. Ordering him away was now the furthest thing from her mind.

She reached for him, threading her fingers through his hair. The need to touch him was so intense she couldn't decide where to place her hands next, only that she had to feel his skin next to hers. His mouth was demanding, and she met it with equal heat.

"Show me the stockings..." He sounded like he was fighting for control, and it stoked something wild inside her. She trailed her hands down the opening of his shirt and curled her hands into talons before pushing away from him. He sucked in his breath as her nails serrated his skin, but his nostrils flared with arousal.

"Stay," she ordered. "Do not move, or ye shall not see what you want."

"I'll have what I want, lass... when I come and claim it." He was stalking her, looking as powerful and untamed as he had the first time she'd seen him. Only now, the sight sent a surge of need twisting through her belly and on to her passage. Her body knew the delights he might offer her and was eager for her to surrender. She wanted more.

"Lace stockings are for seduction, not brutish tumbling." She stopped and wagged a single finger back and forth. "Stay… right there and wait on my whim." She had no idea where her boldness came from, but it made her voice husky. Temptation flickered in his eyes, along with impatience, but he stopped and fixed her with an intense stare.

Nervousness rippled through her, but it wasn't nearly as powerful as the sense of confidence she was experiencing. She fingered the end of one of the garter's ties, drawing her hands along the silk cord to the ends before turning around and peeking at him over her shoulder.

"Ye look like an enchantress."

She returned to facing him with the tie undone. The dressing robe was gently slipping open to offer him a narrow view of bare skin down the center of her body.

"Ye left yer chemise off…"

She turned back around and heard him snort. When she peeked back at him, he was frowning darkly at her, but there was also a hint of a boy being made to wait, which amused her.

"I did plan to seduce you… before you behaved so atrociously, that is."

One of his eyebrows rose, a challenge beginning to flicker in his eyes.

"If ye want to besmirch me, lass, I can make sure I do a grand job of behaving improperly." He made to act on his words, stepping toward her.

"No, no, no," she scolded in a teasing tone as she pulled the drooping dressing robe back up. "You've had two nights of overwhelming me."

"Two nights ye enjoyed full well."

He was half growling, but she turned and pointed at him. "Tonight it's my turn to dictate the pace."

He looked unconvinced and ready to rush her once more. She shrugged, and the dressing robe slithered over her shoulders, baring them. She hugged the bulky fabric tight to cover her breasts, at least half of them, anyway.

Broen licked his lower lip. "Never let it be said that I'm no' a man who appreciates it when a lass takes the time to test his nerve."

"Somehow... I do believe I am testing your... resolve." She turned, faster this time, so the hem of the dressing gown flared out. She rotated all the way around and back to facing the wall before allowing the garment to slither down her back and puddle around her ankles.

"I'm suddenly no' sorry I cut yer hair."

She jumped around, ready to argue, but froze when she realized she'd played into his hands. An arrogant grin met her stare as he began to toss aside his clothing. He never looked at what he was doing, but maintained eye contact with her.

"I care no' if I ever see another silk dress on ye, but those stockings are something I'll demand... often."

He tossed his shirt as he moved to within a pace of her. Both of their breathing had turned rough and labored, and her senses were suddenly keenly aware of every sound. Her skin was ultrasensitive, begging for his touch, but what demanded his attention most was her passage. She felt empty, so much so that she ached with the need to be filled. Her heart was pounding, and she caught the scent of his skin with her labored breaths. It was heady and intoxicating, sending her spiraling into a dark storm of desire.

"I've reached the end of me strength, lass… Have pity on me now."

"And on me…"

He closed the remaining distance, capturing her in his arms. She cried out, the sound primal and full of enjoyment. Words failed her, her mind overwhelmed by the rush of sensation as he lifted her and flattened her back against the wall. The stone was cool, but it soothed the raging inferno inside her.

"Ye've teased me too much, lass… Now I'm the brute ye so often labeled me."

He cupped her hips, holding her up, and pressed her thighs apart with his body. It was harsh, but she heard herself let out a sound that resembled purring. He growled in response, the head of his cock probing the folds of her sex, which were slick from need and anticipation, welcoming his first thrust with ease.

"Sweet Christ… I cannae slow me pace…" He withdrew and sent his cock back into her with a hard thrust. His body slammed into hers, forcing the air from her lungs. She gasped with satisfaction, half-afraid the pleasure would burst within her before they went much further.

"I didn't ask you to… *brute*." She dug her finger-nails into his shoulders, arching toward his next thrust. Pleasure speared through her, tightening even further as she heard him growl.

"Enchantress."

She wasn't sure if it was a compliment or a curse—or if Broen knew himself, but it fit the moment, feeding the rising frenzy beating inside her. The tempo increased, demanding she keep pace. There was no thought, only instinct and need. Every muscle strained to perform and take her closer to the edge of release. The wall at her back felt nowhere near as solid as the man she clung to.

Pleasure ripped her in two. She was sure of it but didn't care. There was no room for lament, only mind-searing rapture that burned its way through her body and twisted through Broen, wringing release from him as well. He pinned her to the wall as his seed erupted deep inside her. For a long moment, time was frozen.

"I did nae mean to ravish ye," he muttered between soft kisses he trailed over her cheek, "but I am nae sorry."

He cradled her against his chest, carrying her to the turned-down sheets she'd so carefully rubbed with new spring rosemary to welcome him.

"However, it's yer own doing." He laid her down and stood over her, reaching out to stroke one silk lace stocking. "These are wickedness, to be sure. Best to keep them only for me eyes alone."

She laughed and rolled away from his reach. "I knit them, so I'll wear them when I choose." She came up on her knees, and his attention dropped to her breasts.

"Another merit to having yer hair short."

She frowned, reaching up to finger her hair. "I know it had to be done…"

The bed rocked as he joined her, capturing her hands and kissing them before rolling onto his back and taking her along with him.

"I'd have done anything, lass."

Broen woke in the early-morning hours while the chamber was still in darkness. Something sent a tingle down his spine, and he turned to see Argyll staring at the bed. It had been years since he'd seen the spirit, but he recognized the specter from a portrait hanging in the study. Clarrisa muttered in her sleep, clearly sensing the ghost as Argyll reached toward her.

Broen slipped an arm around her and pulled her close. She snuggled against his side as his grandfather's ghost looked at him before fading away. In his gut, he knew he'd seen the last of the spirit, possibly forever.

He wished it would be so simple to settle the rest of his life. Daphne was still contracted to him, and the MacLeods were likely to demand he wed her, for an alliance with the MacLeods wasn't something to lose.

He couldn't. Every fiber of his being rebelled against wedding her.

But that wasn't the only thing he wanted to forbid from happening. Clarrisa muttered as his embrace tightened too much. If only it were so simple to hold her. It wouldn't be. She was coveted, and his country was dissolving into civil war. The future was bleak, so he closed his eyes and savored the sound of Clarrisa's breathing.

Dawn would bring reality to them both.

A snap of someone's fingers woke her. Clarrisa sat straight up.

"Yes, Maud, I have slept too long." The words left her mouth before she was fully awake. She was out of the bed before she finished speaking them, because her matron was fond of using a switch when she was displeased.

"Turn yer backs." Broen's voice was like a bucket of cold water. His men were in the room: Shaw standing with two scrolls, and a pair of younger lads helping their laird to dress. His two gillies turned around, but both boys were already turning red.

The morning air brushed across her bare skin.

"Out." A single word, and it was the laird speaking too.

The gillies made it to the doorway at the same time and became wedged. Shaw gave them a shove through before following.

"Stay in bed next time." Broen's tone had softened, and he leaned down to kiss her lips. "No one will chastise ye here for resting when ye've been up the better portion of the night."

"Well... they should... because... we..."

One of his eyebrows rose. "Because we spent the night together?" His tone was sharpening.

"I recall well that I invited you here."

He chuckled and cupped her face. When he raised her gaze to meet his, tenderness shimmered in his eyes. "'Tis a fine memory, one which will make me want to keep me kilt down for fear of startling the other lasses with how the recollection of ye in those stockings affects me."

"Have you no shame, Broen MacNicols?"

He pressed a kiss against her pouting lips before releasing her to finish dressing. "None. I'm a Highlander, after all. Do nae ye English believe we are cousins to Lucifer himself?"

"Second cousins. For the moment, I believe the French are considered closer kin."

He chuckled at her, a challenge flickering in his eyes. "Something I'll have to be setting ye straight on, lass. Do be here tonight. The cook was nae pleased to have her fine supper wasted when I discovered ye missing."

She stood stunned. "You had the cook prepare a special supper for me?"

He stopped near the doorway. "Do ye believe ye are the only one who feels such a strong pull between us, Clarrisa, or is it that ye doubt I can recognize the value of such a feeling?" He offered her a wink. "I planned to seduce ye but am right pleased ye decided upon the same course of action. We are a good match. There's something for ye to think on until me duties allow me to return to ye."

He left, and Shaw began to speak the moment he realized he had his laird's full attention. Clarrisa stood still, filled with a warmth so intense it engulfed her. Heating her from the inside, it felt like a bubble, but not one that threatened to break.

Happiness... She was incredibly, insanely happy, possibly for the first time in her life. There was nothing she longed for, nothing she had to suffer through, only pure delight.

"Ye're in love."

She jumped, startled by the female tone. Her cheeks turned pink as she realized Daphne had entered the chamber.

"Where is Edme?"

Daphne opened the wardrobe and selected an underdress. "I asked her to allow me to serve ye this morning."

"But you're——"

"Broen's betrothed? Aye, but I refused to wed him, so it is only a matter of time before he goes to the church to have the union dissolved." Daphne gathered the fabric and helped Clarrisa don it.

"A betrothal is not so easily broken."

Daphne tilted her head. "Here in the Highlands, being rejected is grounds enough. Highlanders have pride when it comes to women." She went behind Clarrisa and began lacing the dress closed. "He never looked at me as he does ye."

There was sadness in her tone, which made Clarrisa turn. "I did not plan it. I swear it."

Daphne smiled in spite of the tears glistening in her eyes. "I am the one who owes ye an apology for coming here and allowing ye to leave Broen. The feeling ye have for each other is precious and rare. The Grants had to turn me out, and I cannae go home to me father—but that did nae give me the right to try and destroy yer happiness."

"What will you do, if not marry Broen?"

Daphne returned to the wardrobe and lifted a dress. When she turned, she was smiling, the tears vanished from her eyes. "Broen has promised no' to turn me out. For the first time in me life, I can try to find a man who sees me as a woman instead of the dowry me father has promised. I can go to another of his holdings if ye prefer. I shall understand."

"No, you will stay. Never have I put out anyone, and I shall not begin now." It was a horrible threat she'd lived with her entire life. Daphne stared into her eyes, understanding dawning on her.

Clarrisa reached out and took her hands. "We shall be sisters. If you can bear with me while I learn how to treat a sister, for I have never had one."

Daphne pulled her to her and hugged her. The embrace was awkward for a moment, but Clarrisa was too happy to worry about right or wrong. There was only the glow of contentment inside her. She returned the hug, and the moment was complete.

She was happy.

❧

"So this is what your hall looks like," Clarrisa muttered that evening.

Broen frowned at her teasing. "Highlander brutes do nae sup like civilized men. The hall is a confusing place for me... In fact... I am nae sure what to do now that ye have clothing on."

She swatted his shoulder. "I called you a brute with just cause."

He pulled her close. "Ye called me lover with just cause too."

"The pair of ye are killing me appetite." Faolan Chisholms appeared in the doorway and shouted up the main aisle at them. Conversation died as the Chisholms laird walked toward the high table with two of his captains flanking him.

"A fact we have in common," Broen answered once his fellow laird was close enough to keep his comment between them.

Faolan stuck out his lower lip. "Me feelings are wounded."

"I doubt it," Clarrisa muttered.

Faolan jerked his attention to her, his eyes wide, but he clasped his hand over his heart.

"Sit down, ye pretentious clod," Broen ordered. "And leave me woman alone."

More than one maid lifted her head in response. They stared while Clarrisa felt her cheeks heating. Faolan took a chair beside Broen and slapped the tabletop.

"I'm going to enjoy yer hospitality, Broen, indeed I am, for ye've taken me on a merry chase these last few weeks."

Broen smirked and covered her hand with his. More of his people took notice of them, many of them leaning toward one another to whisper. Her face felt like it was on fire. Faolan studied her over the rim of a mug. For a moment she was torn between the need to reject the public display of ownership, simply because her pride was demanding it, but on the other hand, the look in Faolan's eyes kept her silent. The man was studying her, waiting for any hint that she might be his prize for the taking.

She stood, gaining a glare from Broen. "I'll bid you good night."

"Sit down, Clarrisa."

There was a warning edging his words. He caught her wrist, his grip tight.

"Here is another thing I believe Englishmen and Scotsmen have in common..." she muttered while the staff found reasons to step closer to the table. "They do not need women about when they are drinking."

Faolan grinned and raised his mug to her. "I believe I hate ye, Broen, for any woman who can liken me to an Englishman and have me agreeing is surely perfection."

Broen didn't want to release her hand. She lowered herself, and he was forced to relinquish his grip or have their hands smack the tabletop. His fingers slid down her hand while a look of longing flickered in his eyes. It touched the same feeling inside herself, the need to be near him, no matter the consequences.

"I will se ye later, lass."

It was a firm promise, one that stoked her passions and her tender feelings for him. She lowered her eyelashes, fluttering them for the first time in her life and realized she was simpering. He watched her leave the hall—in fact, most everyone did—but it was Broen's stare she felt the weight of.

"It's wonderful to see them sitting together as friends again."

Daphne was hiding beyond the arched entryway, her face a radiant mask of joy while she stared at Faolan and Broen.

"Go sit with them."

Daphne tore her gaze from the high table and shook her head, but Clarrisa shook hers faster.

"Do it and shame them as they deserve. Let them thank you for having more sense than they did."

Daphne only smiled. "Men do nae like admitting when they've been wrong. 'Tis enough to see them reconciled."

"No, it isn't." Clarrisa wasn't sure where her boldness came from, only that a spark of rebellion was lighting a fire inside her. She grasped Daphne's hand and tugged her through the doorway. They'd made it only two paces before both Broen and Faolan looked up to investigate who was arriving.

"We are going to sit with them and enjoy the peace you helped bring about."

"Are ye sure ye have no Scots blood in ye, Clarrisa?" Daphne asked with a soft sound of amusement. "Ye certainly have more spirit than I'd ever thought an Englishwoman might."

Clarrisa leaned toward her to keep her reply between them. "But when it comes to women, it matters not what blood we have. It's the knowledge of how to deal with insufferable men that makes us kindred souls."

Daphne giggled, and Clarrisa joined her. They both sealed their lips but failed to mask their amusement when they reached the end of the aisle and stopped to offer deference.

"I'm afraid to know what the pair of ye find so amusing," Broen announced.

"Well, I'm terrified," Faolan added.

Behind the two lairds, their captains grinned. Clarrisa opened her hands in an innocent motion. "That's very disheartening to hear, after all the trouble Daphne has gone to in order to see the pair of you sitting so nicely by each other's side. I hear life in the convent is very somber, the food bland, and the beds but wood planks."

"The ticking was so thin I might as well have been sleeping on the wood," Daphne muttered, but there was no meekness about her tone. "I, however, am not disheartened to hear the pair of ye are suffering some misgivings."

She swept around the table and sat when Shaw pulled a chair out for her. Clarrisa sat beside her while

Faolan and Broen studied them both. Tension prickled along her nape, for they were making a public display and both men were lairds.

But Broen stood and lifted his mug. The hall grew quiet.

"I owe Daphne Grant a debt of gratitude. She had the sense to realize the match between us was destructive to the peace between the Chisholms and the MacNicols. We will seek an annulment, but she has earned me respect and should be treated so."

The MacNicols people looked unsure, but Faolan stood as well.

"And I owe her twice as much for bringing me to me senses. I consider her me sister and will hold to that if anyone forgets how I believe she should be treated."

The hall began to fill with the sound of men hitting the tops of the tables. The sound rose until it drowned out everything else. But Broen was staring at Clarrisa while his men showed their approval. The laird of the MacNicols inclined his head toward her, offering her respect.

She loved him. Plain and simple and with no way to ignore it.

But you don't want to ignore it...

No, she didn't.

"Ye did a fine thing," Edme muttered.

The head of house must have been watching her, for Edme appeared beside her the moment she left the great hall.

"Daphne Grant needed her position made plain,"

Edme muttered with firm confidence. "Aye, ye did well to force the matter. Ye have a solid spine."

"Thank you." Edme was followed by two of her older staff members, and one younger woman trailed them.

"It isn't necessary to escort me to my chamber."

"We are nae doing it because the laird set us to watching ye." Edme voiced the fear Clarrisa had been avoiding mentioning. The older woman continued on until they reached the floor where her chamber was and Broen's. Edme stopped at the top of the stairs, eyeing her expectantly.

"Oh... well..." She paused, staring at the door of Broen's chamber. Every obstacle was removed now, the only barrier the mind-set her kin had tried to mold her into living her entire life serving.

That everything she did must have a purpose or a price.

Well, she was going to Broen's bed without a promise, and that was her word on the matter. The moment she stepped toward the door, Edme's staff rushed forward and opened the huge double doors.

"Oh fie upon you, Broen MacNicols. How did you get in there ahead of me?"

The man smiled arrogantly at her, his doublet and hat already lying discarded on a chair.

"This is a Scottish castle, lass. There is more than one entrance into this chamber." He closed the distance between them, and she heard the door shut firmly behind them. He gently cupped her chin. "I'd have scaled the exterior of the keep in order to see ye choose me bed of yer own will."

She shivered, his touch unleashing a flood of
sensation. He touched his lips to hers in a tender kiss
that stole her breath. Gooseflesh rose along her limbs
while her nipples puckered and her belly began to
heat with desire.

"But that does nae mean I am no' planning on
ravishing ye."

He bent over and tossed her over his shoulder
before she recovered from the kiss. A solid smack
landed on her bottom before he spun her around in a
circle and tossed her onto the bed. She rolled over in
a tangle of skirts and lifted one hand to point at him.

"Brute."

&

The door of the chamber opened at dawn.

"Get yer mistress out of bed," Edme announced
with a glee Clarrisa had never heard from the
woman before.

"Get ye gone," Broen growled, but the women
ripped the covers off them and pulled Clarrisa from
where she'd been lying beside him.

"It's May Day, and if ye want a lusty tumble, my
son, ye'll have to chase her for it!"

The women laughed while tossing her clothing
over her head and securing it quickly. Someone
brushed her short hair and placed a garland of new
spring greens on her.

"Let's go, my lambs! The morning dew will wait
for no one!"

Edme hurried them down the hallway and stairs.
Their bare feet made slapping sounds on the stone, but

they giggled in spite of the chill, because it was tradition to go without footwear on May morn. The bell was ringing in the church, and girls were streaming out of their homes. Most had their hair unbound and flowing behind them; everyone had a garland of greens on their heads. The men lined up along the roads and cheered them on.

But it was the women who went into the woods, seeking the morning dew among the new leaves. They bathed their faces and laughed. Superstition claimed the dew would keep them youthful forever. Once the sun rose, they hurried back to the village, drawn by the sound of music. The men were playing near the maypole, and the entire village was turned out to enjoy the festive moment.

"Is nae it grand?" Daphne muttered when she came close to Clarrisa. "I adore May Day!"

She danced away to the beat of the drums, becoming lost in the crowd of merrymakers. But Clarrisa felt her cheeks heat when Broen came into view. He looked just as strong and untamed as he had the first time she'd seen him, his shirt rolled up to display his forearms and the corded muscles she'd stroked. His blue eyes were fixed on her, and the morning light flickered off the sapphire set into the pommel of his sword. He was a dangerous man and expected to survive by his strength alone.

But he was also a tender lover.

The crowd dancing around the maypole was beginning to thin. Couples slipped away to celebrate the more wicked traditions of the festival. The May Queen was still dancing, but she was surrounded by

young men who were all doing their best to entice
her into leaving with them. The church preached
against May Day, but the tradition went back further
than anyone recalled. On one hand, no one wanted to
take the chance that bad luck might befall them if they
didn't dance around the maypole; on the other hand,
it was a fine day of festival, and no one wanted to give
it up, even if it was nothing but hollow superstition.

If the May Queen conceived, it would be considered a sign of a plentiful harvest. Clarrisa envied the
girl for a moment. Her life was not complicated by
the need to maintain her virginity in order to catch a
good husband. Whoever she allowed to lead her into
the woods would gladly wed her if she ripened with
a babe. Every boy competing for her attention knew
the village would expect a wedding, and still they
crowded around the May Queen.

But Broen MacNicols was looking at Clarrisa.

There was a wicked gleam in his eyes, and now that
he was closer, she could see that he was in the mood
to take up Edme's challenge.

She gasped, her belly tightening with anticipation.
A hot, wicked sense of excitement rippled through
her, settling in her passage. The heat traveled up
into her cheeks, setting off a blush that gained a grin
from Broen.

A smug, arrogant one.

She propped her hands on her hips and tried to
decide how to best the man. He was too sure of
her favor; it was May Day, after all. So she joined
the dancers, merging into the crowd. They stepped
together in time to the music and swept along anyone

not moving fast enough. She lost sight of Broen as she circled the maypole. The beat of the drums seemed to increase the pulse of need throbbing in her clitoris. When she danced close to the edge of the circle, she dashed out of the crowd and into the woods with her skirts held high.

Her heart was beating so fast she should have been worried, but all it did was make her light-headed. She looked back over her shoulder and shrieked when she caught sight of Broen. He was chasing her, his expression a mask of determination.

Well, she would not make it simple. Once she reached the woods, she darted between the trees with ease. She heard him mutter something in Gaelic.

"That will cost you a penitence." She took refuge behind a tree and turned to face him.

"A mere drop in the bucket compared to what I'll owe for what I plan to do with ye once I catch ye." He stalked her around the tree, both of them breathing hard.

"So certain... Maybe I am not in the mood to entertain your whims," she teased him pertly.

One fair eyebrow rose. "Ah... a challenge from the fair lass..." His expression darkened dangerously. "Are ye saying ye do nae want a taste of this?"

He raised his kilt, giving her a plain view of his erect cock. She should have found his actions vulgar, but the hunger burning in her passage doubled, her body feeling empty. She forgot to continue moving around the tree and ended up leaning against it while taking the opportunity to look at the piece of forbidden flesh. His cock was thick and long, and she recalled very well how much having it inside her had satisfied the need raging through her.

He dropped his kilt and reached out to grasp her wrist while she was distracted. She shrieked when he yanked her toward him, but it wasn't a sound of fright. Instead it felt like she was too excited to contain all the emotion inside her.

"What have I caught?" he roared with victory. "A lass ripe for tumbling."

He pressed a hard kiss against her mouth, but she returned it with equal strength. Her heartbeat had slowed but wasn't completely normal, and she didn't want to let the moment die. She wanted his strength, wanted him to ravish her.

He chuckled darkly, the sound rumbling through his chest as she gripped his head and kissed him. He caught the sides of her skirts and boldly lifted them until he could flatten his hands against her bare thighs. She shivered, overwhelmed by the sensation of his hands against such an intimate area. Her clitoris begged for attention, and she arched her back, shutting her eyes as he stroked her from hip to midthigh and then reached farther back to caress her bottom.

"I thought ravishing happened much faster."

He gripped each side of her bottom, sending another spike of need through her. "Demanding, are nae ye?"

"As much so as you," she countered.

He drew his hands around to her thighs once more. "Aye, ye're that, all right, Clarrisa of the house of York."

He lifted her off her feet, drawing a startled gasp from her lips. He pressed her back against the tree and kept her there with his body pressed against hers. He tossed her skirts aside and raised his kilt with more ease than she liked.

"Do nae frown, woman. I am nae quite as practiced in this art as ye are thinking."

"I do not believe…"

He thrust smoothly into her, interrupting her thought process. A soft moan rose from her as she gripped his shoulders and savored the delight of being filled. It was delight too, a feeling of enjoyment so intense there was nothing else that mattered.

"I believe we both would rather be engaged in the business of ravishing…"

His tone was thick with need. His hands returned to her thighs and supported her while he made good on his promise. The pace was hard and fast with no hesitation, only the pair of them moving in unison to feed their need.

He cursed against when his seed erupted. She was struggling to draw breath, digging her fingers into his shoulders.

"That was too damned fast." His head was buried against her neck, and both their hearts hammered away from the frantic pace they'd both employed.

"Well… if you cannot keep up, Broen…"

He lifted his head and eyed her. "There is spirit, and then there is hellish temperament."

He let her legs down and pulled his sword off his back. He leaned it against the tree before lying down on the new spring grass growing between the tree trunks.

"Come, lass. Come lie with me in true May Day tradition." He offered her his hand, and she took it.

Soon she was nestled against his side, with her head pillowed on his shoulder. For a moment, they listened to the sounds of the birds calling to one another and the breeze gently rustling the new leaves. The grass smelled sweet and fresh. Somewhere, the earth was newly turned, and there was the scent of her lover's skin too.

"Gaining an annulment will take time." Broen stroked her hip. "Perhaps a long time."

"I know," she muttered.

He raised her face so she could lock stares with him. "Will ye wait, Clarrisa? I'll no' ask yer kin, for I cannae respect them for sending ye to be the king's broodmare. So I'm asking ye to give me yer bond."

He could do so much better, but he knew that. She might do better too, at least if she measured her success by titles or power.

"I'll wait."

There was no other answer, but her heart filled with happiness again when he smiled at her.

"I believe I'm falling in love with ye, Clarrisa, so it's a good thing ye agreed."

"Oh, is it now?"

He pressed her down when she tried to sit up all the way. "Aye, it is, for I'd have had to keep ye locked in me keep until I was sure."

"And now that I've agreed to stay?" she asked.

"I'll build another wall around me keep to ensure ye are well secured, for I do nae think I could bear to lose ye. I hope ye shall no' miss yer home in England too greatly."

"Oh, I was never anywhere for more than a season.

My uncle feared I'd grow fond of one place over another, and he wanted to make sure I was willing to go wherever he directed. He also feared the Lancasters would overrun his lands."

She meant it as a pleasant comment, but Broen stiffened. She lifted her head and witnessed his frowning. "It doesn't matter."

"I'm sorry ye do nae know what a home is, lass."

He meant it—was angry on her behalf—and it touched her heart. He cared about her feelings, the single thing no one in her life had done since her mother died.

"Maybe you can teach me."

He smiled and pressed her head back onto his shoulder. "I'd like to, lass."

She smiled, hearing the echo of his promise as she drifted off into sleep. Broen MacNicols would do more than try; he'd succeed. She was sure of it.

❧

"Norris Sutherland is at the gate!"

Broen stiffened and set her aside. He stepped in front of her, shielding her from the retainer who was running up the aisle toward them. The man stopped, laboring for breath.

"Norris Sutherland and his men are at the gate. He demands ye meet him."

"Then he shall have it." Broen sounded savage. "Two weeks was nae long enough for him to stay away from me gates."

"Broen…"

"Mount up, lads!"

Broen turned to face her and cupped her face with a hand. It looked like he was trying to memorize her face, his gaze was so intense.

"Be here when I return, Clarrisa, as ye promised?"

It was a question. She heard it in his tone and nodded before she'd even thought about it. There was nothing to contemplate. Without a doubt, she never wanted to leave his side. The last two weeks had been pure bliss.

He was gone in another second, the longer pleats of his kilt swaying as he moved quickly across the hall. The men who'd been enjoying their meals all rose to follow him. Many paused to kiss their wives and children, but as the sound of horses came from the yard, all that was heard in the hall were muttered prayers.

"Maybe I'm just getting used to it, but it seems like this lot looks a bit meaner than the last two armies we faced." Shaw's voice lacked true humor. Broen couldn't blame him, because he agreed. Norris's men did look ready to draw blood, but Norris took to the center of the field, leaving his men behind.

"The man still has archers," Shaw warned.

"And I still will nae be called a coward." Broen kneed his stallion and let the animal have its freedom. Normally he enjoyed the surge of speed; today, all it did was twist the tension between his shoulder blades.

"What do ye want, Norris?"

"The look on yer face dares me to say 'the York woman.'"

Broen cursed. "Over me dead body."

Norris grew serious, staring at him for a long moment. "Are ye sure ye want to be so attached to her, Broen?"

"It is nae a question anymore. Those who want to quarrel with it will have to recall they had the chance to stand up when yer father asked for a man to step forward. I stole her, and I'm keeping her."

"As yer leman?" Norris asked soberly. "Her family will nae give up a dowry easily."

"They can keep it. I have what I want. I plan to wed her as soon as I gain an annulment," Broen insisted. "Ye're the one with the noble title to worry about bringing home a bride with more than her charms."

"Kindly do nae remind me. Me father does so often enough."

"If ye are nae here for Clarrisa, what brings ye with yer men looking ready to die?"

Norris reached into his doublet and pulled out a letter. A broken wax seal was still half-attached. "Lord Home has called to the Highlanders. The royalists are massing near Sauchieburn."

He offered the letter, and Broen took it. The words were there, the ones that would tear him away from Clarrisa—possibly forever, if the battle didn't go well for him.

"Then we go and pray for an end to this madness."

He looked up at Deigh, battling the urge to go back inside and turn his back on the war getting ready to rage. It was not his way—had never been—but he was tempted to kiss Clarrisa once more before he rode out to uphold his duty.

A young gillie brought the news back to Deigh Tower. Women cried, and Edme collapsed into a chair. The few retainers left behind lowered the gate.

"The waiting will be hard to bear," Edme muttered. Tears glistened in her eyes. Clarrisa took her hand, soothing it gently.

"It will not be so terrible, for we'll have each other."

Edme nodded, but the woman didn't agree. She was going through the motions just as Clarrisa was. All the inhabitants of the castle shared the strain of knowing their fates were tied to the men who had just ridden out. There would be no mercy for the kin of traitors, and that would be their lot if the royalists won.

Clarrisa sat in the dark long after she'd pinched out the candle. How could it be so short a time since Broen had lain in the bed with her? Now it was a cold, desolate place that offered no haven nor comfort. Sleep didn't come for hours, and even then, it was troubled. She saw the king's face, with lust flickering in his eyes. Her sole comfort was the knowledge that she'd given her purity to the man of her choice.

A man worthy of it. The choice might cost her her head when James found her, but she would not regret it. If Broen died, she'd rather join him than live to further James's ambition.

❧

"Ye can stare at the camp all day, but ye'll be left wondering if we have enough men or no'… Just like the rest of us." Norris's voice betrayed his frustration. The moment was too dark, too brooding for anything such as hope to brighten it. Well, there was one thing that would lift all their spirits—victory.

"I never thought the day would come when the MacNicols would rise up against their king," Broen muttered.

"Or that ye'd lead them," Norris finished. "A sentiment I share. Yet here I am, drawn here for the same reasons ye are. No matter how justified I remind myself I am, it still sticks in me throat."

"Aye." Broen ducked under the open flaps of the canvas tent that Norris lived out of. It was a large pavilion but not overly grand. Only a fool announced his fortune or title in a military camp. Or possibly a king.

Across the camp, the pavilion of the prince was flying the royal standard. Such was a clear statement from the young James, one his father couldn't fail to understand, but there were rumors of talks between the prince and his father. There must have been substance to them, because no call to arms had been given.

"Eat with me, Broen. 'Tis a sad man who sups alone," Norris remarked when one of his men brought in bowls of steaming soup.

"A sadder man who lets his friend eat his last meal alone," Broen remarked.

"Aye, it might be that for both of us."

The fare was bland and rustic, but it was hot, which was more than what a good number of the waiting ranks of men could expect. Every day they camped, the conditions worsened. The stench would rise from waste both animal and human. Food stores were guarded. The bowl of soup in his hand was the only thing Broen had consumed all day. Lack of provisions would take its toll on the strength of the force waiting to clash with the royalists.

"What are ye planning to do with Daphne MacLeod?" Norris asked.

Broen looked at him in surprise, but it quickly faded. "Kael spills details quicker than I'd believe he would."

"I'm his ally, and I was very curious as to why Clarrisa left ye when it was plain it pained her greatly."

Broen leaned forward, pointing a finger at Norris. "Ye're fishing, man. There's a reason I stay far away from court. I've no patience for the games of intrigue."

Norris's expression darkened. "Ye might be surprised to learn how much I agree with ye, but fate was nae so kind to me on where she placed me in this life. I have to play the games of court. Me clan would suffer if I did so poorly."

"But no' with me," Broen insisted.

"As ye like," Norris responded. "I wanted to know why that English lass left ye, and there were only a few reasons I could come up with. She obviously did nae hate ye, was nae greedy enough to jump at the offer I made for her—"

"Ye did what?" Broen demanded. The tent jerked as two of Norris's retainers hurried inside to see what was happening. Norris waved them away, but they didn't go instantly. They both eyed Broen suspiciously before tugging on the corners of their bonnets.

"Do ye think ye are the only one who has eyes, man?" Norris asked with a smugness that set Broen's temper on edge.

"When it comes to Clarrisa, ye can bloody well aim yers elsewhere."

Norris sat back in his chair, tapping his fingertips against one another. "Why should I do that? Me father has been hounding me for the last two years to bring home a match he'd approve of. A lass guaranteed to ruffle the fancy feathers of the new English king would do that full well."

"Forget about her. She belongs to me." He meant it with every fiber of his being, but Norris raised an eyebrow skeptically.

"Why? Because ye've had her?" He chuckled arrogantly. "I do nae care. She's the daughter of a king."

"She is going to be me wife as soon as the church grants me an annulment. Which I've already started the process for, since I know that will be yer next question."

Norris smiled slowly. Broen cursed, realizing he'd played easily into Norris's hands, spilling information without thinking.

"I do nae care what ye think ye've learned, Norris Sutherland. Tell yer father I'm going to wed her."

"As soon as ye clear up the matter of yer betrothal to Daphne."

Broen smiled slowly. "It will no' be difficult now that the MacLeods are siding with the king."

"We both hope for that." Norris raised an eyebrow. "Daphne is content with yer plan to set her aside?"

Broen nodded. "I'm ashamed to admit she is the only one who saw sense when I was fighting over her with me best friend."

"It is nae the first time such a thing has happened."

Broen nodded. "Aye, but for the sake of greed, I

am ashamed. I count meself a better friend than to allow a dowry to set me against a man I call friend."

"That may not be a good-enough reason for the church. They will likely insist ye repent and wed her."

"I know." Broen growled the words, frustration eating at him. The church would most likely not grant him an annulment easily, because they'd blessed the union. They never liked recanting, because it set the example that what they did might be undone. Unless the bride with such a fine dowry chose the service of Christ instead.

"But I swear I'll wed Clarrisa and no other."

Norris tilted his head. "If ye live past this rebellion we're taking part in."

Commotion stirred outside the tent. Both men were on their feet and leaning out of the door to investigate.

"To arms! To arms! Negotiations have failed!"

The clans were massing, men opening their pouches of blue skin paint. Broen reached out and clasped Norris's arm. "In case I do nae get the chance to wed her"—he reached inside his doublet and withdrew a folded parchment—"promise me ye'll see any child she births before summer's end legitimized as me heir."

Norris clenched his fingers into a tight fist, but Broen sent him a hard look. Between Highlanders, a last request could not be refused, not when it came to the future of the clan.

"Ye're me overlord, Norris, since yer father is nae here. Take the letter, me pledge that Clarrisa came to me pure and that I could no' wed her because of the betrothal, but that I planned to. Do yer duty, man."

Norris grabbed the letter and shouted for his secretary. "We might both be dead before nightfall."

Aye, they might, but at least Broen would go to his grave knowing he'd done right by the woman he'd failed to confess his love to.

Time could be cruel. Each day was an eternity. Clarrisa tried to fill the hours with hard work, but sleep still eluded her when she sought her bed. She was not the only inhabitant of Deigh suffering so. After the supper dishes were cleared away, the women sat on the benches, none of them eager to seek their beds. The youngest children were immune to the unhappiness of their elders, but the hall still seemed too quiet.

They were all waiting. By day, the road was empty. The merchants normally expected during spring were missing too. The fields turned green as the animals carried on.

Yet they still waited.

Dawn became a blessing because it meant she could leave her bed. The floor was no longer icy cold when she walked over to the window to open the shutters.

"I thought ye'd be awake early." Edme spoke quietly. "The cobbler finished yer boots. They are nae made of anything as fine as ye arrived wearing, but they will keep yer feet dry here in the Highlands."

"They are perfect." Clarrisa eagerly pulled on stockings so she might try out the ankle boots. They were made of butternut leather, and the first one slid onto her foot easily. It closed with a long length of leather, which was woven around silver buttons. "The buttons are too fine."

"Nay, it's important to show yer position to any who might think to trifle with ye."

Clarrisa fought off a tightening in her chest. "I don't have position here, and it's the honest truth that I am relieved it is so. I am so tired of being mindful of my actions because someone in my family believes I will cost them their coveted *positions*." She stood and tested the new boots. "I know I am being disrespectful, but I am not sorry."

Edme was smiling when she turned to look at her. The older woman laughed when she caught sight of the confusion on Clarrisa's face.

"Ye're adapting to the Highlands well," she declared. "A feat many a Highlander will claim is impossible for any English person."

Clarrisa smiled, enjoying the praise more than any she'd ever received from Maud. Someone was running up the stairs, their hurried steps pounding louder and louder as they neared. They knocked only once before opening the door.

Daphne stood there, with her face flushed but her eyes full of joy. "The king has been killed in battle, and the prince is to be crowned!"

She was clutching a letter, and Clarrisa reached for it without thinking. "What news of Broen?"

Daphne's smile faded. "There is none."

She spoke the truth, and it chilled Clarrisa's heart. She read the letter twice, searching the bottom for any small mark that might indicate Broen had written it but forgotten to press his signet ring into the seal.

There was nothing. The letter suddenly became horrible, because if someone else had sent them news, it might well be that Broen wasn't alive to see to the task.

No news had been better, for now she felt as though her heart was breaking. A soft sob echoed inside the chamber, and she thought she'd lost control of her emotions, only to realize it was Edme. Tears streamed down her wrinkled cheeks, the same horror Clarrisa struggled against burning brightly in her eyes.

Was he gone? Was the only thing left to her the memory of their brief time together?

"You were right, Edme… We do squander too many chances for joy…"

❦

"He may live, yer grace." The surgeon was tired, and his apron stained with blood.

"But ye do nae know for sure?" Prince James asked, appearing too solemn for his age. The surgeon rubbed his eyes. Well, maybe not too solemn, for the day was grim. Scot had fought against Scot, so all the losses were theirs.

"The wound is nae mortal, but it is deep. His age is in his favor."

"Thank ye for yer time."

The surgeon inclined his head before leaving the massive pavilion. There were men dying in the dirt; the one he'd left behind at least had a bed to rest on—not that it made much difference when it came to his wound. He'd been cut as easily as the other common men.

"My prince, there are other matters that need yer attention now that yer father is dead," Lord Home announced.

James turned on his mentor, startling him with how dark his expression was. "I wanted no part of causing his death."

"A battle cannae be controlled, no' when so many were set against yer father due to his own weaknesses."

James turned to look at the man struggling to draw breath on his bed. His face was white, but he opened his eyes and stared at him.

"Do nae look so grim, me young king. I'm nae listening to the angels just yet."

James sat on the edge of the bed as Lord Home came close. "Is there anything I can do for ye?"

"Aye." He reached inside his doublet and withdrew a parchment stained with his own blood. "I'm bound by me honor to see to this woman. Hold it for me, and see it done if I do no' open me eyes again."

Lord Home took the letter before unfolding it and reading the contents. "The York bastard," he muttered.

"Aye…" Norris confirmed. "Yer word to see to the matter would be welcome."

"I shall," James assured him.

Norris Sutherland held the king's stare for a long moment before his eyelids slid shut.

"We must deal with this immediately," Lord Home insisted.

James turned to look at his adviser. "Laird Sutherland only asked us to see to it in the event he cannot. It is his duty."

Lord Home was already seated before his writing desk. He lifted the lid and retrieved a new piece of parchment.

"Lord Home," James insisted. "We shall respect Laird Sutherland's wishes."

Home looked past him at Norris. "He is gravely wounded, most likely will not live to see the Sabbath day. Besides, his father is Laird Sutherland. It will be his sire ye need to worry about keeping on friendly terms."

The prince stiffened. "Then we shall search for Laird MacNicols."

"He stood next to Norris Sutherland when the royalists swarmed down on our line. I doubt the man survived." Home dipped a quill into an inkwell. "In any case, the York bastard is a threat to ye."

"How can that be so when my father is now dead?" the prince demanded softly. He was searching for the courage to insist on his way. Home put down the quill, and the young man nodded approvingly.

"Yes, I will go and search for Laird MacNicols. It is a simple matter, one I am certain Laird Sutherland would approve of, since it might well be his son's dying request."

"A sound plan, yer grace."

The prince headed for the opening of the pavilion, the royal guards closing around him. Home watched him go, taking a moment to watch the prince take the helmet one of his men offered. The boy was young, too young to understand that blood ties with England were the devil's curse for Scotland. He picked up the quill and dipped it once more. The York bastard must be dealt with.

Such was a burden he'd have to shoulder for the young prince. Once maturity settled upon him, he'd come to understand that the woman could not be left alive.

∽

"Another letter…"

It was one of the kitchen women who ran into the hall. Her cheeks were flushed with excitement.

"The laird is alive! He's sent a letter, and there's men from the prince's own ranks here to escort ye to his side."

She ran up to the high table but froze, nibbling on her lower lip as she looked between Edme and Clarrisa, trying to decide whom to give the letter to. Edme's slip had traveled far now, and there was unlikely a single soul who didn't know she was Broen's mother. Clarrisa pointed toward Edme.

"Nae." The head of house rejected her gesture. "Ye'll be the mistress here soon as the laird returns to wed ye. 'Tis yer right."

"Many things may be, but for this moment, ye are the laird's mother and I am naught."

The letter still remained unclaimed, but the hall was growing silent, the MacNicols leaning in to catch each word.

"Naught but his leman, which means something here in the Highlands," Edme insisted. "An important position."

"So is being his mother," Clarrisa muttered.

Edme frowned, but Clarrisa bore up to the hard stare. "You did tell me you enjoyed your position here, Edme."

Edme grunted and took the letter. "Ye turn me words against me."

She read the letter and frowned when she was finished. "He's sent for ye…"

Daphne reached over and clasped Clarrisa's hand, but there was a deep frown on Edme's face.

"And yet there is no seal."

Edme handed the letter over, both Daphne and Clarrisa leaning in to read it.

> *The battle is won, but I suffered a wound. There are too many in need of attention. Come and care for me. I am sure it shall speed me recovery.*
> *Broen MacNicols.*

There was no seal, but she wanted to believe in the letter. "It's doubtful he had any wax... He does say there are many in need of care. Who could take time to bring him wax while there is suffering?"

"A reasonable thing to think. Still..." Edme tapped the tabletop, clearly debating the request.

"It's hardly a matter for great concern. I'll go and help," Clarrisa muttered. Her heart was filling with joy, and the fact that the other two women weren't sharing it threatened to strangle her budding hope. She couldn't bear going back to fearing Broen was dead.

"It is a matter for concern and contemplation," Edme insisted. "If this letter is written falsely and the laird is dead, our only hope lies in the fact that ye have nae bled."

"Any child I might carry would be illegitimate." Edme slowly smiled, and even Daphne grinned. The maids near the hearth shook their heads as Clarrisa struggled to understand their humor.

"Better illegitimate than the clan forfeited to the crown." Edme spoke firmly. "I could swear that ye have been with no other and that ye were pure when ye went to his bed. It would be enough."

Things were happening too fast. Clarrisa felt her thoughts spinning around too quickly to catch. "Surely there is a cousin."

Edme shook her head. "Why do ye think me child inherited the lairdship? There is no other. And those who come after this bloodline, there are several and sure to be fighting if it comes to that."

"It's why his father came to fetch me back when I refused to honor the marriage agreement," Daphne muttered. "He knew his days were drawing to an end, and it was time his son had an heir." Daphne reached for Edme's hands. "Forgive me."

For a moment, it appeared Edme would deny Daphne her request. There was a hard look in her eyes, but she nodded at last. "I cannae condemn ye for wanting what I craved in me own life: choice. Besides, ye were correct. The match with ye was poisoning me son against his best friend. Ye've a fine heart for thinking of them instead of the position ye would have gained by marrying."

"Well... I want my choice too," Clarrisa declared. "I am going. We are speaking as though we have been sent word of his death, when that is not so. I will not discuss the future without Broen." She felt that remaining inside Deigh would smother her. Edme was frowning, clearly set against the idea, but Clarrisa stood. "I am going," she insisted.

"Ye cannae. As I think upon the matter, I do nae believe Broen would send for ye. The times are too uncertain. He'd want ye here, protected."

Clarrisa shook her head, unwilling to hear any further argument. "If I cannot believe he sent for me because he needs me by his side as greatly as I desire to be there, there is no reason for me to be here when he returns." She turned, unable to stand still any longer.

"Well, I'm going with ye," Daphne announced. Edme slapped the tabletop in her displeasure.

"Do nae encourage her to this rash action."

Daphne nodded agreement but still moved to stand beside Clarrisa. "Sometimes ye have to take rash action for the greater good. If Broen is in need of care, we cannae allow him to think Clarrisa will nae come to him. Neither should we leave him at the mercy of rough care."

Edme sighed. "Ye have me with that argument, but do nae tell the escort who is whom. Keep at least that much private."

Clarrisa felt her belly tighten. It was a mixture of apprehension and excitement. At least it meant an end to waiting. Edme's warning drove home how easy it would be for the men waiting outside to be deceptive. Once she left the tower, she'd be at their mercy.

"We won't," Daphne insisted. "They won't know which of us is English if we keep our lips sealed."

It was a small amount of shelter, but Clarrisa was grateful. Tears stung her eyes, for she felt part of something at last, not just the orphan child tolerated because she might have value someday.

❧

"The pair of ye are the quietest females I've ever met."

Clarrisa and Daphne held their silence, and the captain of their escort shook his head.

"No' that I care, no' a bit. Me duty is to escort ye, naught else."

He turned back to his men while Clarrisa breathed a tiny sigh of relief. Daphne echoed the sound while shooting her a quick look.

The Highlands were behind them now, too far for them to escape back to the protection of Deigh Tower. The twenty men who'd come with the letter kept them surrounded as they marched toward the Lowlands.

The farther south they went, the taller the crops grew. But what drew Clarrisa's attention was the way they were trampled on either side of the road. At first, it was only a few feet, then a full yard, and then several yards on either side of the road were flattened. The destruction marked the path of an army. The fields were empty of people, making for an unsettling feeling. She could feel death on the wind.

The horses smelled the battlefield first—tossing their heads and trying to turn around. Packs of filthy men began to pass them now, their hair marked with dirt and dried blood. They carried their wounded, eyeing their horses hungrily, but her escort held the standard of the prince, and the survivors cleared the road for them. The unlucky were lying on the side of the road where they had fallen and died of their wounds, their clansmen unable to take them home because they had no wagons. Once they crested the next hill, it was clear why there were no wagons for the survivors.

The battlefield was strewn with wreckage. Carts and wagons lay smoldering while the bodies of the fallen were left as a silent testament to the cost of victory. Horses and men alike were twisted in the last moments of their existence. Already the stench was growing unbearable.

"Sweet Mary..." Daphne muttered. Their escort swallowed roughly, gripping their reins tighter.

Clarrisa struggled to hold on to her hope. *She'd know if he was dead...*

Tears stung her eyes as they rode around the edge of the carnage. She was deluding herself. So many men lay staring at the sky, the light gone from their eyes. Crows circled, their cries sending shivers down her spine. Nausea gripped her, but she honestly didn't know if it was the stench or the sight that sickened her most. Shame touched her, for the truth was that her yearning was for Broen. What turned her stomach was the fear that his was among the rotting bodies.

I'd know... I'd feel it in my heart...

She prayed she was right.

"Which one?"

The captain shrugged. "I do nae know, my Lord Home. They both came out, and they are both fair-haired."

Lord Home paced back and forth in front of Clarrisa and Daphne. "Who is the York girl?"

Daphne raised her hand before Clarrisa did.

"No, she isn't. I am," Clarrisa insisted.

Lord Home frowned. "That's a piss-poor English accent if ever I heard one." He delivered a sharp slap to her cheek that popped loudly. Norris opened his eyes where he still rested in a bed behind Lord Home.

"You may both die, if that is your wish," Lord

Home announced, but he was distracted by a commotion that was rising outside the tent. He walked out, disappearing from sight as they heard him join the argument.

"Ye are still playing a dangerous game—both of ye," Norris remarked with more strength than he appeared to have. He looked toward the tent opening. "But once more fate is siding with ye. Come here now."

He sat up, gritting his teeth but making no sound. He pulled a dirk from the inside of his boot. "That's the prince raising a fuss out there. Slit the side of the tent and escape before Home soothes the youth. If yer luck holds, the royal guard will be watching the commotion and ignoring the back of this pavilion."

"If they aren't?" Clarrisa asked.

Norris leaned back on his elbow. "Ye'll miss getting the chance to say yer prayers before Home has ye murdered." He tugged his signet ring off. "Take this. Me men will take care of ye."

"Did you have word of Broen?"

"Nay." He pointed at the canvas wall near the headboard. "Go now, Clarrisa, or ye will nae have the chance to look for yer heart mate."

Daphne wasn't lingering. She took the dirk and rent the canvas, right next to the bed so it would go unnoticed longer.

"Go now," Norris muttered before standing. His face turned white, pain filling his eyes, but he made it to his feet and walked toward the doorway. He stood there, providing them with the chance to leave and giving himself an alibi.

Daphne sucked in a breath before she slipped through the slit. Clarrisa waited but heard no cry for her to halt. Daphne reached back into the tent for her. With a deep breath, Clarrisa followed. No one noticed them, because everyone's attention was on the fight happening in front of the tent.

Clarrisa tightened her hand around the ring as Daphne gripped her wrist and led her between other tents. The fight faded as they searched for the banners of the Earl of Sutherland.

"There…" Daphne muttered. "Pray, Clarrisa, for I have no faith in anything else at the moment."

❦

"Where did they go?" Lord Home demanded.

Norris shivered and looked about the tent as though searching for the women. "I… I heard ye and the prince…" he muttered.

"Ye shall not question him further, Lord Home." James spoke sharply. "The surgeon told ye he was near death."

"So he did," Home replied, but Norris saw the suspicion glittering in his eyes. Norris played his part, lying still, as though his walk to the door had over-taxed him. In truth, he was itching to be free of the tent, but Home would follow him the moment he left. The women needed more time to escape.

So he lay back, allowing the prince to believe him weak. But it was a dangerous game, one that might end in his death if Home decided he knew too much. For the moment, though, he had to stay put. Broen MacNicols owed him a large favor—so long as they were both among the living by dawn, a fact he wasn't entirely sure of.

⚯

"I've got to get ye both away from this camp." Gahan Sutherland was a huge man. His hair was black as midnight, and his hands massive. He turned the ring over several times before slipping it into his pouch.

"Strip out of those dresses." He didn't give them any time to argue, pointing at Clarrisa and Daphne. "And thank Christ both of ye have short hair, or I'd be cutting it off. Ye'll dress as lads—and even that may not be enough to get ye out of this camp as more than corpses. Undress while I fetch ye some clothing."

He was gone only a few moments before he ducked under the rod holding up the top of the tent and threw a bundle of clothing at them. "Get into these and grab me sword and shield before ye attend me outside."

"So now we're lads…" Daphne muttered as she tried to buckle the belt to hold the kilt around her waist.

"You've come a far distance from life in the convent," Clarrisa whispered.

Daphne gasped, but her eyes filled with merriment. She smothered her amusement behind a hand. "Ye're wicked, Clarrisa."

"She is English, nothing more foul on this earth, except perhaps the stench of English royal blood." Lord Home stood in the doorway with his men behind him. "Something I plan to rid this country of."

⚯

She should have been afraid, but all she felt was a sense

of calmness that settled deep, feeling like it was seeping into her bones.

Lord Home motioned his men toward her, but Clarrisa stepped forward. Daphne tried to hold on to her, but she gently twisted her wrist from the girl's grip.

"I am finished with these games," she announced. Surprise flickered in Home's eyes, but she focused on the admiration on the faces of his men. She'd not die a coward.

Once outside the tent, she drew more than one curious stare. "Well now, my Lord Home, shall you slit my throat here for all to see?"

"Be silent, woman," he growled.

Boldness flooded her, sparking a rebellious desire inside her. "I think not. If your plan is to murder me, I believe all should know you are not satisfied by your victory."

"I told ye to be silent!" Lord Home hissed.

"Clarrisa of the house of York doesn't often keep her mouth shut." Clarrisa jerked around, certain Broen's ghost had arrived, because the man had sworn to protect her.

"She does so because she is the daughter of a king." Broen was filthy. His shirt was brown with dried blood, and his kilt sliced in several places. Mud was caked to his boots all the way to his knees, but he was the finest sight she had ever beheld. She launched herself toward him, only to be caught by the royal guards.

"Laird MacNicols… we feared ye dead." Lord Home spoke softly. The man didn't care for how many men were clustered about them. "Let us retire to the royal pavilion."

"As ye like, so long as ye tell yer men to get their hands off *my woman*." Broen's voice was deadly, and he'd raised his sword, his eyes bright with challenge. The royal guards closed around Lord Home, obviously fearing for their master's safety.

The fear she hadn't felt earlier arrived now, choking her. Had she found him only to watch him die because of her careless behavior?

"Now there, me lads… is a fine example of what happens when a Highlander steals a woman." Kael Grant appeared beside Broen, looking as battle-worn and determined. He held his sword up, standing shoulder to shoulder with Broen. "So I suggest ye do what he says. Unlike the rest of ye, the battle has nae really ended for us."

"Put down your swords. To threaten me is to threaten the prince," Lord Home declared.

The guards holding Clarrisa didn't agree; they released her with a shrug. She ran through the space between her and Broen, reaching for the man she'd longed so much for. He held her only for a moment, but she was sure it was a lifetime.

"To hold her is treason, Laird MacNicols, but ye are welcome to share her execution," Home muttered before marching back toward his pavilion. He raised his hand and waved his guards at them, but one look from Broen and the guards tugged on the corners of their bonnets, waiting to follow them to the royal pavilion.

"Clarrisa, lass… why is it ye are never where I leave ye?" He'd pulled her close and buried his head in her hair. She heard him draw in a deep breath, the arm binding her to him quivering. One of the royal guards cleared his throat.

"'Tis a damned sad day when a man returns from death's doorstep and cannae take a moment to enjoy his woman's embrace."

"Aye, it is that, makes me wonder what I've been bleeding for," Kael stridently agreed. Several of the guards looked away, unable to maintain their determined stares.

"A letter arrived. It was signed with your name, Broen. Claiming ye needed me here to tend ye," she explained.

Kael stepped close while Broen still held her to him. "Whose men escorted ye here?" Broen demanded softly. The seriousness in his expression made her shiver because it was clear their situation was as precarious as she believed. Lord Home might have her executed for no other reason than the blood flowing through her veins. But what frightened her was the determination in Broen's eyes to shield her, with his own life if necessary.

"Lord Home's. Norris is there in the royal pavilion. He gave me his signet ring, but we were discovered."

Kael muttered something. "Norris is playing a damned dangerous game to be resting his head there when his own men are here." Broen looked around, his muscles tensing.

Kael shook his head. "We've no chance of success. No' with our men on the other side of the camp and all of us fresh from the field. Better to see if we can play it out. Norris is clearly of the same mind or he'd no' be lying down in that royal pavilion. I'd bet me lairdship on it."

"Aye, and the fact that he gave his signet ring says he can be trusted."

Determination flickered in Broen's eyes, and it gave her confidence, but there was something else there, something that sent a sickening twist of dread through her.

❦

"Where is the prince?" Broen demanded.

"He's gone to confession. His Majesty is besieged by guilt over his father's passing. He'll likely be gone for hours," Lord Home informed them from behind his desk. His tone was smug, and he casually reached for a goblet of wine before looking at them.

The royal guards had had no difficulty in releasing her, but they had also escorted Broen along with her into the pavilion she'd so recently escaped. Fate had a misplaced sense of humor.

"I shall continue to make decisions that have His Majesty's best interests at heart," Lord Home declared.

She could hear him condemning her, but what sickened her was the fact that Broen was standing beside her. That was the horror she could not bear.

"Laird MacNicols does not need to share my fate. I became his mistress to have a place." She almost choked on the words but still forced herself to continue. "My uncle raised me to always consider gaining the best position I might."

"Poppycock," Broen announced. "She's the woman I plan to wed because I damned well want to. Ye're a bloody bastard to go after my woman while I'm out fighting to protect yer interests."

"Don't listen to him... He has a noble heart and wants to protect me," Clarrisa offered quickly. "I duped him into believing I have affection for him, but I couldn't ever have tender feelings for a Scotsman." She tried but failed to put as much disgust in her tone. At least she kept her chin level and her stare unwavering.

Lord Home smiled at her, but it wasn't a pleasant expression. "Rebellion shall not be tolerated, no matter the reason. The prince will be crowned, and only those loyal to him will be left in Scotland."

He looked beyond her. "Slit her throat and run through any man who steps into yer path."

Broen let out a snarl, but he had been disarmed, and the royal guards were all armed with pikes. The men lowered their weapons, pointing the deadly iron tips at them. A sense of calm gripped her, and she stepped forward, confident in her choice. Broen snarled softly and dug his hand into the back of her dress to yank her back.

"Release me, Broen," she muttered her words kindly, but the expression she witnessed on his face was one of the Highlander she'd faced when he first stole her.

"Nae a chance in hell, woman. Ye belong to me, and any man who threatens ye will face me."

He pulled her behind him, and Kael planted a hard hand on her shoulder to yank her behind him as well. Horror gagged her as the royal guards squared their shoulders and stepped forward with their pikes aimed at Broen.

Eight

"WE'VE RECEIVED A RANSOM DEMAND FOR LAIRDS Chisholms and Matthews from the remains of the royalist ranks."

The royal guards jumped, pointing their weapons at the young prince as he came hurrying through the door. The guards escorting him drew their swords, bristling.

"What happens here, Lord Home?" the prince demanded.

"Lord Home was just hearing about the ransom demand from Laird MacNicols and his clever plan to trade Clarrisa of the York family for our men." Norris Sutherland spoke up from behind the prince, pushing himself into a seated position. "Incredibly clever to trade an English royal bastard for good Scots lairds."

The prince smiled. "A wonderful idea, and it warms our heart to see ye recovering."

James turned to stare at her. He moved forward, looking more mature than his fifteen years. "I understand my father wanted to have a son with you."

Norris watched her from behind the prince, warning her with a stern look. Lord Home was quiet, obviously unwilling to admit he'd been making execution decisions without the prince's approval. She lowered herself in front of the prince.

"I did as commanded by my family."

James considered her for a long moment. "Every child owes obedience to their parents. It is written in the scriptures." The prince lost his composure for a moment, grimacing as though he was in pain. "Something I have recently learned I am guilty of not doing. I will forever strive to repent for the sin of being part of my father's death. The circumstances do not excuse me from the commandments."

Everyone in the tent waited for the youth to recover his poise, which he did quickly. He turned and walked to a large chair and sat down in it. Clearly he'd been raised to rule, for he looked like a king at that moment—poised and calm as he considered everyone in the pavilion.

"My prince..." Lord Home muttered. "She is a threat to you. Her kin will only arrange another match for her, with another man who thinks to challenge your place."

"Which is why ye should allow me to wed her," Broen interrupted. "I'll take her into the Highlands, and our children will be loyal to ye. I've proven my loyalty these past few days by fighting on yer behalf."

"But you have a betrothed, Laird MacNicols," Lord Home declared, his skin flushing with agitation. He pointed at Daphne where she stood silently watching the entire exchange. "Daphne MacLeod is bound to you and in just as much need of controlling, for her father fought with the royalists. I'm happy to report he fell in battle and will no longer trouble us, but the man had no sons. The MacLeods need controlling by a laird loyal to our prince. Besides, what the church has blessed cannot be undone so simply."

A strangled gasp came from Daphne. She slapped a hand over her mouth, but her eyes were wide with grief. Tears began to slowly fall down her cheeks.

"A betrothal must be honored." The prince spoke gravely. "There is no way to avoid that truth."

"I failed to honor it," Daphne interjected. "The disgrace is mine. Broen has the right to renounce me for refusing to take my wedding vows."

"As I said, the MacLeod need controlling, beginning with this girl who needs to honor her father's word, but another match can be made for her," Lord Home sputtered. He made a slashing motion with his hand. "MacNicols hopes to breed sons who will have a claim on your throne, and we have no need of men who plan such treason."

There were several snarls in the tent, sending the royal guards reaching for their pikes once more. Clarrisa couldn't tell who made the threatening sounds first, only that Broen, Kael, and Norris were all growling with rage.

"I'm covered in blood still from the battle I waged to see the prince gain his rightful place, and no man will label me a traitor," Broen spit out.

"Ye will nae say any vassal of mine is a traitor while he's been proving the opposite by coming to this field to stand behind ye," Norris argued.

"Enough!" Lord Home barked. "I will hear no more of this. She is a bastard of Edward the Fourth—and a

York one at that. She cannot be allowed to produce another generation to needle us. My prince, there have been countless lives sacrificed to ensure yer position. This is but one more. A necessary one. Have her put to death, immediately."

The royal guards were unsure whom to point their pikes at. They looked between Lord Home and the prince before raising their weapons and stepping back to wait on the whim of their new monarch.

"Ye have served us well, Lord Home, a fact we shall not forget." The prince spoke soberly, but he lifted a hand to keep everyone silent. "But Laird MacNicols has also served me well, and I shall nae repeat the mistakes my father made which led to this sad event of Scot fighting Scot. There will be justice even when the correct course of action goes against our personal wishes."

Broen, Kael, and Norris all nodded and inclined their heads. Clarrisa breathed a sigh of relief, feeling the horrible tension in the room easing. Or perhaps it was only the worry strangling her that released, as the prince appeared to be ready to ensure Broen was recognized for the nobleman he was.

Highlander… She took a moment to soak up the sight of him standing with his fellow Scots.

"The horse I gave my father helped identify him in battle," the prince muttered. "It matters not that I meant well. I helped cause his death, so I shall do penitence." James looked at her. "My lairds who fought so bravely beside me shall be given their due. Ye shall be returned to yer kin in exchange for lairds Chisholms and Matthews."

"Yer Majesty—" Broen raised his voice.

"I respect yer courage, Laird MacNicols, but ye should no more cast off yer duty to yer father. Ye are betrothed to Daphne MacLeod," the prince said.

"She's the daughter of a traitor." It was Norris who spoke up, moving to stand near the prince. "The match agreed upon before sides had to be chosen. It's a fair-enough reason for the match to be renounced."

James looked at Daphne, pausing for another moment. "It's true the scriptures say a child of a traitor is tainted, but if that is so, half our countrymen would be considered unfit to be my subjects. We shall consider them all misguided until now and give them the opportunity to prove themselves. None shall be reproached until they give reason for such. My men shall see to the ransom."

"By God, no one shall—"

There was a heavy thud, and Broen crumpled to the floor. Norris Sutherland tucked a short dagger back into his belt, the hilt of which was a large brass ball. His expression was furious, but resignation flickered in his eyes. "It's best I see to me vassal."

The prince nodded, his eyes wide. Norris's face was white, but he held his ground and looked at Daphne. "Ye'll come along now and take up the duties of caring for the man yer father bound ye to. Since ye are to wed Laird MacNicols, ye're me vassal."

Clarrisa was halfway across the tent when Norris stepped into her path. She froze, raising her gaze from the crumpled form lying on the fine Persian carpets to the face of the man preventing her from touching Broen.

"Ye shall do as commanded, madam. Ye are on Scottish soil, and so subject to the Scottish king's will. Just as I am. Laird MacNicols is me responsibility now."

Norris snapped his fingers, and several of the royal guards came forward. They lifted Broen and carried him from the pavilion. The oddest feeling filled her. It was overwhelming relief, reinforced by the sight of Broen's chest rising and falling until the canvas wall prevented her from seeing him. But she was also filled with white-hot pain, as though part of her were being cut away by the sharpest of knives. She stood there, twisting her hands into the fabric of her dress until her hands ached.

Norris offered his king a lowering of his head before he pointed Kael toward the door and followed him out. She was left facing Lord Home, but the man was busy reading the ransom notice.

She suddenly laughed. A dry, brittle sound of irony.

"What amuses ye?" James asked, some of his somberness lifting now that he wasn't facing his grown subjects. When she turned to look at him, she could see a hint of playfulness on his face.

"Naught, Your Majesty. I am simply glad there is no blood spilled, for I was sure it would happen. I laugh because I am glad to find myself proven wrong."

Lord Home scoffed. "Women have no business speaking their minds in the presence of men. Yer prattle is a waste of our time."

The prince frowned but said nothing. For a moment she felt a kinship with him. She could see in his eyes the same look of resignation she so often felt herself. They were both born into a world full of people who wanted to use them. To survive, they endured what they must and hid their true feelings.

She was not sure she would survive being parted from Broen, but the knowledge that he would live was balm for her wounds. It numbed them enough for her to remain still, when inside part of her was screaming with the need to flee. Yet if she could not go to the side of the man she loved, she cared not where she went.

෴

He had to wake. Broen battled the fatigue demanding he rest, fighting to regain consciousness. When he lifted his eyelids, soft hands held a cup to his lips. His vision was blurry, but he saw the short, fair hair and drank from the cup offered. *Clarrisa…*

He relaxed back into sleep, confident in her arms.

"Are yer tears true?" Norris was taunting her. Daphne raised her face and stood. She left the goblet near the bed Broen was sleeping in, the remains of the sleeping draught pooling in its bottom. She felt the stain of her transgression burning across her soul. He would hate her for her deed, but she would detest herself far more.

"They are, for I'd prefer to have none of this affair."

"Why?" Norris demanded in a soft voice full of arrogance. "It will make ye the wife of a Highland laird, ensure ye are mistress of a fine castle and mother of the next chieftain. A fine position many would like to have."

She was suddenly so angry she didn't care if he was heir to the earldom of Sutherland. She would grant him no submission.

"I want it not. They love each other. Parting them is a sin against the heart God gave us to feel love with. All I have ever brought to Broen is suffering: first when he took to fighting with his best friend over what came with me, and now because the prince used me to separate him from the woman he truly desires. Would that I could make it so he'd renounce me."

His lips twitched, his color better than she seemed to recall. "Well now, Daphne MacLeod, if ye want something else for yerself... ye shall have to take a hand in carving out what ye desire of fate. Most women do nae have the courage for such action."

"And ye doubt I do?" She laughed, stepping closer—so close they were only a single pace apart. There was a fire brewing in her belly, one she didn't understand, but she wanted to let the heat build further. Maybe it would burn away the feeling of being strangled.

"This match is poison."

One of his eyebrows lifted arrogantly. "The prince is set in his thinking. Broen cannae refuse a royal command." He stroked her cheek. "So make the best of it. Take a lover or a dozen once ye've secured yer position by giving him some sons. Since he has affections for another woman, I doubt he'll mind very much."

His touch should have shocked her; instead, it fanned the flames licking at her insides. She needed to break free of every rope binding her, so she smiled at the ripple of sensation traveling across her skin—because it was forbidden.

"Ye understand nothing." She spun away from

him, but Norris grabbed her upper arm and pulled her back against him with a strength that surprised her. He chuckled softly. "Ye are nae weakened," she accused, jerking against his hold and finding herself caught.

"And ye are crying out against fate and her cruel nature instead of taking action."

There was a tone in his voice that made her freeze. "What do ye mean? Speak plainly."

He released her, moving past her until he stood over Broen. He lifted one of his eyelids and studied Broen's pupil. "He'll sleep until sunrise, but nae much longer, no' with his attachment to young Clarrisa eating at him."

Daphne followed Norris, wanting, not actually needing, to know what he wasn't telling her. She could feel something drawing her to him; it was as instinctive as stretching out chilled fingers to be closer to a fire.

Norris turned to face her; his hand cupped her jaw before slipping over the surface of her cheek. It was a bold touch. She lifted her hand but never delivered the slap such forwardness deserved.

"Why are ye toying with me?" she muttered, irritated by the way he was watching her. His green eyes shimmered with a need that tugged at her heart for some reason.

He offered her a dry chuckle and stroked her cheek once again. This time his eyes narrowed as though he was trying to memorize the way her skin felt against his own. "Because I am a blackguard."

She stepped back but didn't move very far away, because she felt the separation between them keenly.

It made no sense, but her instinct was to return to where he could touch her again. "A touch on the cheek hardly labels ye a blackguard."

"I'm a knave for thinking to help ye and my friend Broen by satisfying me own need to touch life." There was heat in his tone; it bordered on desperation, as though he was starving.

"I do nae understand…" But she wanted to. She stepped closer and put her hand on his chest, drawn to the need in his eyes. He quivered, her fingers detecting the tiny response to her touch.

Norris massaged the back of her neck, slowly sliding his fingers along the tender skin. "Watching men die is nae an easy thing. It dries out the soul, sending ye searching for the life that flows through a woman."

He leaned down, touching his lips against hers. She might have retreated, but his kiss seemed to satisfy the cravings inside her. He teased her lips until she mimicked his motions and kissed him back.

"Slap me and leave." He was angry, but it appeared to be with himself. He brushed past her and sat on the bed against the other side of the tent. The ropes creaked as he sat down.

"It's rather hard to slap ye when ye walk away."

He untied one boot and tossed it aside. "Then come here and do yer worst, Daphne…" The second boot followed. "I dare ye to come within me reach, for me stomach has been turned with the sight of too much blood spilled for selfish ambition. I want to feel yer heart beating while I discover what yer lips taste like, and no' because of any affection I feel for ye but for the sake of assuring meself that I'm still alive. So come over here if ye dare." There was an unmistakable challenge in his voice. He opened his doublet and tossed the garment aside with more force than necessary.

"Why do ye dare me? Do ye truly believe I'm so impressed with yer title that I'd no' take ye to task if I wanted to?" She was growing warm and had trouble keeping her attention on his face. He ripped his shirt up and off next. Her discipline failed, and she let her gaze wander over his bare torso. Only a strip of white bandaging kept her from seeing every inch of him exactly as nature had crafted him. *Magnificent...*

"I'm daring ye to do what ye please with yer future, Daphne." He stood once more and pulled on the end of the wide leather belt securing his kilt. It fell down, but he caught it, bending with only a tiny grimace. His cock stood hard and ready, and the man didn't even blush. Instead, he tossed his plaid aside and faced her with a challenge on his face.

"I'm daring ye, Daphne MacLeod, to come lie with me because ye want to choose who will ride ye."

"That is nae why I do nae want to wed Broen. It's because the match me father offered was like poison between him and Faolan. I do nae want such a stain on me conscience."

He shrugged and pushed the bedding aside before lying down. The damned man looked more powerful once he was stretched out—Daphne noticed her mouth had gone strangely dry.

"I warned ye. I'm a blackguard, Daphne." He patted the surface of the bed beside him. "I want ye to come here and let me seek solace against yer sweet flesh. The only courtesy I'm offering is the fact that I will nae overwhelm ye with me greater knowledge of seduction by getting up and chasing ye around this tent."

"But ye could…" She shouldn't have spoken aloud, but the words tumbled past her lips.

"Aye, easily." The words rolled so easily from his lips, but what shocked her was the fact that she did not doubt him. Not one bit. Her belly quivered as she recognized just how easily he could seduce her. The man knew his way around a woman's body and that was for sure.

She propped her hands on her hips. "Someday someone is going to knock some of that smugness out of ye, Norris Sutherland. I've a mind to try me hand at it."

He smiled at her, the rogue in him unrepentant. "Well, it will nae be ye, because ye'll be bearing Broen MacNicols's babes. Unless ye come to me now and give the man the only reason the prince will accept to renounce ye: lack of virtue."

Rejection surged through her. "Do ye think I lack the courage?"

His expression became serious. "I think ye know ye are trapped, and it sickens ye. But the prince is young, and he's unknowingly left ye with a slim opportunity to escape his decree. But such will not come freely. Broen can only renounce ye for losing yer maidenhead, and I'm a blackguard for no' offering to help ye deceive him."

"But ye would welcome me to yer bed."

Norris nodded. "As I said… a blackguard."

"A choice…" she muttered, glancing back at Broen. He wasn't sleeping restfully. The bedding was rumpled about his feet where he kicked at it. He didn't want her, and her pride bristled beneath the weight of the knowledge. Combined with the memory of how he and Faolan had fought over her, she turned back to stare at Norris. Oh, the man was a blackguard, but at the moment he was also her friend because he offered the one thing she wanted most of all.

"Well now, Norris Sutherland, it seems ye do nae know all that much about this seduction matter, for I cannae loosen me dress on me own, and I rather thought seduction included more than simply tossing me skirts… yet ye're the one claiming to be the experienced one."

Something appeared in his eyes. She wasn't exactly sure what it was, because he sat up so fast. Her belly tightened, a bolt of fear spiking through her as the man approached her. He was somehow larger than she'd noticed before, more menacing perhaps.

Yet he was also intriguing. She wanted to know what it was like to feel his heart beating against her. A craving to lose herself in the moment, while she forgot about everything the world around them expected of her, was licking across her skin. He slipped his hands beneath her short hair, gripping the silken threads just hard enough to send little ripples of discomfort along her scalp. She gasped from the intensity of the sensation. It wasn't pain; it was deep enjoyment rising up from some place inside her she'd never noticed before. He pressed his mouth against hers, surprising her with how gentle the kiss was.

Her choice, and she was pleased with it.

❧

"I have not seen you since you were learning to walk."

Sir Richard Scope wore his knighthood proudly. He circled Clarrisa, studying her from head to toe before settling himself down with his comrades once again. They were watching her with a similar familiar glint in their eyes, gauging her worth to their cause. She was still on Scottish soil, but among the English—at least, men who believed themselves to be English. She wasn't sure. After all, they had fought with the prince to overthrow his father in the hopes the young boy would assist them in pushing Henry Tudor off the throne.

"She isn't worth what we gave up for her," one man groused.

"I disagree," Richard answered. "Since the young Scottish prince has given us sanctuary here, we would have had to return his lairds for naught. Now we have another blooded heir to help us push that pretender Henry off the throne."

"She's a bastard, and a female. That will be no help now that Henry has an heir."

Richard picked up a mug and took a swallow. She continued to stand before the three men, no offer of chair or stool for her. Of course not, for she was a commodity to them, something with value to be used to gain what they wished.

"Babies die often. So do women. If Elizabeth of York dies in her next childbed, Edmund shall be king. Clarrisa will be used to secure a good alliance for his cause. We'll dangle her blood in front of the noses of some of these Scots, or perhaps a French lord or two who seek connections with royal houses. There will be someone willing to pay us for her."

Clarrisa stopped listening. Edmund was her cousin, his older brother having been killed in the last battle with Henry Tudor. He was a boy no older than the prince of Scotland and she had never met him. But she felt kinship with him; it seemed he was living a life much like her own.

"She's likely no virgin."

Richard snickered. "Who cares? James Stuart paid for her, and if she produces a child, it will have uses." He snapped his fingers, and one of his men came forward. "Take her and see that she is guarded well until we depart for the tower we've been promised."

Clarrisa left the tent gladly. Outside the day was dying, night falling over the camp. With the wind blowing in their favor, they couldn't smell the stench of death from the battlefield. But she felt it.

Despair ripped at her heart. It threatened to steal her breath, the weight of it so great, it felt as though it might crush her. The Scottish camp was not so far away, but it might as well have been halfway to London. She could not return to Broen. He was as trapped by circumstance as she. The breeze turned her tears cold but she was sure fate was colder. Richard and his friends were busy deciding who to sell her to next.

By morning, the tents were being taken down and a long line of wagons began to carry away the remains of the battle. She mounted a mare while the sun was still only half risen and followed her relatives.

She wanted to kick the sides of the animal and urge it to run back toward the man she loved, but the retainers flanked her, keeping her as surely as any chest of gold they'd discovered. Yet it wasn't the men guarding her she felt she couldn't escape from. It was the certainty that Broen was not free to wed her or even keep her as his leman. Lord Home would surely demand she be taken from Deigh Tower if she returned there.

So it was better to face her fate sooner rather than later. Courage was after all within her power to grasp. She lifted her chin and refused to glance over her shoulder again. Broen's face filled her thoughts anyway. She smiled in triumph because her kin could never force her to relinquish her memories.

Broen ripped himself from slumber's grip at last. He wasn't very well rested, his muscles aching from his restless night. With a curse, he rolled out of bed and tried to decide what it was that had been hounding him all night long.

The tent was low, and he frowned when he looked for his boots. He saw a pair lying on the floor that he didn't recognize. His memory was slow to return, and he rubbed his eyes before reaching for one of the boots.

"I believe that one belongs to me." Norris was still in bed, but the man didn't sound sleepy. In fact, he sounded fully alert, which drew Broen's attention to the man's face. Sure enough, Norris was watching him from the other bed, his green eyes clear and focused. "Daphne put yers under the stool."

Broen didn't reach for his boots. Instead, he watched the rumpled head of blond hair snuggled against Norris's chest begin to stir. Norris stroked the woman's neck gently as she stretched and turned. Daphne blinked and reached up to rub her eyes.

"What in Christ's name is happening here?" Broen exploded.

Daphne opened her eyes wide and sat up. He got a fine view of her small breasts when she left the bedding behind in her haste.

The tent's door flaps were flung open, Norris's men and Shaw all looking in to see why he was yelling.

"Ye tell me what's happening, Broen." He stood and swept Daphne out of the bed. He bundled her in the comforter, leaving the soiled sheet on display.

"God damn ye to hell—" Broen shut his mouth before finishing, the look of relief on Daphne's face distracting him. Glee or fear, he'd have understood, but she gently pushed herself away from Norris and sighed as though a weight had been lifted off her shoulders.

"Close the flaps," Norris barked at his men. "Ye've seen enough."

There was grumbling from Shaw. "Go on, Shaw," Broen muttered before sitting back down and yanking his boots out from where they sat under the stool. The tent flaps closed, and he spied the cup sitting on top of the stool. One sniff and he cursed.

"Ye doused me with a sleeping draught."

"That was my doing," Norris answered as he shrugged into his shirt. "It seemed the only way to keep ye from getting run through when ye went after Clarrisa in defiance of the prince's order."

"Something I'll still be doing. Do nae have any doubt about that, Norris Sutherland."

"And now ye can," Daphne muttered softly. She'd donned her chemise and was lifting her underdress over her head, still looking relieved. No blush stained her cheeks, only firm resolution flickered in her eyes. He'd missed something about her when she'd revealed to him that she was alive—Daphne was no longer a girl. She was a woman willing to shoulder the weight of her own choices. She no longer feared the challenges life presented.

"Christ in heaven, ye did nae have to go to such lengths, Daphne."

"Did I nae?" She turned to stare at him while holding her underdress over her breasts because it needed lacing up her back. "There was no other way to end this contract between us. Ye must renounce me, something ye would nae do without cause."

"I would nae have taken me freedom at the expense of yer good name, woman," Broen muttered with a bitter taste filling his mouth. "It was me duty to resolve the matter, no' yers."

She lifted her overdress from where it rested over the arm of a chair. "I knew ye would say such. So it fell to me to end this before we drove one another to bitterness because neither of us wanted to wed. I'm going home now. Perhaps I am a poor daughter, but I will take me father home to be buried on MacLeod land."

She left the tent, having to wait as Norris's men and his own shifted out of her path. Daphne held her chin high as she went, the open back of her underdress speaking clearly to every man watching. The flaps closed, and Broen slammed his fist into Norris's jaw.

"Damn ye, Norris! Ye should have tied her up and kept her from doing such a thing."

Norris rubbed his jaw but didn't retaliate. Guilt shone in his eyes. "I know well I'm a knave for taking advantage of her, but I am nae a liar. No' now, no' ever, Broen MacNicols. Ye can hate me for the things I do, but ye will never have to wonder if I'm telling ye the truth when ye ask what me position is."

Broen sat down heavily, the bed ropes groaning beneath his weight. He stared at Norris and the soiled sheet, and God help him, he felt relieved, but guilty because Daphne had been the one to resolve the situation.

"I'm a damn bastard too," he muttered.

"Ye're a lucky fool, for I swear I'd no' take a blow from any other." Norris rubbed his jaw before searching for his boots. "But ye're entitled to a few. Lord Home took that damned letter from me doublet when I was too weak to notice. He sent his men up and convinced Clarrisa to leave the protection of Deigh."

"Where is she?" The relief transformed into a raging need to claim the woman he loved. "Where is Clarrisa?"

"They traded her for Faolan last night. I hear the prince has granted her kin sanctuary from Henry Tudor's desire to wipe all York blood off the face of the Earth. They will be staying in Scotland."

Broen stood up, but Norris blocked his path.

"Get out of me way, Norris, or ye'll sample a few more blows from me hand I doubt ye'll be so quick to forgive."

"Stealing her will nae solve yer dilemma. Think, man. This is nae as simple as stealing the woman. Is yer desire for her so great ye'd risk her life as well as yer own? Once ye're dead for treason, it will nae take long for Home to finish her off."

Broen let out a frustrated growl that sent the tent flaps opening again. He waved Shaw away and waited for Norris to do the same with his men.

"There are times I hate needing others too, Broen, but alliances keep our clans strong. I need ye as much as ye need me. Ye're smart enough to know a bride with royal blood must be contracted. And that ye would no' be the only man wanting her wed into yer clan."

"That's a fact, one I plan to make into reality."

But it would not be simple. In fact, it was most likely impossible. But Broen refused to think about the facts. He'd find the way because the thought of failure sent white hot pain through his heart. The steady look on Norris's face assured him he wouldn't have to do it alone. He offered Norris his hand and his friend took it.

"Let's make a plan," Norris muttered.

⬥

"Oh now, I've been so worried about you," Maud muttered. She busied herself with snapping her fingers at the two maids pulling lengths of sheeting off the furniture in the chamber.

"This tower is older but it is made of stone. That gives me good solace, it does, seeing as how we're still in Scotland and on the border of the Highlands no less. God is testing us, I have no doubt."

Clarrisa walked to the window. The keep looked north. *To the Highlands*... All that much better for her to dwell upon happier times.

She busied herself with helping to clean the chamber. It helped her to not dwell upon the fact that her last link with Broen was gone. Her monthly courses had arrived to confirm her brief sojourn into free will had not resulted in a child.

"The master is beginning to receive offers for ye, and ones which include marriage this time," Maud continued to babble. She stopped and rubbed her hands together. "Your obedience has paid off, indeed it has. You'll be a proper wife, of a nobleman possibly..."

Her place, her duty, her fate.

It still wasn't enough to steal the last bit of joy from her heart. The only thing she feared was that it would grow cold with time. Still, for the moment she was grateful for the impulse that had seen her following her heart into Broen's embrace. Love did exist; she'd felt it as sure as holding her hand over a candle flame.

What sobered her was the certain knowledge that she could not expect her future to hold such a wonderful feeling. She'd be fickle to believe she'd love the man Sir Richard sent her to, because true love wasn't something that ever died. She could not discard the feelings burning inside her heart for Broen and expect them to grow for another man at her whim. Love could not be directed, which was why matrons such as Maud spent so many hours trying to prevent their young charges from meeting anyone they might form affection for. It was better to be kept away from temptation, so she might be

content when she was sent off to wed the man who
contracted her.

Clarrisa smiled, because Highlanders such as Broen
obviously didn't obey such rules of common sense.
She preferred him that way. Wild and untamed by
civilization. Well, Broen would have to obey his king;
being a Highlander would not keep him from his duty.

She'd go wherever her kin sent her, because Broen
was likely already wed to Daphne. It would be better
to have her own place too since she couldn't take one
beside the man she loved. Such would be the practical
thing to do.

But she grinned, looking up toward the Highlands.
Amusement tickled her almost beyond her endurance
to maintain her composure as she considered just what
Sir Richard might make of the fact that she was docile,
only because the man she loved was bound to another.

She'd wager the pompous Englishman would
turn purple and choke on his arrogance. Another
pleasant thought.

"A pleasant night to ye, mistress." Clarrisa looked up
because the maids seldom spoke to her beyond a yes or
no response. Like a ghost in the keep, she was there,
but not really the same as the other inhabitants. She
felt as though she was waiting—but for what? The
summer was half gone, and she couldn't distinguish
the days one from another. The excitement in the
maid's tone was the first thing different from the
routine she'd fallen into.

"Thank you."

The girl's eyes were shimmering, and she fingered her skirts for a moment. "Och well... I hear in England a servant does nae speak unless spoken to, but I just want to say how happy I am for ye. The eldest son of the Earl of Sutherland for yer husband. Now there is something to celebrate. Yer kin has done right well for ye. I know more than one clan was hoping to place their laird's daughter there." The girl smiled brightly. "But ye're the daughter of a king, and blood is blood."

"Enough," Maud snapped. "Get on with you."

The girl drew in a stiff breath, her elated expression becoming tense. Clarrisa looked at the old matron suspiciously.

"Sir Richard was going to tell you of your good fortune soon." The note of superiority in her voice kindled Clarrisa's temper. She looked at the maid.

"Thank you for telling me." She raised her voice just enough to make it clear she was putting Maud in her place. "You are very kind."

The girl beamed before lowering herself quickly. Her skirts bounced behind her as she moved quickly out of the chamber.

"Exactly why you have not been told of your impending marriage. The news polishes your pride. You'll become difficult." Maud shook a finger at her. "My position is to ensure you are raised to be properly respectful—"

"You mean subservient to whoever pays the most for me."

Maud began turning red; her mouth opened and closed a few times before she managed to form her thoughts into words. "Now see here. You will remember your place."

"Enough, Maud. Why are you so surprised to hear me speak my mind? It wasn't a docile nature that kept me alive in the Highlands." Clarrisa sat on her bed and took off her slippers. She longed for the boots Ardis had crafted for her, but Maud had taken them away, declaring them rough and uncivilized. "Besides, it cost nothing to be kind to the girl, unless you want it whispered that I believe myself too good for a Scots groom. I don't think it wise to anger those who call this country home."

"What is not wise is the tone you are using. I've devoted myself to helping you gain such an offer, and listen to the way you rail at me like some dockside strumpet." Maud drew in a dramatic breath. "Why, it's a wonder you've been blessed at all. It hardly seems fair when you are such an ungracious child."

"Perhaps if you explained more of the details, I might be less ignorant of my good fortune."

Maud was torn. Clarrisa could see the matron battling the urge to rail at her as the desire to preen over their newest accomplishment grew.

"I should allow Sir Richard to tell you, but perhaps that isn't such a wise plan, seeing as how you are so prone to speaking whatever thought you have. Maybe you are simple-minded, for I know I have tried to teach you to hold your tongue."

Clarrisa bit her lip to maintain her silence, earning herself a nod of approval from the sour matron.

"The Earl of Sutherland has been negotiating with Sir Richard. They opened a bottle of French wine today and looked quite merry."

Maud clapped her hands together as Clarrisa battled the urge to speak her mind once more. She lay down and sighed when Maud pinched the candles out. Darkness was welcome, and she found it the only time when she felt Broen near her. Tonight, though, it felt like even his memory was being tugged away from her. In its place she recalled the way Norris Sutherland had looked at her. Well, it would seem he had his prized mare now.

She rolled over, wiping the tears from her cheeks with a frustrated hiss. Crying was for babes and girls too young to understand the way the world worked. She should be grateful to have a sanctuary so far from Henry Tudor and his quest to wipe out her blood.

What kept her up most of the night was the fear that she'd live to see her children drawn into the struggle for England's crown.

❧

Dunrobin was magnificent. The castle of the Earl of Sutherland was far north, but at least the summer made it a warm journey.

Clarrisa heard the surf long before she realized that the castle dropped off in back. There were three towers in the front, rising into the air some three stories, the center one rising even higher. A half curtain wall protected it, and there were cannons positioned every ten feet along the battlement.

Magnificent and cold-looking. They could be a law unto themselves here, for it would be very costly to march an army all the way up to the walls of this castle—all the while dragging the machines necessary to knock down the thick stone walls.

"Look at that. I feared we'd have to live in a hovel, but none of your relatives have a finer holding. The hallways might be moldy, though…"

Clarrisa had let her hood fall back, and Maud snapped her fingers at her. "Your cheeks are chapped from the wind and pink from the sun. What will your bridegroom think?"

"The man is a Highlander. I understand they like their women a little more natural."

Maud frowned, although it honestly wasn't much of a change from the disapproving expression the matron wore most of the day through. "He's contracted you, which means he has more taste than his barbarian kin. Raise your hood, so you arrive as a lady should."

She would not weep… Clarrisa ordered herself to remain firmly in control of her emotions. She could not go back to Broen, so there was no reason to lament taking her place beside another man. The church might have her, but without a dowry, she could expect no protection. It would only be a matter of time before someone stole her to either murder her or breed her. Wedding Norris Sutherland was better, a wiser choice.

But it still hurt… Every step the mare carried her closer to the man she'd have to lie with as intimately as she had Broen threatened her composure. Now that the moment was upon her, all her well thought out reasons deserted her. Her heart ached, the pain more powerful than she'd ever thought possible. It threatened to crush her with its strength as she fought to draw in even breaths.

The Sutherland retainers leaned over the battle-ments to gain a glimpse of her. Once inside the yard,

maids and other members of the clan found excuses
to come outside the inner buildings to stare at her.
Maud didn't allow her to linger. The matron moved
with more speed than Clarrisa had guessed she had.
She gained only a glimpse of the yard and then up the
stairs into the first keep. The head of house stood with
a large ring of keys secured to her wide leather belt.

"Welcome to Dunrobin Castle. I am Asgree."
Several maids stood behind her, all lined up and
turned out in freshly ironed linen caps. They lowered
themselves, earning a grunt from Maud.

"My charge shall require a bath before tonight's
celebration of her nuptials."

Asgree nodded before leading the way through
the maze of hallways. The castle was larger than it
appeared. At last, they came to a chamber three stories
up. "The earl has said ye shall have this chamber and
the solar above it."

Two maids were waiting in the chamber. They
lowered themselves before straightening back up and
remained poised in position in case they were called
upon. But they didn't look at her.

Edme had never run Deigh with such rigid
formality. Perhaps in time she might change it, but the
reality was, she had little authority among the household staff unless Norris dictated it so. Her husband.

She tried to say the word again, but her mind refused
to acknowledge the firm reality of their union. It was
already done, the vows taken by proxy. Sir Richard was
no fool to allow her outside the keep he controlled until
the union was sealed by the church. All that remained
was the celebration of the union. The bedding.

She turned to look at the large bed on the opposite side of the chamber. The comforter was already turned down. The scent of rosemary rose from it, and amber burned somewhere in the chamber. Perfectly set.

There was nothing to find fault with except her discontentment. She was a fool indeed to recall a stormy May Day when she'd frolicked and lain with her lover. Her lips twitched up as the maids began to disrobe her. Maybe she should sink into her fantasy; it pleased her more than reality. Yet it would be unfair to Norris. No doubt his father was behind their match and he'd had little choice as well.

She took her bath and tried to force herself to enjoy the heather-scented soap. Asgree's staff was flawless in their service, and she stood with her hair drying in the summer breeze before long.

"I did nae know yer hair was short, but I've brought up a caul for ye." Asgree held the small cap gently. It was sewn of silk and adorned with pearls. It would fit over the back of her head, the band sitting behind her ears.

The maids were busy arranging her hair into braids, and then Asgree set the costly cap in place to conceal her short braids. The head of house pinned it in place and stood back to survey her work.

"Ye'll be right pleasing," she announced before the maids continued to dress her. A fine underdress and overdress were lifted above her head and then laced shut. Through it all, Maud watched, but not with the glee Clarrisa had come to expect from the matron. Instead, there was sadness in her eyes. The moment the maids finished, Maud waved them out.

"I know you believe me a harsh woman without any care for happiness, but the world is not a kind place. You needed to be strong enough to endure. Affection for me would have made me happy, but it would not have prepared you for the fate I knew your kin planned for you. At least they have not bound you to an old man. You can enjoy the blessings that are yours if you try. I'm finished now, my task completed. These Scots do not want me near you in case I poison you against their ways. I'm bound for the Lowlands and the promise of a quiet home for the remainder of my days."

The matron turned and left. Clarrisa tried to miss her but failed. It seemed Maud had performed her task well.

I think it sad ye have no place or one ye hold dear... Broen's voice rose from her memory, sending two tears down her cheek.

"Are ye ready?" Asgree asked from outside the chamber door.

"There is no reason for me not to be."

If the head of house found her answer odd, she failed to comment on it. Instead, she turned silently and led the way down the stairs.

❧

The great hall was lit with an abundance of candles. The tables were crowded and the long head table filled with the lairds who owed the Earl of Sutherland allegiance. Their different plaids caught her eye as she paused in the doorway.

Broen was there. *Of course he was*. Three seats to Norris's left with Shaw standing behind him. She should have expected it, but she felt as though her feet were nailed to the floor. Music began to play, and the people seated at the lower tables stood. The scraping of benches being moved back jolted her out of her shock.

Spirit was respected in the Highlands...

She forced herself to begin moving, trying to enjoy the harp's happy melody. The Earl of Sutherland stood to greet her.

"Welcome, Clarrisa of the York family. I'm right proud to see ye arriving to become me son's wife."

She lowered herself, biting her lip to keep her gaze from straying to Broen. She could feel him watching her—only him, really, because everyone else was nothing but a sea of strange faces. The single empty chair at the high table was pulled back for her.

A cheer went up the moment she sat down. Norris reached over and covered her hand with his. Another cheer went through the hall before the feast began.

Since the harvest was beginning, there was an abundance of food. Vegetables and fruits were carried past on large platters. Freshly baked bread and cakes. There were the first of the squashes and plenty of greens along with berries and apples. But when a silver bowl with rare pomegranates was set in front of her and Norris, she was sure the color drained from her face.

Pomegranates were an aphrodisiac, an expensive one because they had to be brought from afar by ship. Lytge Sutherland laughed at her expression and reached for one of the ruby fruits himself. He broke it in two, revealing the plump seeds inside.

"Yer bride needs a bit of encouragement, Son," he announced to the delight of his guests.

"Which is something I'll no' be needing help doing," Norris declared.

His fellow lairds chuckled, raising their goblets before draining them. Every laird had his captain at his back to safeguard him from poison while the feast progressed.

A roasted pig went by to be placed on a table and carved. There was lamb and beef too. All of it made its way on to her plate. Asgree guarded her meal like a hawk, taking away what she picked at and returning with fresh selections to tempt her. Once the meal was well under way, the younger girls took to the aisles to begin dancing. They rose onto their toes and lifted their skirts to show off rapid motions of foot and ankle. All the while, the harps and pipes helped them keep time. More toasts were raised, and the candles burned down while the Sutherland people celebrated.

When Asgree finally tapped her on the shoulder, she was startled because she hadn't realized how late it was growing. *Because you don't want to notice…*

She stood up, and a cheer went through the crowd. A good number of them wore intoxicated grins now.

"Hurry now…" Asgree muttered. "Before the men have time to cause trouble."

"What manner of trouble?" Clarrisa asked once they'd reached the hallways.

Two of the women walking with them laughed. They were not young girls but women of experience, obviously selected to inspect her once she was stripped and ready to be put to bed to ensure she was not deformed.

"Highlanders enjoy a healthy sense of humor. They'd enjoy making Norris retrieve ye from them."

"But he's their laird's son."

"Aye," one of the women said. "But if he cannae outwit them, he's no' fit to lead them."

They all laughed, enjoying the moment. Once back inside the chamber they quickly disrobed her. Clarrisa fought the urge to cover herself with her hands.

"Come now, into bed with ye before the men show up and see more than they should."

Asgree clapped her hands, and the women all stopped staring at her bare form. They helped cover her with the sheets while sending each other knowing smiles. The scent of rosemary filled her senses a moment before the door burst open. Lytge was leaning on his son, clearly besotted.

"There she is, Son! A royal-blooded bride for ye. The Lindsey may be crowing about how their chief was made a duke by the late king, but David Lindsey does nae have a royal-blooded bride! All he has is a title he'll no' pass on to his son if he ever has one."

Norris eyed her, something in his eyes sending a tingle down her back. It wasn't apprehension, but suspicion. His father's retainers gained his attention when they began to pull his kilt off.

"Enough, lads… I'll see to the matter meself."

He might as well have saved his breath, for the men paid him no mind. His father found another set of shoulders to loop his arm over and laughed at his son trying to keep his dignity.

Norris lost; every last article of clothing was stripped from him. His father's men winked at her before they quit the room, singing loudly in the hallway on their way down the stairs.

"The least ye might do is no' enjoy me humiliation, lass," Norris admonished her. He surprised her by reaching for his shirt and shrugging into it.

"Would you prefer to find me weeping?"

One of his fair eyebrows rose. "I expect it. After all, I'm a barbarian Highlander."

"Who worries about his modesty," she muttered demurely before laughing softly. There was nothing remotely near worry on his face; the man was completely at home in his skin. But her hands tightened on the bedding, rejection filling her thoughts. What she knew she had to do didn't seem able to slice through what she didn't want to do.

He frowned at her. "Ye mock me, madam." He pulled the shirt off and let it flutter to the floor. She looked away, gaining a soft chuckle from him.

"Be careful when ye challenge a Highlander, lass."

The bed dipped, and a chill raced across her skin. She couldn't bear it. Yet she must.

"Now here's the second time I've caught ye in bed with a woman who belongs to me without a stitch on, Norris."

Clarrisa jumped and shrieked when Norris rolled right over her. He came up in back of her, draping a strong arm across her body as she stared across the chamber at Broen.

"By rights, this one is contracted to me," Norris announced as he nuzzled her neck.

"But her heart belongs to me," Broen muttered softly. "Get out of her bed."

It was an insane thing to say but she couldn't help smiling.

Norris groaned but rolled back over the top of her and landed on his feet. She sat up, trying to decide what to demand first.

"What... what is happening—"

Norris cupped the back of her head and pressed a hard kiss against her mouth. She sputtered, abandoning her grip on the sheet to push him away. He suddenly flew back, but it was because Broen had hooked his shoulder and yanked him away from her.

Norris laughed at her. "Ye wound me with that look, Clarrisa. No' a single lass has ever complained about me kisses."

She opened her mouth to change that fact but was distracted by Broen. He stood there, close enough to touch, and she realized she couldn't stand not taking the opportunity to feel him against her. She made to rise, but he sat on the bed and pulled her close before she made it onto her knees.

It was perfection, a single moment that fed every longing she'd had since they'd been torn apart. Her hands roamed over him, stroking all the places she recalled.

"Well, I'll just see myself out..." Norris groused.

"That was the understanding," Broen muttered against her neck. He raised his head and looked toward Norris.

"What do you mean... understanding?" she asked, her voice a mere whisper because she feared she was dreaming and might wake any moment to discover Broen a figment of her imagination.

Norris sobered, his expression becoming serious.

"An agreement between friends—and make no mistake, lass, I do nae call many men me friend."

"But it means ye will be shouldering the burden of being called a disobedient daughter, Clarrisa." Broen was forcing his words through clenched teeth. He set her back by her biceps, his expression hard. "It's yer choice. Ye can stay with Norris if ye desire, but to leave him, he'll need to have a reason to renounce ye."

A smile split her lips, joy filling her so full, there was no way to contain it, but she suddenly froze. "What of Daphne?" she forced out at last.

"She made sure I could renounce her," Broen muttered. "By lying with Norris and making sure both his men and mine witnessed the evidence of her lost virtue."

Norris yanked on one of his boots and snorted. "Ye have a way with women, Broen. One I do nae envy."

"Ye took advantage of it sure enough," Broen accused his friend.

Norris shrugged and stood now that his boots were on. He paused for a moment to buckle a pleated kilt around his waist. His staff knew their duties well, for the wool had already been laid out on a table near the door.

"I did," he answered. "And I'll no' apologize either. Ye are nae the only man who finds himself pulled to a woman when he is nae expecting it." He turned and left. Clarrisa stared at the chamber door, too shocked to speak.

"I'll go if ye like, Clarrisa." Broen was forcing his words past gritted teeth once more. "But I wanted ye to know I love ye enough to try and regain ye.

Daphne gave herself to Norris so I could renounce her. I'd never have allowed her to do such a thing—"

"I didn't think you would." There was too much honor in him. He shook his head, refusing to allow her to make excuses for him.

"I wanted to steal ye away again, but Norris was correct. Stealing ye will nae end this. The prince would only insist I return ye to yer kin."

"So he's offering to let me make the same choice Daphne did."

His pride was wounded, and she could see him straining against the walls closing him in. The prince: her kin and his lord. She suddenly laughed, so relieved tears streamed down her cheeks. She kicked the bedding aside and stood, no longer feeling exposed, because Broen was the man she wanted to share herself with.

"Don't hate it. I can see in your eyes how much you detest doing this."

He snarled something in Gaelic and stood, pulling her against him with one hard arm.

"Ye reduce me to allowing another man to help me when what I want most is to take ye away because I cannae face the future without ye." His tone was thick with emotion, the arm binding her to him quivering. Or maybe it was her body quivering, perhaps both.

"I can bear anything if it means being with you, Broen." He shook his head, but she cupped the sides of his face to stop him. "Do not, for neither of us can hate the circumstances of how we have come together, not if we truly love each other."

He slowly nodded. "Because to hate our beginning

is to say we would prefer never to have met. Aye, lass, I cannae say such a thing, for ye're the other half of me." He gently stroked her cheek, looking at her as though he'd longed for her as deeply as she had for him. "But ye are going to marry me, Clarrisa of the York family, just as soon as yer marriage to Norris is annulled due to lack of consummation."

A wicked gleam entered his eyes as he uttered the word "consummation."

"Well now, my fine Highlander, that will leave us time to be lovers before we must become serious about our duties as man and wife."

"Beginning now, lass…"

He kissed her at last, and it felt as though she'd been waiting for that touch of his lips for an eternity. She slid her hands into his hair, wanting to bind him in place and assure herself that he was real. He was. His heart beat strong enough for her to feel it as the scent of his skin filled her senses. Every detail she'd struggled to hold in her memory was there for her to experience anew. It was perfect.

It was love.

⁂

Norris poured himself a goblet of French wine but frowned when its rich aroma filled his senses. None of the enjoyment he normally experienced came with the first sip. He set the goblet aside, trying to decide what was irritating him. Everything had proceeded as planned, yet no sense of satisfaction was arriving to allow him to slip into slumber as a happy man.

He lay back in his bed and felt cold. Frustration was

nipping at him like a rash—one that needed scratching for relief, but after you gave into the urge, pain was your reward. Daphne's face rose from his memory, sending another round of frustration through him. His cock hardened and his mood darkened further.

Why had she been so relieved to leave him? That was what tore at him. The way she'd so easily left his bed after spending the night with him. She'd been pleasured, well and good, and still she'd walked away without so much as a longing look over her shoulder.

He was the heir to the earldom of Sutherland and a Highlander... what did she have to turn her nose up at? Norris stared into the darkness and realized he wanted to know.

A true Highlander went after what he wanted.

About the Author

Mary Wine is a multipublished author in romantic suspense, fantasy, and Western romance. Now her interest in historical reenactment and costuming has inspired her to turn her pen to historical romance. She lives with her husband and sons in Southern California, where the whole family enjoys participating in historical reenactment.

True Highland Spirit

by Amanda Forester

Seduction is a powerful weapon...

Morrigan McNab is a Highland lady, robbed of her birthright and with no choice but to fight alongside her brothers to protect their impoverished clan. When she encounters Sir Jacques Dragonet, she discovers her fiercest opponent...

Sir Jacques Dragonet is a Noble Knight of the Hospitaller Order, willing to give his life to defend Scotland from the English. He can't stop himself from admiring the beautiful Highland lass who wields her weapons as well as he can and endangers his heart even more than his life...

Now they're racing each other to find a priceless relic. No matter who wins this heated rivalry, both will lose unless they can find a way to share the spoils.

The Highlander's Heart

by Amanda Forester

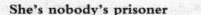

She's nobody's prisoner

Lady Isabelle Tynsdale's flight over the Scottish border would have been the perfect escape, if only she hadn't run straight into the arms of a gorgeous Highland laird. Whether his plan is ransom or seduction, her only hope is to outwit him, or she'll lose herself entirely...

And he's nobody's fool

Laird David Campbell thought Lady Isabelle was going to be easy to handle and profitable too. He never imagined he'd have such a hard time keeping one enticing English countess out of trouble. And out of his heart...

"An engrossing, enthralling, and totally riveting read. Outstanding!"—Jackie Ivie, national bestselling author of *A Knight and White Satin*

For more Amanda Forester books, visit:

www.sourcebooks.com

Sins of the Highlander

by Connie Mason with Mia Marlowe

ABDUCTION

Never had Elspeth Stewart imagined her wedding would be interrupted by a dark-haired stranger charging in on a black stallion, scooping her into his arms, and carrying her off across the wild Scottish highlands. Pressed against his hard chest and nestled between his strong thighs, she ought to have feared for her life. But her captor silenced all protests with a soul-searing kiss, giving Elspeth a glimpse of the pain behind his passion—a pain only she could ease.

OBSESSION

"Mad Rob" MacLaren thought stealing his rival's bride-to-be was the perfect revenge. But Rob never reckoned that this beautiful, innocent lass would awaken the part of him he thought dead and buried with his wife. Against all reason, he longed to introduce the luscious Elspeth to the pleasures of the flesh, to make her his, and only his, forever.

"Ms. Mason always provides a hot romance."—RT Book Reviews

www.sourcebooks.com

The Return of Black Douglas

by Elaine Coffman

❧

He'll help a woman in need, no matter where she came from…

Alysandir Mackinnon rules his clan with a fair but iron fist. He has no time for softness or, as he sees it, weakness. But when he encounters a bewitching young beauty who may or may not be a dangerous spy, but is surely in mortal danger, he's compelled to help…

She's always wondered if she was born in the wrong time…

Thrown back in time to the tumultuous, dangerous Scottish Highlands of the sixteenth century, Isobella Douglas has a lot to learn about her ancestors, herself, and her place in the world. Especially when she encounters a Highland laird who puts modern men to shame…

Each one has secrets to keep, until they begin to strike a chord in each other's hearts that's never been touched before…

For more Elaine Coffman, visit:

www.sourcebooks.com